DA VINCI'S LAST SUPPER

THE FORGOTTEN TALE

PAUL ARROWSMITH

I dedicate this book to my three children, Rachael, Daniel & Samuel.

ACKNOWLEDGMENTS

I am deeply indebted to the following people for their support and encouragement, which proved invaluable during the years spent writing this novel. For their comments and editorial advice in early drafts, I thank Caroline Ryder, Fintan O Higgins and Fiona Blair. For doing a formidable job of editing the manuscript, I offer a special mention to Robert Endeacott.

In addition, I am thankful to my proof reader, Joanna Peios, and to my dear friend Flavia Cerrone, for her help with various Italian translations and advice. I wish to thank Professor Martin Kemp and Dr. Matthew Landrus of Oxford University, whose time and insights into the life of Leonardo da Vinci helped shape my novel. I am grateful to the Direzione Regionale Musei Lombardia for granting me a prolonged stay to view 'The Last Supper,' at Santa Maria delle Grazie, to the Uffizi Gallery in Florence for providing helpful information regarding the early life of Leonardo da Vinci, and to the Czartoryski Museum in Krakow Poland for granting me a private viewing of 'Lady with an Ermine.'

The following deserve to be acknowledged; my former drama tutors Kevin Rowntree for first inspiring me to write this story, and Andy Willoughby for his candid advice that I was a better writer than I was an actor. A special tribute is also reserved for my former screenwriting tutor and mentor Alby James.

To my children Rachael, Danny and Sam, I thank you for always believing your father would eventually get a book deal. The same applies to my mother, Pam, who has been a great source of support, so too my sisters Ruth, Lisa, Susie and brother David. Finally, to all my friends in Leeds, Darlington, London, around the UK and across the globe who have journeyed with me, and always provided encouragement you know who you are and I thank you a thousand times over.

CHAPTER ONE

A CRISP BREEZE SLOPED OFF THE SNOW-CAPPED LOMBARDY Alps and blew into Milan, causing the daffodils Leonardo da Vinci walked past to sway in the wind as they displayed their spring splendour, while the smell from an orange grove lining his path wafted up his nostrils. His gait was long and purposeful, while his reddish-brown hair and beard, speckled with streaks of grey, flapped in the wind.

A tall man, standing head and shoulders above many of his peers, Leonardo was undeniably handsome. His appearance oft aroused envy in less attractive members of his sex, while women on the other hand had been known to swoon in his presence. His fingers were slender and calloused at the tips and when he shook your hand he did so firmly, perhaps too firmly for lesser men. Below the furrows of his forehead, Leonardo's strikingly blue eyes could convey either the calm of wisdom, or that a riot of thought was taking place inside his extraordinary brain.

'Irksome fools! Meddlers, peddlers and thieves!' he muttered, the sound of which carried to none but his own ears. Clasped between Leonardo's fingers was the source of this verbal consternation, a Ducal summons. Earlier that morning he had discussed with his senior apprentice Francesco, a polite and amiable youth, which primer to use on the ancona for the second commission of the *Virgin of the Rocks*. No paint had been applied to its surface, only the pin-pricked outline of a sketch.

'I painted them perfection,' he complained to Francesco. 'And do those miserable monks thank me? God forbid, they do not.'

Leonardo, along with the de Predis brothers Ambrogio and Evangelista, had been commissioned by the Confraternity of the Immaculate Conception in Milan to paint a wood panelled ancona. The two brothers were given the minor work of the side panels with Leonardo assigned to the larger central panel. The brethren of the Confraternity were vociferous in their disapproval of Leonardo's contribution. By a succession of court edicts, contested over a period of years, and pleas to the Duke of Milan, Leonardo finally had his hands forced into yielding up a second panel for the Confraternity. The original, the Duke kept for himself after taking a liking to its misty moodiness.

While Leonardo and Francesco discussed how best to proceed, they were interrupted by the arrival of a court official bearing a summons for Leonardo from his patron, Ludovico Sforza, the Duke of Milan, or Il Moro (The Moor) as he was better known. Il Moro was a stocky and pugnacious individual with limited education yet boundless ambition. He aspired for Milan to be the greatest city in Italy. To surpass Florence, Leonardo's home city renowned for art and commerce; Rome (home to a corrupt papacy); and Venice, which Il Moro loathed due to its refusal to acknowledge him as the rightful ruler of Milan.

Blowing out his exasperation with each step he took in answer to his summons, Leonardo cared little for the court of Il Moro. Experience had taught him that when courtiers were polite, it served only to lure their unsuspecting victim in to some trap. He had long since reached the conclusion: for courtiers to be hostile was bad but for them to be friendly was even worse.

Clutching the summons while still complaining under his breath about the sheer inconvenience, Leonardo wound his way through Milan's cobbled streets. He recalled that during his ten years in Milan he had received only four previous summonses from Il Moro, three of which bore the influence of some devious courtier pent on mischief.

Ordinarily he took the long way around from his studio in the south on journeys to his patron's abode, the Castello Sforzesco, thus avoiding the Lazzaretto. Yet this morning Leonardo, walking at a fearsome pace, entered the notorious slum of Milan. His appearance registered with its superstitious inhabitants, most of whom believed him to be a necromancer and by looks, whispers, frantic gestures and gasps of surprise, notice of his arrival soon spread.

The streets of the Lazzaretto were covered with a vile layer of human excrement mixed with that of dogs and other animals. For its unfortunate inhabitants, the stench clung to them in life and only departed upon their demise. For it was death you smelt as you passed this way, the slow, relentless aroma of humanity rotting.

Food was mostly decayed before it reached these parts and along with brick, mortar, wood, glass and clothes, soon became a part of the disease that was known as the Lazzaretto. Leonardo cursed his luck that the black sludge, made worse after a night of rain, seeped its way between the toes of his sandals and splattered up the calves of his legs.

It was a commonly held belief that Leonardo was in cahoots with the Devil, an attitude fuelled by the numerous inventions Leonardo sought to find buyers for amongst the business establishment of Milan. His self-propelled cart had been widely seen in the city. Whereas the educated scoffed that such a machine could have any practical usage, commoners saw the hand of the red-horned one in building something that would put ordinary folks out of a job. To further fuel their misgivings of Leonardo's 'witchcraft', there were rumours of the many outlandish props and costumes he designed for various functions at the Castello Sforzesco.

Exiting the Lazaretto, he entered the Via Castello, the main cobbled concourse that led towards the Castello Sforzesco. Proudly resplendent in red stone, the castello lay atop a hillock and was designed more after the manner of a Turkish castle than a European one. The walls were made of dark red stone but, although sturdy, they lacked the thickness of traditional castle walls seen elsewhere in Europe. A moat ran around the perimeter surrounded by high walls with oblong turrets at each corner, while an additional turret jutted out of the middle of each wall.

Veering off the path, Leonardo ambled down to the water's edge. He sat down heavily and like a child, dangled first one foot in the moat and then the other until the filth from the Lazaretto had been expunged from his feet. Merchants lined Leonardo's way back up the path by the Castello Sforzesco, selling fruit, vegetables and clothes of local and exotic origin for the fashionable buyer, pots and pans, chickens, livestock and numerous trinkets. Today there were special offers to be had on secret incantations to protect against leprosy, sold by a man whose skin was so grimy it was hardly an endorsement of the product he was selling.

Further along the path, hawkers dressed like Benedictines were selling ornaments of saints, supposedly blessed by the Pope. A chicken seller and an alchemist vied loudly for Leonardo's attention. He ignored both and instead bought a red apple from an honest looking peasant woman. He had long ceased to partake of meat, frequently telling his bemused friends, 'I do not wish my body to be a tomb for other animals.'

Leonardo's attention was caught by a gonfalon blowing in

the breeze above a turret, one emblazoned with the Sforza coat of arms. Divided into four, it showed two blue snakes wearing crowns and a man emerging from the mouths of the snakes alongside two eagles also wearing gold crowns. Leonardo passed beneath the turret and into the forecourt of the Castello Sforzesco.

The courtyard was littered with an array of smaller buildings including a high stone store house guarded by two soldiers. A kitchen, where a cart of fresh produce was being unloaded by a couple of ruddy-faced servant boys. Outside the soldiers' dormitory, off-duty soldiers drank grappa and played cards under the midday sun. To the left of the dormitory were the stables, where eager recruits brushed down the shiny coats of proud horses. Finally, there was the magnificent Palace, with its imposing fluted colonnade, each column tall and imperious like a soldier standing to attention.

Facing Leonardo was a well-tended herb garden. Passing along its western border he breathed in the essential fragrance of Lombardy: sweet basil, thyme, rosemary and oregano. Two elderly merchants doffed their caps as he walked by. A little further down the path, a young captain was doing his best to win the admiration of a young lady who held in her hand an embroidered handkerchief. The maiden blushed appropriately at the advances of the young captain, who looked splendid in a green cape depicting his family insignia of a gold lion. While the youngsters danced their *pas de deux* an elderly aunt dressed in black stood at a discreet distance, hawkishly eyeing the captain's every move. The lovers were oblivious to his presence, but the old girl caught Leonardo's eye and winked mischievously.

Arriving at the long broad steps that led into the palace, Leonardo reluctantly took them in his stride. At the top, Il Moro's palace guard moved aside, the blue feathers atop their blackened iron helmets blowing in the wind. Leonardo barely heeded them as he proceeded down the long stone corridor where he passed more soldiers wearing the black leggings, blue tunic and iron plated body armour of Il Moro's private guard.

The sight of the Sala delle Asse that he himself had painted, momentarily lifted his spirits. Cast in a mid-morning sun, the woodland landscape of intricate branches wove upwards, spiralling around each other, decorating the ceiling and vault as though by some magical incantation. He gazed at the thousands of leaves that dangled from branches arching first in one direction then another. Every leaf slightly different in tone and shade as the shadow seduced each one or left them exposed to an imaginary sun that glistened off each leaf creating a cascade of greens, reds and yellows and every conceivable combination of hue in-between.

Seated opposite him, a solemn-looking fellow in his fifties in black merchant's robes twitched nervously before rising to his feet.

'Nasty business, the price of bread. Those Poles in Krakow are charging me hand over fist for a pound of salt and his Lordship still thinks I'm taking advantage of the good Milanese bakers. If they have to charge more for bread, don't blame me. I'm just doing my best to make an honest living.' Leonardo nodded his sympathies and rose from his seat just as Il Moro's secretary was instructing an official to admit him. Leonardo strode forward and bowed before his patron.

'With what may I assist my good Lord on this fine spring day, the lowering of the price of bread?' Il Moro smiled at Leonardo's unashamed impudence.

'If only you could perform such a miracle Leonardo, the whole of Milan would be in your debt,' replied Il Moro.

'Indeed so,' interjected the secretary to the Duke of Milan, attempting to sound affable when his tone of voice implied the opposite. He was a round, greasy-haired man with an equally greasy disposition. Through years of wet-nursing Il Moro through the intricacies of diplomatic protocol, he had built up a position of considerable trust from the Duke, and with it a sizable portion of envy in the hearts of Il Moro's courtiers.

'What I have in mind maestro Leonardo, is a new commission!' announced Il Moro with considerable gusto. 'A portrait of my mistress Cecilia Gallerani, in honour of her great beauty, as well as several functions she performs for my pleasure.' A remark which caused his secretary to snigger, while several courtiers over-hearing guffawed.

'My Lord, as you are aware, the dear brothers of the Confraternity of the Immaculate Conception have at your ruling an ancona of the Virgin needed from me. In addition to the new engineering plans, you have instructed me to oversee the design and construction of a new well inside the castello. I do not know when I will have time to engage the young lady in her portrait. Would it not be more appropriate if on this occasion another artist was asked?'

Il Moro rose to his feet. 'When you have two things of rare value, it is prudent to see whether by joining them together, one can create some lasting memorial. Cecilia is a woman unlike any other in my court and, I would be bold enough to say, unlike any found in the whole of Italy. You too, Leonardo, whatever your private eccentricities, are unique.' To emphasize his point, Il Moro stepped down from his throne and leaned forward. 'I know how highly you prize your art, always seeking to create perfection. Therefore, I insist you paint Cecilia's portrait.'

'My Lord, if it pleases you, you can send the young lady to my studio at noon on Tuesday.' Leonardo bowed and stepping backwards departed.

Cecilia Gallerani, the young lady whose portrait had been commissioned, was a fair-skinned beauty admired by both men and women alike. She had long slender limbs, a graceful figure and the face of a siren. Few women were equal in terms of their pleasing shape, graceful disposition and hospitable manner of her character. Cecilia was also a scholar. In addition to Latin and her native Tuscan dialect she was fluent in French, German and Spanish. Her keen intellect was put to good use by hosting regular gatherings of Milan's intelligentsia. At these evenings, held once a quarter as befits the natural cycle of the seasons, the art of philosophy was regularly studied and debated.

'To be-blessed with intelligence is the greatest of all God's gifts,' said Cecilia on one occasion. 'For the intelligent have a greater appreciation of the mysteries of life.' Her listeners, all men, would murmur approval while stroking their beards and nodding benignly in the direction of this Athena who had been resurrected from antiquity for their benefit.

Cecilia's father, Fazio Gallerani had been a former ambassador until being forced into bankruptcy. The shame of this had caused his health to fail. Not long after her father's burial, and encouraged by her six brothers, the virginal Cecilia was brought to Il Moro's attention. Besotted with his sixteen-year old mistress, Il Moro paraded her around court to the alarm of his advisors.

It was his secretary who gingerly approached him late one night when Cecilia had retired to bed.

'Sire, I have spoken this night to a trusted advisor to Ercole 1 d'Este, and he has assured me if the Duke were to discover you have a mistress he... he would not grant the hand of his daughter Beatrice in marriage.'

'Satan's breath, what Duke does not have a mistress!'

'One who wishes to be recognised as the rightful ruler of Milan.'

The secretary lowered his head, anticipating that if Il Moro were to strike him, it would be the top of his head that would take the force of the blow and not his face.

Irrespective of how reluctant she was to become a Duke's mistress, particularly one who had recently announced his engagement to one of the most influential families in Italy, over time she found Il Moro possessed certain attractive qualities. He spoke to her with more respect than he normally showed his courtiers and allowed her to continue being tutored. Although he had never read Aristotle, Pliny or St Thomas Aquinas, if he found her engaged in a book, he would ask after its nature and listen intently to her summary of the contents.

One of Il Moro's saving graces was that he liked music and was a fine dancer, a quality that pleased her particularly when functions were held for visiting dignitaries. Such occasions gave her an opportunity to demonstrate her linguistic skills as well as illicit any information or gossip she could later relay to Il Moro, who hoped the delicate tongue of his pretty mistress would prise from his guests what he never could. It was a game Cecilia enjoyed, with the exception of drunken foreigners who sought to seduce her.

Alone in his room, Leonardo pondered the outcome of his meeting with the Duke and, as was his custom, allowed his mind to ruminate: *Is the painting of mistresses all Il Moro considers me suitable for? Will he ever commission from me a master work? Something that would stand the test of time as testimony to my superiority as an artist.* His mood turned melancholy, and rather like the pitter-patter of rain that beat against his window, doubts assailed his mind.

CHAPTER TWO

CECILIA SEEMED INCAPABLE OF SITTING STILL. AN ATTACK OF acute agitation gripped her slender frame, causing her head to bob like an apple in a bucket and her hair to snag as her maidservant combed it. Her maid Maria, like the Virgin, was blessed with faith and patience. She had black curls hanging just above her shoulders and exquisite pale green eyes that a mercenary had once described as the colour of the Aegean Sea, though she herself had never been fortunate enough to see the sea.

It took some time for Maria to untangle the knots in the fine strands of Cecilia's red hair. Eventually satisfied that she was suitable for presentation, Cecilia eyed herself in a mirror. Her shapely figure accentuated by her resplendent hair, held upright by a pretty pearled comb, momentarily transfixed Maria.

'Do I look presentable?' Cecilia asked.

'Mistress, you were born to wear that dress, truly,' replied Maria, snapping out of
her trance.

In the south of the city, Leonardo busied himself with tidying his personal studio, while his apprentices set about preparing the workshop in readiness for their esteemed visitor. Only ever catching rare glimpses of Cecilia from a distance on his various assignments around the castello, matters of appearance and how he would capture her on canvas were utmost on his mind.

News of Cecilia's arrival was delivered to him in his private studio, one reserved for portrait painting by Francesco, who entered with a boyish grin; his admiring words tinged with wonderment.

'She's beautiful, maestro, more so than any woman I have ever seen.'

'Of course, she's beautiful,' rebuked Leonardo. 'If you were a Duke would you take pig to bed with you?' Francesco said no more, distracted by the notion of taking such a woman to bed.

Forcing a smile, Leonardo entered his workshop and opened his mouth to speak, but upon surveying the sublime figure of perfection facing him, he for once was dumbstruck.

'Is anything the matter?' Cecilia quietly asked.

'Leonardo da Vinci,' he said falteringly. 'At your service, my lady.'

'I am Cecilia Gallerani.' She curtseyed. 'It is a great honour to meet you, maestro.'

Leonardo took her extended hand and let his fingers linger on hers. Transfixed by the moment, it took him a little too long before he realised the lady whose hand he held was not alone. She was accompanied by Maria, a stern-looking court official and two armed guards.

'Are they also to be present when I am engaged in painting your portrait, my lady?' The court official cleared his throat, but before he could speak Cecilia addressed Leonardo.

'No maestro, they will wait here in your workshop while you paint me in your private studio.'

'Excellent!' Leonardo said with just a little too much gusto, enough for the court official to register a degree of disapproval.

'My lady,' said the court official in response to Leonardo's declaration. 'I am charged with issuing the maestro with a warning. Il Moro will not hesitate…'

'I am sure,' Cecilia said, taking a light hold of Leonardo's arm, 'the maestro is mindful of his obligations to his Lord.' Leonardo dutifully nodded his honest intent.

'I am fully aware of my responsibilities. Rest assured, the lady Cecilia will be perfectly safe in my hands.' He bowed to ease any lingering suspicion in the mind of the official.

'This way, my lady.'

'Cecilia, please call me Cecilia.'

Leonardo smiled as the last 'Cecilia' left her lips and the solemn oath he had just sworn was drowned out by the sound of her name cascading around his ears. He breathed deeply and escorted her out of his workshop.

The guards showed little interest in the proceedings, being much more interested in Leonardo's construction of an armoured vehicle. Circular in dimension it was divided into twenty sections of metal that were stretched out like a fan, below each sheet protruded a metal pipe from out of which missiles would be fired. Although it was only a miniature incorporating puppets to operate its mechanical devices, the guards could clearly see its military purpose. But what use a commander would find for such a bizarre contraption they knew not.

Throughout the discourse between the court official, Cecilia and Leonardo, Maria had quivered with fear. She had fixed her gaze firmly upon said magician, while in her hands she clasped a small silver cross that she hoped would grant both her and her mistress protection.

Leonardo guided Cecilia inside his personal studio, reserved for painting portraits, the workshop being far too noisy with all manner of distractions. His personal studio was small consisting of a writing table with a bulky journal atop it, a wooden chair, a large south facing window, a bookshelf and various easels, some with canvases on them and some without. Propped up alongside the wall below the window were several drawings. Cecilia stood motionless, waiting, while Leonardo fiddled with some papers.

'Now that we have been introduced, is there any particular idea that springs to mind as to how you wish to paint me?' she enquired, keen to know what the maestro had in mind.

'I always have ideas; the question is whether they are any good,' he replied.

Cecilia idly picked up one of the many drawings strewn across the workbench. It depicted five grotesque men in a circle. Their hideous deformity provoked amusement from Cecilia, in particular, one whose lower face resembled that of a duck.

'I promise not to make you look like any of these,' he quipped. Cecilia giggled, embarrassed that of all the drawings on display she had selected this one.

'Where would you like me to stand?' she asked, toying with a strand of hair.

'Over here by the window.'

Cecilia moved to where Leonardo had indicated but as she took her place she noticed a look of agitation on his face.

'Is anything the matter?'

'The light…'

'Oh, I am sorry,' Cecilia said.

'It is hardly your fault Cecilia if the morning is overcast.' The hairs on the back of Cecilia's neck tingled as she absorbed the sound of her name spoken on his lips for the first time.

Leonardo picked up a magnifying glass and ran it over Cecilia's neck, shoulders and
the tops of her breasts. 'Your skin has a luminous quality,' noted Leonardo.

'Is that a good thing?' she blushed.

'It means the light will fall more evenly and make the flesh seem more alive. I take it

you want to look alive?' She giggled in the flirtatious manner of all women when in the company of a man whom they are becoming more infatuated with each passing moment.

'Good. We seem to have established an important principle. I am to paint you looking like these grotesque gargoyles,' he said, taking hold of the caricatures she still held in her hand.

'I see you are a man of some humour.'

'If we are to be trapped in this room for long hours, the ability to amuse each other will make life easier.'

'Oh, I am quite sure we will find ways to do that,' replied Cecilia with a warm smile. Embarrassed, Leonardo turned away to gaze out of the window that dominated the south-facing wall.

Waiting patiently for instruction, Cecilia took the opportunity to study him closely. Leonardo stood erect with the pride of a man comfortable in his own inclinations and habits. Cecilia wondered what his vices were and whether the love of a woman was one of them. She watched the fingers of his right-hand curl around his beard, first the little finger, then the ring finger, followed by the big finger and the index finger as he slowly stroked his beard with a slow compulsive rhythm.

'I know you do not have a wife, but surely a man of your attractiveness has no shortage of lovers.'

'There are some things I prefer to keep secret.' Bruised by his rather curt response, Cecilia looked to the floor in the hope the maestro would not notice her blushes, which went unnoticed, for he was too busy admiring the contours of her body as she stood half in light and half in shadow due to a cloud passing overhead. Wishing to prolong their time further, he picked up some charcoal and began to draw her portrait. Staring at her body, Leonardo's mind battled with unfamiliar temptations: *Have I not seen desire in her face? Her beauty truly is worthy of all the accolades afforded her. If only my arms could hold such an exquisite goddess.* The lady in question held her composure like some Athenian statue, the only movement being the rhythmic rise and fall of her bosom.

His musings were interrupted by an ominous April cloud stealing what light remained from the sun.

'We have been defeated by the elements. Cecilia, would it be too much of an inconvenience to ask you to return at the same hour tomorrow?'

'I think that will be fine,' she replied, trying to hide her disappointment that their encounter was over so quickly. 'Perhaps in a day or two, the gods will shine on us.'

When they returned to the workshop, the court official jumped up and eyed both for evidence of any misdemeanour. 'Is everything in order?' he snapped.

'Everything, apart from the weather,' Cecilia replied as pleasantly as possible. As if to reinforce her assertion, the heavens opened. Leonardo stood in the doorway, a hand outstretched to catch the raindrops that beat upon his hand. Cecilia nodded to Maria, who opened a white silk parasol. 'Good day, maestro,' she said, departing with her escort.

Soon after her departure, an agitated Leonardo paced about his workshop, drawing looks of puzzlement from his apprentices and derision from Salai.

What's up with you?' he said, 'Got an itch up your crack?' Salai had wide eyes and a chubby face that shone like the proverbial cherub. He was blessed with thick gold ringlets curling around his bronzed cheeks, while his azure eyes sparkled with mischief. His feet and hands were swift, and he was a deft hand at picking pockets, an art he had learned on the rough streets of Milan.

When he had first come into Leonardo's care, Salai was even wilder and more foul-mouthed. Indeed, one of the maestro's best customers, Signor Agusto Montafarno, was trying on a costume for a gala celebration that Leonardo had designed and made when the little vagrant took advantage of the situation to engage in the theft of the signor's purse. The poor man was so vexed at this betrayal he was adamant that Salai should be hauled before the courts. It took every ounce of persuasive energy from Leonardo to forestall this eventuality. Nonetheless, the good signor swore he would never do business with Leonardo as long as 'the little devil' remained under his roof.

Salai's peasant father was a drunkard who drifted between sporadic periods in work followed by longer periods out of work. Salai's mother had died when he was very young. Shortly after her death, the boy's father had left him to fend for himself, abandoning him like an unwanted mongrel. Salai soon learned that if you wanted food you must steal to acquire it. A chance encounter drew Salai and Leonardo together. Leonardo had not been looking for a son, indeed he was indifferent to the notion of taking a wife and raising a family. In truth, he relished telling his friends, 'marriage was like putting your hand into a bag of snakes in the hope of pulling out an eel.'

One winter's morning, when the wind and the rain were fleeing down the mountains, Leonardo opened his workshop door to find a child propped up asleep in the doorway. Above the door was an overhang that offered some protection from the rain. The rags it wore barely covered its flesh, which was red raw from the elements. Noticing the child's fingers and lips had turned blue, and its face was bleached of colour, Leonardo picked the child up and carried it inside his workshop. The child barely managed to open its eyes, so weak was it from cold and hunger. Leonardo laid the child down upon his bed. The feeble creature mustered the strength to kick out and scream.

'Get off me! Don't hurt me! Leave me!' But then, as if waking from a trance, the creature stopped its wild thrashing and lay panting, staring up at Leonardo. It was only then that Leonardo was able to ascertain the frightened wretch before him was a boy and, if not for the filth that smothered his body, a handsome one.

In a short time, Salai came to live in Leonardo's household as his adopted son. It was an act of generosity that took the maestro's friends by surprise. Having been abandoned himself at the age of five when he was removed from his mother's home by his father and sent to live with his uncle, Leonardo knew something of the pain of abandonment and rejection and had much sympathy with the plight of the child. Even when the boy proved to be a nuisance, Leonardo showed himself to be a forgiving even indulgent father.

In a thoughtful frame of mind, Leonardo walked to and fro around his workshop, an oblong building with three large south-facing latticed windows that opened outward onto the street outside. There was a standard door at one end of the workshop and, at the other, a large double door for loading materials and for carrying out large finished pieces. Two workbenches were fitted into the studio. One was on the wall opposite the window, crammed with a variety of instruments and work tools it ran the full length of the room. The second, being smaller, was tucked alongside the wall by the door one ordinarily entered through. There was a kiln and a small furnace near to the shorter workbench plus two basins of water. The floor was covered in terracotta tiles. Upon them was a faded pattern, and in parts green olive trees were still vaguely visible.

The training of apprentices had never been an ambition of Leonardo's and he made use of the few he appointed sparingly. In one corner, by the large double doors, was a device shaped like a wheel with what appeared to be a wooden wizard's hat split into lattice-shaped panels that had metal pipes protruding all around it. Next to this stood a box-like machine, woven with interlocking mechanical coils and springs, a self-propelled cart.

'You're boring me,' said Salai, frustrated at watching his papa march silently up and down the length of the workshop. He picked up a vial of red paint and threw it against the cartoon for the *Virgin of the Rocks*, before he hurried on his way.

Leonardo picked up a cloth, dabbed it in a little water and set about cleaning the red paint Salai had splattered across the left-hand corner of the ancona.

'Would you like me to do that maestro?' Francesco asked. Leonardo ushered him away with a wave of his hands.

Having cleaned the paint, Leonardo retired to his room, lay on his bed, stretched out his legs and closed his eyes. His mind raced as it pictured Cecilia's graceful figure and heaving bosom, her piercing eyes and inviting lips, the contours of her dress that accentuated those parts of her body unseen by all but her lover. Aroused by sensual feelings he had long since denied himself he wrote in his journal: *A man who cannot control his appetites is no better than a dog.* He put down his quill and sighed: 'Oh Cecilia, what is to become of me? You have seduced me in mind if not in body.'

CHAPTER THREE

The mere mention of Father Rodrigo of Salamanca was enough to strike fear into the hearts of many an honest Catholic. Amongst the Spaniard's various papal duties was that of 'Inquisitor', a role he relished as he traversed Italy with a license to condemn those he perceived guilty of crimes against the Church. He had ordered the execution of more souls than he could recall. It had only been a few winters previous, when still in Spain, Father Rodrigo had been called upon to investigate allegations of heresy and witchcraft.

Late one November night, he had arrived with a small band of soldiers under his command during a heavy downpour at the ancient town of Cartagena. Abbot Ferdinand, who had sent for him, was waiting with a remnant of faithful monks and nuns in a state of desperation inside a small stone church on the outskirts of the port when Father Rodrigo arrived. Abbot Ferdinand told their sorry tale of blood and feathers on the floor of the Monastery of the Blessed Virgin atop the hill overlooking the town. A jewelled crucifix had been torn from the wall above the monastery altar and positioned in a pentagram, upside down and dipped in blood. The monks and nuns occupying the monastery were drunk and naked and indulging in all manner of Devil worship and licentious behaviour.

'The vile song of witches has been heard throughout the night, terrifying the townsfolk,' the Abbot had claimed. 'Many have fled along the coast to relatives.'

Father Rodrigo considered their comments carefully, along with the horrific accounts the Abbot and his companions told of how Satan had seized the minds of many they once considered brothers and sisters in Christ.

Of the weeks that followed it was Abbot Ferdinand, along with the poor frightened monks and nuns Father Rodrigo had first encountered, who were the first to be found guilty of heresy. It was Father Rodrigo who signed their death warrants and who stood proudly to the right of the hangman when each one of these innocent Catholics was executed. The power he wielded, he did so with zeal, deriving satisfaction from the fear he struck into innocent and guilty alike. Such a reputation proved invaluable to the Pope when sending the surly Spanish priest on diplomatic missions.

Having been thwarted on several occasions by Il Moro's powerful brother Cardinal Ascanio Sforza, who was Vice-Chancellor of the Holy Roman Church, the notorious Inquisitor had a particular disdain for the House of Sforza. The conniving Cardinal had used his influence to hinder the Inquisitor when he had laid accusations of heresy against several prominent individuals, who Father Rodrigo suspected had paid handsomely for the Cardinal's protection. Therefore, when he was informed by His Holiness that his next diplomatic mission was to Cardinal Sforza's usurper of a brother, Ludovico Sforza, Duke of Milan, his black heart beat with menace.

Even Il Moro was not inclined to look the blood-stained Priest in the eye when he arrived in Milan one windswept winter's day to fulfil his business from Rome.

'If you wish the Holy Father's blessing, we would like to see a commission of deep religious significance handed to an artist in whom there is evidence of piety,' said Father Rodrigo of Salamanca.

'Leonardo is my artist in residence, I am sure he is worthy,' Il Moro said with the slightest quiver in his voice, one not lost on the smirking Inquisitor.

'Leonardo is a bastard and a sodomite!' was Father Rodrigo's terse reply.

'Every artist in Italy is either a bastard, a sodomite or both,' replied Il Moro.

'My Lord, rumours abound that Leonardo secretly uses cadavers. Any man practising such diabolism cannot be considered worthy to depict Christ.'

'I have also heard it said that Leonardo flies around the rooftops of Milan with a broom between his legs, but in all my nights observing the stars from my balcony I have yet to see such a sight. If I paid attention to every piece of tittle-tattle that swept past my ears, then I'd be more worried that either the Pope or the King of France has designs to take my land.' Bowing slightly, Father Rodrigo continued in a more conciliatory tone.

'Well, my Lord, if you will vouch for the man, I will pass your recommendation to His Holiness.'

In the pretence of warming his hands over a blazing log fire, Il Moro turned his back upon his papal emissary. 'A room has been prepared for you,' he said, studying the flickering flames.

'I thank you for your hospitality,' replied the priest. The proud Spaniard promptly turned on his heels leaving Il Moro to breathe a sigh of relief.

'That man could curdle the milk in a dead goat,' he said to his secretary, who stepped up once their unwholesome guest had vanished from sight.

The following morning, the Inquisitor attended the early

morning service of Lauds, where he was dissatisfied with every detail of the ritual. The incense was not pure enough; the prayers were said too quickly; some of the chants were out of tune. Afterwards, he lambasted the poor priest officiating, meticulously pointing out to the startled man, who was deaf in one ear, a list of his shortcomings. Unfortunately, due to the poor man's disability, the sting in Father Rodrigo's venom was somewhat wasted. Frustrated, the Inquisitor gave up and took route to the stables, saddled his horse and, in full force of a downpour, commenced his return journey to Rome.

'Rain, rain and more blasted rain!' Father Rodrigo complained to the young novice who had been assigned to accompany him on his journey. 'Only an Englishman would feel welcome here,' he said as he passed out of the southern gate without so much as a backwards glance.

During his return journey to Rome, Father Rodrigo rued the decline of the Catholic Church's influence under the reign of Pope Alexander VI (Rodrigo Borgia), a despot who owed his rise to the Papal throne to a successful arrangement he had undertaken with Il Moro's brother, Cardinal Ascanio Sforza. It was the good Cardinal's clandestine activities that secured Rodrigo Borgia the necessary votes to become Pope. Of course, the Cardinal's brother, Ludovico benefited substantially from his brother's favourable position and new-found wealth.

After a gruelling journey when the rain he had encountered in Milan followed him for the greater part of his return to Rome, Father Rodrigo of Salamanca entered the ornate office of the Pope where he grudgingly bowed and kissed the sacred Fisherman's ring.

'How was Milan?' enquired the Pope.

'Wet, Your Holiness.'

'And Il Moro? Is he satisfied with a Papal blessing for his commission?'

'God has delivered to Rome the greatest artists in the land.

You should make it a condition of your Papal approval that it is an artist from Rome who is sent to Milan to fulfil so important a commission.'

'If Il Moro wants an artist from Rome, let him approach us formally and we will agree terms. If no such approach is made, then he has other artists at his disposal.'

'By others you mean that bastard Leonardo da Vinci,' uttered Father Rodrigo.

'Italy is a land of bastards. Why, I have even fathered a few myself.' His Holiness

replied, relishing the chance to watch his Inquisitor squirm uncomfortably. 'Now go. I will speak no more on this.'

Marching out of the Pope's private chambers, Father Rodrigo passed a bronze statue of Our Lord upon the cross and fell prostrate before it. 'My Lord, he has defiled the Holy office and made a mockery of your name. He is a usurper to the throne of Saint Peter. By the cross and all the holy saints may I live to see the day when a righteous Pope governs your Church.'

The devout Father rose to his feet and kissed the silver crucifix around his neck. He had heard the rumours of regular evenings of debauchery where drunken revellers spurred on by prostitutes were awarded marks out of ten for virility by seeing who among them could ejaculate the furthest. If that were not enough, Pope Alexander VI openly kept a mistress, Vannozza (Giovanna) dei Cattanei. Their bastard children not only stayed in the Vatican, they were even promoted to office.

Even though Rodrigo Borgia was a Spaniard, Father Rodrigo felt ashamed that a fellow countryman so demeaned the Papacy with such vile behaviour. With trembling lips, he proceeded through the east wing of the Curia, comforting himself with the thought that there were others like him in Rome who had not sullied themselves with drunkenness and immorality. Men like Cardinal Giuliano della

Rovere who loathed the Borgia Pope, believed that along with Cardinal Sforza they had conspired to prevent him from being elected to Papal office. The brass knocker on Cardinal Rovere's door was shaped like the head of a lion. Rodrigo slammed it so hard the oak door juddered. It was only after he had knocked several times that the Cardinal sheepishly opened the door.

'Welcome Father,' said Cardinal Rovere. 'My apologies for the delay in answering, but these are troubled days in Saint Peter's.' Cardinal Rovere was a stern looking man with an uncompromising air and a long white beard who, in his scarlet Cardinal's robes, fitted in perfectly with the opulence of his surroundings. Upon his walls hung a richly embroidered tapestry of the battle of Ostia and the elaborately tailored silk-thread Chasuble that had been worn by his uncle, Pope Sixtus IV, on his coronation as Pope. Father Rodrigo poured out his frustrations.

'I rejoiced at the sight of white smoke over Saint Peter's, believing it was you who had taken the Papal sceptre. Now my heart grows wearier by the day, witnessing the evils done in the name of the Church.' Father Rodrigo suddenly stopped. He knew he could speak openly in front of Cardinal Rovere but in his enthusiasm, he forgot to take into account another who was present, Cardinal Alessandro Orsini, a thin rakish Vatican stalwart.

'I assure you, Father Rodrigo, Cardinal Orsini is a man to be trusted.' Satisfied, the Spaniard continued. 'Bastards, thieves, fornicators, sodomites and heretics of every hue are commonplace in our blessed city. Unless we act to stop the likes of the Borgias and the Sforzas, the very institution of the Church will be threatened.'

Cardinal Orsini filled a gold goblet with wine, which he passed to the distressed Spaniard. 'My son, when God looks down upon this earth, let me assure you he is well pleased by the purity of your words and actions.'

'There are those in the Vatican who now conspire to take my life,' said a stern-faced Cardinal Rovere. 'But I believe God will preserve it for this divine purpose, to rid the world of Rodrigo Borgia. On that day, I will be made Pope. Until then, it is not safe for me here, and for that reason, I leave soon for the Court of Avignon. There, I plan to form an alliance with King Charles VIII of France and lure him into some pretext for declaring war upon Pope Alexander VI, and in return secure the Duchy of Milan for the French and Naples too, which he has long held aspirations for.'

Cardinal Orsini leant in to speak. 'This time Cardinal Sforza's wealth won't save him. He will come to ruin once the French take Milan from his murdering dog of a brother, and Rodrigo Borgia is stripped of the Papacy.'

There was never any proof Cardinal Sforza had committed the crime of simony, yet rumours abounded that Rodrigo Borgia had paid handsomely with four cartloads of silver for the Cardinal's assistance in bribing sufficient numbers of The Sacred College of Cardinals, to cast their vote for Rodrigo Borgia.

'When God pronounces his judgment upon the Borgias and Sforzas, what punishment do you forecast?' the Inquisitor asked. Cardinal Rovere placed a hand over Father Rodrigo's and clasped it firmly.

'My dear friend, the trial of such slippery individuals would need to be judged by a man of calibre, one who could not be bribed. I had hoped you would be willing to oversee such proceedings?' Humbled by his mentor's request, Father Rodrigo bowed.

'Your Grace,' he said as he kissed the Cardinal's sapphire ring. 'It would be an honour to root out and punish the enemies of the Church.' He kissed the Cardinal's ring a second time and then raised his gold goblet to Cardinal Rovere. 'To your health, wealth and future success.'

Feeling rejuvenated, the scheming Father finally left

Cardinal Rovere's office. Speaking to himself, he knelt down before a gilded gold cross. 'Sforza or not, I swear before Almighty God, I will see Il Moro hung as a heretic. As for that Florentine bastard da Vinci, he too will feel the wind beneath his swinging feet.'

CHAPTER FOUR

In the year following the commencement of Cecilia's portrait, Leonardo had been so preoccupied by his patron's demands it remained unfinished. Throughout the summer he was busy overseeing the design and construction of a new well within the castello's walls. In addition, Il Moro's wife Beatrice d' Este, had insisted upon a theatrical production to celebrate her birthday, to which Leonardo had been called upon to plan and make both the costumes and a great variety of props.

Compared to Cecilia, Leonardo considered Beatrice to be a plain woman of simple tastes. The daughter of Ercole d' Este, Duke of Ferrara, she was well suited to the duteous role of Il Moro's wife. She was however, perceptive enough to suspect her husband had a mistress hidden somewhere in the castello grounds. Her misgivings were not eased by his furious response whenever she broached him on this subject. Therefore, Beatrice's watchfulness, combined with Leonardo's busy schedule, meant that it was often a month or more between each sitting for Cecilia's portrait. This situation suited Leonardo well, for it allowed his phlegmatic nature time to reassert his vow of celibacy and curb the rush of carnal inclinations she had stirred within him.

One morning Cecilia arrived unannounced in a state of panic.

'The court is alive with gossip that Ercole d'Este has found out Il Moro has been unfaithful to his daughter. Oh my dear, what will become of me?'

'Are you alarmed that your position is a tenuous one?' asked Leonardo.

'The position of any woman is tenuous but at least a married woman has some security. A mistress has none.'

'What repercussions do you fear?'

'Ercole d'Este has some sway with the Venetians, who still do not recognize Il Moro as the rightful ruler of Milan. Il Moro wants Beatrice and her father to embark upon a diplomatic mission to help persuade the Doge to recognize him as Milan's rightful ruler. But if she finds out about me, she will certainly not embark upon any such mission and neither will her father.'

'Then you need hope your presence will remain a secret otherwise he will be forced to turn you out.'

'If he turns me out then I am ruined,' said a teary Cecilia.

'You will find a husband I am sure.'

'Is that a proposal?' she said. Cheered by the remark, Leonardo laughed and wiped the tear from her eye.

'My dearest angel, I am not a good prospect for you. Now, enough of this chatter we have work to do. Please, take your place by the window.'

For the rest of the afternoon, Leonardo worked in silence. While he concentrated on the contours of Cecilia's dress and the technical demands of painting the delicate folds in the material, Cecilia thought of what manner of husband Leonardo might make in the event she was turned out by Beatrice: Surely a man of such sure hands would know how to please a woman.

The morning did not progress well as an anxious Cecilia found herself unable to relax and focus her attention on standing poised as instructed. Much to the maestro's frustration, she moaned at his constant rearranging of her posture. Resigned to the fact he was wasting his efforts, the artist put down his brush and headed towards the door.

'Come, there is something I wish to show you.' Together they entered the main workshop and, accompanied by the stares of apprentices and Cecilia's palace entourage, marched through the large double doors at the opposite end. Once outside they took the steps to the roof where Leonardo opened a small wooden shed and ushered her inside. Cecilia found herself looking at a large, complex wood-framed construction.

'What is it? she asked.

'It's an ornithopter, from the Greek meaning bird wing. I intend to see if a man can fly by aid of such a device.'

Central to the ornithopter was a large plank to lie upon and from this position operate the numerous pulleys attached to two foot-pedals. The mullioned wings were made from willow, for its lightness and flexibility. The wings were covered in the finest linen available. Leonardo deemed it necessary for the fabric to be thin enough to allow air to pass through. Cecilia attempted to lift one end of a wing up, an act that required a great deal of effort.

'It is not possible for a man to fly by means of this apparatus, Leonardo. No man, save Hercules, could generate enough power to lift the ornithopter off the ground if he was strapped into it.'

'Regrettably, I am aware of this.'

'I am sure the mathematician Luca Pacioli would be willing to assist you in your efforts. I will introduce you to him tonight.'

It was early in the evening when Leonardo arrived to deliver his inaugural address to the group of intellectuals and academics that Cecilia hosted quarterly. He knew several by name including his friend Franchino Gaffurius, the head of music at the Duomo, a handsome man with shoulder-length brown hair and luminous brown eyes. In honour of their friendship, Leonardo had painted Franchino, who held in his hands a section of music he had composed, a Mass in honour of the city's patron saint, Saint Ambrose. Also present was Donato Bramante, architect to Il Moro, who was currently engaged in the final stages of construction for the Duke's personal chapel of Santa Maria delle Grazie. Their paths often crossed in work matters.

A delighted Cecilia introduced Leonardo to the ten men present. Il Moro's artist in residence oozed confidence as he nodded politely to each man before he began his presentation.

'Gentleman, I am honoured to speak to you this evening on a subject of great importance to me: flight. Yet if man is to understand the nature of flight, he first need comprehend the art of swimming. Have you ever noticed,' he asked his audience, 'how the hands of a swimmer when they strike the water, cause the body of the swimmer to glide forward in a contrary movement? I, therefore, assert it is the same with the wings of a bird in the air. The atmosphere is an element capable of being compressed within itself when it is struck by something moving at a greater rate of speed than its own velocity.'

Several murmurs of approval emanated from the group and one or two caught Cecilia's eye to indicate their guest had thus far impressed.

'My learned colleagues, my conclusion is – a man suitably equipped with a mechanical device could, through correct design and construction of an ornithopter, overcome the resistance of the air and rise above the ground.'

'Impossible!' proclaimed Professor Tedesco, a rotund bald gentleman who was also appointed to the Royal Court as its Professor of History. 'I have never heard anything so ridiculous!' he said, seeking approval from his colleagues.

Another man, wearing the priestly apparel of a Franciscan, stood up and spoke in a deep voice. All conversations came to a stop. 'Gentlemen, gentlemen, why object? Doctor Mirabilis (Francis Bacon), a man of considerable intellect and fame, did he not also advocate that man could, given the proper scientific tools, fly? Therefore, I say let maestro Leonardo speak.' His words carried weight with his listeners. Leonardo nodded politely to his rescuer and continued his theorizing on the mechanics of flight.

Leonardo presented before the Society Philosophic several of his drawings that revealed in intricate detail his various mechanisms, measurements and plans for a manned ornithopter including: how the wings emulated those of a bird and were designed to be flexible and for air to pass through the mullioned fabric; and where a man was intended to sit and operate the pulleys that would facilitate flight. Clearly evident to the esteemed company of men was the level of intelligence that had gone into each of the designs submitted. Leonardo went on to answer their questions thoroughly, explaining the workings of his machine. While others scoffed at the thought such machines would ever be practically demonstrated, others marvelled that a man noted for his art had such a grasp of science.

An emboldened Leonardo picked up his numerous diagrams and concluded his presentation by reasserting his fundamental maxim.

'It is my belief that one day man will master the skies just as he has mastered land and sea. For once you have tasted flight you will walk the earth with your eyes turned skywards, for there you have been and there you will long to return.'

During the course of the evening, Professor Tedesco wearied of the remarkable claims Leonardo postulated. The professor huffed and puffed in his chair until finally he spewed forth his bile.

'You are not a man of letters, are you? The boasts you make you do so without the necessary academic credentials to support them.' The room fell silent. Leonardo's eyes narrowed, and his voice bristled with indignation.

'I have been invited here to speak on matters of science. I contend most strongly that no human investigation can be called true science without passing through strict mathematical tests, as opposed to fastidious reliance upon the untested words of others.'

Professor Tedesco's face flushed crimson with anger. 'Hundreds of years of wisdom are the basis, the rock of our knowledge. Are you so arrogant as to claim you are superior to the learned minds we have taught from antiquity to the present day?'

A thin, angular man began a long list of revered names from antiquity. Aristotle and Plato, Ptolemy and Pliny, and ending with St Thomas Aquinas.

'It is utterly preposterous,' said the thin man, 'that we should be asked to lay aside our academic history and heed to your un-learned assumptions.' Unruffled by this interruption, Leonardo rebutted the angry professor calmly.

'Before we claim that something is a law in nature, we must first test our hypothesis many times over. Where men of learning in the past have stated such and such is a law or principle that governs nature, we should not maintain such an opinion if the truth of our experiments differs from long-established views.'

The room descended into academic squabbles. On one hand were those led by Professor Tedesco, who stuck rigidly to classical teaching and rejected as nonsense all modern thinking. While on the other, Leonardo, his priestly ally and Cecilia, who had been enraptured by Leonardo's presentation, led the chorus for change.

When the proceedings were all but over and the debate subsided, Leonardo's deep-voiced champion introduced himself.

'I am Father Luca Pacioli. It is my pleasure to meet you, Leonardo. You have not disappointed.'

'But you too, Father Luca, if I may be so bold, have a reputation.'

Luca Pacioli was considered the finest mathematician of his day, not only in Italy but throughout Europe, and recently appointed to teach mathematics at the Royal Court.

Cecilia entertained her other guests as graciously as was expected of her, but her mind was on Leonardo. When she finally approached him, he was still deep in discussion with Father Pacioli.

'I am pleased you have made each other's acquaintance.' The two men smiled and bowed. Noticing a court attendant in his blue and silver regalia enter the room, Cecilia gently took hold of Leonardo's right hand. 'My carriage awaits. I know from the many comments passed to me that you have made a lasting impression. I hope you will grace us with your presence again. Goodnight gentlemen.'

Leonardo departed soon after, accompanied for some distance by Luca who was staying in monastic quarters to the south of the city. Together they discussed the mechanics of flight, during which the priest-turned-mathematician made it clear he would very much like to inspect Leonardo's ornithopter. It was a suggestion wholly agreeable to its inventor and so, before the two went their separate ways, they arranged to meet at a more opportune time to exchange ideas.

While approaching his workshop, a commotion from the street caused Leonardo to realise something was amiss. Pushing his way through the melee, he demanded to know the reason a throng of people were gathered on his doorstep. An aristocratic gentleman in his early thirties sporting a fine moustache stepped forward.

'Maestro Leonardo, I am Giovanni Visconti.' He bowed flamboyantly. 'I wish our meeting were under more pleasant circumstances, but a serious crime has taken place, the robbery of my young cousin, Alberto Visconti. The young brigand who committed this outrageous act has locked himself away in your private quarters.'

'Is it Salai?' asked Leonardo, knowing the question was foolish.

'Indeed maestro,' replied Giovanni Visconti. A downcast Leonardo shook his head.

'My humble apologies,' he said, bowing.

After some persuasion, Salai abandoned his refuge. The guilty youth was not in a position to deny involvement, for in Leonardo's bedroom they found a cloak belonging to the robbed youth. Leonardo paid Giovanni Visconti the amount that had been stolen, with a little usury to prevent Salai being hauled before the courts and sentenced to the Duke's fields as a mud basher.

When the crowd had left, and all the other apprentices had finally retired to bed, Leonardo sat Salai down in the kitchen.

'What more can I do to persuade you that you need no longer steal or mix with thieves? Talk to me Salai, what is it that makes you persist with such actions?'

'I don't know, papa. Perhaps I am afraid that one day you will abandon me and I will return to the streets.'

'Salai, listen to me. I am not your father, I will never abandon you.' Tears slid down the boy's face. 'I'm sorry papa.'

Later that evening, her passions aroused, Cecilia flung open her bedroom door the moment she heard footsteps outside. She dragged the Duke inside, not allowing him breath before she hungrily kissed him. Il Moro needed no encouragement and sought to carry her up in his arms. To his surprise, she skilfully side-stepped him, spun him around, placed her right foot between his two feet and pushed him hard with both hands in the chest. Il Moro collapsed onto the bed and before he had time to react Cecilia lifted her white knee-length linen camisole, jumped up and straddled him.

'My Lord, you had better satisfy me tonight or I will banish you from my room for good.'

His ardour kindled, Il Moro needed no further invitation and flung himself on top of Cecilia. Tearing off her camisole he planted a firm hand on each of her pert breasts. While he frantically made love to her, she imagined Leonardo's artistic hands had come to take possession of her and recalled how Leonardo had gently spoken her name. In response to the sound of his voice echoing inside her mind she tossed her head from side to side, kicking up her red hair and closing her eyes. Her lover, oblivious to his mistress's fantasies, rode her with all the gusto he could muster. She longed to scream Leonardo's name but bit into her knuckles to stop herself from doing so. As their frenetic lovemaking reached its zenith, Il Moro grunted into Cecilia's ear while a hand violently spanked her chalk-white derriere. His energy spent, he collapsed on top of her, perspiring and breathing deeply.

'If this is what happens when I neglect you, I can see the benefits of making you wait more often,' he said. A satiated Cecilia surrendered to Il Moro's arm too exhausted to move.

Her room was carpeted by a large Indian rug depicting men wearing coloured turbans who rode upon elephants in pursuit of a tiger. The tiger's gold and orange stripes were a source of great fascination, along with the beautiful tropical birds that flew hither and thither to escape the clash between pursuers and pursued. By the window sat a blue and cream chaise longue, long enough to sit three people. Opposite, on the far wall was a carved Indian rosewood vanity unit with a mirror held in place by a silver border. Beside the vanity was a matching wardrobe, both were carved in ornate interlocking curves like braided hair in a style distinctly oriental in origin. A large window opened out to a balcony. This offered on one side a view of the castello, while the other a spectacular view of Milan. Cecilia preferred the view of Milan and was fond of taking in the night air whilst looking out across the city.

After his exertions, Il Moro drew his arm over Cecilia's body and snuggled up to her, a rare gesture of affection.

'I have news,' he said softly. 'For some time now, I have considered plans to have an important commission painted in Santa Maria delle Grazie but I have hesitated from making an announcement until work there was finalized.'

'I am sure maestro Leonardo would welcome such a commission.'

'I'm sure he would but Father Rodrigo thinks a Roman artist might be more suitable.'

'Why pay for an artist from Rome? You have Leonardo who surpasses anything Rome has to offer.'

'We will speak more on this another time. I will sleep in your room tonight and see what the morning has to offer.'

While Cecilia's mind raced with the Duke's news, Leonardo slept uneasily. The wind whistled down the street outside his window, conjuring up strange sounds that echoed in his mind and gave weight to the amnesia that regularly stole the sleep from his body. Cold loneliness seized him, just as it had done many years ago as a motherless child who rarely had contact with either his father or siblings. It had returned to him when he had been imprisoned in Florence. And again, in Milan, there were nights when he found it hard to shake off the gloom that engulfed him. Doubts assailed his mind: *Lord, will I ever be commissioned to paint something worthy of my talent? Or, will fate forever conspire against me as it did in Florence?* Morose and restless he rose from his bed, lit a candle and, using a quill, wrote in his journal: *Oh wretched life, what must a man do to be free from your many miseries.*

CHAPTER FIVE

When Maria arrived with breakfast of fresh bread, cheese and warm milk, the naked Cecilia was frantically searching for something. The Duke had gone long before Cecilia's eyes saw daylight.

'Confound the girl, where has she tidied it away?' she complained. Then, realising she was no longer alone, she let out such a squeal of surprise that Maria jumped, inadvertently spilling milk over Cecilia's prized Indian rug.

'I am sorry, my lady,' spluttered Maria, 'I didn't mean to startle you.' She placed the tray upon a small table of exotic design and began to wipe the carpet with the hem of her grey dress.

'Don't worry about that, leave it. Have you seen my quill?'

'But the carpet will smell,' implored Maria. 'Your quill? No, I have not,' she said as she continued to clean the spillage.

Cecilia looked at the breakfast. 'Are you hungry?' she asked and then broke the bread in half and handed a piece to her dress maid. Maria eagerly accepted, biting into the bread only after her mistress had begun to eat hers. Compared to the blackened, salty, teeth-cracking bread Maria was accustomed to, this bread melted in her mouth. On rare occasions, particularly when the Duke had held a banquet and there was food left over, her mama was able to bring home fresh bread, the best cheese and on a couple of instances sweet pastries with honey and cherries. Maria was thankful that she got to eat meat an average of once a month, making her considerably better off than the average family in Milan who only got to eat meat on special occasions. Even this was a luxury for a vast swathe of the population who rarely, if ever, tasted meat from one year to the next.

Cecilia perched on the edge of her rosewood bed, swinging her slender legs.

'Maria, can you keep a secret?' she asked.

When she was younger she and her best friend Sabrina, who also lived in the staff quarters, had had lots of secrets between them, most were the innocent fancies of children at play.

'I have not been asked to keep a secret since I was a child, my lady.'

'Perhaps another day then,' Cecilia responded, to Maria's relief.

'But...' Cecilia continued, jumping off the bed. 'I need you to help put into action a little plan of mine. You are to return to your quarters and bring me a long winter cloak, the longer the better. When you have done that you are to assist me vacate the castello disguised as a servant girl and accompany me to Leonardo's workshop.'

'Mistress, please. If I am caught, me and all my family will be whipped and beaten and flung into the street.'

'I'm sorry, what am I thinking? Cecilia said, having realized Maria was right. 'I will go alone if you are willing to fetch a suitable cloak.'

Maria agreed and departed to fulfil her clandestine errand, returning a short while later with a dark brown cloak with rabbit fur along the edges and an inner lining of horse hair.

'May the blessed Saint Ambrose smile upon you,' Cecilia said, thanking her maid. Maria nodded and left her mistress to her schemes.

Very carefully, Cecilia opened her door and looked left down the corridor that ran the length of the upper east wing, which were used by Il Moro's high-ranking officials, his secretary, treasurer, and garrison commander. They were up and busy attending to their many duties well before the pampered Cecilia emerged from her room, but today demanded her caution. Her spine tingled, and her hands perspired as she took one step then another towards the servants' back staircase, no more than ten or twelve steps from her room.

Steeling her nerves before she began her descent, Cecilia wrapped the cloak tight around her. She lifted one end to use as a hood to conceal her head and began to tip-toe her way down the uneven stone stairs. She was wearing the plainest black dress she could find, along with an old pair of black boots. When she reached the penultimate step, she paused to check if she could hear anyone nearby. Satisfied the way was clear, she took the final step and turned right. She would have to pass by the kitchen on her way to the door that led outside to the castello forecourt. Beside the clunk of pans and the chopping of vegetables, she could hear the coarse banter of kitchen staff.

'Mary Mother of God, grant me favour.' Cecilia scurried past the kitchen and hoped to God that neither Maria's sister, Agnese, nor her mother would be nearby. Hurrying towards the outside door, she braced herself for the sound of footsteps or a voice from behind, but none came. Cecilia opened the outside door and breathing a sigh of relief stepped into the far side of the courtyard. Nearby was the busy south-facing main gate where traders were plying their custom while buyers milled about. Also that way lay the castello garrison, where soldiers outside were idly playing cards. She decided to head for the south gate. Just as she reached it a quartet of soldiers passing through jostled her.

'Hey boys, what have we here?' leered one.

'Come with me, honey, I'll show you what you're missing,' said another.

'You need a real man, not a servant boy,' sneered a third, groping Cecilia's breasts.

Looking on, the other soldiers laughed their encouragement. Cecilia retaliated with a hefty knee to his groin. 'Why you little bitch!' He wanted revenge, but she was up and away and soon lost in the crowd.

Eventually Cecilia regained her composure. Walking the cobbled streets, she was pleasantly surprised by what little notice common people paid her, even underneath a fur cloak on such a hot June day. Quite inadvertently she found herself paying attention to sights and sounds she ordinarily tended to ignore when escorted to and from the castello to various locations in the city. Now, strange as it would seem, her disguise had torn a veil between her and the populace, the sounds of traders selling their wares, the haggling with prospective buyers over prices, the noise of men cheerfully drinking cheap wine and making bravado at every attractive maiden passing their way. Yet it was the sight of half-naked children with bulging eyes and visible ribcages which provoked a response of compassion that hitherto had not been her custom.

Two of these orphaned wrecks sat on a wall by the Basilica of Sant'Eustorgio. Here on Sundays, Wednesdays and Fridays, the good-hearted ladies and priests of the parish fed the poorest of these wretches. Where did they come from? How did they live? Ahead of her, Cecilia could see others had also taken sanctuary on or around the Basilica's walls. All were waiting for a bowl of watery soup and stale bread, but none looked quite as close to death as the two Cecilia stood before. Tears began to run down her cheek.

'What are your names?' she asked, a boy of about six and a girl maybe a year or two older. Then, quite forgetting who she was, Cecilia wrapped her arms around them both and ignoring the grime that covered their sunburnt skin, kissed their gaunt cheeks. 'Oh my little darlings, what can be done for you? If only I could take you home with me,' she sighed. 'Lord, have mercy on these poor children.'

As she held their piteous forms, they laid their heads gently in Cecilia's arms. Eventually, she dragged herself away, placing a coin into the tiny hand of each child. So worn down were they from a lifetime of misery, no word of thanks nor even a smile greeted this gesture.

This encounter so moved her that every Wednesday from this day on she joined the other ladies at the Basilica of Sant' Eustorgio. She would prepare and serve food to the orphaned children or clothe and nurse the bruised bodies of Milan's urchins. Il Moro sought to forbid her from such behaviour, yet she insisted, that as a daughter of Milan, it was her duty to assist those children whom poverty had blighted.

It was a tradition in Leonardo's household for each apprentice to take it in turns to prepare breakfast. This morning the responsibility fell to Piero who, although not as diligent as Francesco, was nonetheless a genial and cheerful youth. He possessed a fine eye for sculpture and the necessary muscular frame to execute this particular skill. Although had had less sleep than usual (due to being kept up late the previous night by Salai's trouble with the Viscontis) his spirits were still keen enough for him to whistle merrily as he set about his duties.

The kitchen was square and comprised of an ornately decorated pine table. There were two pine benches either side of the table, upon each rested a richly-embroidered cushion that Leonardo had made. One was purple and gold and embroidered with a fancy of silver dragon wings, the other was forest green with a gold dragon's heads that breathed fire. On one wall a window faced the street, next to the window was a small pantry filled with coloured jars of all shapes and sizes. On the opposite wall was a large stone fireplace with bronze pans fastened on hooks above it.

Piero had just laid the table when Salai rushed in and knocked all the plates and a bowl of fruit and a small slab of cheese and the bread basket onto the floor.

'You bastard!' Piero raged. Salai laughed and threw a pear at him. Piero ducked out of the way but to Salai's delight a second pear hit him on the nose. The smirk was soon wiped from his face when Piero leapt over the table and wrung his hands around the boy's neck.

'You little shit!' Piero yelled.

'Stop this,' Francesco entered the kitchen and took a hold of Piero's shirt.

'The little bastards had it coming' said Piero. Francesco took hold of Piero's right arm forcing him away from the kicking Salai.

'You're a woman, Piero, a snivelling woman,' taunted Salai, who spat in Piero's face, enraging him even more. Salai received a sturdy punch to his nose in response before Francesco dragged him away and forced him out of the door. 'Salai, go!' he ordered.

Salai departed with the farewell, 'cock-sucking whore!' aimed at Piero.

'I am sick of the little bastard. I'm leaving this madhouse. There are other artists to whom I can be apprenticed.' Piero was a proud youth not known to issue idle threats. Indeed, he was gone by breakfast without even a departing word to his employer.

It was left to Francesco, to regretfully break the news of Piero's departure to Leonardo. His response was to storm into the kitchen.

'After last night's apology I expected you to have turned over a new leaf,' said Leonardo, appalled with his adopted son's earlier behaviour. The boy shrugged his shoulders. 'Why should I care?'

'Because we are family! It is the work that I and these apprentices are engaged in that puts the food in your belly, the clothes on your back and allows you to sleep in a warm dry bed at night and not a cold wet doorway like the one I found you in!' It was the first time Leonardo had thrown his generosity back into Salai's face.

'I simply will not tolerate this kind of behaviour. I have a business to run and no thanks to you I have just lost a good apprentice.' The boy's mouth gaped open and his nostrils flared with anger but his tongue for once stayed silent.

No one heeded Cecilia stealing into the workshop just as Leonardo finished chastising his errant son. She pointed a manicured finger at Salai.

'You ought to show more gratitude to the man who has shown you nothing but kindness.'

'You're only a whore,' the boy sneered.

'Salai! Apologise at once,' rebuked Leonardo.

'Be careful, as boy or not, Il Moro will have your head in a basket,' said Cecilia.

The altercation between mistress and urchin needed to cease, Leonardo turned to Francesco and Nicoli, who had both prudently kept out of the matter.

'To work!' he ordered. He then switched his attention to Salai and fixed his steely eyes upon him. 'As for you! There is a kitchen that needs cleaning, and when you have done that you can prepare breakfast.' Leonardo dismissed the household and led Cecilia by the arm out of the workshop.

'Be careful my friend, that boy may be the ruin of you' Cecilia said.

'I am the closest thing to a father the unfortunate creature has ever had. Although I may not be as skilled a parent as some, I am charged to do all that is in my power to affect a change in him.'

'Do you think it suits me?' she said twirling her cloak around.

'I should think you have a good explanation for arriving on my doorstep so charmingly dressed.'

The moment Cecilia entered Leonardo's personal studio she caught sight of the easel upon which her portrait rested. 'You've finished it!' she cried, prompting Leonardo to quickly place a cover over the portrait and position himself between it and her.

'Why can't I see it now?' she demanded.

'It is certainly not finished. Besides, I doubt you took the effort to come so… dressed… for an early preview of your portrait.'

Like a child suddenly remembering the errand upon which she had been sent, she exclaimed, 'The commission! Il Moro has told me he plans to announce an important commission at Santa Maria delle Grazie.' Leonardo's heart raced with the prospect of finally being commissioned for a master work. Clasping his hands together he paced excitedly around the room.

'This is magnificent news. What else did he say?'

Cecilia took hold of Leonardo's hands and shaking her head said. 'Nothing,' she said in a manner that was less than convincing.

'You cannot lie to me. I know there is something you are not telling me.'

'He mentioned that it may fall to an artist from Rome.'

'Il Moro will not go to Rome for an artist as he would have to pay His Holiness for the privilege. What else did he say?'

'He stayed the night, which is unusual, and left this morning at dawn.' For a moment Leonardo was lost in quiet contemplation.

'Il Moro merely wished to put a wasp in your head and is

probably laughing to himself right now knowing you would have word sent to me one way or another.'

'You think he is playing games?'

'You ought to know by now Cecilia, to men of power everything is a game.

CHAPTER SIX

IN THE PLEASANT LITTLE VILLAGE OF TREVIGLIO, NESTLED IN
the fertile valley between the rivers Adda and Serio, Alessandro, a weaver by trade, ambled his way past terracotta
rooftops and thatched cottages. Dressed in a knee-length
smock of dark blue with sandals on his feet, his face and arms
were bronzed from working in the sun. He was a handsome
man, muscular with curled blond hair and at thirty years old,
considered unusual not to be married. He attributed this to
never having met the right woman, until recently, others
attributed this to his desire to play with the ladies as opposed
to marry one.

The girl who was the object of his desires was named
Letizia, a tanned beauty aged nineteen who was blessed with
an inquisitive nature and an appetite for life. Her wavy
chestnut hair and dusky almond eyes were complemented by
two passionate red lips. Despite her pleasant features she had
the earthy appearance of a young woman accustomed to hard
labour. During the long summer months, Letizia worked from
dawn till dusk in the vineyards of Treviglio. Calloused fingers
and scratched forearms bore testimony to her employment.

Due to her outright refusal to romance the men of her

village whom she described as dull and plodding, Letizia too, had acquired an unwarranted reputation, as a fussy little madam with ideas above her station.

'Your younger sister Sabrina is not yet seventeen and she is already married. At this rate Roberta will be married before you,' were the words her mother had scolded her with less than a month ago. Since the death of her father three years ago from consumption, Letizia had become painfully aware of how grief could turn even the most mild-mannered of women into a tyrant.

When thoughts of marriage had previously occurred to Alessandro, the time needed to win a woman's affection plus the necessary formalities of arranging a dowry with her relatives, to say nothing of the many requirements of the church, had caused him to give up. Having traversed the period of a man's life where he had sown his wild oats with every willing maiden who passed his way, the thought of finally settling down with a fine woman appealed to him. Regrettably, none of the respectable young women from Bergamo, the town he called home, would entertain his approaches.

Since learning his trade from a child sat upon his father's knee, Alessandro had never thought to become anything else. Having finished his apprenticeship, he moved from Canegrate to Bergamo, where his skill was sufficient for him to make a modest income weaving for several noble families and merchants who sold his wares in Milan and Venice. With only one uncle to call family, Alessandro's parents, siblings and relatives having perished in 1485 of the sweating sickness – he lived alone in a simple manner. His one pastime was wrestling, an activity he excelled at and trained several evenings a week with his best friend, Marco.

Every year on May twenty sixth the village of Alessandro's birth celebrated the appearance of the Virgin Mary to a local girl, Giannetta de'Vacchi. She had been picking herbs in a meadow when this heavenly visitation had taken place. Consequently, villagers from far and wide annually made pilgrimage to Canegrate for a special celebratory Mass. Like many religious events, it was also an occasion of merriment and feasting. Letizia, accompanied by others from her village, walked the journey from Treviglio the day before the Holy Remembrance to sample the atmosphere.

Ordinarily, Letizia would not have stopped to watch bouts of wrestling, however her closest friend Christina wanted to watch the major bout of the day. One where the reigning champion Alessandro, grappled with a man much larger than he as he defended his title against a much-fancied opponent. The larger man tossed Alessandro from side to side then brought his knee up sharply to Alessandro's ribcage, the force of which lifted him momentarily off the ground. His opponent grabbed a handful of Alessandro's hair and spun him around, he then yanked up the reigning champion's left arm and wrenched it sharply around. Alessandro flipped his body over in an effort to release his arm before he fell to the dusty ground.

Men in the crowd cheered or jeered depending on their allegiance. Bets were hastily exchanged as opinion swung heavily in favour of the larger man. Alessandro reeled from a punch, blood spurted from his nose causing Letizia to wince and turn her face away. The defending champion's senses spun. The challenger grinned as he moved in for the crucial blow. While he attempted to wrap his brawny arms around the champion – in a swift movement of arms and legs the larger man unexpectedly found himself off-balance. Alessandro struck. Using the man's weight against him he deftly threw his opponent face down in the dirt. He drew his forearms tightly over his opponent's neck, squeezing the breath out of him. Pinned to the floor and unable to withstand the pressure of Alessandro's grasp, his rival submitted. The majority of spectators began chanting Alessandro's name.

Letizia too cheered and, seeing a flower vendor nearby, dashed over to the old lady and purchased a small garland.

Impulsively she found herself standing before Alessandro. He bowed his head to enable her to place the garland around his neck.

'I am honoured to receive such a gift from so beautiful a lady.'

'You must be ever so strong,' she gushed, placing a hand lightly on his biceps.

'Wrestling is not just about strength,' he explained. 'It is about skill and knowing how to tip your opponent off balance.'

'I suspect many a thing in life is about knowing how to tip your opponent off balance,' she added. Alessandro felt his knees wobble under the gaze of her warm smile.

'My name is Alessandro, I am honoured to meet you.'

'And I am Letizia,' she said with a flirtatious smile.

The following morning, they met again and chose to stroll by the leafy poplars that lined the short distance from the piazza to the lazy river Adda. This time the handsome couple were accompanied by Letizia's mother and several other black-cloaked widows, who followed behind at a discreet distance. It would not be acceptable on such a holy day for a young couple to be accused of impropriety.

Alessandro bent down and picked up a bunch of wild bluebells and handed them to Letizia. 'You have such sweet eyes,' said Alessandro to a blushing Letizia. Each step by the banks of the river Adda carried the couple further along a canopy of blossom trees swaying gently in the swirl that swept off the river. Letizia smiled at the man by her side. He was handsome, with his blond locks flowing down over his shoulders. Seized by a thirst for daring, she did something quite contrary to her nature; she kissed Alessandro firmly on his surprised lips.

'God forgive me,' her mother wailed. 'I have raised a harlot.'

'Letizia!' Alessandro raised his voice loud enough for the pious ladies behind to hear his words and breathe a sigh of relief.

Later that evening, just as the sun began to set over the village, bathing its pilgrims in a soft orange glow, the bells of the sanctuary rang out to invite the devoted inside. The shadow of its domed tower cast a net around all who entered it, gathering up a long trail of people enticing them inside the sanctuary's twin arched porticos. High above the entrance on a bronze pole hung a banner that blew in the breeze. The expertly crafted banner depicted a girl picking a flower with the Holy Virgin beside her.

Oblivious to the gossiping around them, Alessandro and Letizia sat next to each other amongst the festival goers for the evening Mass in honour of the Holy Virgin. The highlight of the evening would prove to be the revelations to the assembly of a frail, old lady. As she was helped from her seat of honour, a hush fell over the congregation.

'I was a good girl, honest and hard-working. I was not particularly devoted. When you neither read nor write it is difficult to be pious. Father Thomas always said I was attentive to scripture and had a good memory. The Lord knows my memory is not what it used to be. Yet of that day, if I close my eyes, I see it more clearly than my fading eyes see you. I was ambling through a meadow on a beautiful day as I often did. I had just bent down to pick up some herbs when I became aware I was not alone. It was the heat I felt first, a glow of heat. I looked up and there before me stood a woman with the most peaceful expression I ever saw. She was wearing a long tunic. Though the tunic itself was blue, it shone from a light from deep within her. Around her head was a golden halo. I knew instantly it was the Blessed Virgin Mary. My knees shook, and I fell to the ground. Mary spoke to me. It was like a thousand nightingales singing. *Don't be afraid,* she said, *I bring you a message of peace, for war will end and prosperity will come to all.* At this, she bent down and touched the earth. As soon as her hand touched the ground, water sprang up like a fountain, it splashed my body where I lay. When I looked up she was gone but the water remained. I ran to tell Father Thomas and when we returned water was still springing freely. He looked at the earth where the Blessed Mary had stood and it was scorched, not black, but with a golden ring. Since that day, people have come from far and wide to drink of these waters and many wondrous miracles have been wrought to the glory of God. I am Giannetta de'Vacchi. I am old now but when I was a girl I saw the Holy Virgin. God be praised.'

The dear woman was led back to her seat of honour while, in the congregation, men and women wiped tears from their eyes. Being a devout girl, Letizia regarded it as a good omen she had met Alessandro on a day of holy remembrance.

Days after their first meeting, Alessandro embarked upon his first journey from Bergamo to Treviglio where it had been arranged for him to have dinner with Letizia and her mother. Afterwards, he would retire for the night to the home of Father Alfredo who would accommodate him in a spare room.

The cottage Letizia called home was neat and tidy and furnished with care. A basic table and four chairs, each with a pretty embroidered cushion atop it, a hearth for cooking and warming the house with, and several pans, pots and cooking utensils. Scattered around the room were a few dainty fancies of needlework and embroidery.

While Alessandro sauntered into the village of Treviglio, the noisy Roberta quizzed her elder sister relentlessly.

'Is he handsome?'

'Very,' answered Letizia, busy seasoning the polenta with a liberal dollop of nutmeg.

'In what manner is he handsome?'

'Roberta, go and find something useful to do,' scolded her mother.

'Leave her be, mama, I don't mind,' said Letizia, who once more looked out of the window. Her pulse raced momentarily to see Alessandro ambling towards the house.

'Alessandro!' she called gleefully as she ran outside to greet him. They eagerly embraced, Letizia took him by the hand and all but dragged him to her home to meet her family.

'This is my youngest sister, Roberta. She has been looking forward to meeting you.'

'A pleasure to make your acquaintance.' Alessandro made a show of kissing the young girl upon the hand. Roberta responded with a fit of giggles and ran outside into the street.

Alessandro savoured each mouthful of his polenta with heartfelt affection for the woman who had made it. After dinner, Alessandro and Letizia sat together outside on the porch. She brought him wine, sat down beside him and took hold of his hand. He looked down at her slender fingers locked around his own and he squeezed them gently. He noted how warm her hand felt, paying attention to a couple of the calluses on her fingers he could feel brush against his own.

'Tell me Alessandro,' Letizia said, 'do you make a good income as a weaver?'

'I have sufficient for my means and for those of a wife and children. Do you find your work in the vineyards to your liking?' asked Alessandro.

'The work is hard, but I have proven myself knowledge-able in viticulture and have progressed to not only tending to the vineyard and picking grapes but assisting with the fermen-tation and barrelling.'

Seated on the porch after a hearty meal enjoying each other's conversation was a scene they were to repeat once a week for the next month, during which Alessandro's longing for Letizia grew and her fondness for him became more apparent with each visit. Desiring to prove himself a chaste man, he chose not to attempt to seduce her.

After Alessandro's eighth visit, they once again found themselves of a pleasant evening taking in the tranquillity of village life. Alessandro glanced at Letizia, just as a breeze blew, causing the moonlight to cascade through the folds of her dark hair. His heart pounded, as he took a sharp intake of breath, knelt down beside her and cupped her hands in his.

'Letizia, will you do me the honour of marrying me?' A moment's hesitation. Her heart, heavy with trepidation, pounded in her chest before she gave her reply.

'Yes.'

Before anything else could be said, there was a high-pitched squeal from Roberta as she and her mama landed on the porch. There were hugs and kisses and handshakes and a mug or two of fiery grappa before Alessandro finally left to sleep the night at Father Alfredo's.

CHAPTER SEVEN

On a glorious summer's day in August 1491, the villagers of Treviglio turned out in style for the marriage of Letizia and Alessandro. In addition, a lively crowd of Alessandro's neighbours made the journey from Bergamo especially for the occasion. Trees were swathed in ribbons made of strips of white cloth and adorned with garlands of flowers. Encouraged by the exuberant Roberta, children played and skipped, their laughter a perfect accompaniment to the day.

Letizia's red bridal dress was tucked in neatly around her waist, fanned outwards from her hips and trailed around her feet. Sadly, however, it had seen better days, but her resourceful friends had sewn on motifs of birds to hide the worst of the ravages of moths and time. Over her face, she wore a white patterned lace veil, embroidered by Sabrina to prevent anyone giving her the *mal'occhio* (the evil eye) on her wedding day. In her hair, she wore a crown of rosemary as a token of her love for Alessandro. To keep at bay the jealousies of any spurned woman who had resorted to witchcraft, she wore a blue *corno* (horn amulet) around her neck. Her mama had insisted upon the *corno*, a family heirloom handed down through several generations. She had also asked Father

Alfredo to ensure the nuns be kept from the village in fear of a portent to death. Being familiar with the many superstitions of his flock, he relented and wrote to the Abbess requesting she abided by his instruction.

Villagers applauded and cheered as bride and bridesmaids passed them on their way to the Basilica of San Martino. Letizia did her best to smile only her mind was plagued by troubling thoughts. The strange creeping sensation that had caused her to hesitate the night Alessandro proposed, once again inflicted her. Snapping out of her mood Letizia declared.

'You're the best friends any bride could wish for. I love you all.'

Outside the Basilica of San Martino, Alessandro fiddled nervously with his clothes. His jacket and britches had been purchased several summers ago. Regrettably they had remained in a drawer. Now that he had need of them, creases stubbornly remained in spite of repeated pressing. He fiddled with a lump of iron in his pocket, one his friend Marco had given to him to ward off the evil eye.

'Perhaps she isn't coming,' taunted Marco. 'Maybe a nobleman passed her on the road and kidnapped her.'

'Stop this,' pleaded Alessandro.

'It would seem, my friend, it is your lot in life to remain a bachelor, but at least there is plenty of wine for you to drown your sorrows.' Those within earshot grinned at Marco's teasing, while a worried Alessandro looked nervously down the road to see if there was any sign of Letizia... but there was none.

The bride and bridal party eventually reached the doors of the church. The relief on Alessandro's face was palpable. Stood resolutely in front of the church was Father Alfredo, who hit his staff twice upon the solid oak doors of the church and immediately brought the excited chatter to a standstill.

Alessandro handed the traditional bouquet of lilies and

roses he had nervously been custodian of to Letizia. She thanked him with a smile as broad as the church doors and sniffed their fragrance before passing them to her sister, Sabrina. Father Alfredo stepped forward and indicated for Alessandro and Letizia to kneel. The good Father then handed the couple a candle each. They each lit their candle from the symbolic flame held by a young novice. Father Alfredo then led prayers to Saint Andrew, the patron saint of marriage and to Saint Valentine, the patron saint of love.

Marco brought forth a cushion, upon which rested a gold wedding ring. Father Alfredo propped his staff against the Basilica's doors, took the cushion in one hand and placed his other atop the ring.

'O merciful Lord, bless this ring. May they be ever faithful to one another, remain in your peace, and together in your great love may they live and grow. Bless their union with children and may they live to see their children's children. Amen.' A nervous Alessandro took the small gold ring between his forefinger and thumb and slipped it over Letizia's ring finger. Looking heavenward, Father Alfredo placed their hands together.

'Let us pray.' Neither bride nor groom heard Father Alfredo's closing prayer, so engrossed were they in each other's gaze. The ceremony concluded and the guests burst into cheers as Alessandro kissed Letizia with the kind of zeal reserved for a man just married. Letizia's head swirled with a thousand pleasant emotions as Alessandro's lips pressed firmly against hers. Tears of joy wound their way down the cheeks of Letizia's sisters and her dear mama, who blew her nose rather loudly into her handkerchief, bringing a moment's mirth to the occasion.

'It is time,' Father Alfredo said, hitting his staff twice against the Basilica's doors, which the women of the village had decorated in garlands of flowers that were draped along the edges of the church door and held in place by a rope that had been threaded around the entrance and tied to the candle hooks. Father Alfredo opened the doors of the Basilica of San Martino to allow the newlyweds and all outside to enter for a celebratory Mass.

CHAPTER EIGHT

DUE TO HER FATHER'S ILL HEALTH, BEATRICE WAS CALLED away, thus presenting Il Moro with the opportunity in her absence to celebrate the unveiling of Cecilia's portrait. Il Moro had ordered his secretary to draw up a list of trusted courtiers and nobles whose discretion could be relied upon. Instruction had been given to those courtiers and maidservants loyal to Beatrice, forbidding them to enter the Palace until her return. Amongst the invited were Cecilia's six brothers, finely dressed and chatting merrily to bystanders.

'Business is flourishing!' Federico Stefano declared. 'Much more of this and I shall have to take a wife.'

Cecilia, the centre of all this attention, had not yet arrived. In truth she was still preparing herself for *la grande entrata*.

Several members of the Society Philosophic were in attendance including Luca Pacioli and Franchino Gaffurius. Franchino wore a red doublet jacket, whereas Luca wore his grandiose black robes and habit reserved for special occasions.

Resplendent in a black doublet jacket with padded shoulders trimmed in blue silk and a large white ruff, Il Moro strutted to and fro amongst his guests. Upon his head he wore a magnificent round red leather hat adorned with a white feather, his tights had one leg in red, to match his hat, and the other in black and white stripes to match his doublet and ruff.

This summer, dresses were usually of one colour, orange, peach and azure blue being popular this season. All were elaborately designed and embroidered by the finest dressmakers Milan had to offer. Extravagantly shaped hats, adorned with the pretty motifs and dainties, were draped in silk and lace netting that trailed off to a narrow point at the tip proved fashionable with the ladies of Milan.

The secretary checked his list and was pleased to inform Il Moro that all invited were present except the Cappaldi family, whose father had recently passed away and were still observing a period of mourning. Being mindful of Il Moro's temperament the Cappaldis still sent their eldest son, who Il Moro paid his respects to and being in an unusually generous mood, granted him permission to leave.

As he departed with the secretary, a murmur of excitement rippled around the room, speculation that he had gone to welcome Leonardo. In fact, he swiftly returned accompanied by the royal tailor and two of the tailor's sons, their arms laden with clothes.

'What is this man doing here?' demanded Il Moro.

'You arranged for him to visit today, your Lordship,' squirmed the secretary. The tailor bowed to Il Moro, unsure of the situation but decisive in his show of respect to the Duke. 'Whatever for?'

'The forthcoming visit of the Queen of Hungary, my Lord.'

'Send him away,' said an irate Il Moro.

Mindful of Il Moro's temper, the tailor remained bowed as low as was possible for him to do so within the bounds of dignity. He was a small squat fellow with a large round head, his breathing hurried and uncomfortable. The secretary motioned to dismiss him, the tailor continued to keep his head down as he stepped backwards, his face flush with embarrassment.

'Is the wench beautiful?' Il Moro demanded.

'To whom are you referring, my Lord?' the secretary asked.

'The Queen of Hungary!' bellowed Il Moro, to the amusement of a number of courtiers who had long harboured jealousies against the now red-faced secretary.

'In my humble opinion Sire, Queen Esther is an immutable goddess.'

Il Moro beckoned the bemused tailor forward, who likewise ushered his sons either side of him to hold out various garments for display. Il Moro carefully examined each garment and finally made his selection before he sat back upon his throne. The tailor stepped forward with a piece of chalk and looking at Il Moro marked the cloth for measurement.

'A splendid garment my Lord, the very latest in French fashion.' Before the tailor or anyone had time to react, Il Moro rose to his feet and slapped the poor man in the face.

'French!' his roar reverberated across the Sala delle Asse. 'You dare bring me clothes from my enemy?' mercilessly striking him again with such force the persecuted tailor fell to the floor.

The tailor's two young sons looked on in horror. The clothes they had held were dropped to the floor and they fled from the room to the accompaniment of sniggers. Il Moro meanwhile stamped up and down on the discarded clothes.

'My Lord, perhaps the tailor is a French spy,' suggested the secretary, feigning innocence in the remark before he clapped his hands, prompting several of Il Moro's stern-faced guards to step forward. Il Moro looked to the heavens.

'My God, I am surrounded by traitors!' he said, drawing his sword from its silver scabbard only to hold it precariously over the tailor's head.

'Mercy my Lord, mercy!' the tailor said as he scrambled on all fours repeatedly kissing Il Moro's feet. 'Please, I beseech you for the love of my wife and many many children, mercy.'

Just as Il Moro brought his sword over the man's neck there came a cry...

'No!' All turned to witness Cecilia, earnestly walk towards Il Moro as quickly as the twin necessities of decorum and expediency allowed. Cecilia bowed low.

'My Lord, please... away,' she placed a delicate hand upon the handle of his sword hand and held it there hoping to restrain him from violence. The secretary, who was not enamoured with Cecilia, declared,

'With all respect my Lady, this man is a French spy.'

Cecilia laughed.

'He is no more a French spy than you or I.' She turned to the quivering tailor and raised him to his feet. 'I promise you my Lord, this man means you no harm.'

Leonardo entered the Sala delle Asse accompanied by Francesco, who held an easel under his arm. Sensing an unfavourable atmosphere, Leonardo took hold of his apprentice's shoulder to prevent him from proceeding further. Cecilia saw the pair enter and gave Leonardo the most imperceptible of acknowledgements before turning her attention back to Il Moro.

'My sunshine throughout the day, I implore you, this man is a mere tailor. He thinks in fabrics, colour, style, texture, not of politics, diplomacy, or war.' Subdued by Cecilia's words, Il Moro placed his sword back into its scabbard.

'Go tailor, and next time bring me something stylishly Milanese, and not from my enemies the French.' Then, spinning the frightened man around, he kicked him up the backside and yelled, 'Or I'll give you French alright, with my foot up your arse!'

The hapless tailor, in a similar manner to his sons, abandoned his garments and fled the court with the sound of guffaws resounding in his ears.

Cecilia leant towards Il Moro and whispered discreetly into his ear while she pointed to where Leonardo had patiently decided to bide his time.

'Leonardo! Do you have it?' an excited Il Moro shouted across the Sala delle Asse. Leonardo and Francesco made their way inside. Francesco erected the easel, ensuring the cloth continued to conceal the portrait. Leonardo stepped forward and bowed before Il Moro.

'If I am not mistaken my Lord, you appear a trifle distracted,' he said with a grin.

'Be quick with you Leonardo, I am in no mood to jest.'

Leonardo looked to Francesco to ensure all was ready. Satisfied, he bowed again, and declared.

'Noble ladies and gentlemen, it is always rewarding for an artist to see those upon whose generosity he so heavily relies, appreciate his endeavours. Out of time-honoured necessity, I salute your unquestionable sense of taste and dear munificence to one so unfortunately encumbered by life's prejudices such as I.' While the assembled dignitaries of Milan contemplated if they had just been insulted or flattered, with an elaborate flourish of his hand, Leonardo removed the cloth.

'My Lord, ladies and gentlemen, I present to you, Cecilia Gallerani.' Gasps filled the air vanquishing all prior thoughts – Cecilia's very character and mannerisms – the sensual way she appeared to chew her bottom lip, the delicate texture of her skin, hair resplendent in all its fiery hue, the proud manner in which she stood were all clearly displayed on canvas. Yet it was the eyes of the portrait that drew you towards her, the subject's gaze followed all who looked upon it. Someone began to applaud, it was Cecilia. Il Moro, wanting to please his mistress, followed suit and once his seal of approval had been given, a paean of praise ignited the Sala Delle Asse. Only the secretary was lukewarm in his response.

Cecilia stood beside her portrait – a flawless reflection in a mirror.

'I do not know which one I shall take to my bed tonight, such is the likeness.' Il Moro boasted.

'Take both my Lord,' quipped Leonardo, much to everyone's amusement as he soaked up the plaudits as easily as a sponge soaks up water. 'Magnificent.' 'Splendid.' 'Truly sublime.' 'Perfection.' 'A work of genius.' He particularly liked the latter and vigorously shook the hand of its speaker, his dear friend Franchino Gaffurius, who added, 'I am convinced your paintings Leonardo will live on long after my music has been forgotten.'

Leonardo noted the delight on Il Moro's face as he surveyed Cecilia's portrait and concluded there was no better moment to strike.

'My Lord, I am pleased you approve of my efforts, not only of the lady Cecilia, but here too upon the ceiling and vault of the Sala delle Asse I have displayed my craftsmanship as an artist *par excellence*. Therefore, if I may be so bold, I hear you have plans for Santa Maria delle Grazie concerning a new commission you have in mind.'

'A private matter, maestro,' interrupted the secretary, disliking Leonardo's impertinence. Il Moro raised his hand to silence him. 'Come, Leonardo, there is something I wish to show you.' He turned on his heels and paced out of the Sala delle Asse with Leonardo at his shoulder, he carried onwards along the palace corridor, out by the veranda with its fluted columns and into the forecourt of the castello, his four guards close behind. The bemused secretary, in an effort to catch up, waddled ungainly after them. So too the gathered dignitaries, quite taken by surprise, took up the rear as they scurried along like rats following a pied piper.

'One of the many disappointments of being such a wise and masterful ruler as God has ordained me, is witnessing the ludicrous fawning of men seeking to curry favour and approval. Many of my conniving courtiers would happily wipe my arse if they thought it would bring them some advantage. I am impressed, Leonardo, that the only arse you wipe is your own,' said Il Moro, with a firm slap on Leonardo's back.

Walking beside Il Moro as they marched through the streets with his guards close to hand, Leonardo witnessed the panic in the eyes of many a citizen. Men doffed their hats and dropped on one knee, women curtseyed and waved their tattered handkerchiefs in respect. But from the shadows and dark enclaves came anonymous and derisive whispers – 'butcher,' 'thief,' 'usurper.'

When they entered the Via delle Santa Maria, Il Moro pointed to the newly finished Basilica of Santa Maria delle Grazie. 'There Leonardo, doesn't she look splendid?'

Before them stood an orange-red brick basilica of oblong design with a large round outer tower of grand proportions intersected by circular walls, which along with its triangular front façade and high buttress walls gave the basilica an impregnable almost fortress style appearance. As well as being a place of worship, it also housed a small monastery with living quarters, a kitchen and a refectory. Il Moro entered by a side door that lead into a small garden forecourt, taking the monks at rest in the afternoon sun quite by surprise. Walking past the forecourt's colonnades, he stepped into the refectory. Inside, monks were so engrossed in their meals they initially failed to realise they were suddenly in the presence of esteemed company. Il Moro gestured for them to continue eating then nodded towards a bare stone wall at the far end of the refectory.

'Leonardo, it has long been my ambition to see painted a memorial to honour our Lord and the House of Sforza. Upon this wall, I commission you to paint the Last Supper of our Lord and Saviour Jesus.' Leonardo walked cautiously forward and rested the palms of his hands against the refectory wall and graciously offered a silent prayer to heaven: '*God, you have granted me my miracle.*'

'My Lord,' Leonardo said, turning back to face the Duke and assembled dignitaries. 'Upon this wall I will paint such a work of art it will stir the hearts of man for generations.'

CHAPTER NINE

WHILE MOST OF MILAN SLEPT, A TALL FIGURE ENTERED THE refectory of Santa Maria delle Grazie. A lone monk secretly watched him make his way into the garden and proceed towards the refectory. The restless monk, a novice, had been unable to sleep due to the heat of summer and tried to cool off beneath the branches of an olive tree. Barefoot, he followed the shadowy figure. In the gloom of the refectory he could see the stranger had long hair and was holding a candle up to the far wall. In the long, narrow room, the stranger's voice echoed.

'Speak to me, Jesus, speak to me and I will listen. Come forth from this wall and speak. Peter, speak to me. Andrew, speak. James, son of Zebedee, John the beloved, brother of James, show me your favour and speak. Philip, Bartholomew, doubting Thomas, do not forsake me, speak.'

The young novice was of course familiar with the names of the twelve disciples, as recorded in the Gospel of Matthew, but he wondered at this strange ritual.

'Matthew, James, Thaddeus, Simon, speak and I will listen.' The stranger held his head against the wall as if waiting for an answer.

'Judas, even you! Come to me, Judas, tell me your secrets.' The man knelt and placed the candle beside him. He stretched out his hands to touch the wall, where he remained for several minutes as if anticipating a reply.

The monk decided the man meant no harm, and as quietly as he had arrived, he departed to leave the man to his unusual protestation to return to his place under the olive tree. He quietly mumbled his devotions and soon fell sleep. When he awoke a few hours later, there was no sign of the strange visitor. His immediate thought as his bleary eyes met the haze of the early morning sun was to wonder if it had all been a dream.

CHAPTER TEN

DUE TO A BITTERLY COLD WINTER, LEONARDO HAD BEEN forced to wait until the spring of 1492 before he could begin work on priming the refectory wall at Santa Maria delle Grazie. Aided by Francesco and Nicoli, a promising new apprentice, Leonardo applied his experimental gesso to the wall of the refectory. Off-white in colour, gesso was made from animal glue and traditionally mixed with chalk. Here, however, the maestro instructed his apprentices to stir in pitch mastic with the aim of creating a hard surface that would withstand deterioration to the painting from moisture in the air and would therefore allow him to paint at his usual pedestrian pace. Ten layers of normal gesso, applied thinly, was sufficient to prime a surface but no one had ever attempted such a large-scale painting using an unproven substance before.

'Keep it nice and even,' Leonardo instructed the duo. Francesco knew well the peculiarities of the maestro and quickly adapted to the application of the gesso. The younger Nicoli, inexperienced and lacking in confidence, struggled.

'Is this thin enough, maestro?' he asked.

'Watch me,' Leonardo responded. Taking some of the

gesso in a trowel, in a right to left movement he spread it evenly over a patch of the wall.

'Now you try.' The apprentice applied his trowel in a sweeping motion as he applied the gesso. 'Good Nicoli.' The youth smiled, pleased his efforts had gained the maestro's approval. 'Romano, more water!' yelled Leonardo. Romano was a stocky boy of twelve with thick black curls. 'Coming, maestro,' the boy replied as he heaved a bucket of water over.

Picking off some plaster from his trowel, Nicoli flicked it at Romano, causing him to stumble as it hit him on the nose. He quickly retaliated; a wet sponge thrown at his tormentor. The Prior of Santa Maria delle Grazie, Vicenzo, walked through the refectory door just in time to witness their tomfoolery. 'This is a house of God not a street for playing in! Maestro, have your apprentices treat the Lord's House with respect.' Before Leonardo could answer, Prior Vicenzo departed, muttering to himself in Latin. Prior Vicenzo was a short-tempered man in his mid-fifties, his belly indicating a love of wine and rich food. He wore the black cloak of the Dominican order over his white habit and was an imposing figure as he strutted around Santa Maria delle Grazie.

A few weeks and numerous applications later, the preparation of the wall with Leonardo's experimental gesso was finished. It then needed three months to dry before any paint could be applied to the refectory wall. To aid the drying process, the doors and windows of the refectory were left open at night.

'What if some thief took the opportunity to rob us?' the Prior demanded.

'If you wish to place a watch, I have no objections,' Leonardo replied walking away.

'Place a watch!' a vexed Prior Vicenzo yelled at the departing artist.

A week later, Leonardo departed his workshop with a sack slung over his back, while a thick brown leather belt with a pouch and hammer attached to it was wrapped around his waist. Looking like any artisan, he walked through the Piazza del Duomo. The bustle of market stalls filled one corner of the piazza as traders and customers haggled over prices. In the far corner, young men from Milan's military academy were being put through their fencing exercises by an old soldier sporting an impressive grey beard. Holding his feathered silver helmet in one hand, and a gleaming sword in the other, he barked his orders.

A crowd had gathered around a troupe of *Commedia dell'Arte* players who had taken prime location in the centre of the piazza. Leonardo stopped to observe the actors dressed in striped black and white costumes and elaborate zanni masks with bizarre elongated noses.

To the amusement of their audience the French king, Charles VIII, was being played by an excitable cocker spaniel that wagged its tail with considerable enthusiasm. The gist of the tale was that the avaricious King Charles VIII of France was divided in his affections: should he court the ugly old Doge of Venice or the treacherous Borgia that sat upon the Papal throne? The whorish Pope was played by Colombina, whose breasts were exposed as she strutted about arms akimbo.

The Doge beckoned to the dog. 'I may be an old fart,' he pleaded, 'but the bulge in my codpiece can still satisfy a young hussy!' He got down on all fours and cocked his leg in the direction of the spaniel, who seemed mightily impressed. The French king licked the Doge and was just about to mount him when there was a shout of, 'Heel pup!' from Colombina, who lifted her skirt up and over the spaniel. 'You don't want to ruin your appetite on a decrepit old man who's not long for this world when I have pleasures a French king has never tasted before.' She kicked the Doge out of the way, who promptly keeled over as if dead, arms and legs held rigid like a corpse. Provocatively, Colombina lifted her skirt back up and the

French king came yelping out and barked at the Doge before jumping into Colombina's lap, at which the crowd and Leonardo roared with laughter. The players took their bow. Leonardo, tickled by the folly he had witnessed, obliged the mischievous troupe with a couple of small coins and walked on.

On one corner of the piazza was a noticeboard, where officials nailed bulletins, city edicts or details of wanted criminals, as well as occasional announcements. Putting down his sack, Leonardo pulled out a bulletin, one expertly written by his hand, and nailed the parchment to a noticeboard on the perimeter of the Piazza del Duomo. A small group of curious citizens approached.

'Can you read?' enquired one.

'Indeed, I can,' answered Leonardo.

'Who might you be?' asked another.

'You don't look like an official.'

'I am the maestro, Leonardo da Vinci.'

'Never heard of you, what are you doing with them bulletins?'

'You have never heard of him?' a man with no teeth said, incredulously. 'How long have you been in Milan? He's the Resident Artist to Il Moro.'

'I am indeed,' admitted Leonardo.

'What does this bulletin of yours say then, maestro?' asked a woman with a carbuncle on her nose.

With a pompous air, Leonardo read out the words of his notice:

Leonardo da Vinci seeks men of sound mind and body and of godly features to audition to be painted as the figure of our dear Lord and Saviour Jesus Christ. The man chosen will receive the sum of two months' salary. Those wishing to be considered must be aged between twenty-five and thirty-five and be of good reputation. Applicants must be in possession of their teeth, clean-faced and hair washed, and to arrive on the first Monday of the new month at Santa Maria delle Grazie. Honourably yours, the maestro Leonardo da Vinci. Resident Artist to the Duke of Milan.

Leonardo looked up at bemused faces staring back at him. First to speak was the toothless man, 'This strikes me as improper maestro, to choose a man to be painted as Jesus.'

'You can't take an ordinary man and paint him as Jesus,' said the woman with the carbuncle on her nose. In response, the toothless man took hold of Leonardo's cloak.

'Tell me, has Il Moro granted you permission for this nonsense? Or the Archbishop? There could be trouble.' Others murmured their agreement.

'Friends, friends,' implored Leonardo, 'Everything is in order, I assure you.' He left the crowd to their discussions and hurried on his way to pin more of his bulletins to notice boards elsewhere in the city.

Within the hour, a band of ruffians swigged down mugs of cheap wine as they sat outside the tavern at the north end of the Piazza del Duomo.

'Are you going to show your ugly wart-riddled face to the maestro then?' a man with more neck than face asked of his friend.

'Me? Not likely! Can't imagine our Lord looking like the far end of a donkey, can you?' His reply drew various heehaw noises from his drinking companions.

'I'll wager three bits it won't be long before the maestro has a papal bull shoved up his arse! I'd like to see him conjure his way out of that!' laughed the man with multiple warts.

CHAPTER ELEVEN

LIKE MANY PREGNANT WOMEN, LETIZIA WAS HAVING A RESTLESS night. On her mind preyed Alessandro's complaints that as business was so poor in Bergamo he contemplated leaving his home to secure work. 'Wife I am convinced I have better prospects of finding work as a weaver in Milan rather than Venice where guilds run by local families strictly control trade.'

She had settled well into her new home on the outskirts of Bergamo, just a short walk from the road to Milan, and had done an admirable job of transforming Alessandro's cottage into a suitable place to raise a family. She had planted roses and some geraniums in the front garden, along with rosemary, oregano and garlic. In the back garden she had grown a selection of vegetables and fruit, spinach, onions, cabbage, various berries and a peach and apple tree. An olive tree that Alessandro had neglected had fruited under Letizia's care, providing a useful income.

Inside the cottage, the touch of a woman was evident: a vase of flowers on a shelf by the front window, a neat white lace tablecloth and several embroidered representations of biblical scenes made by her own hands now hung upon the walls. The largest was a colourful scene depicting Moses and Elijah descending from heaven to give strength to Jesus as he prayed on Mount Carmel. Now she prayed the good Lord would give strength to her husband. Strength to resist the fear of poverty that was tightening itself like a noose around his neck, and giving thought to the unthinkable, that he would leave his wife of less than a year to seek employment in Milan.

CHAPTER TWELVE

IT WAS A NIGHT AS BLACK AS PITCH WHEN THE MOON ABOVE was shrouded by cloud. Nevertheless, it failed to deter Prior Vicenzo, who walked earnestly like a man who had spent the evening contending with Lucifer and who now believed he had him on the run. Accompanying him was a novice, Paulo, a ruddy-faced youth of seventeen who was prone to wilful streaks of disobedience.

'Come boy quick,' urged Prior Vicenzo. 'We will have this plot foiled and the Devil wringing his tail before the night is out.' Due to the many bulletins he was holding, Paulo was in no position to reply to his irate superior, for he could barely see the direction he was staggering in. Despite his tender years he had some sympathy with Leonardo's cause. Had he not been born the second son of his family, and thus by a long tradition destined for the priesthood, he would like to have chosen the path of an artist.

In one corner of the Piazza San Carlo they found the object of the Prior's wrath: another of Leonardo's bulletins, which Vicenzo furiously ripped down.

'That's one less, let us find the rest before the dawn

summons us to prayers.' He placed the bulletin on top of the others Paulo already held in his increasingly weary arms.

While the God-fearing folk of Milan slept, Leonardo was roused from his bed by four of Il Moro's guards who, forsaking the pleasantries of knocking on the front door, kicked it in. Squirming on his bed believing his death was upon him, they presented Leonardo with a ducal summons. Their boots echoed loudly off the path as Leonardo was frog-marched barefoot wearing only his nightshirt through the streets of Milan.

This was not the first time Leonardo had been dragged by armed guards through the streets. The first occurred when still in his youth and recently released from his apprenticeship to his maestro Verrocchio in Florence. On that occasion he had been paraded through the streets of Florence where all and sundry jeered and mocked, pelting him with whatever object they saw fit. It was a day to haunt him forever. Once inside the courthouse, and after a judge had commanded the baying crowd to be silent, Leonardo was sentenced by a trio of judges to imprisonment. Along with three other young men he was accused of sodomy with one Jacopo Salterelli, a sixteen-year-old male prostitute, a crime punishable by indefinite incarceration, burning at the stake or banishment. One of his co-accused was Lionardo de Tornabuoni, nephew of Lorenzo the Magnificent, de-facto ruler of the Republic of Florence.

There had been a party at the home of Lionardo de Tornabuoni, attended by all five men along with others of the fashionable Florentine elite. As the night wore on and the wine flowed, someone had become intimate with Jacopo Salterelli. Since the man in question had worn a party mask, his identity was unknown.

'I left early,' claimed Leonardo to the Judges.

'No, no,' insisted Leonardo de Tornabuoni. 'You returned later in the company of several male prostitutes, one of them being Jacopo.'

'I have committed no crime,' Leonardo pleaded. Yet his protestations were dismissed.

Dragged away by two burly guards, Leonardo was flung head first into his prison deep in the bowels of Florence's Palazzo della Signoria. Behind him, he heard the prison door slam shut and the jangle of a key in the lock. Darkness clung to him with a sickening air, while the prison's rancid smell attacked his nostrils as violently as any fist to the nose.

'My God, don't let me die,' he cried. From inside his prison, a slow mocking laugh answered him. Leonardo could vaguely make out the shape of a man chained to a wall on the far side of his cell. He presumed it was a man, though its appearance looked more animal, all hair, wild eyes and teeth that grimaced with menace as he cursed and screeched. The man rattled his chains and shook his head violently.

Fatigued Leonardo sank to the floor, yet no angel appeared in his dungeon to soothe his soul like Daniel in the lions' den. Tonight, and every other night of his imprisonment, God and his angels were silent.

On one long, lonely night, when the chained companion in his room mumbled his agonies more than most and the ticks in the straw had bitten him half to death, Leonardo made a vow: *If I survive this ordeal, neither man nor woman will touch my body again. I have no need of the agonies love brings.*

Leonardo endured a difficult two months before the court hearing. Eventually, the charge of sodomy against all four men was dismissed by the judges for lack of evidence. The prevailing gossip was that the whole fiasco was a plot to discredit the Medici family.

Within the year, Leonardo was overlooked by the Medici family for a lucrative opportunity to be one of the Florentine artists sent to Rome to work on various commissions assigned by the Vatican. Leonardo was indignant and sought out his old maestro, Verrocchio.

'The Medicis have ostracized me.'

'Demand for places was such that there would always be those who were disappointed,' Verrocchio argued but in truth, he knew that the Medici had deliberately excluded Leonardo, who they blamed for the embarrassing debacle of their nephew's imprisonment.

'Where will you go?' Verrocchio asked. Leonardo waved a letter in his hand.

'Milan. I have heard Il Moro is in need of my skills, and I have written to him offering my services.'

'But what of your unfinished commissions?'

'Florence has no business with me. Therefore, I will have no business with Florence.'

Once again, Leonardo was made to suffer the ignominy of an armed escort, only now it was Milan's turn to heap shame upon him. Mercilessly Il Moro's guards took every vantage to make his journey to the Castello Sforzesco a miserable one. They spat, struck him with fists and feet and trod purposely with hard leather-heeled boots on the maestro's toes, which were now bruised and bloodied.

Clandestinely following a short distance behind Leonardo and his armed escort, the cunning Salai, stuck close to the shadows as he watched his papa pushed and shoved inside the Castello Sforzesco courtyard, then up the steps of the palace where he disappeared inside.

Two soldiers pushed Leonardo into a room, where he was met by an incandescent Il Moro, who slapped him across the face with one of the bulletins.

'What is the meaning of this?' declared an irate Duke. 'Have you any grasp the trouble you have stirred up? I detest that Borgia bastard but the last thing we need, with the French threatening to march into Milan, is trouble with the Vatican, isn't that so, your Grace?'

Inside the room, and suitably grave-faced was Archbishop Arcimboldi, ordinarily, he was a gentle man by nature, but not tonight. 'It is indeed so, my Lord,' responded the Archbishop, flashing the artist a look displeasure. 'What explanation do you have for your actions?' he asked.

Leonardo looked anxiously around the room as the two most powerful men in Milan waited for his account. Purple drapes hung from the walls while a purple curtain shut out what little light shone from a starless night. In the centre of the room, two silver stands, each shaped like a hand and bearing lit candles, cast a flickering pallor over the room. A cowed Leonardo looked down at the bulletin that had fallen to his feet.

'My Lord, your Grace, I acted in all innocence,' he replied.

'Innocence!' barked Il Moro.

'I am an artist my Lord, and naïve about…'

'You are many things Leonardo,' the Archbishop said, 'but naïve? Do not insult our

intelligence with so ludicrous a defence.'

The colour drained from the questioned artist's face. As for his stomach, it knotted so tightly he felt as if he was being strangled around the waist.

'Forgive me, your Grace,' he replied in a hoarse whisper.

'To what purpose did you see fit to audition men to represent the face of Christ our Lord?' demanded the Archbishop. It was not the first time those in authority had questioned his creative impulses – the Medici too had occasion to demonstrate their displeasure, now the authorities of Milan saw fit to take him to task.

'Your Grace, I did not trust my imagination to surpass what nature in the form of man has already provided. Why go to the weakness and fragility of the mind to bring forth an image of the divine?'

'I see,' said the Archbishop dryly. 'Perhaps if you were more diligent in your faith the thought may have occurred to you that in the very least you should have consulted the Church.'

'My Lord, your Grace, I humbly apologize. Scripture teaches that each man is created in the image of God, therefore what better example of Christ would there be than to paint a man whose face and demeanour personified our Lord?'

'My son,' the Archbishop said, resting his hand upon Leonardo's bowed head. 'It is not for you to decide if depicting a man as Christ is permissible, such responsibilities fall to the Church to decide.' Leonardo's shamed head faced the floor: *How I long for an era where artists are free to pursue their vision free from the whims of wizened old men.*

'Your Grace,' he began, paying heed to the delicate intonation of his voice. 'Forgive my presumption.' Raising his head, he looked directly into the Archbishop's eyes. 'My proposition to find a godly man to portray as our Lord was done without any intention to compromise the Church.' Leonardo then bowed, while the Archbishop pondered his sincerity.

'That may be so,' he said. 'But there are other considerations, particularly where the question of blasphemy arises.'

'Blasphemy?' cried Leonardo.

Shaken by the Archbishop's declaration, the blood drained from Leonardo's face. Having read Dante's Inferno, he knew all too well the horrors that awaited those in hell who were deemed heretics, and like all Catholics, just how grave an accusation of blasphemy if proven could be.

The Archbishop's reply was measured and his tone conciliatory.

'Because man is imperfect, and Christ is perfect. And many who came to see me today are appalled that you could even consider painting a man born in sin to depict the Sinless One.'

'I admit your Grace, I had not considered some would view my proposal in such a way.'

'We are exhorted in scripture not to make graven images.

Therefore, painting a man as our Lord and Saviour is seen by some within the Church as an act of blasphemy.'

'But your Grace, artists for centuries have painted images of Christ.'

'Indeed, that is true, but those images have sprung forth from centuries of tradition and have not born the image of an actual man.'

'Your Grace, it was Saint Irenaeus who said, 'the glory of God is a man fully alive.''

'I am aware of the teachings of Saint Irenaeus,' he replied curtly.

'Please, your Grace, I have a vision for *The Last Supper* that will surpass anything seen before. I plead with you, allow me to pursue the vision I have for Christ and judge me once the painting is complete. If I am proven to be wrong in using an honest and dignified man to depict Christ, I will return the money and a new artist can be hired to paint a more conventional painting. If I am right, then you will have a painting that will be the envy of Italy.'

Patiently he watched as the elderly guardian for the souls of Milan took out his rosary beads, deftly wove them in and around his fingers, while he muttered under his breath a prayer in Latin. After an eternity of silence, during which Leonardo prayed to every saint his memory could recall to intercede on his behalf, the Archbishop finally opened his mouth. 'If his Lordship has no objection, then neither do I.'

'I have no objection,' said Il Moro.

'Good,' replied the Archbishop. 'Then we can all retire to our beds.'

Il Moro stepped forward and gripped Leonardo's shoulder. Stooping down he whispered into his ear. 'By God's bones Leonardo, if this painting proves to be less than you claim, I will pluck your pubic hairs out one by one and when I'm done, I'll have my guards bugger you up the arse.'

Shaken by Il Moro's threat, one Leonardo had no doubt

was real, he quickly made his way along a narrow corridor guarded at either end by soldiers belonging to Il Moro's personal guard. He walked down a flight of stairs, and out into another corridor, one unlit by torches. Thankfully a clear moon and cloudless sky offered sufficient light for him to ease his way along the castello's inner sanctum. Suddenly an arm grabbed hold of him and shoved him into an alcove.

'You're alive, thank God,' Cecilia said quietly as she wrapped her arms around him. She kissed him on the lips then slipped off the cream linen nightdress she was wearing and stood before him naked. He gazed at Cecilia's exquisite body. Her fair skin glistened in the moonlight like a Roman statue. Legs like the finest marble were within his grasp, while the faint glow of light perfectly accentuated her petite breasts enticing Leonardo to break his vow of celibacy.

'I know you are pleased to see me,' Cecilia said, as she clasped hold of his hands and placed them seductively upon her breasts. Her auburn hair, cascaded over her neck, came to rest just above his fingers.

She hooked a slender leg around him and nuzzled into his greying blonde beard while he lovingly caressed her hair. He had forgotten the last time he had felt a woman's heart beat against his own. As a youth in Florence, there had been moments of being carried away by the intoxicating scent of a young maid. Such memories flickered back to life as Cecilia, breathing upon his neck, clung to him for what seemed like an eternity.

'I cannot pursue you, Cecilia, to do so would be folly.' He said, as he forced himself to break the silence of their embrace.

'My love, do not be so hasty to refuse so noble a gesture.'

'I have escaped the prospect of death once already this night. As much as my flesh desires you, my head is adamant, if we were discovered... it would surely result in both our deaths. Mine I could accept as the price of the devotion I hold for you, but I forbid myself to see your life snuffed out, not in one so young, who may yet find a husband.'

'Forgive me. I… I could not bear the notion that you would be taken from me without first having made love to you.' She kissed him delicately on the cheek then took hold of her nightdress and slipped it back on.

'What am I to do?' Leonardo asked. 'When I made a Christ Child, the Medicis put me in prison, now if I represent him again I am treated worse.' Cecilia placed a gentle hand on his cheek. 'I must go,' he said, politely removing her hand from his face.

With long deep breaths, knowing her desires for the man she loved may never be fulfilled, she ruefully watched each stride Leonardo made until they took him from view. Just as she turned to make her way back up the servant's staircase, Salai stepped out from his hiding place.

'Show me your cunt,' he said. A stunned Cecilia looked into his wicked face.

'You disgusting little…'

'If you don't, I will tell Il Moro about you and Papa.' Cecilia raised a hand and set out to strike him… Guards,' he said. Cecilia came to an abrupt halt. 'Your cunt,' he repeated with malice. Feeling intense shame, her head bowed low, she slowly raised her nightdress.

CHAPTER THIRTEEN

The first Monday of July in the summer of 1492 arrived. A cool south easterly breeze blew down from the mountains, just enough to take the sting out of the summer heat and give the good people of Milan a spring in their step. Even the populace of the Lazzaretto seemed to lift their feet off the filthy streets with a little more ease.

Although weary from his night of spiritual warfare, it was not his bed that Prior Vicenzo sought, instead he sat at his desk and wrote: *Most gracious Father Rodrigo of Salamanca, greetings in the name of the Holy Church. It is upon a grave matter that I now write to you. Leonardo da Vinci, from birth a bastard and hence more prone to wickedness than one born in wedlock, has devised a most pernicious and blasphemous plan. To select a man from the populace of Milan and to paint this man's image as that of our Lord and Saviour Jesus Christ for inclusion into the recently commissioned painting of The Last Supper. Please come urgently to aid me in my fight against the evil that has been unleashed in this city. Your trusted brother, Prior Vicenzo.*

At the far side of Santa Maria delle Grazie, monks and apprentices crowded around a latticed window and jostled for vantage as they peered outside into the street. Below them, a queue of about twenty men had gathered along the cobbled path by the refectory door. The men were in their twenties or early thirties and, whether blacksmith or merchant, each was dressed in his finest clothes.

'It's a scandal!' a monk with a weather-beaten face exclaimed.

'An absolute disgrace,' said an elderly monk.

'Why? What's wrong with it?' Salai asked, smirking.

'Fool!' replied the elderly monk, giving Salai a clout around the head.

'Has anyone seen da Vinci?' boomed the voice of Prior Vicenzo. The startled monks
jumped at his sudden appearance. 'No Prior,' they uttered in unison.

'Don't Prior me in that tone of voice,' he snapped. Prior Vicenzo pushed them aside and opened the window. 'You should be ashamed of yourselves,' he shouted to the queue of men lined up by the refectory. The men looked up at him, some sheepishly turned their faces away, but most had no mind to take note of the vexed Prior. 'And if you have no shame, then may it fall on the heads of your poor mothers.' He crossed himself before taking hold of the large wooden cross hung around his neck, kissing it and mumbling to himself in Latin. 'Be off with you!' he ordered as he waved his cross about rather like a wizard casting a spell. A few did skulk away, yet the majority remained, defiant. The Prior turned his head back inside the Church and puffed out his cheeks.

'By the time I've finished with that miserable fellow da Vinci he'll wish he had never set foot in Milan!'

'And why would that be?' sounded a man's voice from behind. All turned around to witness the man Prior Vicenzo considered not far short of the Devil incarnate, who held several of the offending scrolls tucked underneath his arms. The Prior's body heaved.

'Blasphemy!' he spluttered. Leonardo remained unmoved as he waited for the Prior to regain his composure. 'Mark my words,' said the Prior, as he unforgivingly wagged his finger towards those queuing outside his refectory, 'nothing good will come of this.'

CHAPTER FOURTEEN

O<small>UTSIDE THE WEAVER'S COTTAGE, WHERE A BLANKET OF THICK</small> clouds veiled the town and blocked the light of the moon, Alessandro pronounced his intentions to Letizia.

'Do you think God would show us mercy if I waited for a miracle to feed my family when He has granted me strength enough to walk to Milan and seek work there?' Letizia's eyes watered with sadness with each word spoken by her husband.

'Perhaps business will spring back as it has done before,' she suggested.

'If it does then next year we will be in a stronger position. But, for now there is work in Milan. Letizia, you must trust me. Allow me to leave with your blessing.' The tears fell from Letizia's eyes.

'When will you be back?' she asked. Alessandro wrapped his arms around his wife to comfort her. 'Winter.'

'After the birth of our child?'

'I have no choice. In Milan God may smile on me. If he does, rest assured I will send for you.'

'Then go in the knowledge you have a wife who holds you dear to her heart,' said Letizia.

Early the following morning when the morning mist still

clung to the earth, Letizia embraced Alessandro in the vain hope of deriving what little comfort she could, but alas, such was the sadness of their departing, even the arms of her husband failed to quell the dull sadness that rested heavily upon her heart.

The road to Milan was notorious for gangs of bravados who prowled the highway. These easily identifiable ruffians, with their caps or capes the colour of the local landowners who employed them, plagued the roads. Such was the frequency of attacks, people would travel in groups for protection rather than risk travelling alone.

Along with food, a sleeping mat and a little money, Alessandro packed a long knife in readiness to defend himself against such parasites. Having set off at dawn, he had encountered few persons on his journey, the odd farmer in a field and a few Dominican monks in their distinctive black habits. A constant drizzle had accompanied him throughout the morning and he thought perhaps the rain had deterred travellers.

By midday the weather had brightened and the frequency of people on the road increased. Merchants with their wagons and guards armed with cudgels passed him every half hour. Riders, too, were becoming more frequent. Alessandro bumped into a small party of pilgrims making their way to Milan, eager to pay homage at the Basilica di Sant'Ambrogio to Saint Ambrose. For a while they walked together. All sympathized with Alessandro's plight, wishing God's blessing upon his endeavours and the rest of the Blessed Virgin's upon his beloved wife.

Early in the afternoon, he approached a low wooden gate. Three men leaned against it. They wore blue caps with a pheasant feather protruding from the side. Alessandro slowed his pace.

'Are you going somewhere stranger?' one of the bravados demanded. He bore a heavy scar down one side of his face, while his eyes were darkened by the many violent crimes he had committed.

'To Milan,' Alessandro replied, trying to hide his fear.

'We don't allow your kind to pass this way,' spoke another.

'Be a good peasant and go back to shovelling shit.'

'What you got in that bag?' the smallest of the three men demanded.

'Got a tongue in your head, ignorant yokel?' sneered the first man who then made to snatch Alessandro's sack. Alessandro though was faster, punching him with such force the man was sent staggering backwards to collide with his colleagues. The men floundered on top of each other, slipping in the mud. The small man looked on startled. Alessandro fastened his eyes upon him and the man backed away. The two remaining ruffians eventually managed to hold each other upright.

'Right yer dumb bastard, let me at you,' cursed the gashed-faced man, but Alessandro was ready for him and brandished his knife.

'I'm going to Milan,' he stated. The gashed-face man nervously opened the gate and pointed straight ahead. Alessandro hurried on his way, stealing half a glance over his shoulder to ensure the thugs weren't following him.

Eagerly he ate up the miles until he ascended a small grassy hillock. Here Alessandro came face to face with the skyline of Milan. He paused to admire the magnificent structures that dotted the horizon. The tallest being the Duomo whose white towers seemed to him to be a beacon of hope welcoming him into this great city. His heart leapt and his weary legs found new strength as he pressed on until, walking beneath a turret displaying a large gonfalon of the Sforza crest, he entered the city.

The architecture of Milan fascinated Alessandro. With its intricate designs and the many adornments of crosses, gargoyles, coats of arms and fashionable gothic follies carved into the masonry like patterns on a cloth. On the half-dozen previous occasions work caused him to visit Milan, he had confined himself to the row of weaver's merchants by the Piazza Mercanti. Due to the pressing need to sell his merchandise, time had denied the opportunity to peruse the city at his leisure. Now with the afternoon at his disposal, he wandered around Milan like a man without such constraints, confident he would soon secure gainful employment.

His attention was galvanized by the sight of several inhabitants of the Lazzaretto with their soiled rags, bulging eyes and gaunt faces. A fearful thought struck him, perhaps he had arrived too late and poverty and disease had already gripped the city. The appearance of a baker carrying a large basket of bread on his head, walking happily on his way, offered him hope that this was not the case.

Alessandro turned down a busy, narrow street. As is familiar with all cities, people pushed and barged their way past him, while he, still overawed by the newness of his surroundings, got in their way. The street opened out into a quadrant with a dozen Roman arches ringing all four sides. Each arch housed a business. Alessandro made his way towards a blacksmith stoking his forge.

'Do you have any work?' he asked of the blacksmith, who barely gave Alessandro a glance as he threw down a pile of tinder.

'You're new in town, aren't you?' he said. He was a small man in his mid-forties with a burn scar running halfway down one side of his bare torso from his collarbone to his navel. 'What do you do, peasant, farmer?'

'No,' replied Alessandro, 'I'm a weaver.'

'I've got no work for you. You need to be at the market by the Duomo first thing in the morning, that's when anyone looking for work hires.'

'Thank you kindly,' replied a grinning Alessandro.

'Now piss off, can't you see I'm a busy man?'

Alessandro continued to ask each of the businesses in the square for work. Most gave him vulgar rebuttals. Undeterred, he walked through alleyways and backstreets asking whoever he saw.

Emerging from one of the narrow streets that surrounded the Palazzo Marino, Alessandro caught a glimpse of the gothic glory of the Duomo, resplendent in the late afternoon sun, where the light danced off its white walls from a myriad of angles like crystallized frost.

'Surely, only in Heaven will there be found a more splendid building,' he exclaimed. He walked slowly around the Duomo to admire it from every angle, noting each angel carved into its huge stone walls. He counted the windows and re-counted them. Fascinated by the on-going construction work he marvelled at the men who, high up on scaffolds, were busy with elaborate pulleys and mechanical wonders to lift blocks of stone to be added to the octagonal cupola. He strained his neck as he gazed up to view their work and squinted in the afternoon sun.

When the last vestiges of daylight finally faded, and the shadows of the Duomo became one with the encroaching night, the only souls who remained close to its sanctified walls were the homeless who sought sanctuary under the Duomo's towers. Out of his bag, Alessandro removed a thin blanket and a mat. Nearby, brothers from the Order of Saint Ambrose distributed coarse horsehair blankets.

Feeling the need to acquaint himself with his neighbours, he struck up a conversation with a family nearby and learned they had arrived only three days previously.

'Disease struck half my crops. What we were able to salvage was stolen from us by bravados. I'm ruined,' the head of the family said.

'He's a hard worker,' exclaimed his proud wife. 'But what can a man do for his family when the lawless go unpunished? We plan to earn enough money to return home and plant new crops in the spring.' Their two young daughters, aged four and six, sat silently as their parents presented their sorry account.

'It is a tragedy all too common,' Alessandro empathized, recalling his own encounter with such vagabonds. Consoling them with the promise he would pray to Saint Ambrose to restore their fortunes he bade them good night. Wrapping his blanket around him, he shuffled about until he was neatly tucked into an alcove. He then prayed to the Blessed Virgin and Saint Ambrose to protect his wife and bless his endeavours before tiredness overtook him.

It came as some surprise to Alessandro to learn that cities are noisy places at night. The bells rang out from the Duomo on the hour every hour, to be routinely replied to by the howling of dogs and the cursing of their owners. A wife quarrelling about twenty paces away pierced the night with her high-pitched caterwauling. Her drunk husband sought to drag her away, but she lashed out with her fists.

'If I chose to take a man with wood between his legs, what's that to you?'

'Well then, I at least ought to have the chap pay, that way we can both be happy.'

Their screaming and fighting was responded to by the angry curses of those, like Alessandro, who were rudely awakened. Being new to Milan, he had yet to learn that the first thing poverty in a city strips you of is your privacy.

When the dawn broke, Alessandro felt a sense of relief that he had survived his first night. He took some bread he had kept aside for breakfast, and having eaten, gathered up his mat and blanket and sniffed the early morning air before setting off to find work. At the head of the Piazza del Duomo about thirty men had gathered. An assortment of carts arrived, and foremen plucked out the lucky ones from the crowd. In the jostle for places, Alessandro found himself alongside the father he had spoken to the previous night. A foreman shouted and pointed in Alessandro's direction, but before he could respond, the man next to him stepped up and took his place. Alessandro was too polite to protest and bided his time hoping for a second opportunity, but no further invitation came. As the carts with their hired men drove off, Alessandro was left with the others who had been denied work.

He initially felt resentment towards the father who had assumed his place, yet he reasoned the man's need was such God would reward his act of grace. He recalled the words of his own father whose advice had been that it was 'unbecoming for a man to wallow in pity'. Therefore, with renewed vigour, he set off with some confidence that with a little toil and effort he would secure work. Arriving in a street just off the Piazza Mercanti, he entered a weaver's shop where he approached a handsome merchant in his early thirties.

'Good morning, sir, I am a weaver from Bergamo recently arrived in Milan and looking for work. Are you hiring?'

'I'm sorry,' he politely replied, 'but I have had to lay off weavers because the cost of material has risen threefold this past year and ordinary people cannot afford to buy.' Undeterred, Alessandro stopped at every merchant's shop that lined the Piazza Mercanti, where once again the same sorry tale was relayed of spiralling costs and men laid off.

The following day, Alessandro resolved to strike off in the direction of the Naviglio Martesana. The canal was lined with storehouses and merchants' yards and potentially a good place to inquire for work. He walked past several barges laden with stone, which would later be used to aid the construction of the Duomo. In one yard, men stripped to their waists hauled the stone with pulleys from the boats and loaded them on low-slung carts. Alessandro pushed back a wooden gate, entered the yard and approached a colossus of a man whose thick neck was almost as wide as a tree trunk.

'Are you hiring?' he asked the man. 'I'm strong and able bodied.'

'Be off with you, vagabond!' the huge man yelled.

'Sir, please, I'm new to Milan and seeking employment,' pleaded Alessandro. The

man picked up a rock and threw it at him, missing his head by a hair's breadth.

He tried more merchants' yards and buildings and, although not pelted with rocks, he suffered more verbal barrages from foremen who were, as one put it: 'Tired of feckless beggars.'

Back in Bergamo, Letizia held her hands tight together in prayer and with closed eyes, tilted her head heavenwards: *Saint Ambrose, may your face smile upon my dear husband.* Laying tearfully upon her bed, the babe inside her womb kicked for the first time. She imagined her baby saying: 'All will be well mama, trust to God.'

The morning after his wife's prayer, Alessandro woke with an ache in his stomach, so he joined the throng of those waiting for a bowl of gruel and a hunk of black bread from the monks of Saint Ambrose. The gruel was served from a large vat that contained the decomposing remains of onion, carrot and leak. It tasted bitter and left a sliver of grease on his tongue. Yet to a man whose lips had not touched food in three days, even this meagre ration was welcome. He devoured his bread with relish, licking the crumbs that clung to his sweaty palms.

Leaving the Piazza del Duomo, he deliberately avoided the faces of the starving whose fretful eyes desperately scanned the stone floor, scratching and scraping in the dirt for any crumbs that might have slipped through their fingers. Alessandro stepped over several gaunt figures, face down on the ground, weeping and cursing, driven mad by the kind of torment only hunger can induce.

Heading back towards the Naviglio Martesana, he passed a warehouse where men were loading bags from carts. 'I'm looking for work,' Alessandro announced to the foreman. The foreman turned away to bark instructions to a man struggling to carry a bag.

'Drop that and it's more than you'll earn in a year.' Eager to show his willingness, Alessandro ran to the man's aid and helped him with the bag. When the bag had been safely deposited and just as Alessandro was about to return to his conversation, the foreman yelled further instructions. 'Everything on cart three is to be brought in and placed over there,' indicating a spot on the other side of the yard. Alessandro summoned up his remaining strength and did as instructed.

He worked there loading bags onto carts until midday when he was fed some fresh bread and cheese and handed a battered cup of watered-down wine, which he savoured as if it was wine from the renowned vineyards of Tuscany. At the end of his day, the warehouse foreman handed him a coin, enough to buy bread for the night and perhaps several days if he ate frugally.

Later in the afternoon, Alessandro entered the Piazza del Duomo. His attention was suddenly drawn by a man hurtling towards him. Behind the man could be heard cries for help with several men in pursuit of the man heading in Alessandro's direction. He was a scrawny creature with deep sunken eyes. Without thinking, Alessandro neatly sidestepped the man and threw him skilfully over his left shoulder onto the ground. When the startled man attempted to get to his feet, Alessandro placed a foot firmly upon his chest.

'You bastard!' the captured man yelled. An aristocratic gentleman with a neatly trimmed beard and a protruding belly arrived panting for breath with an escort of two soldiers.

'I believe this belongs to me,' he said, snatching a large brown leather purse from the thief's clutches. 'Which of you fellows put this vagabond down?' he demanded.

'He did, sire,' said a pretty young fruit seller who smiled sweetly at Alessandro.

'Young man,' the aristocrat said to Alessandro, 'I am in your debt. What is your name and state your business?'

'My name is Alessandro, sir. I am a weaver from Bergamo and only recently arrived in Milan looking for work.' Never having addressed an aristocrat before, Alessandro bowed lower than decorum required, much to the amusement of those watching.

'You're a long way from home, my boy. Take this in acceptance of my gratitude.' He removed a small silver coin from his purse and placed into Alessandro's hand. Overjoyed at such a gesture he thanked the gentleman numerous times.

'He'll hang,' said the fruit seller, still clinging to Alessandro's arm. Even though she was fair of countenance, her tone of voice implied she had witnessed more than her fair share of misery. 'I'm hungry, are you?' she said, lifting her dress slightly off the left side of her shoulder to reveal the outline of her ample bosom.

'What is your name?' Alessandro asked.

'Isabella,' she replied, smiling widely and flicking her raven hair back across her face.

'Well, Isabella, do you know where we can get something to eat?'

'I know just the place.' Isabella took hold of Alessandro's hand and led him down a
dirty alleyway.

They had only ventured a few steps when out of a window a woman threw the contents of a piss pot into the street that splashed against their feet. 'Bastard! Look where you're throwing your shit, yer lazy bitch!' screamed Isabella. She led him a little further on and stopped at an alcove near to where two alleyways merged. Dropping her fruit basket to the floor, she pushed Alessandro up against the wall, wrapped one arm around his waist and with her other hand she thrust down his pants and grabbed hold of his penis.

'For half that silver coin, you can have me.' Terrified,

Alessandro pushed her away, but she was more persistent than he bargained for and pressed her body against his while hitching up her skirt. 'I'm only trying to do us a favour. We both need to eat and we both need a good humping now and again.' Alessandro was flustered.

'I never invited you for… I thought you wanted something to eat.'

'Something to eat? You mean you didn't know what this was about?'

'You're a fruit seller,' Alessandro protested.

'Yes, amongst other things.' For one so slim it took a great deal of force for Alessandro to finally free himself from her grasp and flee.

After stumbling through a maze of narrow streets, Alessandro emerged opposite the Basilica of Sant'Eustorgio. He knew nothing of the Basilica's eminent position in church history, where long-held tradition maintained it is the final resting place for the relics of the Three Magi. Neither did he notice the unique design of its star-shaped bell tower. What did catch his eye was a bread vendor. Alessandro picked up two large loaves of bread and proudly presented his silver coin.

'Have you got anything smaller?' the vendor asked. It was the first time in his life Alessandro had ever been asked such a question. He felt rich. The vendor scratched his head and rummaged around for change in his pocket. Thanking the vendor, Alessandro took his bread and change. He had only taken a few bites when two children with lank black hair and hungry eyes, fell at his feet.

'Please, bread, sir.' Alessandro broke off half a loaf and handed it to the thankful urchins. Moving on, he quickly ate his bread before anybody else could relieve him of it. Grateful for his good fortune he decided to light a candle inside the Basilica of Sant'Eustorgio. Having prayed his customary prayers for the protection of Letizia, and for success at finding work, he returned to his alcove by the Duomo more content than he had been since his arrival in Milan. He exchanged pleasantries with others who too slept by the Duomo, then at nightfall he ate a small piece of his bread, pulled out his blanket and mat ready to curl up under the stars.

When morning arrived, Alessandro set off towards the warehouse where he had secured work the previous day. However, upon his arrival he found only a skeleton workforce and no sign of business. He looked for the foreman but his search was in vain. He approached an old, bald man who stood lazily by the warehouse's large double doors.

'Excuse me friend, are you hiring today?'

'You're asking the wrong man,' the old man said whilst scratching his crotch. 'The master is away and has taken the foreman.' Alessandro thanked him and with his usual optimism, carried on walking east. He passed several similar properties that too were shut up. The only signs of life were guards armed with cudgels. By the time he had stopped at every warehouse and place of business along the Naviglio Martesana, it was well past midday and the rumble in his stomach told him it was time to eat. Taking shelter under the shade of a willow tree, he sat down and ate the last of his bread.

A cool wind blew through Milan as a tired Alessandro dragged his aching limbs to his alcove by the Duomo. Here, weary and dejected, he took his mat and blanket and curled up by his favoured spot and prayed for divine intervention. The following morning, he once again lined up with men seeking work and, to his surprise, a foreman with a sanguine face asked if any man there was skilled as a weaver. Alessandro replied that he was a weaver from Bergamo. The foreman, who went by the curious name of Doffo, told Alessandro to follow him.

Bounding up and down in a cart passing row upon row of terracotta rooftops they eventually arrived at a small warehouse in the south of the city. The warehouse contained various coloured fabric that the foreman explained his master had purchased ready to be made into coverings for various pieces of furniture his master wanted for his home. The previous weaver had been knocked over by a galloping horse that had broken both his arms.

'Are you able to perform the work?' Doffo asked. Alessandro looked at the fabric and examined each of the pieces of furniture, a chaise longue, six matching dining chairs and a comfortable reading chair.

'I am confident I can,' he replied.

After a brief discussion they agreed on the rate he would be paid. This was to include breakfast, one meal a day and lodgings in a small room attached to the warehouse. Feeling galvanized by his new opportunity, Alessandro set to work. The previous weaver's equipment and loom were made available to him, the foreman having agreed a price for the rental. Alessandro later found out from the weaver who had broken both his arms that the rate he had accepted was lower than the weaver's guild in Milan considered acceptable. This caused Alessandro some consternation because, if it became common knowledge, it could jeopardize his prospects of securing work as a weaver in the city. For a small sum of money, which Alessandro was obliged to pay, the man he had replaced agreed to hold his peace.

Every few days Doffo would call by to check on progress. After a couple of weeks, he informed Alessandro that he and his master were travelling to Venice on business and would be gone for two weeks. Upon confirming they would be travelling via Bergamo, Alessandro asked if he would be so kind as to present his wife with the better part of his wages for the month and tell her he was doing well and missed her. Much to Alessandro's satisfaction, Doffo agreed.

The knowledge that he had been able to secure some money for Letizia filled Alessandro with a sense of satisfaction.

He felt content that like his father, he had the joy of providing for his wife and the child she carried.

By the time Doffo returned, Alessandro had completed the task of covering the dining chairs and it would only be a matter of a few weeks before the reading chair and the chaise longue would be completed. Doffo informed him his heavily pregnant wife was grateful for the money and had secured employment in a nearby vineyard. Doffo gave Alessandro a handkerchief Letizia had embroidered with bluebells and passed on her request that her husband return home as soon as possible.

After finishing work on his last night, the master paid a visit to inspect Alessandro's handiwork. Piero Mancini was a small merchant aged sixty who had a missing finger on his left hand. One that the foreman had previously explained had been cut off by bravados when they had been unable to prize a signet ring from his finger.

Delighted with the quality of Alessandro's work, he paid him his outstanding wages, wished him well and gave him a letter of recommendation. Doffo informed Alessandro that as it would soon be dark, he was welcome to sleep one more night in his work lodgings. Grateful for this kindness, he and Doffo went out to a nearby tavern where they ate, sang, swapped stories about their wives and got merrily drunk.

The following sun-blessed morning, Alessandro packed up his meagre belongings and headed for the nearest public bathhouse. While he languished lazily in the steaming water he was persuaded to buy a remedy to help clean and restore his hair to its natural vibrancy. After working hard these past two and a half months, and not having had a bath since he arrived in Milan, he reasoned a little extravagance was justified. The male bath attendant poured the potion from a small vase. To Alessandro's untrained nose the potion smelled of honeysuckle. In a circular motion the attendant's firm hands massaged Alessandro's scalp, neck and shoulders, producing the desired effect of causing his body to feel revived.

Refreshed and in good spirits he sauntered out into the street brimming with confidence, whistling the tune of a ditty Doffo had taught him the previous evening.

CHAPTER FIFTEEN

ONCE MORE A STEADY STREAM OF MEN GATHERED OUTSIDE Santa Maria delle Grazie. Some arrived with fresh hopes having been turned away at the end of a day when Leonardo's time was insufficient to view them. A pair of strapping apprentice blacksmiths radiated confidence as they joked and teased one another. Amongst the newcomers was a handsome teenager Leonardo had spoken to when posting his bulletins in the city.

'Good morning,' Leonardo said, eagerly shaking the youth's hand. 'Over here by the light if you would be so kind.' The young man nervously obliged. He had a wispy layer of fuzz on his unshaven face while his fair hair mingled with a red blush hung in tight curls that dropped gently over his neck and shoulder blending perfectly with the pale complexion of his virgin skin.

'I'm glad you remembered to come. You are Umberto?'

'Yes, maestro,' the nervous youth replied in falsetto.

'Umberto, sit here for me.'

Leonardo indicated to a nearby stool and stooped down to pose the youth as he desired. 'Hold that position.' He took out a piece of red chalk and feverishly began to draw Umberto's boyish features on the canvas. He had high cheekbones, which combined with his flowing light-coloured hair tinged with a reddish hue and innocent air lent him a feminine look. After a short time had passed the youth's curiosity got the better of him.

'Maestro, do you wish to paint me as Jesus?' Leonardo laughed.

'Jesus? No, Umberto, you are too young to be Jesus. According to scripture the beloved disciple John was a young man still not of an age to pay temple tax. Thus, you are to be John. Now, give Francesco your address and when I am ready I will send for you again.'

'Thank you, maestro,' Umberto replied. 'Even if I am not to be Jesus, it is still an honour to be painted.' Leonardo smiled, recollecting his own youthful exuberance.

While Umberto swaggered on his way with a grin as wide as the studio door, Leonardo turned to Francesco. 'He's perfect, isn't he.'

'I'm not sure finding the other disciples will be quite so easy,' said Francesco. Nonchalantly, Leonardo flicked a paint-brush into the air, caught it and spun it between his fingers and thumb. 'Send in the next man.'

Francesco stepped outside to hear an excited Umberto recount his experience to the men gathered outside the studio. His eager chatter was cut short by the sudden arrival of Prior Vicenzo, whose hands were clasped tightly around the wooden cross that dangled over his neck.

'Mark my words,' he said, pointing his cross towards the studio door. 'Evil lurks in many guises.' Francesco quickly closed the door and went back inside the studio.

'I take it the gracious Prior is afoot,' Leonardo mischievously remarked. In no mood for sarcasm, Francesco ignored him and instead poured himself a mug of water. Before he dared to venture outside again, he looked out of the narrow studio window to see if the Prior had departed and, considering it safe, opened the door.

'I see you still persist with aiding the Devil in his blasphemy!' yelled Prior Vicenzo to a startled Francesco. 'Mass on Sunday,' he hissed before walking away. Behind him, a flustered Francesco heard the maestro chuckle to himself.

'Why are you so amused?' questioned Francesco. 'My eternal salvation is at stake, or so Prior Vicenzo would have me believe.'

'Compose yourself and call in the next man,' replied Leonardo.

Francesco did as he was instructed and called the next person for audition, a handsome young merchant's son with a cultured face and long brown hair.

'What is your name?' Leonardo asked.

'Alberto,' he answered.

'Why do you think you would make a suitable Jesus?'

'My father thinks it is a scandal that a man could be painted as our Lord, but my mother said I am a handsome man and such a position may offer some favourable opportunity.'

Later that afternoon, Cecilia called by Santa Maria delle Grazie, causing a stir amongst the young men gathered outside who grinned like imbeciles. She greeted several politely, allowing them to kiss her dainty hand. Given the heat, Cecilia wore a light peach summer dress with detachable sleeves that exposed her back and the top of her bosom. Maria carried a parasol to shade her lady's skin from the sun. Cecilia entered the makeshift studio at Santa Maria with all the aplomb of a woman in her prime.

'Leonardo, I see many handsome young men outside. Surely you will find your man.' A casual Leonardo turned to the young merchant.

'This man is also handsome yet, as I have sought to engage him in conversation to ascertain the likeness of his soul, he too is found wanting. You may go, Alberto.' Embarrassed, the young man hastily exited the studio.

'That was a little harsh,' Cecilia said, surprised that Leonardo had been so candid.

'A good painter has two primary objectives. Firstly, to paint the physical nature of a man and secondly, the intention of his soul. The former is easy, the latter much harder, but if I am to find a man worthy to be painted as Christ, there must be some quality to his soul.'

'You ask a lot.'

'Francesco, wine for the lady Cecilia.' Francesco, who always welcomed her visits, poured two cups of wine.

'I'm afraid, my lady, I only have wooden cups,' said Francesco.

'Before my fortunes changed. I drank from much worse.' Harbouring a boyish infatuation with Cecilia, Francesco's face burned red as he handed the Duke's mistress her goblet of wine. Privy to Francesco's embarrassment, Cecilia smiled indulgently. Knowing she and Leonardo were close, the self-conscious apprentice made his excuse and went outside.

Extending his hand, Leonardo touched the tip of Cecilia's hair. 'You look like a rose in bloom, my sweet.'

'You are the only man who speaks to me with such tenderness,' she said, taking hold of Leonardo's hand.

'Surely Il Moro…

'Il Moro tells me my breasts are ripe for eating and that I have the arse of a peach.'

'Well, I shall have to bow to his superior knowledge,' said Leonardo smiling.

With some reluctance she released her hand from Leonardo's. 'Il Moro has asked to be informed of your progress. What shall I report?'

'Tell him I am confident I will find a suitable Jesus… soon,' Leonardo added with as much conviction as he could muster.

'Very encouraging,' Cecilia said, clapping her hands approvingly.

No sooner had Cecilia departed than the twin evils of melancholy and fear surfaced. Together they whispered in his ear that his search for a virtuous soul to depict as Christ was futile. He peered out of the window at the half-dozen men queuing for an audition and one by one sized-up their appearance: *Too tall, too ugly, too scrawny, fish lips, carbuncle, bald.* He sighed, none of them struck him as men who possessed the quality of soul he was searching for.

'Surely Francesco,' he said turning to face his apprentice, who was poised in the doorway ready to admit the next hopeful, 'there must be better specimens than these?'

CHAPTER SIXTEEN

THE FOLLOWING DAYS FEWER MEN ASSEMBLED OUTSIDE THE makeshift studio at Santa Maria delle Grazie than had gathered in the first month of Leonardo's auditions. The complaint spread abroad that the exacting standards set by maestro Leonardo would likely exclude the venerable Saint Ambrose (if he were alive.) Still a smattering of noble sons arrived, confident that with their superior breeding, one of them would be chosen as Jesus. One young noble, Cesare was the most favoured.

'We will hold the biggest party in Milan once you are crowned Jesus,' his closest friend Donatello declared. Cesare, Donatello and their companions had decided upon this venture after gossip at the home of the distinguished Ambrossini family had turned to Leonardo's search for a Jesus.

The august Senior Ambrossini, declared. 'I have never witnessed such folly in all my eighty years living. A man to be painted as Christ? And from the common stock of Milan? Utter nonsense!'

'Were such a specimen present amongst the rank and file of the city's common folk, we would be a city of saints,'

Giuseppe Rigatoni said. And as head of the city council's finances, he ought to know well the moral fibre of its citizens.

'Perhaps the wrong calibre of men are frequenting Leonardo's studio? Perhaps some of our fine young noble sons ought to press their claim,' Lady Ambrossini declared, much to the annoyance of her husband who was still muttering to himself.

'Well if that is the case, on Milan's honour, my companions and I will seek out the maestro Leonardo tomorrow,' responded Cesare.

Cesare had hair as black as a crow's feathers that hung to his shoulder in tight ringlets. He smiled often, and his comely face set off by two exquisite brown eyes was in perfect proportion, as too was the rest of his fine physique. While the young man and his companions continued their exuberant chatter, Francesco appeared and announced the first audition of the day. 'Cesare! Cesare!' hollered his collaborators smiling broadly. Cesare bowed to his friends and followed Francesco back in to the studio.

When Leonardo's eyes feasted upon the young man, his heart momentarily broke rhythm. 'Please, step this way. I am the maestro Leonardo da Vinci, whom do I have the honour of addressing?' Cesare swung aside his red cape and bowed.

'I am Cesare Scaligeri, second cousin to the Duke of Verona,' he said as he clipped the heels of his boots together and making a show he placed his right hand upon his chest. No one else auditioned so far held claim to such prestigious pedigree. Leonardo was quite taken aback by the manner in which he had been addressed.

'Please, if you would like to remove your cape, we can begin,' he said in his most formal tone of voice. 'Francesco?' The apprentice followed his master's cue and hurried forward to take the young man's cape and place it over the spare easel.

'Cesare, please move over here where the light is better and sit on this stool?' Leonardo requested.

'Upon this?' Cesare said, eyeing the stool with disgust.

'I would rather you did. I intend to paint our Lord reclining at a table.' Leonardo took hold of Cesare's shoulders and moved him into position. 'Try to shift your weight slightly onto your left leg.'

'Like so?'

'Excellent. Now tip your head ever so gently to the right.' Cesare obliged the artist and raised his head in a haughty manner.

My dear mama says I was born with the look of the gods. I am sure you agree?'

Such a streak of pride unnerved Leonardo, nevertheless he dismissed it as merely a youthful boast.

After a morning of experimenting with Cesare's positioning, Leonardo came to the conclusion that despite the young nobleman's blessed appearance, he had the attitude of a man not accustomed to humility or piety of soul.

'I am afraid this is not working as I had hoped,' he said, disappointed. 'You may leave.'

'How dare you dismiss me like a common servant?' responded the indignant Cesare.

'Your cape,' said Leonardo, handing it to the young man. Cesare snatched it from him and marched, red-faced into the street.

Outside the studio, the departure of the spurned Cesare, who cursed the maestro amidst gesticulating to his comrades, mounted his horse and galloped off in haste, knocking an elderly woman aside in the process. The manner of his parting was greeted with gasps of surprise. Feeling their cause a hopeless one, several men walked away deeming their chance of success futile. Yet a handful of optimists stayed, their belief that with the competition thinning, their chance of success had exponentially increased.

'He will never find a Jesus,' said a disgruntled baker, who along with the others who had witnessed the departure of

Cesare, took themselves off to the tavern. 'I swear to God, even Saint Ambrose would fail to please the maestro,' he said, continuing with his complaint.

While the men grumbled into their fiery grappa, Leonardo felt a cold shiver creep up his spine as doubt once again plagued his mind.

'Surely Francesco, there is a man worthy of my art?' Francesco looked across at his maestro, who was trying hard to conceal his frustration.

'I think perhaps you seek the impossible,' replied Francesco.

Later, knelt by his bedside, a depressed Leonardo, sullen and fighting the thought his search for 'Jesus' was futile, summoned what faith he could muster and muttered a half-hearted prayer to the Almighty: Grant me my destiny and send a man of integrity to my aid, and I will paint no more for ambition but to serve only you, Lord.

The following morning, he rose at dawn before anyone else and after writing a note for Francesco, departed for the refectory of Santa Maria delle Grazie. Upon his arrival there were no men waiting to be auditioned. He reasoned that perhaps his impatience had got the better of him and men would soon arrive, but none came. He waited until noon, by which time Francesco had arrived with a light lunch of apples and cheese. The youth had sufficient wits about him to not provoke his mentor with meaningless questions.

In frustration, Leonardo snapped a brush in two. 'I'm going home, care to come?' In his mind he angrily fired off a list of complaints to God: *Why did you not answer me? Do you not care if I cannot find a man to paint as Jesus? Do you too consider it blasphemy? What wrong have I done that you deny me so?*

Arriving home, Leonardo went straight to his room and was not seen again until breakfast the following day, where Francesco observed no change in his downcast countenance. Once more they arrived at Santa Maria to find no men waiting. Leonardo beat his fist against the wall. 'God in heaven, why?' Unlocking the door, he thrust it open and marched inside. Having no desire to bear the brunt of the maestro's anger, Francesco sat outside on the step.

After a couple of hours Leonardo reappeared. 'People of accomplishment rarely sit back and wait for things to happen. They go out and make things happen. Therefore, if the man I aim to paint as Jesus will not come to me, then I will come to him.'

Feverishly Leonardo spent the next few hours scouring the streets of Milan. He approached several merchants, none of whom upon closer inspection satisfied his exacting standards. A baker, a barber, a tanner, and even a bailiff, but none pleased him. More significantly, attitudes towards the maestro were oft unfavourable. Gossip had spread regarding the rude manner he had dismissed some who had waited days patiently, only to be dismissed with barely a glance. A few took Leonardo aside to harangue him demanding why he rejected men known to be of good character. Several hours later a weary Leonardo headed back to his studio at Santa Maria. Francesco poured a goblet of wine and handed it to his master, who took it without uttering a word of thanks.

'I am tired Francesco of having to defend my decision to common folk who understand nothing of my artistic vision.'

As the last rays of a golden orange light filtered their way through the studio window there was a knock at the open door.

'We're finished for the day, come back tomorrow,' Francesco said, paying no heed to the figure in the doorway. The man drooped his head, but just as he was set to turn away, Leonardo looked up. The light behind bathed the man in shades of yellow, causing the outline of his silhouette to shimmer in a golden glow.

'Stop! Move to the left. More!' Leonardo ordered. He bounded across the floor grabbing the man's shoulders, moving him abruptly from side to side to observe his reflections in the light.

'What is your name?'

'Alessandro, sir.' Leonardo leapt on top of the stool to check the angle of the light from above. A residue of oil in Alessandro's hair reflected like a droplet of honey as the sun caught it, sending a ripple of light that weaved its way through Alessandro's pristine locks.

Leonardo stood enthralled. 'More, more to the right,' gesticulating frantically with his hands until Alessandro was once again bathed in sunlight.

'I am looking for work, are you hiring?' Alessandro asked nervously.

'Perfect,' Leonardo said, jumping off the stool. 'You will make a fine Jesus.'

Ignorant of the purpose for Leonardo's studio, and fearing he had stumbled upon a madman, Alessandro fled. Leonardo gave chase. Francesco followed too but stopped a few steps outside the studio thinking it unwise to leave it at the mercy of thieves.

'Alessandro, stop!' Leonardo yelled hard on his heels. Unfamiliar with his surroundings, Alessandro ran into a dead-end. His pursuer had him cornered.

'Why did you run away?' Leonardo asked.

'Please, let me go.'

'Two months wages to paint you?'

'Paint me? Who are you? I have no money.'

'Three then.'

'Three? I don't understand.'

'I am the maestro, Leonardo da Vinci, Artist in Residence to the Duke of Milan, and recently commissioned to paint the last supper of Christ our Lord.'

'But what has this got to do with me? I am just a weaver.'

'I am giving you the chance to be immortalized as the face

of Jesus. Speak man, what is your answer?' It was a question that flabbergasted the uneducated Alessandro.

'Why would you choose to paint anyone as Jesus, least of all me?'

'You are an honest man, Alessandro, I can see that quality clearly in your face and I suspect you have other qualities that make you perfect to be painted as Christ.'

'There is much to consider.'

'Six months' wages and that is my final offer.'

'Let me have a moment alone,' Alessandro requested, walking a few paces away to ponder the maestro's divine proposition: *Six months' wages is a princely sum of money to be paid. How would Letizia respond? (Money is money, my sweet.)* He stood awhile longer contemplating his wife and whether the opportunity presented truly was the answer to his prayers. 'Did you say six months' wages?'

'I did.'

'And the Church agrees?' Leonardo nodded that it was indeed so. 'Well… if Holy Mother Church agrees then so do I,' replied Alessandro much to Leonardo's relief who eagerly shook the hand of his newly acquired Jesus.

Back inside the studio, there was insufficient light for Leonardo to attempt any preliminary sketches. Francesco gave Leonardo's newly appointed muse a cup of wine along with some bread, cheese and an apple. Alessandro explained between mouthfuls the events that had caused him to seek opportunities in Milan. He outlined his many attempts to find work, the rejections he had endured, the spitting and stoning he had encountered. He spoke of his resolve not to fall into destitution and how, in answer to prayer, he had found favour from the foreman Doffo and his master. Lastly, he spoke of Letizia and the child she carried, and of his hope to save enough money to return home and provide for his family.

'I see you are a man of some determination, Alessandro,' said Leonardo.

'Thank you kindly, maestro. My wife is a woman of great faith and since marrying her my own faith has increased.'

'She sounds like a remarkable woman.'

'She is,' Alessandro said proudly. 'What of you maestro, do you have a wife?'

'No, I have found women to be a mystery that eludes even a man of my intellect. I do, however, have a mistress.'

'I imagine she is beautiful like some of the painted ladies I have seen since arriving in Milan.'

'Not so Alessandro. You are my mistress.'

'I am?' a nervous Alessandro asked. Leonardo laughed.

'Everyone I paint or sketch or make a model of is my mistress.'

'What do you mean?'

'Art, nature, life, the thirst for knowledge, these are my mistresses. For I consider that the desire for knowledge is natural to good men. More wine?' Alessandro held out his cup as a broad smile filled his face. 'I love those who can smile in trouble,' Leonardo said, placing a hand upon the weaver's shoulder. 'Your patience and faith has been rewarded, tonight you will sleep at my workshop. Tomorrow, Francesco will find a room for you nearby. I will cover the expense.'

Back home at the workshop, Alessandro proved quite a teller of tales and entertained Leonardo's apprentices with stories of his wrestling feats. To prove a point, he jokingly threw Salai over his shoulder, much to the boy's amusement. Once they had eaten and talked some more, a few cushions and a spare blanket were placed on the floor in the kitchen to suffice as Alessandro's bed.

Grateful that his search was over, Leonardo knelt by his bed: *I give you thanks Almighty God that you have seen fit to answer my prayer.*

CHAPTER SEVENTEEN

EVEN THOUGH IT WAS THE TAIL END OF SUMMER, MORNING FOR Alessandro came with all the joys of spring. He woke at dawn, as was his custom. He looked inside the pantry and gazed longingly at a rich-smelling peppered salami. Dragging himself away, he opened the door that led into the main workshop. Noticing Leonardo's self-propelled cart, he marvelled at the intricate coils and spring and wondered what manner of man the maestro was that he could invent such a strange instrument. He leaned over to take a closer look at the layer of coils that wound their way back and forth and stretched out a hand only to quickly withdrew it lest he be the cause of some mishap. He walked over to a long workbench where propped up on top was a painting. Between its chubby fingers a plump baby Jesus sat on the Madonna's lap holding in his fingers a flower. Hearing movement he decided it was best to return to the kitchen.

'Good morning, Alessandro, did you sleep well?' Francesco enquired.

'Yes thank you, though curiosity got the better of me and I went for a wander.'

'Here, have some bread and help yourself to some salami.' Alessandro gladly cut a piece of the salami.

'Did you see anything of interest when you were in there?' Francesco said, passing Alessandro some bread.

'A painting Francesco. Our Lord was certainly well fed as a child.' Francesco smiled, amused at the peasant's simple understanding.

'I thought Letizia would marvel that a man could paint so accurately the bond between a woman and child.'

'Yes, the Madonna,' responded Francesco.

'I have never seen anything like it.'

'No, neither has the rest of Italy.'

Later that morning, Alessandro accompanied Leonardo, along with the two younger apprentices to Santa Maria delle Grazie. Nicoli helped to set up the room, opening the windows to let in the sunlight and ensuring all the pens, ink and paper were at hand. Romano, with little to do, browsed through the sketches of the men his maestro had rejected as Jesus. Studying them in detail, he concluded that each portrait lacked something. With the confidence of youth, he dared offer his opinion.

'Maestro, if you please, may I speak?'

'What is it, Romano?

'When I look at these drawings, I think I see why you have selected Alessandro as Christ.'

'You do?' Leonardo fixed his attention upon his youngest apprentice.

Romano held up one of his maestro's drawings and pointed to the eyes.

'His eyes have the look of an innocent man in a lonely place burdened by some great sadness, such as our Lord must have had the night he broke bread with the disciples knowing it was to be his last.'

'My dear boy I applaud you. You are learning to look at the world through the eyes of an artist.' Never having received such a compliment before, Romano was delighted. 'Take the rest of the day off and enjoy yourself. Nicoli, you can go too.' Gleefully the two boys darted into the street leaving Leonardo and Alessandro alone.

'You are like a father to them,' Alessandro remarked.

'Between a master and his apprentices, it is natural such bonds form.'

Inside the room that substituted as Leonardo's makeshift studio, Alessandro ran his eye over the space in which his place in history had been promised by the maestro. It was about six strides from end to end and, due to a large bulge in the centre of the wall, was in one part only three strides wide. Alessandro shuffled in his seat. At home in Bergamo, he was used to sitting on a stool to weave, so being made to pose for long periods was not particularly irksome. What he did find unsettling was Leonardo's preference to work in silence.

While Alessandro's mind drifted off to thoughts of Letizia and the money he hoped to soon send her way, which intermingled with the carnal thoughts of a husband's longing for his wife, Leonardo's mind grappled with much weightier matters: *If I cast too much shadow on the face of Jesus, it will look as if he has something to hide. Not enough and he will look like a man without cares.* Stroking his beard in a methodical manner he pondered the nature of light and shadow, while outside in the streets of Milan word spread that a Jesus had been found.

Deep in the heart of the Castello Sforzesco, Maria scampered up the servant's staircase and burst into Cecilia's room. 'My lady, my lady, have you heard? The maestro has found a Jesus!'

Even the Duke's sycophantic secretary could not resist the impulse to gossip.

'My Lord, I have received news that the maestro has found a Jesus.'

'Well, go ask the dear chap if he can turn water into wine,'

Il Moro replied, raising a flurry of titters amongst his courtiers.

All morning a steady stream of curious Milanese gathered outside Santa Maria delle Grazie. By mid-afternoon the crowd was large enough and loud enough to affect Leonardo's concentration. The noise aroused the curiosity of Alessandro, who left his stool to peer unseen out of the window.

'What do they want, maestro?'

'They want you, of course.'

'But why?'

'Even they don't know the answer to that question.' There was a frantic knock on the door. 'Go away!' yelled Leonardo.

'Maestro it is I, Francesco.' As Leonardo unlocked the door to let his apprentice in, those outside surged forward to try and steal a glance at the Jesus standing within. Leonardo and Francesco needed to push against the door to stop people intruding.

'Did you get a room?'

'It is just two streets away. They are expecting Alessandro tonight.'

The noise outside became even more intolerable. A crowd of perhaps fifty or more eager souls had gathered. Most were peasants with nothing better to do than entertain their superficial curiosity. A few were merchants and their wives, some of whom had previously auditioned, all keen to know what manner of man the maestro had chosen. Leonardo laid down his silverpoint pen and looked out of the window. He turned to Francesco.

'Go back to the workshop and attend to Salai, Nicoli and Romano. I will remain with Alessandro. Once their curiosity has been satisfied, I'll see he finds his way safely to his accommodation.'

With Francesco's departure expectations rose within the crowd of people. When the door to the studio finally opened, it was Leonardo whose face they saw first. 'Jesus! Jesus!' they yelled. Leonardo stared out at them. 'Jesus! Jesus!' the surging crowd shouted all the more.

'Calm, calm!' Leonardo pleaded. 'The man I have appointed as Jesus is Alessandro da Canegrate.' Leonardo took Alessandro by the arm and led him gently out of the studio.

People rushed forward to introduce themselves and shake Alessandro's hand. He was asked many times where he came from and what was his occupation. All seemed genuine and friendly and eager to hear everything he had to say. Most were happy to reach out a hand and exchange a few pleasantries. Several women blew him kisses and asked if he were married, questions an embarrassed Alessandro ignored.

Having answered more questions in one day than he could recall answering thus far in his entire life, Alessandro's tongue was dry as parch and his throat hoarse from having repeated his thanks to so many strangers.

'The day will soon be over, and all this excitement has given me a thirst,' said Carlo, a baker, who had previously been auditioned to be Jesus. 'There is a tavern nearby, please come with us and celebrate your good fortune.' Carlo was joined by others who took hold of Alessandro and, much to Leonardo's irritation, ushered him towards the tavern.

The owner of the tavern, Philippe the hunchback on account of his deformity had never experienced such a rush of customers as now descended upon his establishment. He sought out Alessandro and thrust a mug of his best wine into his hands.

'Welcome friend, an honour to meet you.'

'Alessandro per Jesus!' those nearby toasted. Two prostitutes approached and stood either side of Alessandro, each taking the liberty to press their bodies lustily into his.

'You can give me a blessing anytime,' said the elder, a woman in her forties, who grabbed her crotch and swung her hips in front of Alessandro. Leonardo stepped forward.

'Have you no shame? Be off with you!' he said. The two prostitutes begrudgingly withdrew to entice richer customers who had entered the tavern.

Tired of coarse jokes and the pawing adulation of Alessandro, Leonardo, resentful that the attention was on *his Jesus* and not himself, looked for a means to escape and approached Carlo. 'Carlo, I have a favour to ask of you.'

'If I can accommodate your request maestro, it will be my pleasure,' Carlo replied.

'I have acquired a room for Alessandro, not far from here on Via Rosa. Eduardo the Spaniard is the landlord.'

'I know the place. I take it you wish to see that Alessandro finds his way safely there?'

'Are you able?'

'I am able.'

'In that case, Carlo, take this for your trouble,' he said handing him a small coin. 'If you will be so kind, remind Alessandro I require him to be at Santa Maria delle Grazie first thing in the morning.'

With a strong sense of revulsion regarding the common company necessity had required him to keep, Leonardo brushed himself down and walked briskly away: *The man is without talent, yet they greet him like a conquering hero. Bah! The ignorant are nothing more than fillers of piss pots.*

CHAPTER EIGHTEEN

LIFE ASSUMED A FAMILIAR PATTERN FOR ALESSANDRO, BY DAY he attended Leonardo's makeshift studio at Santa Maria, and by night he often found himself drinking with his new-found friends at the tavern by the castello. On other occasions, members of the mercantile class welcomed him into their homes where he was given a seat of honour at their table. More than once he found himself the object of desire from some wealthy lady whose husband was much older and spent much of his time away on business.

One such woman was Constanza Mancini, whose husband was Piero Mancini, the wealthy merchant Alessandro had worked for as a weaver. She sent a message for Alessandro to visit her home under the pretext that there was a small tear in the fabric of one of the pieces of furniture. She was an attractive woman, not yet thirty and married to a man twice her age. When Alessandro arrived at the house, the servants had been dismissed. Wearing only an evening gown, Constanza led him into the lounge where she kissed him passionately.

'Make love to me,' she begged, reaching up to kiss him a second time. 'My husband is old and fails to satisfy me. Come, no one need ever know.' There was not a moment's hesitation in Alessandro's response, he straightaway left the house and breathed not a word of her indiscretion to anyone.

In nearly every home he was invited, gifts were given to him: leather gloves, a fine pair of boots, trinkets of silver and even an expensive ornate cross inlaid with mother of pearl from Milan's richest banker, Giuseppe Rigatoni. The clothes he kept but most of the jewellery he sold for money, which he gave to Doffo to pass on to Letizia on his next visit to Bergamo. It was from Doffo he learned the good news that his wife had given birth to a healthy boy.

'This calls for a celebration!' Doffo said. Alessandro agreed, and the two men headed for the tavern to toast Alessandro's son. Soon the whole tavern was toasting Alessandro's news. In a corner of the room, entertaining various customers was the fruit seller Isabella. She had begun a conversation with Alessandro, one he was reluctant to continue. Making his excuses, he returned to Doffo and his friends. Feeling spurned once again, she swigged down what remained of her drink and stomped angrily outside.

Unwilling to turn down the many offers of a toast to his son's health, Alessandro stayed late in to the night and needed to be carried to his lodgings by Doffo, who laid him on the bed and left. Not long after Doffo departed, Alessandro heard his door open. He lifted his head off the bed. Through his blurred vision he could see his visitor was not Doffo. Alessandro tried to focus, but his uninvited guest was compiled of undistinguishable blots of colour that merged together. Whoever it was took hold of a bottle of grappa from atop a table and took a swig.

'Mary Mother of God!' they blasphemed. It was the voice of a woman, one vaguely familiar. 'A bald man would grow hair again after drinking this.'

'What do you want?' Alessandro managed to ask before

the room span and he held his head in his hands hoping it would stop.

'You denied me payment once before,' the intruder complained. Stripping off her clothes she pushed Alessandro down on to his bed. 'I won't let you get away with it a second time.'

The dazzle of the morning light hit Alessandro's pulsating head like a hammer. Yet it was the smell that first alerted him to the realization he was not alone. He sniffed an unfamiliar scent but did not open his eyes for fear of the blinding pain of daylight. He lazily stretched out a hand and brushed against a body. He half opened an eye. Spread-eagled on his bed was a naked woman. He leaned across to get a better view. It was the familiar yet unwelcome face of Isabella.

'Oh God, what have I done? Letizia. Letizia,' he repeated. His anguished words gave way to the vomit that entered his mouth, which he spewed into the piss pot. He crawled by the bed shaking, while the woman who had induced this fretful condition slept. Overcome with a profound sense of guilt, he hastily dressed and stumbled outside into the street. His only thoughts were of Letizia; only her words, her face, her forgiving arms could heal the anguish that ravaged his soul.

His feet fell one in front of the other like lead weights that dragged him down further into a pit of despair. With no sense of direction, only an urgency to get as far away as possible from the accursed scene of another woman's nakedness, he hurried on oblivious to all he passed. His head, overwhelmed by shame, felt as if it would burst. He leant against a wall as once more his stomach wretched its contents into the street, yet onwards he lurched like a madman with neither thought nor apology for those he bumped into.

Passing the Duomo, Alessandro felt drawn to find solace for his soul and stepped inside. Upon entering, he made for the gold statue of Mary and fell down weeping at her feet. A

priest approached and, having witnessed many such outpour-
ings of grief, placed a comforting arm around him. '

'Do you wish to confess my child?' Through his tears,
Alessandro nodded. The priest had forgiving blue eyes and a
kindly face. Taking Alessandro by the shoulders he helped to
him to his feet and half-carried him to the door of a confessional. Dividing the confessional was a thick red curtain.
Alessandro sat on one side and the priest the other.

'Does your confession relate to one of the Ten Command-
ments my child?' the priest inquired.

'Yes Father,' blurted Alessandro.

'Christ died for all our sins, my child. Do not be afraid,
confess and be forgiven.' 'Father, last night I returned with a
friend, Doffo to my lodgings. I was drunk, Father, we were
both drunk. My friend laid me on the bed and left.'

'Go on,' the priest said, in a manner he suspected what
was coming next.

'The door opened. At first, I thought it was Doffo. But it
wasn't, it was Isabella.'

'You knew this woman? You have had dealings with her
before?'

'I met her once before and she tried to seduce me but I
ran away.'

'And what of last night? Did you run away then?'

'No Father, I was too drunk.'

'So you slept with this Jezebel?'

'May God forgive me.'

'You are a married man?'

'I am, Father.'

'You defiled your marriage vows for a common harlot?
Shame on you!'

The previously mild-mannered priest had vanished, to be
replaced by one with spittle round the edges of his mouth as
he spat his accusation. 'May God have mercy on your beloved
wife, adulterer!'

'But Father, I do not know if we committed adultery. I was so drunk I cannot remember anything until waking up this morning.'

'Don't argue with me. You slept with her, therefore you have committed adultery.'

'Father, what must I do to be forgiven?'

'Are you repentant of your sins, my child?' The priest's hand reached through the curtain and gripped Alessandro's knee.

'May God have mercy on my wretched soul,' bleat a truly wretched Alessandro.

'Your penance is to attend the first Mass of the day for a month and to abstain from strong drink for the same period. To say the 'Hail Mary' fifty times per day, twenty of which must be with prostrations, and to shun all contact with this woman. God has forgiven you.'

In a state of consternation, Leonardo walked to the door and peered into the street.

'Go and see if he has slept in,' Leonardo instructed of Francesco, who ran off down the path. While he waited for news of Alessandro's whereabouts, Leonardo cast his eye over the few sketches he had made. What concerned him most was the angle at which he would place Jesus' head in relation to the rest of his body and just as importantly, his proximity to the other disciples. The eyes of Christ had to fall on neutral ground. Having made the statement 'one of you will betray me' his eyes could not be seen to focus on an individual disciple.

When Francesco returned without Alessandro it had already turned midday. Leonardo decided there was no point pacing the floor and that he would be better off returning home. Francesco had just stepped outside the studio when he saw Alessandro walking towards them.

'Maestro,' Francesco said, tapping Leonardo on the shoulder.

'I'm sorry, maestro,' Alessandro said quietly. 'But I cannot be your Jesus. How can a man who has disgraced himself step into the shoes of the Lord of grace?' Leonardo and Francesco exchanged a look of surprise at the poetic cadence of Alessandro's words.

'What has happened since I last saw you?' Leonardo asked.

'I am guilty of an unspeakable wickedness,' the weaver's voice broke with emotion.

'Alessandro, you have nothing to fear from us,' said Francesco. 'Please, what has happened?'

'Yesterday, I received word that my wife Letizia has given birth to a son. To celebrate, I went to the tavern… Oh God forgive me… I am undone. I cannot be your Jesus, I fear the responsibility that has been thrust upon me is greater than my poor character can bear.'

'Alessandro,' said Francesco, 'all men feel at some point in their life fear the responsibility upon them is too burdensome.' To emphasize his point, he repeated, 'All men,' and placed an arm around the distressed Alessandro. 'When God examines our hearts, there is no man who does not feel guilt over some act he has committed.' He looked for support from his maestro, but Leonardo's ashen face showed his terror that his 'Jesus' was on the brink of abandoning him.

'Maestro,' pleaded Francesco. Leonardo gulped, and wiped his bottom lip with his tongue. 'Francesco speaks the truth. Even I carry my fair share of shame.'

'Really, maestro? It is some comfort to know I am not alone.'

'Alessandro,' Francesco said gently, 'did not our Lord forgive Saint Peter after he had denied him three times? Therefore, if God in his mercy can forgive us, we ought rightly to be able to forgive ourselves.' Leonardo marvelled at the wisdom of his young apprentice and wondered if he had missed his vocation. Aided by Francesco, Alessandro stood to his feet and wiped away the tears on to his tunic.

'Come, let us speak no more of it,' said Leonardo.

The kindness shown to him by the maestro did more to heal the pain in Alessandro's soul than the stern voice of the priest to whom he had made his sorry confession. Leonardo too, for once, was grateful that his apprentice had saved the day. He thanked God, Francesco had been mindful of Alessandro's pain, and therefore been able to offer comfort, where all that was shouting loudly in his own mind was panic. He pondered why he was oft prone to doubt God when the Almighty had placed within his reach men, and a youth, who possessed faith.

Later the same evening, Leonardo sat on a chair, one of a trio he had painstakingly carved with a large Maltese cross on the back of each. Being a balmy night, he had placed the seats outside his workshop where he shared a jug of wine and a plate of olives with Franchino, director of music at the Duomo and the mathematician and Franciscan friar Luca Pacioli. The moon above was just a quarter of the way through its lunar cycle and only a pale light fell on to the street. A torch placed over a hook by the door cast its glow upon the men as they spoke.

'For a moment I thought he was going to walk out and I would have to start my search afresh,' explained Leonardo.

'You are always too dramatic my friend,' said Luca.

'It is the nature of artists to be dramatic,' commented Franchino. 'I think every artist, whether painter, poet or musician, longs to create something that will be remembered after his death. Isn't that so Leonardo?'

'I am of the opinion, it is a sad man who goes to the grave with no visible reminder or evidence of him ever having lived.'

'That may be true, but in painting *The Last Supper*, what is your inspiration?' asked Luca.

'I wish to paint a miracle,' Leonardo replied without hesitation.

'To work miracles is for the Divine,' replied Luca.

'Surely the creation of art is a miracle,' said Leonardo.

'Not all would agree with such lofty ambitions,' replied Luca. 'Paul the Apostle admonished us to do whatever our hands find to do as unto the Lord and not unto man. So, I put it to you Leonardo, in painting *The Last Supper*, whose glory do you seek, that of man or that of God?' Luca's deep voice reverberated down the cobbled street while Leonardo shifted uncomfortably in his seat. 'Come, how do you answer?'

A bead of perspiration dropped off Leonardo's forehead and his palms turned moist with sweat. His mind harked back to his former prayer to the Almighty when he had declared he would 'no longer paint for ambition.' His intonation tinged with guilt he eventually answered, 'Surely it is possible to have both.'

CHAPTER NINETEEN

Dawn came and while most of Milan slept, Alessandro, desiring to show his penitent state to the Almighty, made his way to first Mass at Santa Maria delle Grazie. He genuflected, lit a candle in honour of the Holy Virgin and prayed that God would grant Letizia and his son good health. Looking around, he marvelled at the eerie way the light cast its long tentacles over the incense filled altar.

While Francesco assigned Romano and Nicoli the task of reassembling Leonardo's spring propelled armoured vehicle they were disturbed by a tap on the door as two officious looking men entered. One was a young man a similar age to Francesco, the other, a man in his fifties, sported a neatly groomed grey beard, wore a black legal cloak and walked with a slight stoop. He addressed Francesco formally.

'Is this the workshop of Leonardo da Vinci, son of Ser Piero?'

'It is indeed,' replied Francesco. 'Whom do I have the honour of addressing?'

'I am Senior Prodi from Florence and this is my son.'

'Please enter. I will fetch the maestro.'

At the far end of the workshop, Leonardo was painting a small statue of a horse.

'Maestro, you have a visitor. A Senior Prodi from Florence.'

'From Florence, you say?' asked Leonardo, a little intrigued. He put down the statue and made his way to the workshop entrance.

'You are a long way from home. May I offer you some wine?' Anticipating this request, Francesco was already on his way to the kitchen.

'If you would be so kind,' Leonardo indicated for Senior Prodi and his son to follow him. 'Please be seated. What news of Florence?'

'There is a mad monk stirring up strife,' replied Senior Prodi's son.

'Please forgive my son's impertinence,' interjected Senior Prodi.

'Senior Prodi, may I inquire as to the nature of your visit?'

'As you will have gathered from my attire, I am a lawyer and I represent the monks of San Donato a Scopeto.' Francesco entered with a tray and three goblets of wine which he offered first to their guests.

'To your health, sir,' Leonardo said politely.

'Good wine,' ventured Senior Prodi's son.

'Life's too short to drink bad wine,' replied Leonardo.

'I have in my possession a document detailing the court action against you for failing to complete the commission with which you were entrusted.' Leonardo took the document from Senior Prodi and placed it nonchalantly on the table behind him.

He had been in a similar position before with the monks of Saint Bartolomeo in Florence over his failure to complete *Annunciation* and again in Milan with the brothers of the Immaculate Conception concerning the original *Madonna of the Rocks*. Senior Prodi narrowed his eyes as he spoke. 'You have until the end of the year to fulfil the terms of the commission or face court proceedings.' He drank the last of his wine and rose to his feet. 'Good day,' he said, ushering his son out of the workshop, whose fascination with Leonardo's self-propelled cart caused him to be distracted from his father's business.

'Come, Francesco, we have been delayed long enough.' Francesco picked up the document. 'What are you going to do about this?'

'Do? Nothing. Il Moro would never sanction a request that I return to Florence now, not even if it were personally signed by Lorenzo the Magnificent.'

'But what if there is a court case?'

'If there is a court case, it will tell me no more than the contents of this document,' Leonardo said, taking the document from Francesco and waving it about. 'That I return the payments received or complete the painting by a given date. However, as far as I am concerned the matter is closed.'

He tossed the document onto the table and, picking up the quills, paper, silverpoint pen and inks, walked to the door. 'Well? What are you waiting for?' he said, as he hurried out into the street.

When they arrived at Santa Maria delle Grazie, Alessandro was patiently waiting. As he opened the door, Leonardo mumbled an apology for their lateness and quickly set to work. While Leonardo painted, Francesco played the lute. Strumming gently, he noted Alessandro's downcast demeanour. Thinking it best not to comment, he left him ponder in peace, hoping the melodic tone of his playing would help soothe the nature of Alessandro's anguish.

After the morning they ate lunch, washed down with a little wine, during which Alessandro, deep in thought asked, 'Maestro, would you write a letter from me to send to my wife?'

'Certainly Alessandro, but I think I can do better than

that. How would you like to learn to read and write your own letter to your dear wife?'

'That would be most kind of you, maestro.'

'Then let us begin now.'

Leonardo put down the drawing of Alessandro and picked up a new sheet of paper on which he began to write the alphabet. Underneath the alphabet, he wrote Alessandro's name and commenced teaching the basics of literacy to his eager pupil.

'It is a remarkable thing,' said Alessandro, 'that all the words we speak are made up of combinations of so few letters. Surely there is a lot I must learn.'

Each day after Alessandro's sitting, Leonardo would take an hour or two to instruct him in the art of learning to read and write. Above all, Leonardo was pleased with Alessandro's temperament and aptitude to learn, something his adopted son Salai lacked when it came to his lessons. However, all did not progress smoothly, for Alessandro rung his hands and shook his head in sheer frustration on numerous occasions. Where lesser men would have been inclined to scold their pupil, Leonardo was ever the patient teacher who realised that teaching a man at thirty to read and write would require much more tolerance than teaching a child who was not yet set in their ways.

'Confound it, I shall never get the hang of double consonants!' declared the discouraged pupil.

'Patience, my friend. Everything comes to he who perseveres.'

Alessandro struggled to the point of almost giving up. However, Leonardo insisted if Alessandro mastered the art of writing, a new world would be opened up to him. For Leonardo was fond of insisting that there were two worlds. 'One that we see with our eyes, and one that the knowledge contained in books opens up to us. And he that lives without the latter is poorer for of it.'

'I know you are right, maestro, but at this rate Letizia will be old before I have even written my first letter.'

During these hours, Alessandro learned much about Leonardo. In contrast to his own happy childhood, he learnt the maestro had been marred by feelings of rejection and abandonment by his father. Whereas Alessandro had spent many a playful summer with his siblings, he learned that Leonardo had remarkably little or no contact with his for much of his childhood, and since moving to Milan had not received even a single letter. Above all else, the one factor Alessandro grew to understand was that being born illegitimate carried a stigma Leonardo had sought to hide by means of his many talents.

The letter Alessandro eventually wrote for Letizia, although brief, was one that had taken a whole day for him to compose: *My dearest Leti, I pray you and our son are both healthy. All is well in Milan. I am prospering and have written this letter by my own hand. I shall come to you when my time working for the maestro, Leonardo da Vinci, Artist in Residence to the Duke of Milan is over. I love you and miss you.*

Your dear husband Alessandro.

As the afternoon drew to a close Carlo, one of Alessandro's friends from the tavern, visited the studio.

'I'm going for a game of bocce, care to join me?'

'I had thought about going to Mass later,' Alessandro said.

'Weren't you in church this morning? I think one Mass a day is sufficient!' replied Leonardo. Alessandro yielded. 'If I have your permission?'

'Go and have fun and I will see you again in the morning.'

The game of bocce was being played on a patch of dried grass just outside the castello walls and was watched by a small crowd of friends and passers-by. Carlo and Alessandro had each won two games. Now into their final match, Carlo stepped up to take his decisive throw. He spat into his hands and prayed the gambler's silent plea. He released the boccia which flew out of his hand towards the pallino. The boccia hit the pallino and came to a halt nestled between two of Alessandro's bocce. All hinged on the final ball.

'There must be a prize at stake, what will you wager? A bottle of grappa?' asked Carlo. Alessandro agreed, then with a practised flick of the wrist threw his final bocce with just the right amount of back-spin for it to land a hairs-breath from the pallino. The crowd clapped and cheered. 'I owe you a bottle of grappa,' Carlo said, and then as if by instinct, the small group of friends headed towards the tavern near to the castello.

Preying on Alessandro's mind were the words of the priest ordering him to abstain from strong drink. He wondered how he could squirm his way out of drinking with his friends. Anxiously he fiddled with his collar, while sweat moistened his forehead. Sensing his unease, Carlo turned to him. 'Are you well?' he asked. 'You look like you've seen a ghost.'

'I feel a little faint Carlo, perhaps it is best if I go for a lie down.'

'What about the wager?'

'Don't worry, I'll give you a chance to win back the bottle another time.'

Satisfied his sins were still forgiven, and that he had caused no offence to his friend, Alessandro made his way to his lodgings. On his way he encountered Leonardo.

'Why are you not with your friends enjoying the evening?' he asked.

'A man who is drunk is inclined to make mistakes he lives to regret,' replied Alessandro.

'And what is it you regret, Alessandro?'

'What do you regret, maestro?'

'Me? Oh I regret that I am so preoccupied with my many ideas and inventions, they leave me with little time to devote to my friends and those I love.'

'And who do you love?'
'That, my friend, is a secret known only to God.'

CHAPTER TWENTY

DAMP HUNG IN THE AIR AND A COLD DRIZZLE STUCK TO THE face of worshippers as they walked to the Basilica di Sant'Ambrogio. Every year on October sixteenth there was a Mass to honour Saint Ambrose, the patron saint of Milan and his victory over the Roman General Magnus Clemens Maximus. In 383AD, the General had usurped power from Rome in Britain and Gaul and his army advanced into Italy. Without a single person being killed, Milan was saved by the bravery of its Bishop, who brokered a deal between General Maximus and Emperor Valentinian II.

Since arriving in Milan, Alessandro had heard the story of St Ambrose many times, when as a babe asleep in his cradle, bees had landed on his face and, rather than sting the sleeping baby, they left behind on his cheek a droplet of honey to indicate the Lord's favour upon his life. To mark the auspicious occasion, Alessandro had purchased clothes especially for the Mass. He wore a white linen shirt with navy blue cuffs and collar with large blue buttons sewn down the front, and a pair of matching blue breeches that gathered just below the knee where a pair of black leather boots began. Unfamiliar with more fashionable garments, Alessandro wore his new clothes clumsily.

'Hey! You there, you're Jesus!' called out a man missing half a leg. He wobbled excitedly on his crutch, 'Jesus of Milan,' he cried out several times. A woman walking nearby joined in the calls and pointed and stabbed her fingers (ruined by a life of grinding corn), at Alessandro as she pursued him down the street. 'Jesus of Milan' she yelled, shrieking like a dervish.

Soon he was joined by others who shook his hand and added their voices to the cries of 'Jesus of Milan'. Alessandro sought to pass through the people and return home, but there was such a crowd pressing upon him, his way was barred. Some were perplexed by the jabbing fingers and babbling tongues of those who circled the courtyard of the Basilica di Sant'Ambrogio. Most, however, wanted nothing more than to exchange a greeting or shake Alessandro's hand.

Francesco, who had also come to pay homage to Saint Ambrose, avoided the crowd clamouring around Alessandro. At first, he thought Alessandro wavered and looked uncomfortable at the attention he received. Yet their apparent friendliness and good Milanese humour caused Alessandro to warm to their ovations. Francesco looked on as a stocky merchant with a kind face slapped Alessandro on the shoulder.

'Bless you, Jesus of Milan,' the man said, thrusting his wife and three children in to Alessandro's path for their hands to be shaken.

The cries of the throng who squeezed into the red-cobbled courtyard were becoming louder and more persistent. Surrounding the courtyard on all four sides was a red-bricked Romanesque portico with three ornate arches. Standing in the centre arch was the Archbishop of Milan, who looked out at the jostling crowd with bewilderment. Accompanying the old Bishop was Prior Marco, the head priest at the Basilica di

Sant'Ambrogio, a fiery little preacher with thin lips whose eyes looked through you rather than at you. Il Moro, too, was present, accompanied by his wife Beatrice. Standing with the monks from Santa Maria delle Grazie was Prior Vincenzo, whose face wore an expression of abject horror as he witnessed Leonardo's lackey lapping up the lurid attention of the crowd. Finally, there was the Papal Inquisitor, Father Rodrigo of Salamanca, who had only arrived in town the previous day, and in whose cassock pocket lay Prior Vicenzo's letter, which he had read so many times he could now recite word for word.

'Who is that man?' the Archbishop asked. A priest holding a large, jewel-encrusted gold cross stepped forward. 'Your Grace, he is the man chosen by the maestro Leonardo to be Jesus.'

'There must be a word to describe this madness,' mumbled the Archbishop.

'There is,' countered the black-eyed Inquisitor, 'blasphemy!'

The hairs on the back of Father Rodrigo's neck bristled with indignation. Eyeing the crowd with utter disdain, his jaw locked, his eyebrows narrowed while the knuckles of his hand turned white.

Hidden in the depths of the swirling throng was a woman and her daughter. Both wore rags and walked barefoot. The woman looked like a product of the Lazaretto. Her skin was grimy, and her hair was pitted with muck. The girl aged about seven was emaciated and cross-eyed. Neither looked as though food had passed their lips in days.

'What's all the noise, mama?' the girl asked.

'See that man over there?' the mother replied, pointing a bony finger covered by sores in Alessandro's direction. 'That man is Jesus, my love, come to visit the poor of Milan.'

Pushing her daughter through the crowd, the woman edged closer and closer to a beaming Alessandro, who was repeating, 'God bless you' to those who shoved and pushed him towards the entrance of the Basilica.

Hunched behind a pillar, Francesco peered out at the crowd, he felt perplexed and a little perturbed. He played with the idea of going to speak to Alessandro with the intent of persuading him to leave, but the fervour of the crowd was so unrestrained he doubted his effort would succeed. When Alessandro was ten yards away from the Archbishop, the woman with the child apprehended him.

'My daughter is ill. Pray for her,' she pleaded, pushing the child towards Alessandro. Those standing nearby fell silent. The mother knelt, several people close by also knelt, while others reverently made the sign of the cross and stood back to give Alessandro room. Gingerly, Alessandro placed his left hand on top of the girl's head and made the sign of the cross with his right.

'In the name of the Father, Son and Holy Spirit, bless this child.' Overcome with emotion the girl collapsed into Alessandro's arms. Gently he whispered into the child's ear, raised her upright and passed the girl back to her mother. The child looked into the tearful eyes of her mama.

'Am I better now?' the girl asked. The weeping mother clasped her child tight to her chest.

'A miracle! A miracle! God be praised!' shouted several people standing nearby. Alessandro stared open-mouthed into his hands while all around him people fell to their knees. 'He's a Saint!' yelled a cripple standing nearby. People clamoured for Alessandro to touch them. 'Pray for me, too,' they begged. When he did some fell down as if slain.

Witnessing such events from behind his pillar, Francesco wondered at their meaning and observed how Alessandro's expression changed from shock to one of delight. Galvanized by his recently acquired 'power,' he began to move through the crowd like some bygone prophet, even the rain ceased, which only added to the fervour of the crowd.

Tears streamed down faces, hands were raised towards

heaven, the joyous lips of hundreds repeated 'a miracle'. Some whispered this news, others screamed it aloud. In a matter of minutes, the courtyard of Sant'Ambrogio resembled a scene from the Gospels. Scattered all around were hundreds of prostrate people, praying, weeping, clapping, convulsing, singing, confessing or rocking gently back and forth with glazed expressions.

Startled by the sight he was witnessing, and fearing the crowd pressing ever closer, Il Moro and Beatrice retreated inside the Basilica and watched events unfold from behind the safety of a window. Prior Vicenzo, dreading the effect Alessandro's apparent 'miracle' would have upon the younger and more impressionable of his monks, also ushered them inside the Basilica.

While common folk poured out their devotion to God, and gratitude to his servant who had granted them their miracle, Alessandro, for a few brief moments, felt what it was to be divine. It was clear to Francesco, the cautious and down to earth Alessandro he had come to know, was before his very eyes being transformed into a man intoxicated by spiritual forces.

Unable to grasp a reason for this gospel-like scene, the ties that keep a man lucid, sane and bound to the earth were dissipating in the face of each person, who in stupefied wonder praised his name or keeled over under the influence of his power. Alessandro's mind began to unravel. No longer a weaver, or a subject to be painted, he was to be worshipped! In the whirlwind of devotion and delirium that greeted his every word and action, words that no mortal should utter found their way onto Alessandro's lips. 'I am a worker of miracles. I am... Jesus of Milan.' Alessandro flung his hands towards heaven and in a loud voice declared, 'Jesus of Milan!' Others repeated the phrase until soon the courtyard reverberated with the sound of a thousand-people declaring it aloud.

Lost in a sea of worship, Alessandro began to look upon those around him, not as fellow citizens, but as adoring subjects.

A beggar, his hands aloft praising God, strayed too close to Father Rodrigo and suffered a boot in the face. The Inquisitor turned to the Archbishop who was gazing out at the crowd with a mixture of reverence and fear.

'Your city is a haven of blasphemy. Call out the guards!' Father Rodrigo ordered. The Archbishop didn't hear him.

'Father Rodrigo,' said the Archbishop, 'have you ever witnessed such a spectacle in your life?'

'You fool! This is the work of the Devil. Call out the guards and have this crowd whipped.' The enraged priest sought to approach Alessandro but was obstructed by the crowd. 'Damn you all to hell!' he yelled at those barring his way. The Archbishop indicated his disapproval and several priests rushed over to Father Rodrigo and took hold of him. Much to his chagrin, the apoplectic Spaniard was eventually ushered inside the Basilica di Sant'Ambrogio.

In the cobblestone courtyard, merchants and bankers emptied their pockets and gave all their money to the starving inhabitants of the Lazaretto. Inside the porticos, small groups of people gathered around priests with requests for confession and prayer. With tear stained eyes and shaking hands these common folks hugged the priests until they had received a blessing.

Watching these scenes of religious ecstasy, Francesco kept to himself and chose to stay cowering behind a pillar. When gleeful people, drunk on the delirium of the crowd approached him, he fearfully moved out of their way. From his vantage point, he saw a merchant's wife fall to the floor, screaming as she foamed at the mouth, and he wondered at the strangeness of the power that had seized Alessandro. Into the hands of the mother whose daughter had been healed, Francesco saw an elderly gentleman place a bag of coins. The woman then made her way out through the crowd, passing only feet away from him as she exited the courtyard.

Alessandro turned around to see the Archbishop standing before him. Silence fell amongst the crowd.

'My son, I think it is time we talked.' He took Alessandro firmly by the arm and together they entered the Basilica.

In a daze, Francesco returned home where he found the maestro in the act of firing the kiln.

'You are back early,' Leonardo remarked with some surprise.

'Maestro,' Francesco said nervously, as he reached out to pull up a chair. 'I think you ought to take a seat. I have news concerning Alessandro.'

CHAPTER TWENTY-ONE

It was a long exhausting day for the old Archbishop, who once again found a queue of people outside his office. Some came to testify to their own miracle, others were distressed and had come to seek advice as to whether God or the Devil had been at work. Some seethed with anger, adamant their dearly beloved Saint Ambrose would have been mortified had he witnessed such lunacy. None were more roused to anger than Father Rodrigo of Salamanca.

'I have witnessed men of perverse mind before,' said Father Rodrigo to his eager accomplice, Prior Vicenzo. 'They are always men of intellect who by deception and use of the dark arts impose their satanic philosophies upon weaker minds.'

'The maestro da Vinci has remarkable powers of persuasion. Do you believe them forged in the fires of hell?' asked the dour Prior.

'Undoubtedly.' The Spaniard took out his rosary beads and began to mumble a prayer in Latin. Seeing the earnest manner of his guest, Prior Vicenzo took hold of the wooden cross around his neck and followed the example of his superior in prayer.

'The key is to strike before friends of that Florentine bastard can rally to his support.'

'Have you a plan?' asked the Prior keen to know more.

'Before the Holy Virgin and all the saints of heaven, I will not rest until he and his idolatrous protégé are charged with blasphemy.'

'I am confident I can enlist the support of Father Marco,' said Prior Vicenzo. 'As the head priest at Sant'Ambrogio, his opinion will carry weight with the other priests of the city.'

'Then I suggest you rally the support of the clergy, and I will tackle the matter of persuading Il Moro to release Leonardo to stand trial for blasphemy.'

Once safely back at his lodgings, Father Rodrigo stripped to the waist and removed from his cassock a small whip with bits of bone stitched into the leather strands. Taking the whip in his right hand, he flayed his back reciting the Sacred Magisterium. In his mind flashed images of the scene he had witnessed in the courtyard of Sant'Ambrogio. In response he whipped himself harder, lay prostrate on the floor and begged God for mercy. Exhausted, he drifted off to an uneasy sleep. When he awoke, the sun was just peeping out above the Torre dei Monaci bell towers opposite his room. His first thought was of Il Moro and how to secure permission for Leonardo and Alessandro to stand trial for blasphemy.

The stench of burning flesh that clogged the back of your throat and made a man's nostrils twitch did not perturb the phlegmatic Inquisitor. In Father Rodrigo's soul burned the conviction that Milan was a city ripe for judgement, and that there were many who would suffer the pains of death before the city was cleansed of its vile ways. Then, today being a Monday, the scowling priest knelt by his bed and, taking out his rosary beads, recited the first of the Joyful Mysteries. 'Beloved Mary, by your obedience in saying "yes" you opened the blessing of Heaven and achieved the will of the Father.

Blessed art thou forever.' Once nourished and sustained by his devotions, Father Rodrigo exited his room.

A chill wind surged down the concourse that connected Sant'Ambrogio to the Castello Sforzesco, bringing with it the occasional blast of rain. Father Rodrigo gathered his cloak around him. A gust of wind kicked up a pile of dirt and flung it in his face, spluttering, he managed to spit the grit from his mouth. He wrapped the hood of his black cloak over his mouth and nose and drew it under his eyes. In the mind of Father Rodrigo, even Milan's inclement weather was evidence of the sin into which the city had fallen.

Righteous indignation boiled in his veins while the thud of his boots rang off the ` castello's stone steps as Father Rodrigo pushed passed the guards and into the Sala delle Asse. Il Moro shuffled on his throne beside Beatrice who, having heard fearful tales of Father Rodrigo's temper and his propensity for burning people at the stake, covered her pale face with a veil and reached out a shaking hand to that of her husband.

'The Devil has come to your city,' accused an assertive Father Rodrigo.

'If I may be so bold,' responded Il Moro with as much authority as he could muster, 'the Devil has not come to my city.'

'Milan is teetering on the precipice of idolatry and will soon fall into the pit.'

The colour drained from Il Moro's face as he steadfastly clung to his wife's fingers. His secretary, seeking to placate Father Rodrigo, bowed before the priest.

'I am sure the good people of Milan have no desire to be flung...'

'Choose your next words carefully,' interrupted Father Rodrigo, 'I am in no mood to `bandy words with a sycophant.' The secretary lowered his head.

'My apologies Father,' he meekly replied as he discreetly scurried away.

'Your city is beset by blasphemy. Men and woman run wildly after an evil conjured up by that malevolent bastard da Vinci, who you have too long protected. I have witnessed with my own eyes the people of this city falling down and worshipping a man. A mere weaver whom the maestro appointed to be his Jesus and now this man has committed blasphemy by allowing himself to be worshipped. Therefore, by the papal authority vested in me, I demand Leonardo da Vinci and Alessandro da Canegrate be handed over to me to stand trial for blasphemy.'

Father Rodrigo thrust the document detailing his demands into the hands of Il Moro.

'These are grave allegations, priest, which I will consider carefully.'

'Do not suppose your brother's position in Rome offers you favour.'

'Are you threatening me?' asked a dumbfounded Il Moro.

'I do not threaten people, I issue decrees ordering men to stand trial for crimes against `Holy Mother Church and when they are found guilty, I sentence them to death.'

'What has the Archbishop to say on the charges you bring?'

'The Archbishop knows it is not in his interests to arouse the anger of a Papal `Emissary.'

'Before I release Leonardo into your charge, I first want the man to be given the opportunity to defend his reputation.

'One way or another, he will stand trial.' The priest turned on his heel. His black cloak clung to the floor and rather like a slug leaving behind a trail of slime, marched triumphantly out of the Sala delle Asse.

CHAPTER TWENTY-TWO

A WEARY IL MORO RELAYED THE EVENTS OF THE DAY TO Cecilia, whose head swam making her faint of breath while tears she dare not shed filled her eyes.

'Have faith, woman, I have no desire to lose a prize like the maestro.'

'What is your plan my Lord?'

'By asserting Milan is a city rife with blasphemy, Father Rodrigo has committed a direct indictment against myself and the Archbishop. He has overstretched his hand and made it a political decision. That is something I will not allow, not from some jumped up priest who thinks he can come traipsing into my city stirring up strife. We have already witnessed what one mad man of the cloth has done to Florence, I will not let another zealous bigot do the same to Milan.'

Mindful that his wife had doubled her efforts to root out his suspected infidelities, Il Moro chose not to prolong his visit.

Gathering her wits, Cecilia called for Maria and presented her with a note she was to take immediately to Leonardo, imploring him to meet her at Il Moro's prayer room inside Santa Maria delle Grazie. Once her maid had been dispatched, Cecilia vent her emotions. She ran to the balcony for air where she almost collapsed with grief. The sky was filled with a long trail of orange and pink plumes that tailed off into the distance bathing the city in shades of soft pastel. It was a soothing sight that ordinarily would have gladdened her heart but tonight she laid prostrate on the cold floor and sobbed. When she could cry no more, she returned to her room and searched for Maria's old cloak, which her kind maid had allowed her to keep for just such an eventuality.

Rarely did Cecelia venture from the castello's grounds once night arrived, yet her urgency of the moment outweighed any concerns she had for her own safety. With the hood pulled over her face, she wrapped the cloak about her and slipped out of the castello in the same manner as her last secret enterprise, in the disguise of a servant girl.

On the doorstep of Santa Maria delle Grazie, Cecilia glanced about her. Satisfied she had not been followed, she entered. Inside, what meagre illumination there was came from two bronze candle stands placed slightly in front of the gold and jewel encrusted alter, causing the gold of the altar to ripple with movement as the flames flickered across it. She shivered in the eerie stillness while she looked for signs of life as the candles cast long tentacles of light that penetrated the lofty emptiness of the Basilica's apse. She rested her hand against one of the cold stone pillars: *Dear God, I pray he has received my message.*

Girding her soul for fear of disappointment, she genuflected twice before she walked slowly forward towards Il Moro's private prayer room and opened the door. Before her was blackness so thick that her eyes failed to take in her surroundings. She let out a muffled cry as in the darkness a hand took hold of her.

'Shh, it's me. Why on earth have you sent for me at this hour?' Leonardo whispered.

'To save you from certain death.'

'Why? Who would have me killed?'

'Father Rodrigo plans to see both you and Alessandro burned at the stake for blasphemy.'

Cecilia could not see Leonardo's face. Had she been able to do so, she would have been surprised by the calmness of his expression.

'There is another way, Leonardo,' continued Cecilia. 'You have no choice but to flee to France.'

'France? I have no desire to flee like a dog to France.'

'Then you will be tried for blasphemy.'

'My sweet, I plead with you to take heart,' Leonardo said, as he reached out to wrap her in his arms. 'Be convinced of this... it is not my end to be burned at the stake by some fanatic.'

'I could not live if you were to die.' Leonardo responded to Cecilia's declaration with a kiss on her forehead. 'Go home and be at peace,' he said.

Cecilia kissed Leonardo's hand and reluctantly left him in the blackness to contemplate his future. From where his confidence came Leonardo knew not, but as he prayed in the darkness, he had an inner conviction that the hour of his death was not yet upon him.

Unbeknown to Leonardo, Prior Vicenzo had earlier seen him enter Il Moro's prayer room. Intrigued, he hid inside a confessional and waited to see who else might arrive. Shortly afterwards he observed Cecilia enter. The malcontent Prior waited a moment or two then crept out of Santa Maria delle Grazie. Filled with spite and a desire to cause mischief he waddled in haste towards the Castello Sforzesco.

On the stroke of midnight, Leonardo walked out of the basilica and straight into the arms of Il Moro's guards who flung him to the ground.

'Down!' they ordered. 'Il Moro does not take kindly to servants cavorting with his mistress,' the chief guard said, his sword poised above Leonardo's neck. A satisfied smirk snaked across the Prior's face as he stepped out of the shadows.

'You are not long for this world da Vinci,' he hissed. 'When I see you again, you will be either swinging from a rope or burning atop a fiery stake.'

'You fool!' Leonardo shouted. They were the last words he spoke before a guard brought the butt of his sword down upon his head.

CHAPTER TWENTY-THREE

WHEN LEONARDO CAME TO HE WAS LAID ON THE FLOOR, HIS hands bound behind his back and tied to a wooden stake that ran the length of his body. His head throbbed. He tried to look up to see where he was, but as he was trussed up like a pig on a spit, his visibility extended as far as the end of his feet in one direction and no further than a stone wall in the other. Struggling to find a better view, he attempted to pivot to one side when the night was shattered by the high-pitched wail of a woman's screams from within the Sala delle Asse.

'You are my mistress!' shouted Il Moro. 'Not some common whore who opens her legs for any old bastard!' Two guards gripped an arm each as Il Moro punched Cecilia in the mouth. Blood oozed from a split lip.

'My Lord, I beg you, Leonardo never laid a finger on me.'

'Lying slut!' Il Moro said, as he thumped her in the stomach. She doubled over in distress, but the guards yanked her upright and shook her like a doll.

'We did not make love,' Cecilia said, between gasps of breath. 'I swear upon my father's grave.'

'How dare you answer me back?' Il Moro screamed, pushing her to the ground. She fell heavily, her head striking the hard floor. Il Moro kicked her in the right side, breaking a rib. Choking back tears, Cecilia opened her mouth to speak, but all she could do was splutter up blood and spittle that dripped down her porcelain chin.

'I went to warn him to flee to France,' she feebly protested. 'I have no lover my Lord but you. I beg you, do not kill Leonardo, to do so would only serve the plans of that scheming Spaniard.'

'Do not try to hide behind my loathing of that Papal menace.'

'My Lord, I tell you the truth.' She clung to his legs vainly hoping he would cease his violence but instead he pulled her head back with one hand and clasped tight around her throat with the other.

'I will rip your throat out with my bare hands if you so much as touch another man. Confess! Before I kill you and have the maestro strung up by his balls and his head impaled on a pike.'

'Please my Lord,' Cecilia gasped, 'I went only to warn Leonardo of the plot against him.'

'Then why did you go sneaking off dressed like some scullery maid in the dead of night?'

'How else was I to get word to him? You would never have consented for me to visit the maestro at so late an hour.'

'Do you think me a fool?' he asked, taking a knife from his belt and holding it to her throat. 'How many times have you donned such garb in order to sneak out and whore your body?'

'Never, my Lord, never. I am your property and if you kill me, you kill one who has been faithful to you.' Il Moro withdrew the knife and stepped slowly away to consider her words. 'Leave us,' he ordered the guards. They cast a sideways glance at the wretched figure on the floor and left.

Her hands shaking, Cecilia wiped away blood from her mouth and chin and proceeded to straighten out her dress.

She then drew her hands through her hair to comb some semblance of shape into them: 'If I am to die', she said to herself, 'I will do so with as much dignity as I can muster.' While she contemplated her lot in life, whether she would live to see another sunrise, Il Moro breathed nasally, as if Vesuvius was about to erupt.

Pity was an emotion alien to Il Moro's nature, yet as Cecilia awaited her fate, it was pity he felt, and it discomforted him. In her favour was the knowledge that in all the years he had known the maestro, he had never taken a lover, and had lived faithful to his vow of celibacy. 'You may go,' Il Moro finally said, with a dismissive wave of the hand. Cecilia bowed her head then carrying her bruises and broken rib retired to her room.

Leaving the Sala delle Asse, Il Moro, ill at ease over his sympathetic act, paused to stand beside the two fluted columns that separated the palace from the courtyard. Out in the courtyard soldiers mocked and poked Leonardo with sticks or boots. They were so engrossed in their game they did not heed Il Moro's approach.

'Pick him up!' Quickly the men raised a dazed Leonardo to his feet, his hands still tied behind his back and fastened to the stake. His clothes were stained with blood and he would have fallen but for the intervention of a guard who held him upright.

'Did you dip your wick in my mistress's pantry?' Il Moro demanded.

'Cecilia…' but Leonardo was unable to complete the sentence for his spinning head
lolled idly on his neck.

'Speak! What were the pair of you plotting?'

'France,' was all Leonardo could mutter before his eyes closed and his knees crumbled. Il Moro raised Leonardo up by the scruff of his hair.

'Are you and Cecilia lovers?'

'I have no need of the pleasures love brings,' Leonardo said as his head flopped forward into the hand of Il Moro. 'If you are lying, you have more to fear from the wrath of a Sforza than some jumped up priest holding a burning torch.'

Pushing himself up on the arms of the soldiers either side of him, Leonardo recited a verse from his days in Florence.

'Though he can't stand to attention, he still laughs with joy forever. Who'd be happy, let him be so. Nothing's sure about tomorrow.'

'The man's lost his wits,' said Il Moro, who scrutinized his Artist in Residence with the kind of repugnant expression he usually reserved for the insane. 'Throw him in the dungeon overnight. Perhaps come morning we'll get some sense out of him.'

The dungeon was lined with straw and heavy with the stench of rat urine. The chief guard untied the rope binding Leonardo's hands and removed the stake. Leonardo slumped to the floor where overcome by drowsiness, he fell into a deep sleep. A fat rat scurried over and licked the blood oozing from his wound and nibbled his torn flesh.

Several times Leonardo awoke. At first, he thought he was amidst a nightmare about his time imprisoned in Florence, only the nauseating smell that greeted him was enough to confirm it was no nightmare. Each time he racked his brain for answers as how or why he came to be bound in such a manner, the pain in his head was too severe to concentrate and he soon drifted back into unconsciousness.

When morning came, Il Moro, in the face of interference from Rome, wished to emphasize his rule over the Duchy of Milan, was attired in his ducal regalia: a long purple robe finished in ermine fur around the collar and sleeves. Upon his head he wore the Iron Crown of Monza said to have been fashioned from the nails used in the cross of Christ. The crown was made of a thin metal strip, plated in gold and encrusted with rubies and other precious stones.

Gathered with the Duke was the Archbishop, Father Rodrigo of Salamanca and his faithful subordinate, Prior Vicenzo. Prior Marco of the Basilica of Sant'Ambrogio was also in attendance. Making up those present were several prominent figures of Il Moro's court. All had come to hear Father Rodrigo cross-examine Leonardo and state his case to have him tried for blasphemy.

The Papal Inquisitor had reluctantly agreed to question Leonardo in Il Moro's court and allow the artist the opportunity to explain his actions before formal proceedings and charges were made against him. Satisfied his mistress had not betrayed him, Il Moro regretted the beating the guards had given Leonardo, for his night in the dungeon now played into Father Rodrigo's hands. Seeing Leonardo's dishevelled state, a smirk of satisfaction slithered across Father Rodrigo lips.

'Has your infatuation with poetry ceased, Leonardo?' Il Moro had recovered his good humour.

'My Lord, I haven't the faintest idea to what you are referring.'

'It is a common tactic amongst the guilty,' insisted Father Rodrigo. 'One I have encountered many times. Flagellation and torture usually restore a person's memory.'

'Why should I be tortured? What crime have I committed?' Leonardo swayed on his feet and the glorious mural in the Sala delle Asse with its myriad forms of life became a blur.

'This man is clearly unwell. Call the physician,' demanded the Archbishop, looking for some pretext to postpone the proceedings.

'A physician? What use is a doctor to a blasphemer?' replied Father Rodrigo.

'No conclusion has been reached regarding the accusation of blasphemy and a sick man deserves the attention of a physician,' replied the Archbishop, annoyed. The debate was cut short by Leonardo vomiting.

'God damn you, man!' said Il Moro but then, realising he

had blasphemed in front of the Archbishop, mumbled a half-hearted apology.

A stool was brought for Leonardo to sit upon, along with a cup of water. His head flopped, and his hands fell limp by his side. The searing pain from the butt of the sword inflicted upon him the previous night made his every thought difficult. Try as he may to hone into the accusations of Father Rodrigo and listen to the debate in Il Moro's court, the ache in his skull and the numbness he felt made concentration nigh impossible.

'Can we proceed with the matter in hand? Namely releasing Leonardo into my authority, where he will be charged with blasphemy and ordered to stand trial for his crimes.' The stern voice of Father Rodrigo echoed around the room. Fighting through pain and nausea Leonardo lifted his head.

'I have committed no such crime.' Leonardo's eyes rolled in their sockets and, as soon as he had spoken, his head drooped down. Father Rodrigo took hold of Leonardo's hair and yanked him upright.

'Confess!' Father Rodrigo slapped Leonardo hard across the face. 'Confess or be damned!'

'I am a Christian,' spluttered Leonardo, who fell backwards on to the floor.

The physician entered just in time to see Leonardo's arms and legs flail wildly about in a flurry of uncoordinated movements. Then, as suddenly as they had started, they ceased and remained by his side rigid. The physician ran over to examine the lifeless maestro.

'Is he dead?' asked Il Moro.

'If he is, then it is the fires of hell that await him,' said Father Rodrigo.

The Archbishop, using his gold staff, made the sign of the cross over the still body of Leonardo. 'May God have mercy on his soul,' he solemnly pronounced.

He is unconscious, my Lord,' the physician said. 'He needs to be moved to the infirmary where I can best attend to him.'

'See to it,' said Il Moro.

'This is a ploy. Throw a bucket of cold water over him,' said Father Rodrigo, his mood becoming more agitated by the second.

'Excuse me, Father, but water will not rouse this man. He will die if you seek to question him further.'

'Physician do not contradict me. I order you to rouse this man.' Spittle flew from the mouth of Father Rodrigo showering the physician in the face. The Archbishop stepped towards the Papal Inquisitor. 'The maestro is in need of a physician. Therefore, I declare this examination over.' In order to assert his authority, he banged his staff twice upon the floor.

'It is I, your Grace, who have authority here and I am not finished with this heretic!' bellowed Father Rodrigo.

'In my court, I make the decisions. Physician, see to the maestro,' ordered Il Moro.

The physician stepped forward and indicated to several servants who rushed over. Each took a limb of Leonardo's and quickly carried him out of the Sala delle Asse.

'If he dies, I will demand compensation from Rome,' said Il Moro.

'You will receive no compensation for a man with a charge against the Church hanging over his head.'

'Where is the evidence of blasphemy?' asked the Archbishop. 'You will receive no confession from the maestro, save by torture, and I will not allow a sick man to be tortured. Not in my city. We…' he said pointing to those gathered, '… were all present that morning in Sant'Ambrogio. Whereas I agree, what we witnessed was difficult to describe. But if you had been standing by the Sea of Galilee when our Lord performed his miracles, would you not also be overawed, afraid and question whether God or the Devil had been present?'

The Archbishop's argument resonated with his listeners who murmured their approval. Only Father Rodrigo and Prior Vicenzo were inclined to disagree.

'Archbishop, I agree that what we witnessed was, as you say, difficult to describe,' said Father Rodrigo, adopting a more conciliatory tone. 'But the accusation I make, I do so because with my own eyes and ears I saw and heard people clamouring to touch the weaver known as Alessandro, proclaiming his glory, not that of God's. I furthermore insist the whole sorry spectacle, could and should have been avoided, by forbidding the maestro to choose a mere man, a peasant, to be painted as our Lord.'

'Artists have for centuries used models to paint the Holy Virgin,' stated the Archbishop. 'And the Church has not accused them of blasphemy. By granting permission for Leonardo to take a man of sound principals and moral standing to paint as our Lord may break with the traditions of the Church, but I do not consider his intentions were ever blasphemous.'

'And the spectacle we all witnessed at the Basilica of Sant'Ambrogio, what name does your Grace have for that?'

'That, Father Rodrigo, was godly ecstasy,' replied the Archbishop.

'Godly ecstasy! What nonsense. Upon my return to Rome, I will have another artist dispatched to complete *The Last Supper*,' said Father Rodrigo. A remark that rankled Il Moro, who had endured enough of his malcontent papal menace.

'I am the maestro's patron and it is I who will decide whether he is released from the commission or not,' Il Moro replied.

Prior Marco, who until now had kept quiet, finally broke his silence.

'Nothing so far has been mentioned concerning the man painted as Christ, Alessandro, whom I have spoken to and found to be a man of good character and faith. If you condemn the maestro, will you condemn him too?' Father Rodrigo rounded upon Father Marco.

'Can you not see how they have acted in cahoots to deceive you?' The Archbishop, exasperated with Father Rodrigo, faced his papal tormentor.

'As Archbishop of Milan, I renounce the charges you have brought against the maestro Leonardo da Vinci and declare that he has no crime to answer to.'

'You are a disgrace,' said Father Rodrigo. But the Archbishop was insistent.

'Since the appointment of the weaver Alessandro as the maestro's Jesus, attendances at Mass at Sant'Ambrogio and the Duomo have risen, and even Prior Vicenzo has confirmed it is the same in Santa Maria. I ask you, what kind of heresy is it that leads to greater devotion amongst the faithful?'

'Let us seize the devotion of the people and turn it to our benefit,' said Father Marco.

'We can hold up this man Alessandro as an example of godliness for the common man to follow.'

'An excellent idea,' replied the Archbishop.

'Rome will hear of this!' boomed Father Rodrigo, who incandescent with rage, stormed out of Il Moro's court with Prior Vicenzo hanging off his coat tails.

Il Moro let out a sigh of relief and turning to a gaggle of whispering servants yelled,

'Wine you lazy bastards and quick about it.'

CHAPTER TWENTY-FOUR

'YOU WANT ME TO PERFORM ANOTHER MIRACLE?' IT WAS CLEAR Alessandro had failed to grasp what the Archbishop had said to him. Beside His Grace, seated upon a tall high-backed gold painted chair, were Il Moro, his secretary and Father Marco. They were gathered in the Archbishop's private office in the Duomo, a lavishly decorated room with a thick red carpet and an elaborately carved wood-panelled ceiling. Covering the wall behind the Archbishop was a large mural depicting the miracle of Saint Ambrose as a baby. A hive of bees hung from a sycamore tree above his head while on his cheek was a thick droplet of honey.

Choosing his words carefully, the Archbishop began a second time.

'My good man, one miracle has been sufficient to galvanize the populace to faith. God has used your appointment as Leonardo's Jesus to bring about an increase of piety in the people of this noble city. Therefore, to acknowledge their devotion, this coming Sunday we will present you to the city's population, a common man, like our Lord, whose example they would do well to follow.'

'I am honoured, your Grace,' said Alessandro.

'And whatever that Florentine miser has offered you as payment, I will double,' declared Il Moro. The secretary handed a pouch of coins to Alessandro, whose eyes lit up as he took them in his hand.

'The Church, too, would not employ your services without adequate recompense,' said the Archbishop handing an even larger pouch of coins to Alessandro, who thanked his benefactors repeatedly. Father Marco took gentle hold of Alessandro and escorted him, still bowing, out of the Duomo.

With his pockets bulging, Alessandro's immediate reaction was to pay the maestro a visit. In what should have been a journey of no more than half an hour, he instead heard the church bells ring twice. Every time he saw a man walking towards him, he thought he saw the eyes of a thief and he turned around and walked the other way or crossed the street. When he eventually found his way to Leonardo's workshop, he was met by Francesco.

'Have you not heard? The maestro is unconscious and being attended to in the infirmary by the Duke's physician.'

'My God, no.' Alessandro's hand shook, and his face drained of colour.

'Here Alessandro, sit down,' the youth said, pulling out a seat.

'Shall I go to him, Francesco? If I pray for him, he is sure to recover,' said Alessandro with the enthusiasm of a child.

'No one is permitted to see him. Not even I have been. I think all you can do is pray.' Alessandro looked off into the distance and nodded his head.

'Was there another reason for your visit?' asked Francesco.

'The Duke and the Archbishop gave me these.' He held up his money bags. 'Can I trust you?' Alessandro asked.

'Of course.'

'I cannot go walking around Milan with such a princely sum of money tucked in my jacket, who knows what vagabond may seek to snatch it from me? Can I leave it here with you? I am sure it is safer here in the hands of you and the maestro than in my place at Via Rose.'

What about putting it in a bank?'

'God forbid, I don't trust those thieving rascals. Won't you keep it safely here till I have need of it.'

'I will personally ensure it is kept safe,' replied Francesco. 'Have you eaten, Alessandro? Would you like me to prepare some food and a little wine?'

'Thank you, you are a good boy.'

While Alessandro waited, his thoughts drifted to the conversation with His Grace: *You are to be honoured before the people*. Dwelling upon such lofty views his mind became filled with deluded mysteries. He saw the Lord dressed in white placing upon his head a crown of gold and heard a gentle voice whisper 'Jesus of Milan'. A wave of euphoria swept over him and a tear of joy wove their way down his cheek. His body felt limp and his hands flopped by his side. He wanted to speak but was so immersed in his apparition that words failed him.

When Francesco returned, Alessandro had his mouth open wide and wore a look of stupefied wonder. 'Are you sure you're alright?' asked Francesco, placing some bread, cheese and a mug of wine down on a table.

'I have seen a vision, Francesco, of our Lord placing upon my head a crown of gold and declaring that I am the Jesus of Milan.'

'You seem to be experiencing many a wondrous thing of late.' Francesco eyed his guest perplexed that one with no education had been chosen as the recipient of such divine phenomena. Tired and wary Alessandro's eyes began to droop. 'I insist you stay the night,' said Francesco.

After a sound night's sleep and partaking of a hearty breakfast that Francesco had prepared, a much-relieved Alessandro departed. Walking down the Via Rosa, Alessandro paid no attention to two aristocratic women heading towards him, until the court official escorting them pointed in his direction. The ladies had painted pale faces and wore flowing yellow dresses, cut revealingly across the bust. Their dresses did not trail along the floor as was the custom, but were raised slightly off the ground, just enough to show a flash of an ankle. They wore long white gloves, and both had their hair tied up with pretty combs and ornaments. One had curly red hair, mischievous blue eyes and a dainty face. The other had blonde hair, eyes the colour of emeralds and wore a large emerald necklace with a thick chain made of gold that rested atop her ample breasts. Alessandro made to move aside when he was deliberately hindered.

'You must be the man all Milan is talking about?' the blonde said, tapping her embroidered lace fan off Alessandro's chest.

'Isn't he divine?' oozed the redhead.

'He is rather pretty for a country bumpkin,' said the blonde.

'Who are you? What do you want with me?' Alessandro protested, as each took hold of an arm and marched him off down the street. 'Where are you taking me?' They ignored him and continued onwards.

'I wonder if he makes love like a pig,' said the redhead.

'I once made love to a French man, does that count as a pig?' the blonde replied.

'My God! Tell me more,' demanded her accomplice.

'It was at a banquet Il Moro held for a French Lord while you were away in Verona. A rather handsome young general had been eyeing me up all evening and demanded dances at every available opportunity. The Duke asked if I would bed him and try to find out what the wily old Lord was up to. So I did, and told Il Moro everything the young general…'

'I don't care about the politics,' interrupted the red head. 'What was he like in bed?' 'Lousy, all grunts and no rhythm,' she said laughing hoarsely.

'Who are you?' Alessandro demanded to know, digging in his heels and bringing them to an abrupt halt.

'I am Caterina Rossetti, only daughter of Senior Umberto Rossetti,' said the redhead. 'And this delicious creature on your left is Belinda Arcimboldo, whose uncle happens to be the Archbishop.'

Caterina Rossetti and Belinda Arcimboldo were inseparable and notorious. The daughters of wealthy aristocrats their raucous behaviour had heaped considerable shame upon their respective families. Caterina, the redhead, although smaller and more softly spoken, was the leader and mastermind of their infamous exploits. Belinda, a year younger than her companion was a seasoned hedonist, but a lazy one, who would not have achieved quite the reputation she had if it were not for her accomplice.

Two things struck Caterina as strange. The generous amount of money she was being paid to toy with Alessandro and the identity of her paymaster.

'If he possesses the character of our Lord, then like our Lord he will be able to resist temptation,' had been Father Rodrigo of Salamanca's words to her. 'If not, I charge you to discredit him by whatever means necessary. Are you in agreement?' the priest asked. Caterina, who was accustomed to dealing in the devious ways of the world, whipped out a small knife from inside her dress and pinned it to the priest's throat, drawing a thin sliver of blood.

'I accept your terms,' Caterina said. 'But if I find you plan to deceive me, I will put out a contract on your life and hire every mercenary in Italy to hunt you down like a dog.'

Caterina and Belinda glided effortlessly but slowly, given the cumbersome nature of the dresses they were wearing until they eventually arrived at a house with a large marble Roman portico, set back in its own private garden. The garden was festooned with orange and cherry trees. Caterina stopped to open a bronze gate, in the middle were three roses depicting the Rossetti family crest.

The widowed Senior Rossetti was away on business for much of the year, leaving his wayward daughter the run of the family mansion. An elderly aunt, her dead mama's sister, also resided on the premises, but she was too old and blind to subdue her niece.

Upon entering the large and ostentatious lounge, Caterina, in her brusque aristocratic manner, ordered the servants to prepare a bath for Alessandro.

'You fetch the pumice stone, sponges and strigil.' To another, 'Don't spill the hot water you clumsy fool.' And to a third, 'Hurry with the perfumed oils.'

Female servants carried into the room a large bronze bath, which they proceeded to fill from urns being heated over a fire. The room was wide and spacious, even the fireplace was bigger than Alessandro's room in Via Rose. Behind him was a long, carved rosewood table with fourteen high-backed chairs placed around it, each covered in red velvet. Along one wall was a tall rosewood cupboard, full of jars of herbs and spices.

A young servant girl of no more than fifteen years was made to rub Alessandro down with a sponge. She applied the pumice stone to clean the dirt and smooth his rough skin. Having done that, she used the strigil to scoop up the dirty skin and rubbed it dry with a cloth. The servant girl appeared in awe of Alessandro. Nervously, she said,

'Forgive me, Jesus, if I scrub too hard.' Once Caterina was happy the scented oils of roses, cloves and cinnamon had replaced the smell of the street, she ordered the servant girl to wrap Alessandro in towels and dry him down by the fireplace. Alessandro's skin glistened in the soft firelight and the masculine outline of his torso, accentuated by the oils, shimmered with lustful promise. Belinda felt the tingle of sexual craving surge down her spine and settle inside her moist vagina.

By the time Caterina had locked the door, and the last echo of the servants' footsteps could be heard retreating down the corridor, Belinda was halfway out of her dress and, with a little help from Caterina, was soon relieved of her rigid bone corset. Her waist, accustomed to life inside a corset, was slender compared to those of the common women Alessandro had thus far seen in a state of undress. Tossing back her hair and throwing the combs aside, Belinda stood naked from the waist up, her blonde locks cascading down her smooth neck and coming to rest on the crest of her bounteous bosom. Alessandro had never seen such pale breasts before and he stared at her soft white flesh accentuated by two blossom pink nipples. While he stood gawping, Caterina unfastened the back of her dress and turned to Belinda, who helped her out of both dress and corset until she too was naked from the waist up. Caterina's svelte figure and porcelain breasts were petite, like those adorning many a Roman statue. A rapt Alessandro eyed their perky exquisiteness with a confusing mixture of lust and trepidation.

Wrapping a hand around Belinda's waist, Caterina drew her close and kissed her lips. Transfixed by both curiosity and fear, Alessandro froze to the spot as he watched while the two women embraced with a passionate kiss. Once his faculties returned he ran to the door.

'Heaven have mercy on my poor soul. I have fallen under the spell of witches.'

'Witches!' laughed Belinda.

'Please, let me go,' Alessandro pleaded, fumbling frantically with the locked door.

Caterina gathered up Alessandro's clothes and threw them into the fire. He tried to rescue them, but it was too late, the flames had consumed them.

'What do you want with me?' he pleaded. Removing her white linen undergarment, a naked Caterina sauntered over to Alessandro. Her skin was white as chalk and her red pubic hairs glowed in the firelight rendering him dumbstruck. None of the common women he had known had the marble features of the two goddesses who stood before him in all their aristocratic prime.

'Consider us as a reward for your faithfulness,' spoke the delicate tongue of Caterina. 'We are a gift from the people of Milan.' She reached out a hand towards him. 'Come, don't be afraid. We have been instructed by a Prince of the Church to satisfy your every desire. You are Jesus of Milan. A man of great importance who is to be honoured before the people, and we…we are angels sent to serve you. Look, here is a ring, a token of the esteem you are held in.' The ring was silver and bore the Rossetti crest.

Caterina stretched out her arm to Alessandro, who paused, his mind swirling with a myriad of thoughts: *'What of my wife, Letizia?'* *'Surely the church would not give such gifts if it were sin.'* *'She is indeed an angel and I am after all a man to be honoured.'*

Mesmerised by her porcelain skin he cast a lecherous eye over Caterina's nakedness.

CHAPTER TWENTY-FIVE

RATHER THAN HEAD SOUTH FOR ROME, FATHER RODRIGO OF Salamanca turned north. Taking the Alpine pass he headed into France and the Court of King Charles in the Loire Valley. Here Cardinal Giuliano della Rovere had fled aiming to foment strife between France and the Borgia Pope.

Given the inclement weather, Father Rodrigo's journey was arduous, made worse when one windswept afternoon he was waylaid by bravados. Undeterred, he called down fire and brimstone upon their heads and as luck would have it, his curses were answered by torrential rain, which poured forth their fury amidst a thunder clap so loud a horse belonging to one of the bandits keeled over dead and the others bolted. The bandits were so awestruck by this display of divine retribution they fell to their knees and begged forgiveness from Father Rodrigo, who took out his whip and flogged them as they fled away crying out to heaven for mercy. The young novice accompanying Father Rodrigo believed he was in the hands of a rare holy man and swore lifelong allegiance to his master.

Unfortunately for Father Rodrigo, his horse died shortly after this incident and so the last two weeks of his journey were spent on foot. Several days walking over rough terrain took their toll on his blistered feet. Such was the pain and discomfort he felt by the time they reached the Loire Valley his mood was so black he believed the French should be damned as a nation.

The Château d'Amboise, where the court of King Charles VIII resided, was not to Father Rodrigo's liking. Its grey stone walls and clumsy design were crude compared to the palaces of Rome. Extensions and renovations were under construction, presided over by two Italian stone masons. The grounds and formal garden were also being restyled by an Italian.

The priest Father Pacello da Mercogliano, a genial man with huge hands had

been given the responsibility of attending to the needs of Father Rodrigo.

Etienne de Vesc was regarded as the most influential man in Court. He oozed Gallic charm and was the kind of courtier who would betroth his own daughter to the Devil if he thought it would advance a cause he was pursuing. An increase of French influence in Italy was an aspiration of his, therefore, meetings were held between Cardinal Rovere and Etienne de Vesc designed to investigate ways by which the Borgia Pope could be deposed and replaced by Cardinal Rovere, who would then allow the army of King Charles to claim the crown of Naples and take Milan. King Charles had a vague claim to Naples through his paternal grandmother, Maria of Anjou. Milan was important for strategic reasons and Cardinal Rovere, who hated the Sforzas, had a desire to see it fall into French hands and witness Il Moro and his brother, Cardinal Ascanio, stripped of their power and influence.

The private chambers of Cardinal Rovere were not as ostentatiously decorated as his former Vatican quarters, all the same, his room in the château was well maintained. The dour Cardinal had nothing but praise for his hosts.

'The King is a simple man, unsuited to the affairs of state, preferring to leave them to his sister, Anne of Beaujeu, and that silver-haired fox Etienne de Vesc, whom you have met.'

'How do you find the French?' asked Father Rodrigo.

'The French see themselves as the natural masters of Europe, yet they lack the cultural and academic lineage of Rome or Vienna. Besides, they are too often thwarted by the brutish British, whom they are forever at war with, and like the Romans before them are never able to subdue.'

'Do you think they will invade Italy and place you upon Saint Peter's throne?'

'Rome cannot endure the ignominy that Borgia heaps upon her. Retribution must be swift, decisive and merciless.'

'I pray God will cause your plans to prosper,' Father Rodrigo said, bowing low to kiss the Cardinal's ruby ring.

'From what you have told me it is not only Rome that needs purging of iniquity, but Milan too. Yet that is hardly surprising considering it is Sforza who sits enthroned there.'

'Perhaps not for long,' replied Father Rodrigo.

CHAPTER TWENTY-SIX

WHILE LEONARDO REMAINED UNCONSCIOUS, WORD SPREAD IN Milan's many basilicas that on the second Mass of the forthcoming Sunday, Alessandro would be blessed before the people on the steps of the Duomo.

The elderly matriarch of the Gonzaga family hung her head in shame that her nephew Il Moro had endorsed such a farce.

'It is all the doing of that Florentine bastard,' she complained. 'He has bewitched your uncle.'

'It is the Devil in him, or so the Lazerines would have you believe,' said her granddaughter Bianca.

'Perhaps there is more truth in the minds of the ignorant than we give them credit for,' remarked her stern-faced grandmother.

In the home of Maria, family and neighbours crowded into her parent's hovel to gossip.

'My mistress is most upset over the maestro's condition. The Duke has forbidden her to visit him in the infirmary and she spends her day confined to her quarters in tears,' explained Maria.

'Maria, I think you are a brave girl. If my daughter were

dress maid to the Duke's mistress, I would be beside myself with worry that she would ever meet the maestro,' said Camilla, a portly lady with few teeth who worked as a cook in the kitchens with Maria's mother.

'Oh, she has met him several times, haven't you my sweet?' Maria's father interjected.

'God have mercy!' cried Camilla. 'And what of this 'Jesus of Milan,' have you met him too?'

'Alessandro? Yes. Until a few months ago he was sleeping by the Duomo under the protection of the priests.'

'It is a thing to be marvelled at,' suggested Maria's father. 'To be plucked from obscurity and catapulted to such giddy heights.'

A biting autumn wind blew down from the mountains, heralding winter was on its way. Huddled over a fire deep in conversation with a bunch of regulars in the tavern by the castello were two of Alessandro's friends, Emilio and Carlo.

'Perhaps the Inquisitor has taken him to Rome?' said Emilio.

'No, he came for bigger fish than your Jesus,' replied a grey-haired merchant.

'Then where is he?' demanded the landlord, Philippe the hunchback.

'As I said, he's on the back of a cart bound for Rome,' said Emilio.

'How can that be if the Archbishop intends to present him on the steps of the Duomo this Sunday?' insisted Carlo.

'Maybe he's found a woman?' suggested Philippe.

'I know every whore in Milan,' Carlo laughed. 'If Alessandro has found himself a woman, I would know.'

The morning was all but over when Alessandro woke in a bed of clean Flemish sheets with not one but two women asleep beside him. 'Good morning, my blond Adonis,' Belinda said, taking hold of Alessandro and turning his head towards her to kiss him. Before she could, Alessandro turned away and stepped out of the bed.

'Is it adultery to fornicate with an angel?' the naïve Alessandro asked. 'I mean, have I wronged Letizia?'

Caterina, being the more skilful when it came to playing games with docile men replied, 'Would a Prince of the Church offer us as gifts to you, angels no less, if there was any sin? No Alessandro, he would not. Even His Holiness is known to have a mistress, and would the Church allow such a thing if there was sin? Of course not. You are free of responsibility Alessandro.' Her slippery tongue appeased her not so educated guest, who ceased his questions and sat down on the bed.

'You are a Saint,' insisted Caterina 'the great Jesus of Milan,' and the most important man in the city.' Stretching out his arms Alessandro gazed heavenwards. His lips trembled as the words 'Jesus of Milan' tumbled from his mouth along with a shower of spittle. Each time he repeated the phrase his body quivered with divine delirium.

Observing him, a concerned Belinda took Caterina aside. 'What if he becomes mad?' Belinda asked.

'Father Rodrigo said to ruin him by any means necessary.' Caterina whispered. 'And was it not Euripides who said: *he whom the gods would destroy they first make mad?*'

When the day of his blessing finally arrived, it was a cold unsettled day. An unforgiving wind hit parishioners in the face as they made their way to the Duomo. The most devout had arrived at dawn for the first Mass of the day and many had lingered on to witness the Archbishop's presentation of Alessandro. When Alessandro entered the Piazza del Duomo from the western corner, beaming from ear to ear and dressed like some bizarre character in a troupe of Commedia dell' Arte players, gasps of disbelief greeted him.

Prior Vicenzo, forsaking his duties at Santa Maria, arrived at the Piazza del Duomo with one intention, to forestall the Archbishop's plan and pronounce Alessandro a heretic. The moment Alessandro strolled proudly through the crowd, bowing or genuflecting as he made his way, Prior Vicenzo struck. 'Heretic!' he screamed as loudly as he could. But alas it was to no avail, such was the noise of the crowd hemmed into the Piazza shouting 'Jesus of Milan,' one lone voice bellowing against a thousand was like trying to blow out a candle at a hundred paces.

On either side of Alessandro were Caterina and Belinda, who given the inclement weather had chosen to dress more modestly, whilst Alessandro paraded through the throng wearing a clownish purple and red silk coat with matching britches that Caterina had specially purchased from the Duke's tailor.

'I doubt Jesus will have much success converting those two,' Il Moro sniggered to his grinning secretary. The remark was overheard by the Archbishop, whose face had reddened at the sight of the man he wanted to portray as a paragon of virtue arriving in the company of his notorious niece and her even more corrupt accomplice.

'Good morning, uncle,' cooed Belinda.

'Was it your idea to dress him like a court jester?' asked the Archbishop to Caterina, who fluttered her eyelids. 'Harlot!' His Grace added venomously.

'Your Grace, I am deeply offended,' replied Caterina, enjoying the attention.

'Get out of my sight the pair of you. I will not present Alessandro before this city with you two poised on his shoulder. As for you, young man, you would do well to avoid the company of these two she-devils.'

Despite an extensive search, the woman with the child whom Alessandro had healed had not been found. The rumour spread that she had left Milan to return to her village. Nevertheless, the Archbishop felt compelled by the expectation of the masses to continue with the blessing of Alessandro.

Indeed, many had come hoping to witness some new divine intervention. The Archbishop held up his right hand and silence descended.

'Good citizens of Milan, may God in his abundant mercy bless you.' His voice was loud, authorative and clear. 'Today we pay tribute to a young man whose faith and devotion you would do well to heed. Like our Lord, he is a humble man who has known hard times. Yet God has seen fit to elevate him to a place of honour. Alessandro, step forward.' A starry-eyed Alessandro did as he was instructed. 'Kneel,' said the Archbishop.

Alessandro dutifully obeyed. The Archbishop dipped his hand in a bowl of holy water held by a priest and made the sign of the cross upon Alessandro's head. 'In the name of the Father, Son and Holy Ghost, we give thanks for your life and godliness. God be praised.' The crowd burst into applause amid shouts of 'God be praised' and 'Milan for a thousand years'.

In the depths of his being Alessandro felt an over-whelming sense of euphoria. His mind, filled to the brim with the triumphant shouts of the crowd declaring 'Jesus of Milan' in his ears, only caused him to feel even more that he was chosen to be a symbol of worship. He looked heavenward and, in his trance-like state he saw an angel come down from heaven and extend an arm towards him. The angel wore a white robe and looked like Caterina. Above her shone a gold halo that the 'Caterinaesque' angel took off and placed over Alessandro's head.

'Rise, Alessandro, and go in the strength of God,' declared the Archbishop as he reached down to raise Alessandro to his feet. Il Moro took hold of Alessandro's arm and, holding it aloft yelled, 'Jesus of Milan.'

'Jesus of Milan,' the ecstatic crowd repeated. For a moment events looked as if they might replicate the madness that had occurred in the courtyard of the Basilica di Sant'Ambrogio. Arms were flailing heavenwards, citizens genuflected and embraced each other. Tears wove down a thousand cheeks, some in torrents of euphoria others in gentle sobs.

Sensing the tide of emotion had swung away from jubilation to take on a more fervent disposition, the Archbishop signalled to the Duomo's trumpeters to sound an alarm. With the banner of Saint Ambrose flapping in the wind, three trumpeters rang out a long high-pitched note that brought the commotion in the Piazza del Duomo to a standstill. Priests opened the door of the Duomo, and the entourage on the steps turned around and headed for the open doors. Recognizing the Archbishop had called them to Mass, the crowd quickly curtailed their celebrating and made their way inside the Duomo for the second Mass of the day.

CHAPTER TWENTY-SEVEN

THE VERY HOUR ALESSANDRO WAS BEING BLESSED UPON THE steps of the Duomo, Leonardo woke from his state of unconsciousness. The Duke's physician instructed the maestro to remain in his care until satisfied there was no danger of a relapse. An inability to take orders had always been a failing of Leonardo's, and refusing to heed his advice, he insisted on returning home. Yet, when he stood to his feet, the room spun and his knees crumbled. The good physician guided him back to his bed.

'Now will you listen to me? You are weak, and it will be several days before you are well enough to return home.' The physician ordered some weak broth from the castello's kitchen and water for his patient, who reluctantly agreed to remain in his care.

Hearing that Leonardo had woken from his fretful condition, Cecilia begged Il Moro to let her pay the maestro a visit. He gave his consent with the proviso that the physician be present throughout. She agreed, and once Beatrice had left the castello for her daily prayers at Santa Maria delle Grazie, Cecilia made her way to the infirmary. Upon her arrival, she found Leonardo awake but in a weakened condition and the physician administrating a poultice to his patient's bruised head.

'Oh my dear friend,' she said, taking hold of Leonardo's hand and kissing it. 'How are you?'

'Apart from feeling dizzy and weak whenever I stand up, I am in good health.'

'You are alive. Thanks be to God!'

'Father Rodrigo, does he...'

'Has gone back to Rome...' she replied. 'I hope we will not see him again.'

After a week, Leonardo's health improved enough for him to be discharged from hospital. Not wishing any harm to befall his patient, the physician accompanied Leonardo on his journey back to his workshop. Later the same day, Alessandro returned to pay a brief visit to his old abode on Via Rose. While there, he heard from the landlord Eduardo the Spaniard, who had been left a message from Francesco, that the maestro had returned home. Alessandro packed up his few belongings and hurried to Leonardo's workshop.

When he arrived panting for breath, he spoke first to Francesco who led him through to the kitchen where Leonardo was enjoying a watered-down glass of wine. The physician insisted strong drink was not good for a man in his frail condition. Overjoyed, Alessandro threw his arms around Leonardo.

'God has answered my prayers,' he said.

'I am alive and well and, apart from a little tiredness, feel no ill effects.'

'I swear that priest, if I can call him such, was hell-bent on seeing both of you hang,' said the physician.

'I doubt we have heard the last of Father Rodrigo,' said Leonardo. 'Men like him have a nasty habit of kicking back.' Alessandro fidgeted nervously with his collar as Leonardo continued with his train of thought. 'Let us pray events elsewhere in Italy keep him from Milan.'

'My friend,' said the physician noticing Alessandro's irritated frame of mind, 'you will do well to lead a quiet life and be mindful of the company you keep.'

'Like you, I am a healer now, a worker of miracles who has been blessed on the steps of the Duomo by the Archbishop.' Alessandro said in a voice that betrayed his new-found arrogance. 'I do not think Father Rodrigo has ever performed a miracle.'

'If you are crazy enough to think that, you will end up dangling from the end of a

rope,' replied Leonardo.

'Maestro, I do not wish to cause you distress, but events have moved on. I am…'

'Deluded, if I'm not mistaken,' snapped Leonardo.

'I will be at your studio tomorrow morning as usual, but tonight I am the guest of honour at the home of the Visconti family. Good day gentlemen,' Alessandro said as he departed.

A troubled Leonardo turned to his physician. 'I awoke, only to find the rest of the world is still asleep.'

Mindful of the events that had taken place at Sant'Ambrogio, Leonardo was yet to decide whether God, the Devil or blind hysteria had led to the incident that elevated Alessandro so highly. After the physician had left, Leonardo poured himself a half-goblet of wine and topped it up with a little water.

'Francesco, sit with me,' he said to his senior apprentice.

'You look a little pale, perhaps you ought to lie down,' the youth replied.

'I am perplexed. For all the many services I have performed for the betterment of the citizens of Milan, it is a barely literate weaver who commands the praise of the populous.'

'Maestro, it is of no concern to you if they run after a

weaver,' Francesco said, concerned that for all his elevated intelligence, Leonardo had fallen into resentment.

'Clearly, Alessandro is no longer the meek soul who anxiously poked his head over the threshold of my studio door,' said Leonardo.

'Let the fickle have their hero maestro. Such matters ought not to be of any interest to you.'

'You are right Francesco, envy is beneath good men. Still, long after the antics of a weaver are forgotten, I intend for my art to live on.'

'Then put aside all thoughts concerning Alessandro and create something worthy of God.'

The following morning Leonardo, who lent for support on Francesco's arm, made his way to the studio room at Santa Maria delle Grazie. They had not long been there when Alessandro arrived. After a few pleasantries, Leonardo set to work, however, in less than an hour he was seized by a dizzy spell and was helped to the stool which Alessandro vacated.

'Water,' said a feeble Leonardo.

'Shall I pray for strength to return to your body?' asked Alessandro. Leonardo dismissed this request with a wave of his hand.

'Here maestro, drink this,' said Francesco, handing Leonardo a mug of water. The artist's face looked pale and grey. Together, Francesco taking one arm and Alessandro the other, lifted the maestro to his feet.

'Take me home,' he said. After several faltering moments when they had to stop for Leonardo to salvage the vigour to continue walking, all three men arrived back at Leonardo's workshop. They laid him upon his bed and propped up a cushion.

While Francesco went to fetch some water, Leonardo took Alessandro by the hand.

'Tell me, what does it feel like to perform a miracle?' he asked.

'Maestro, it feels like heaven is in your fingertips.'

'I have always thought the sign of a true artist is if heaven resides in their fingertips.'

'Then we are one and the same.'

'No Alessandro, we are not the same. My brush with death has taught me one invaluable lesson. Be you weaver or artist, if God grants you the joy of performing even one miraculous thing in your life, it is not an occasion to boast or think yourself superior. It is merely the Creator revealing to you what it is to be fully alive.' An indignant Alessandro rose to his feet.

'It is time I was going. I wish you a speedy recovery,' he said, departing in a foul mood.

Wearing a white toga and with a laurel wreath upon her head, Caterina, dressed as a Roman Emperor, prepared for a night of debauchery. Her guests were all dressed as famous figures from antiquity. Among them were Cesare Scaligeri, Il Moro's secretary, and the very young and virginal Bianca Gonzaga, who Caterina had a mind to initiate in the act of love. They were dressed respectively as Alexander the Great, Socrates and Helen of Troy.

Nymphs specially selected by Caterina from the finest brothel in Milan handed out large silver goblets of wine to each guest. Both men and women rewarded the nymphs with a squeeze of either their breasts, buttocks or both. Before matters got out of hand, Caterina brought in Alessandro. Hoots of derision greeted his entrance. He wore only a simple loincloth and upon his head was crowned a floral wreath.

'He's our very own miracle worker,' boasted Belinda.

'I bet he is,' replied Cleopatra, stroking a hand over Alessandro's naked torso.

'I'm in need of a miracle,' teased Venus, exposing her breasts.

'You, my dear cousin, couldn't afford him,' replied Caterina.

Il Moro's secretary planted a kiss on Alessandro's cheek.

'Perhaps not, but I could,' he bragged. 'Maybe it's not one of your little whores he needs, but a fat meaty salami,' continued the secretary planting a kiss on Alessandro.

A nymph poured a goblet of wine into Alessandro's mouth, as the wine flowed down his chin, the eager girl proceeded to lap it up with her tongue.

While the musicians, who Caterina insisted perform nude, for which she paid them triple, struck up a jaunty frottola, half-naked nymphs banging tambourines danced wildly about gleefully discarding their clothes. Giggling, Bianca rose to her feet.

'I do not have gold or perfume,' she said. 'Instead my Lord, I give you...my virgin body!' She threw off her Helen of Troy robes and naked as the day she was born flung her hands in the air and danced up and down. 'Make a woman of me,' she begged and thrust herself into Alessandro's arms.

Besides the noisy coupling of Alessandro and Bianca, who screamed excessively as she cast off the garment of her virginity, Alexander the Great, Minerva, Mark Anthony and Cleopatra set about relieving each other of their clothing. Soon everyone in the room was fornicating, be they Lord, Lady or nymph. While the band played on, the sound of their instruments was nigh on drowned out by the cacophony of moans and groans from Caterina's entourage, who abandoned all moral constraint in pursuit of their licentious activities.

Once the carnal desires of Caterina's guests had been satisfied, it was time to retire to the dining room where a veritable feast had been prepared. A pleasing aroma filled the room. Spread out on the long rosewood dining table were choice cuts of roast pork, rabbit seasoned with thyme and oregano and a chicken cooked in oil and garlic. There was a good range of cheeses, including one distinctive rich smelling goat's cheese that proved very popular. An ample supply of wine from the Rossetti vineyard soon had Caterina's guests well on the way to being drunk. For dessert there were several plates of cheery pastries, sugared almonds and a large bowl of fruit. Once their hunger had been satisfied, the guests retreated to the parlour, where Caterina had more surprises up her sleeve.

After a night indulging the excesses of the flesh, Alessandro crawled out of Caterina's bed before either she or Belinda were awake. He staggered out of the Rossetti estate with a head that felt as though a stone mason were chipping away inside of it. Lurching from side to side Alessandro entered the studio.

'It is the third time this week you have entered my studio in this state,' said Leonardo. 'Francesco! Water!'

'I'm an important man now...' Before he could finish, Leonardo snatched the vase from Francesco, and threw water in Alessandro's face.

'Get out and return when you are sober!'

Watching his errant Jesus depart, Leonardo was seized by a sense of impending doom. His hand stroked the sketches he had made of Alessandro. In them there was the clear indication of world-weariness and sense of isolation, even though he would be surrounded by his disciples, in his eyes you saw Christ alone with his destiny. Now, there was something new in the drawings he made an attitude that ran contrary to the naïve Alessandro he first saw.

Later the same day Cecilia paid Leonardo a visit. Her court official stuck close to her side as Leonardo took the opportunity to confide to his muse.

'I have pondered how long can I continue to let him sit as Jesus, as he teeters on the brink of drunkenness under Caterina's influence. What is to be done with him?' Leonardo asked of Cecilia. 'I fear he has become deluded.'

'Many a man is deluded,' remarked the court official.

'Do you think him in danger of losing those qualities that first attracted you to him?' Cecilia asked. Leonardo tugged thoughtfully on his beard while he walked around the studio watched by Cecilia, the court official and her guards.

'I fear they mock a genius and crown a fool,' he said solemnly.

'But you gave them the fool,' replied Cecilia, a remark that only served to compound Leonardo's predicament.

CHAPTER TWENTY-EIGHT

It became a habit of Alessandro's to stop strangers in the street offering to pray for them. Some welcomed this intervention, others were embarrassed by it, while a few were openly hostile.

On one occasion he insisted Caterina's servants' line up so that he could pronounce a blessing over each. To one he prophesized… 'A faithful husband and a long life,' to another (the girl who had bathed him), 'May your womb be fruitful and bring forth many children,' and to one of Caterina's footmen, 'May you know riches beyond measure.'

Caterina was greatly amused by the whole charade as most of her simple-minded servants took the proceeding rather seriously.

'And what blessing would you pronounce over me?' the delectable Belinda asked.

'That would be simple' said Alessandro as he took her by the hand, 'For you and Lady Caterina to dwell with me in eternity.' Caterina could barely keep a straight face at the absurdity of Alessandro's utterance, and to mask her laughter coughed violently into her embroidered handkerchief.

Learning from Francesco that his aunt had died,

Alessandro asked to be taken to the house to pray that she be raised from the dead.

'If my aunt's name was Lazarus and not Bonita, perhaps such a thing could be possible,' replied Francesco wearily. Not wanting to continue the conversation, he made his excuses and returned to his work. When Alessandro left for the day, a concerned Francesco took Leonardo aside.

'What is to be made of the many reports of miracles that Alessandro is rumoured to have performed. Do you believe them?'

'I was not there at the Basilica di Sant'Ambrogio so cannot comment. But a miracle, like any sign from nature, would need to be examined and proven beyond doubt before I could believe in such a thing.'

'So… you are like the disciple Thomas, demanding proof.'

'No, I am a man of science demanding evidence.'

While Caterina hosted another night of excess, one attended by the usual crowd of debauched guests, she noisily entered the parlour while everyone was fornicating and demanded they all stop. In her hand, she held a large earthen jar.

'I am sorry, my dear friends, but I shall have to call a halt to the evening. We are regrettably out of wine.' While several people groaned their displeasure, most responded that she was forgiven for her error and the party should go on. Belinda, knowing the plans of her lover, cried, Perhaps Jesus of Milan can turn water into wine for us?' All looked to Alessandro.

Caterina held out a ladle to him that contained water. She then asked him to bless the water and drink it, which he did. Caterina took the ladle back off Alessandro and scooped out a drink from the earthen jar – the ladle contained wine! There was such a cry of surprise that Caterina and Belinda could hardly contain their amusement. If their guests believed the earthen jar had contained water all along instead of wine, so be it.

When morning arrived, Alessandro, hungover and shielding his eyes from the sun, staggered along the cobbled streets of Milan and stumbled into Leonardo's studio. Before he could be scolded for arriving still under the influence, he eagerly relayed the event of the night before.

'If I am still drunk, how many men can boast they are drunk on water they have turned into wine?'

'You are making a mockery of your position. Where has your humility gone? Where is the hard-working family man I appointed?' reasoned Leonardo.

'I have other obligations now,' Alessandro argued. 'You are not the only one who has demands upon my time.'

'Go!' demanded Leonardo. 'I am in no mood to paint a drunk. Come back sober tomorrow or suffer the consequences.' A stunned Alessandro, too hungover to argue and feeling in need of his bed, sauntered off without a second thought to Leonardo's warning.

The following day a rumour swept through the streets that 'Jesus of Milan' was to receive the sick and the lame by the door of Santa Maria delle Grazie. By midday, a crowd of more than a hundred had gathered outside the church walls. Some came hobbling on crutches, others were carried on stretchers by friends and family. Monks assigned to the seminary at Santa Maria passed amongst them distributing bread and water and listening to each tale of misery these weary folks were all too keen to communicate. Yet despite their suffering, many wore bright smiles and, even though the biting wind from the mountains tore mercilessly through their thin rags, hope had risen in their hearts.

Prior Vicenzo was indignant when the news was relayed to him. He opened the window in his office and called down in a loud voice. 'Be gone, beggars!' An elderly one-legged man dressed in dirty military rags hobbled on his crutch to below the Prior's window. '

Good Father, I am an old soldier who lost his leg

defending this city from the Venetians. I come in faith hoping Almighty God will grant me a miracle.' Many of those nearby murmured their approval at the brave veteran's words. Muttering in Latin, the Prior closed his window. 'They have lost their wits,' he hissed at Paulo.

Inside Leonardo's studio, a hungover Alessandro looked out at the gathering crowd.

'They have come expecting another miracle. A miracle!' he repeated, merging his words into an incoherent drawl.

'Beware the fickleness of the crowd, Alessandro, they…'

'People nowadays call me Jesus,' he reached out a hand as if to bless Leonardo.

'Get your hand off me.'

'You're just jealous it's me they have come to seek and not you.'

'Don't forget you are just a weaver and, when this is all over, you will go back to being a weaver.'

'Francesco, have a word with him, he's becoming a bore,' joked Alessandro.

'Stay put,' Leonardo ordered, pointing a finger at his senior apprentice.

Alessandro stumbled over a stool and landed heavily on his behind, only to roll around laughing heartily at his drunken error.

'Get out!' yelled Leonardo. 'You have disgraced yourself one too many times.'

'I never took you for a jealous man, maestro. But sure as God made little green apples, it is jealousy that drives you now.' Leonardo peered firstly in Alessandro's direction then out of the window at the rag-tag of peasant bodies congregated in the street outside.

'Where flies gather in numbers, a corpse is never far away,' Leonardo said.

A moment later, the refectory door was flung open as a furious Prior Vicenzo entered. 'The Devil has taken residence in my church!' he barked, kicking Alessandro hard in the ribs. Holding aloft a large wooden cross, the Prior marched towards Leonardo, who backed into the wall behind him. He hit Leonardo hard across the face with the cross. Leonardo fell to one knee. Prior Vicenzo hit him again, this time over the back with the bottom of the wooden cross. Before the Prior could hit him a third time, Leonardo rolled swiftly out of the way as the wooden cross missed its target and came crashing down onto the stone floor. 'Blasphemer!' the Prior yelled, swinging the cross again at Leonardo, who ducked out of the way as it whistled past his head. Alessandro laughed. The colour drained from Francesco's face and he fled the refectory just as Salai arrived in the doorway. Alessandro, still laughing, received another kick in the ribs from the Prior, who screamed at Alessandro. 'I shall beat the Devil in you until it is crying out for mercy!'

Salai settled comfortably against the wall by the refectory door and watched with amusement as his adoptive father jumped hastily to his right as once more the Prior's cross missed him by a whisker, smashing into a row of clay jars full of paint. Blues, reds and yellows went flying across the refectory floor in a kaleidoscope of violence.

'Bravo!' yelled Salai, clapping his hands. Enraged, Prior Vicenzo charged across the room towards Salai, who found the sight of a priest wielding a heavy wooden cross not the least disconcerting. Just as the Prior, cursing in Latin, lifted the cross high above his head, Salai neatly ducked under it and head-butted the Prior in the stomach, sending him flying backwards through the air and landing with a thump. Salai struggled to pick up the cumbersome cross then, mustering his strength, swung it at the winded Prior, giving him a glancing blow to the head.

'Damn you to eternity,' cursed the Prior, who staggered to his feet as Salai once more swung the cross at him. But before it hit the Prior, the hand of Leonardo reached out and grabbed hold of it. 'That's enough, Salai.'

'Fat bastard,' muttered the boy.

'Go!' yelled Leonardo. Salai did as instructed and ran out of the studio. 'Prior

Vicenzo, you have made your point. Now leave before you make an even bigger fool of yourself.'

Leonardo stretched out a hand towards the Prior, who reluctantly took hold of it as Leonardo helped him to his feet. The Prior wiped the dust from his tunic then, without looking back skulked head down out of the refectory, muttered something inaudible in Latin while leaving the instrument of his wrath behind.

'It's true what they say about priests, isn't it?' said Alessandro. 'They serve God with their sermons and the Devil with their tempers.' There was a fire in Leonardo's eyes as he turned slowly around.

'I thought I told you to get out!'

'What do you mean?'

'Your services are no longer required.'

'But the painting, it isn't finished.

'I can finish the painting without you. Now go!'

'But I'm Jesus of Milan.' Alessandro pointed fiercely towards the window. 'Their Jesus!'

'You're nothing more than a peasant!' barked Leonardo.

'How dare you!' replied Alessandro, who squared up to the red-faced artist in residence. 'Don't you know I am a man of honour, blessed by the Archbishop and respected throughout the city?'

A furious Leonardo grabbed Alessandro by the scruff of his neck. 'I appointed you and it is in my power to discharge you.' All his pent-up frustration burst as with considerable force he pushed his wayward model backwards. 'You have become a fool Alessandro, and I will not tolerate the company of fools.'

Leonardo bent down to pick up Prior Vincenzo's discarded wooden cross, then parrying the cross in front of him he repeatedly jabbed Alessandro as one might jab a mad dog and ushered him towards the door. The weaver fell to his knees.

'Maestro, I beg you. I'm Jesus, your Jesus, please...' Leonardo raised the cross above his head, just as he brought it down, Alessandro dived through the refectory door. The cross smashed in to two where only a moment ago Alessandro had knelt.

Shaking, Alessandro stumbled through the courtyard that connected the refectory to the Basilica of Santa Maria delle Grazie and entered the church by a side door. He staggered towards the gold altar, wrapped his arms around it and, looking up to the heavens declared, 'Jesus of Milan.' His words echoed from archway to archway in such a manner it seemed the very building resounded in praises to his name. In the incense-filled clouds, peppered with wafts of sunlight filtering through a stain-glass window, Alessandro thought he saw angels singing 'Jesus of Milan' in heavenly voices that reverberated around the basilica-like a divine aria. He stood in awe of his heavenly hallucination.

The next voice he heard was that of the young novice, Father Paulo.

'Come Alessandro, the people are waiting.' The young priest took Alessandro by the arm and led him down the central aisle of the Basilica, the clouds of golden smoke parting before him like a sign, or so it seemed to Alessandro. No sooner had Father Paulo opened the door than the waiting throng surged forward, knocking the priest aside in their eagerness to touch Alessandro.

'Jesus!' they shouted. Their eyes bulged wide and their dirty fingers stretched out to grasp hold of the deluded weaver. In the melee that ensued, some of the weaker were trampled underfoot, but no one seemed to care, compassion was a forgotten attribute in the scramble for a miracle. Like the prophets of old, Alessandro planted his hands atop the heads of those who flung themselves at his feet and uttered what few words he knew in Latin, 'Benedicat vos Omnipotens Deus, Pater, et Filius, et Spiritus Sanctus.'

Each time he prayed, nothing happened. The infirm and their relatives looked around. A lame man cast aside his crutches and attempted to walk, only to fall heavily to the ground. Alessandro looked at his hands and wondered why the miracles failed to materialize. An old woman dressed in black, with a large tumour that covered one side of her face, grasped her knurled fingers tightly around Alessandro's tunic.

'You prayed for the girl and she was healed, now heal me,' she demanded. The crowd fell silent. Alessandro tilted his head backwards and looked heavenwards. Then, placing his hands on top of the woman's head, he prayed, 'Benedicat vos Omnipotens Deus, Pater, et Filius, et Spiritus Sanctus.' The old woman replied, 'Amen' then touched her face, the tumour was still there. 'I had faith in you,' she said. The crowd began to grumble as the hope they had so earnestly stored up in their hearts was replaced at first by confusion, and then like any mob whose purpose has been thwarted, their mood turned ugly.

'Charlatan,' hissed the old woman, who slapped Alessandro hard across the face. Stung by the force of her venom he recoiled, but before he could recover another blow struck him, one from the crutch wielded by the lame soldier who had earlier argued with Prior Vicenzo. 'Charlatan!' he yelled. Hands which only minutes ago had reached out to Alessandro in expectation now fell upon him in a storm of blows as fists pummelled his body.

'Stop this at once!' bellowed Prior Vicenzo, who had observed the events from his window. 'Help him!' he shouted to a group of priests standing nearby. The lame and their relatives continued to mercilessly attack Alessandro. Dirty fingers scratched and ripped at the flesh on his arms and face. His hair was torn out in clumps and so too his beard.

The priests who came to Alessandro's defence ushered him inside Santa Maria delle Grazie, slamming the doors shut as a torrent of stones and shoes crashed against them. Once inside, Paulo dabbed Alessandro's wounds with a strip of cloth, while another priest rubbed a disinfectant balm of almond oil into the wounds. Alessandro didn't stir but laid his head in Father Paulo's lap and closed his eyes. There he remained still, his breathing barely noticeable, yet his thoughts were very much alive: *I am Jesus of Milan. Make them see. I am their Jesus.* At last, the combination of the beating he had received and the potion he had been given to drink, caused Alessandro to drift into a deep sleep.

It was a tiresome day for Leonardo, who the moment he dismissed Alessandro from service doubted whether the action he had taken was just. For once he sought out the advice of Prior Vicenzo.

'The man has become a liability,' said the Prior. 'Furthermore, you are Artist in Residence to Il Moro, and you cannot allow yourself to be embroiled in further scandal. Let him go maestro. God will decide his fate.' While Leonardo weighed up the Prior's words, he decided to seek out Luca, being a man of the cloth, he wondered if he too would be of the same mind as that of the Prior.

'Had someone been able to predict the future, I would have done more to protect the poor man from the madness of the crowd,' Leonardo said to Luca.

'No one could have predicted the turn of events, only God,' responded his friend. 'Each man is responsible for his own sin, deluded or not. You are free of guilt maestro. I truly believe so.' Even the affable Francesco was of a similar mind.

'You gave Alessandro every opportunity, but a deluded drunkard has outlived his usage.'

With heaviness of heart, Leonardo accepted the wisdom

of those he had confided in. Alone in his room, with only his troubled thoughts for company, he slept uneasily: *Could I have shown him more guidance? Have I wronged heaven by taking it upon myself to choose a mere mortal to paint the Divine? Should I have predicted any man, least of all an uneducated peasant, would suffer a malady of the mind?*

The following morning, Father Paulo was knelt in prayer beside Alessandro's bed, rosary beads flitting deftly between his fingers as he silently mumbled his devotions. Outside, the rain fell heavily, its rhythmic beating off the cobbled stone pavement helped to sooth the torment in Alessandro's troubled mind. He lay there motionless and listened to the rain while the young priest recited his prayers in Latin. When he opened his eyes, and after Father Paulo had cleaned his wound and applied new bandages, Alessandro was given a plain breakfast of bread, cheese and water.

'Have you no wine?' enquired Alessandro.

'The only wine on the premises is altar wine.'

'That will do.'

'Altar wine is only ever to be drunk by Prior Vicenzo during Mass.'

'Bring some to me!' Alessandro hurled his empty wooden plate at Father Paulo, which narrowly missed his head and clattered into the doorframe.

The young priest darted down the corridor while behind him Alessandro screamed his curses. Minutes later, the voice of Prior Vicenzo boomed.

'You ungrateful miscreant! I save you from the mob and you repay me by attacking one of my monks.'

'Mind how you speak to me. Don't you know who I am?'

'You're a peasant and a heretic. Now get out of my church!'

'I am Jesus of Milan and you will answer me with respect.'

'The maestro has no further use for you. The Church has no further use for you. Milan too has no further use for you. If you have any sense left, you will return home to your wife. Now go before I have you thrown out.'

Alessandro pushed Prior Vicenzo out of his way and marched him out of Santa Maria delle Grazie never to darken her doors again.

CHAPTER TWENTY-NINE

In his bloodied clothes (the very ones he wore for his blessing on the steps of the Duomo), Alessandro called upon Caterina, who stood in the entrance to the Rossetti mansion with four manservants resolutely beside her holding cudgels.

'You ridiculous man, do you need me to point out just how tedious you have become?' From her father's banking firm, she had received notice that Father Rodrigo had paid into her account the outstanding monies owed.

'But you are my guardian angel appointed by God to serve me. I demand you fulfil your duty to the people of Milan and take me into your home.'

'If I see you again I shall have you thrown out of the city.' Caterina gave an imperceptible nod to her manservants, who lashed out at Alessandro with their cudgels and chased him off the premises.

Next Alessandro paid a visit to his former landlord Eduardo the Spaniard who, since Alessandro had not slept in his room for over a month, had rented out his old room. He tried the home of Doffo and the warehouse, but there was no sign of him at either place. In desperation he called on Carlo and Emilio hoping he could lodge with one of them.

'When you hobnobbed with the rich did you think to invite us?' asked Carlo, 'no you bloody well didn't.'

'We weren't good enough for you in your fine clothes and pretty women by your side,' accused Emilio. 'But now they've deserted you, like the rich always do when they tire of the poor, you think you can come crawling back to us.' Carlo and Emilio pushed Alessandro aside and went on their way.

Undeterred by rejection, he called on both rich and poor in whose homes he had been entertained but to no avail. Wherever he went, no one would offer him a room for the night. As a chilly November evening drew to a close, Alessandro called at the tavern by the castello. He went from table to table pleading his cause, but it was fruitless, all shook their head, or worse, insulted him. 'From Jesus of Milan to Fool of Milan,' laughed Philippe the landlord. Annoyed at the spectacle he was making of himself, Philippe threw Alessandro out of the tavern.

The only person who came to his aid was Isabella, who allowed him to stay in her filthy hovel on the edge of the Lazaretto. The one thing of worth he possessed was the silver signet ring Caterina had given to him. Exchanged for coin it could have been used to rent a modest room with food for the best part of a year, or more importantly, see his family safely through the winter. Instead, Alessandro sold it for half its value and chose to remain with Isabella.

During the day, Alessandro frequented the many piazzas of Milan, calling out that he had come to heal the sick. He would accost priests, whom he ordered to become his disciples. Whether Isabella accompanied him for amusement, or if she truly believed he possessed divine powers, she was often in attendance when he proclaimed his gospel.

By gossip from Prior Vincenzo's pulpit, word spread that Alessandro da Canegrate had disgraced himself with loose women and drunkenness and consequently was dismissed from service by the maestro. On a nightly basis, Alessandro and Isabella would frolic in taverns and drink until they passed out, often not making it home. Rather like rats drowned in cheap booze their pitiless bodies were washed up on the streets for all to gawk at. Between them, it took only a matter of of months for them to drink their way through Alessandro's money. This was not helped by the fact that Isabella fleeced Alessandro and secreted some of his monies into an old tin hidden under the bed of her hovel. When his money was all gone, Isabella too, like everyone else, threw him out.

The sight of this ragged outcast proclaiming his miracles became a familiar spectacle in the Piazza del Duomo. Occasionally someone would show pity on him and, remembering the height from which he had fallen, toss him a coin or two. Yet, to most people, his very presence caused an uncomfortable shiver. Some blamed the church for elevating an ordinary man to a position of reverence. Yet most blamed the wizard Leonardo, believing the maestro had stolen Alessandro's soul while painting the unfortunate wretch and warned those who auditioned to be painted as disciples to be on their guard for further acts of witchcraft.

A few days later, Leonardo was summoned to the castello over a matter pertaining to a commission Il Moro had long desired he fulfil.

'A noble horse is what I require of you, Leonardo, one made of bronze and bold enough and brave enough to stand as a memorial to my name.'

'Have you the bronze, my Lord?' Leonardo asked, knowing that to cast such a horse would require a sizable amount of the precious metal.

'The bronze shall be made available to you.'

'Then it will be done,' was Leonardo's frank reply. He welcomed a fresh challenge, one that also gave him an excuse to leave aside 'The Last Supper' until a more favourable time.

Leaving the Sala delle Asse, Leonardo happed upon Cecilia.

'How are you Leonardo?' she asked, genuinely concerned. Leonardo cast his eye to the floor and walking on made to ignore her. 'I hear terrible rumours of Alessandro.' Leonardo stopped, for all he counted Cecilia a friend, he had no desire to discuss Alessandro further. He nodded his head and avoiding eye contact replied,

'I have heard them too.' Cecilia could sense the pain in his voice. She longed to embrace him and thus offer some succour to his wounded pride. Yet mindful they were both in sight of the Sala delle Asse, she instead placed her hand gently upon his shoulder.

'You blame yourself?'

'I feel I have done the wretch a disservice and at times I am almost compelled to take him back into my home and see if he can be cured of his malady.'

'Thanks no less to Caterina Rossetti, the man was lost long before you dismissed him from service. You have done all you can. Now leave it to providence to decide his destiny.'

On his way home, Leonardo pondered Cecilia's words and meditated on his position: *It is too late to interfere once again in Alessandro's life, nonetheless, why can I not shake off these feelings of guilt that gnaw at my soul?* Since dismissing Alessandro, Leonardo had lost his stomach for *The Last Supper* and, instead, concentrated his efforts upon Il Moro's long forgotten folly: a giant Sforza horse.

'I need to give the people of Milan something to help them forget the madness of Alessandro,' Leonardo said to Francesco. For several weeks, Leonardo toiled away on various drawings of horses and frequently visited the castello's stables to draw some of the Duke's noble steeds. With some enthusiasm, Leonardo strode into the Sala delle Asse late one afternoon to present his initial cast of the Sforza horse to Il Moro, who looked at it disdainfully.

'This,' he snarled, 'is like some docile animal a woman

might ride.' He thrust the offending horse back into Leonardo's hands.

'Thank you, my Lord, for pointing out to me what should have been obvious,' responded a subdued Leonardo.

'All too frequently maestro, you forget the nature of the man you serve,' interjected Il Moro's conniving secretary.

Ordinarily, thoughts of violence did not occur to Leonardo, yet the secretary with his sycophantic fawning was one man he would gladly punch. Instead, he wished them both a pleasant day and returned home to begin his efforts afresh. After several failed attempts, which were dismissed as not noble or warrior-like enough, Leonardo visited the castello once more, seeking Il Moro's approval for his latest endeavour.

'Splendid work, maestro,' said Il Moro. 'Bring me a horse like this to ride and I shall set out to conquer France.'

Leaving the castello, Leonardo headed towards the Abacus School to meet with Luca, who taught mathematics there to the sons of Milan's well-heeled merchants. The blue sky was peppered with wafts of white clouds, while a fresh wind breezed its way through Leonardo's flowing hair and whipped it in front of his eyes. He pulled his hair aside and took a deep breath as he strode into the school, a long red brick building with a sloping roof that had on the east side an ornate corridor of a dozen Roman porticos. Nestled above the arch of each portico was a high fluted window, some of which had shutters on them. By the central portico, there was a plinth with a small marble statue of Saint Ambrose. Leonardo passed through an oak door that lay next to the plinth and down a dimly lit corridor passing a noisy bunch of students hurrying to their classes.

He found Luca in a moderately sized study filled with bookshelves. In the centre of the room lay a large, old wooden desk strewn with tools for geometry and algebra. Seated on a wooden chair at the far end of the table, Leonardo found the professor busy writing his treatise, *Summa de arithmetica, geome-*

tria, proportioni et proportionalita. A sample of his ground-breaking accounts ledger was left loitering on his desk. Leonardo picked it up.

'I will make one for you, Leonardo. I am sure it will greatly benefit Francesco in his ordering of your affairs,' suggested Luca. 'Hipocras?' he asked, pouring a warm cup of mulled wine for himself and Leonardo.

'Thank you,' said Leonardo taking the cup.

'Now, to what do I owe the pleasure of this visit?' Luca asked. Leonardo placed his small iron horse on the table and took a sip of his drink. Luca picked up the horse.

'Is this your final design?' he asked.

'Yes,' answered Leonardo. 'Rather proud looking, isn't he?'

'Wonderful. I cannot wait to see the completed statue.'

'Will you check these for me? They're the calculations to determine the amount of bronze I will need.' Absorbing the contents, Luca glided his hands gently over the scroll.

'You intend to make the Sforza horse this size? Is such a feat possible?' questioned Luca.

'I believe I possess sufficient skill to execute the task.'

'I will check the calculations for you and bring them to you within the week'

After finishing his drink, Leonardo left Luca, who put his treatise to one side and reaching for his pen and calculus, began immediately to check Leonardo's calculations.

CHAPTER THIRTY

THE RUMOURS LETIZIA HAD HEARD FROM PILGRIMS PASSING through Bergamo on their way home gravely troubled her mind, enough to cause her sleepless nights. Some said the man appointed as Jesus by the Duke's Artist in Residence, the maestro Leonardo da Vinci, dined in the homes of the wealthy and was dressed like a Lord. Others declared he had lost his wits and was wandering the streets of Milan a homeless beggar. Knowing from Alessandro's letter that he had been under the employ of this man only served to disturb Letizia more and give rise to the fear that the man she loved had met some terrible fate.

In need of godly counsel and advice, Letizia sought out her local priest Father Gregory, a young priest who had arrived at Bergamo not long after she had moved into her marital home.

'Father, I am plagued by gossip that my husband has met some terrible fate.'

'I too have heard such rumours,' Father Gregory said. 'As protector of your soul, I took the liberty of writing to a priest I know in Milan and today received a reply. By all accounts it would seem this man who some call 'Jesus of Milan,' is indeed your husband.' Letizia's head dropped into her hands and her stomach churned with such force she thought she would vomit. 'Mary Mother of God, give me strength,' she said tearfully. Noting her disposition, the young priest fetched some water for her to drink.

'Here, take this,' he said, pressing the cup against her lips. Letizia supped a little between her gentle sobbing. 'What have you in mind my child?'

'Please pray God's protection upon the life of my child and I as we journey to Milan. Perhaps there I will be reconciled with my husband.'

'You have my blessing. Go in peace.'

The sun had barely risen from its earthly cradle on the first Tuesday of February when Letizia and her five-month-old son slipped out of their cottage in Bergamo. She had named him Stephano after her father. The baby was clothed in a linen swaddle that covered him from his neck to toe. On his head there was a white linen coif, which was held tight against his face to protect him from the elements. On the front of her body, Letizia had a makeshift hoist to support Stephano while, on her back, she had a small wicker backpack into which she had packed a few clothes, some food for their journey and a little money. She wore her warmest woollen tunic and over that a coat of rabbit fur. Father Gregory's housekeeper had an old pair of boots she had kindly loaned to Letizia. They were a shade too big, nonetheless, she was grateful for them.

The only people out so early in the day were farmers in their fields tending to their livestock. One of these farmers informed her he was on his way to market at her home village of Treviglio. She had visited there only once since the birth of her son. Now her mind wandered to the place of her childhood, reawakening the same premonitory feelings that had engulfed her the day Alessandro proposed, and again before he had left for Milan. A heaviness of heart descended upon her spirit. The blow she felt was as physical as any delivered by human hand and, under the weight of her sack and her son, Letizia's knees crumpled beneath her.

'Sweet Mary, Mother of God, give strength to your humble servant.' Her sweat mingled with tears and the winter drizzle that slid down her face. As if in sympathy, the infant began to cry. Instinctively, Letizia opened her cloak and took the babe to suckle. Sheltering under a sprawling evergreen she fed Stephano. While the rain worsened, and the path began to run with little rivers of muddy water, Letizia hummed lullabies until the infant in her arms cooed and burped and a smile appeared on his innocent face. The rain eventually ceased and like the hearty Lombardy girl she was, Letizia drove herself onwards.

When company finally arrived, she was grateful for it, a small band of Dominican monks making their way to Milan. They were a merry band of brothers, quite content to make a fuss over the infant she carried and frequently breaking into song. At midday, they stopped for lunch at a farm outhouse and Letizia enquired as to whether any of them had heard of this 'Jesus of Milan.'

'I have heard some say he is a worker of miracles,' replied an elderly monk who wore spectacles on the rim of his large hooked nose.

'It is idolatry,' replied a stern looking monk. His words were met with nods and murmurs of approval.

'How can it be blasphemy if people give thanks to God?' retorted the elderly monk. Their leader, Father Bernard, was a kind man, thin as a rake, with eyes that sparkled when he spoke. 'My dear child,' he said, 'the road you are on is unsafe for a woman with a baby. I insist you remain under our protection until we reach Milan.'

CHAPTER THIRTY-ONE

THE MONKS OF SAINT AMBROSE, NOT WISHING TO DENY ANY man a meal, obligingly fed Alessandro a bowl of gruel. It contained more vegetables than usual and even a little meat, courtesy of the leftovers from a feast held at the Archbishop's home to honour those patrons who had donated funds to the building of the Duomo. Feeling the need to rest, Alessandro took a blanket from a monk and curled up in a corner of the Duomo and fell asleep. Later that evening when he woke from his nap, the sky was filled with long wisps of pink clouds like outstretched tentacles that pointed towards the golden globe that dipped on the horizon. He watched the sun slip lazily out of sight, and the clouds turn at first to grey and then black.

It was a cool evening, one with few people about. Wandering the quiet streets, he found none willing to let him pray for them. After knocking on doors and pronouncing one of his deranged sermons on the edge of the Lazaretto, he was chased away by an irate woman and her husband. He exited a narrow street by the castello and, when he had stopped panting, his attention was arrested by the sound of singing coming from the tavern near to the castello.

A murmur of disgruntled voices echoed across the room

as notice of Alessandro's presence spread. Still dressed in the
fine colourful suit Caterina had bought him in the autumn,
which was now blackened by grime, Alessandro bore only a
passing resemblance to the man who had spent many an
evening there the previous summer. Grinning like an imbecile
he held out a begging hand.

'What do you want?' Philippe barked.

'Have you anything to eat?' Alessandro asked.

'It so happens I do,' he replied, spinning Alessandro
around, 'The leather off my boot!' Philippe kicked Alessandro
hard up the backside.

As Alessandro fell forward, Philippe, aided by Carlo,
seized him and threw him out of the door and straight into a
pack of bravados who were passing. The force of Alessandro
colliding with them sent two of these ruffians flailing to the
floor.

'Fool! Bastard! Filthy beggar!' they yelled.

'Jesus of Milan!' Alessandro screamed, believing that
somehow this would save him. One of the men, who had been
knocked to the floor, rose to his feet and stood between
Alessandro and his companions. He had a mark carved on his
forehead to indicate he had been branded a criminal. 'Stop!'
the branded criminal shouted to his companions. He took
hold of Alessandro and pinned him against the tavern wall.
'Are you the Jesus of Milan we've heard so much about?' he
asked, while his twisted mouth snarled in Alessandro's face.

'Benedicat vos Omnipotens Deus, Pater, et Filius, et Spiritus San...'

Alessandro didn't finish his sentence as another man
pulled a long knife across his neck and would have slit his
throat if not for a kick to the ribs from a third man that sent
Alessandro sprawling away from the trajectory of the blade. A
thick leather boot smashed into Alessandro's jaw, the sound of
it breaking sent a shudder down Carlo's spine.

Scrambling on all fours, Alessandro reached up a hand

towards the heavens, just as a bravado came at him with a long thin knife. The blade went clean through the palm of Alessandro's left hand. The wounded man gave his assailant such a look of madness, he backed away without withdrawing the knife. Snarling like a rabid dog, Alessandro impaled his right hand over the knife so that both hands were pierced through. No scream passed his lips, rather his body shock with crazed frenzy. Horrified at his act of self-mutilation, his dumbstruck attackers backed away.

'Jesus of Milan,' Alessandro hissed through his broken jaw while holding out his pierced palms. The bravado whose knife had pierced Alessandro, tried to pull the knife from his hands, but his efforts were met without success. It took two bravados, one to force Alessandro's head and body back, in order for the second to have enough leverage to withdraw the knife. Removing the last of his torn rags, Alessandro stood before them naked with his blood-stained hands outstretched in the shape of a cross.

Struck speechless Alessandro's attackers warily stepped around him and made their way into the tavern. Only one remained, the man branded a criminal. He pulled out a short, thick knife and plunged it into Alessandro's right side. Alessandro fell to his knees, blood oozed from his wound, its crimson stream stained the ground. Carlo looked on aghast as more blood spluttered from Alessandro's mouth and gathered in pools on the cobbled floor. The criminal knelt down beside him. 'Farewell, Jesus of Milan,' he said, spitting in Alessandro's face.

A troubled Carlo made his way towards Alessandro, whose fingers clawed at the ground as he clung desperately to life. Carlo thought of offering the man he once considered a friend some comfort, but a shout from behind caused him to turn away and enter the tavern, giving the gasping Alessandro one final look.

Struggling for breath, Alessandro saw Letizia. She was

bent over the stove in their cottage making his favourite nutmeg polenta. Her chestnut hair dangled over her shoulders and her hips swayed gently as she stirred the pot. She was talking to him though he couldn't hear her words, yet the glint in her eye and the smile on her face were enough for him to know that they were the words of a teasing lover. As Alessandro reached out a hand, Letizia dissolved into the inviting light of the afterlife. Instantly a brilliant glow bathed his body, filling him with warmth from the soles of his feet to the tip of his head.

'Rise, Jesus of Milan,' said a voice that sounded like many waters and filled his body with peace. 'You have been chosen to avenge the wrong done to me.' The sound of the voice soothed the pain in his body and Alessandro felt strength enter him. He looked at his pierced hands. Instead of blood flowing from his wounds, he saw a golden light shine from the palms of his hands. The blood that had collected in pools glistened like molten gold as it weaved its way down the path. Alessandro's body burned with fire, his whole being consumed by the light that encapsulated him. Whether his vision lasted moments or hours he knew not, only when it finally past he was no longer face down in the dirt but standing with his bloodied hands raised heavenwards. Staggering forward, Alessandro gave no thought to the direction in which he stumbled, while in his ears rang his divine summons.

'Rise. Chosen. Avenge.'

A raging thirst gripped him, and he headed for the nearest water font at the Piazza del Duomo. Under a clear sky awash with stars and a chill wind, a naked Alessandro, leaving a trail of blood behind him, tumbled through deserted alleyways.

Arriving at the Piazza, he dipped his head in the font and drank like a man who had been out in the heat of the summer sun. But no matter how much he drank, his thirst refused to be quenched. Noticing the doors to the Duomo were slightly ajar, he reasoned that perhaps holy water would satisfy his thirst. As he dragged his battered body up the marble steps, the effort was too much for him and he crawled into the Duomo on his hands and knees. Hanging on to the font to the left of the door, Alessandro heaved his body upwards until he was able to plunge his head into the water and drink. Despite drinking all the holy water in the carved marble font, it too failed to abate his cruel thirst.

He raised his head and stared into the empty vastness of the Duomo, the pale light of the moon filtering through the stained-glass windows, blended with the flickering candlelight casting long thin shadows into dark recesses. In the distance, he could see a halo hovering over the golden statue of Christ, beckoning him forwards. Mesmerized, Alessandro, drawing upon his last reserves of energy, staggered down the centre aisle. Exhausted he fell at the gold feet of Christ and kissed them.

'Who is Christ?' he asked, as he clung to the statue smearing it in his blood. 'You have wounds,' he said, placing his hands over the pierced hands of Jesus. 'But, see, I do too.' While Alessandro spoke to the statue, an elderly priest entered from a side room to the right of the altar. Alarmed by the sight that greeted him, he hurriedly made his way forward.

'You there! What do you think you're doing? Move away!' Oblivious to the priest's presence, Alessandro continued to mumble. Each word he uttered sent a stabbing pain through his mouth. 'Water… water…' Alessandro collapsed into the arms of the priest, who precipitously arrived just in time to catch him. The priest looked at the bleeding body in his arms and instantly recognized him. 'Merciful God!' he exclaimed, as he gently placed Alessandro on the grey marble floor.

The priest saw Alessandro's wounds, and fearing he might die, hastily administered Extreme Unction using a little oil he carried in a vial around his belt. Carefully anointing Alessandro's head, he prayed the prayer of absolution and committed a destitute weaver into the safe keeping of Our Saviour. With a heavy heart, he took a red silk cushion from the front pew and placed it underneath Alessandro's head. He paused for a moment, looking in wonderment at the wounds of the naked man who lay in his arms. Then, as quickly as his arthritic legs allowed, he went to rouse help.

CHAPTER THIRTY-TWO

A COLD FOG BLEW INTO MILAN, ONE SO THICK IT CLOGGED Carlo's throat and kept visibility to no more than an arm's length. The superstitious believed such a gloomy sign to be a portent of bad tidings, which would surely befall Milan for the act of wickedness that had occurred the previous night. From those gathered in the tavern the rumour quickly spread that 'Jesus of Milan' had met an unfortunate end, murdered by bravados. Carlo felt pangs of guilt, and when questioned on this by the woman he called his wife, he pleaded ignorance. When she pressed him further, he lost his temper.

'Jupiter's cock woman! Just because I once shared a drink with the man doesn't mean I wipe his arse and know whether he lives or dies.'

Mopping the sweat from Alessandro's brow, Sister Anna, a young nun with full lips and inquisitive brown eyes marvelled at the stigmata of her patient who had remained unconscious throughout the night. Under her grey habit, she had an admirable figure, one Brother Francis, the middle-aged monk who was also in attendance, couldn't help but notice.

'Do you think it is a blessed sign?' Sister Anna asked, clasping the blood-stained right hand of Alessandro.

'Only God knows,' replied Brother Francis, taking hold of Sister Anna's fingers and lifting them off Alessandro's bloodied hand.

'He has a wound in his side too. Surely it is a blessed stigma?'

'"Only God knows,' repeated Brother Francis.

'Will he live?' she asked, while she fiddled with the ring on her left-hand signifying

she was a bride of Christ.

'Only God knows,' replied an unimpressed Brother Francis.

'But he is 'Jesus of Milan,' surely the sign is authentic?' Sister Anna said, her voice rising excitedly with each word she spoke.

'Only God knows,' repeated the dour-faced monk.

'Can't you say anything Brother Francis, other than, "only God knows"?'

Unaccustomed to outbursts from young women, Brother Francis blushed and, on the pretext of going for more medicine, exited the room regretting his earlier lustful thoughts for the feisty nun.

Sister Anna took hold of Alessandro's hand. 'I am your faithful bride. My body promised to you alone.' She kissed his hand repeatedly as she said. 'Purer than glass, whiter than snow, more brilliant than the sun is my love for you.' Swaying backwards and forwards, Sister Anna pressed the bloodied palm of Alessandro right hand tightly to the breast that lay above her pounding heart.

When Brother Francis returned, he caught Sister Anna naked from the waist up pressing her lips against those of the lifeless Alessandro. Aghast, he dropped the balms he had brought, one containing almond oil smashed on the floor and filled the room with its pleasing aroma. In a heightened state of agitation, he rushed at Sister Anna and flung her to the floor.

'You harlot!' he yelled.

'I am a bride of Christ and he is my beloved,' whined Sister Anna, seeking to hold on to Alessandro's right hand. Brother Francis dragged her out of the room and proceeded to kick her down the corridor.

By the time evening arrived, Alessandro had still not regained consciousness. Now, however, he was attended to by two monks. Father Marco had considered it necessary to send instructions to the Abbess of the Poor Clare's convent forbidding any nun to enter the hospital wing of Sant'Ambrogio. Any nun who disobeyed his command would be stripped of Holy Orders and banished from the convent. Sister Anna's punishment for her objectionable actions was to be flogged with a cat of nine tails and for her hair to be shaven off. The Archbishop, alarmed by Alessandro's apparent stigmata, summoned Father Marco to the Duomo.

'What is to be done with this man? He seems ever to haunt us,' said a concerned Archbishop. 'One thing I know for certain Father Marco... news of his whereabouts must never reach beyond the walls of Sant'Ambrogio.'

'I understand, Your Grace. My brothers can be relied upon and I will ensure the sisters of the convent are also held to obedience,' replied Father Marco.

'Good. There is a monastery in the Swiss Alps founded by the Holy Saint Bernard of Montjou, one that is only accessible from April to September. I will write a letter explaining our predicament and request that the Abbott confide Alessandro da Canegrate to the monastery and put him to use. As soon as he is well enough to travel I want you Father Marco, to personally oversee his safe passage.' Father Marco bowed and kissed the Archbishop's ruby ring.

The brothers at Sant'Ambrogio and the sisters of the Poor Clare's convent adhered firmly to the Archbishop's instruction and refrained from mentioning, even among themselves, word of Alessandro. So strictly was this order observed that not even the indomitable Prior Vicenzo caught wind of it, he too, like everyone else, presumed Alessandro dead.

CHAPTER THIRTY-THREE

Ever attentive to gossip, Salai burst into Leonardo's bedroom.

'Papa! Papa! Wake up!'

'What is the meaning of this?'

'Papa, Alessandro is dead! Murdered by bravados outside the tavern by the castello.'

Leonardo felt his stomach sink as he listened to an excitable Salai relay all the gossip he knew pertaining to the demise of the man he had chosen to paint as Christ. His innards plummeted to hitherto unknown depths of guilt with each gory detail Salai imparted. His mind similarly was awash with thoughts of self-reproach: *This is all my doing? I should never have abandoned him to such a fate. Oh God, what will become of me now?*

'Please, leave me in peace now Salai.' Deeply saddened, Leonardo put aside his task for the day, moulding a life-size clay cast of the Sforza horse and wrote a letter of condolence to Letizia, which read:

Greetings Letizia. Although we have never met I feel I know you for your husband talked often about you. It is concerning Alessandro that I write this letter with a heavy heart. I regretfully inform you that he has been taken from us and is now in the safe keeping of Almighty God. I include a sum of monies that belonged to Alessandro, which I now entrust to you. I know it will not ease your pain, but it will perhaps help during the long nights that lay ahead. You are in my prayers, Leonardo da Vinci, Artist in Residence to the Duke of Milan.

He then wrote a second letter, which he gave to Francesco to deliver to the Archbishop informing him of the news he had heard. Troubled by remorse, Leonardo made his way to the Basilica of Santa Maria delle Grazie. His mind was plagued by a sense of responsibility, for had he not insisted upon choosing a model for Jesus, Alessandro would still be alive. His stomach suffered spasms of anxiety whereas his mouth dried under the impact of the shame he bore. Mixed with his sense of blame he also felt humiliated and embarrassed for the man he had appointed to be the paragon of virtue, had been possessed by flaws that ultimately led to a sad and pathetic end. There was anger inside his heart towards Alessandro too, that he had not heeded the warnings given and returned to his wife.

Out in the streets, Salai and Francesco were harangued wherever they went.

'What did the maestro know of the death of Jesus of Milan?'

'Did the maestro order his execution?'

To which they replied, the maestro had not spoken to Alessandro since he was dismissed from service.

Fearing the wrath of God, Carlo, paced up and down the street whilst he attempted to summon the courage to enter Santa Marai delle Grazie and confess his part in Alessandro's murder to a priest. His mind tormented by the belief that if he were to step foot inside the church, the hand of judgment would reach down and punish him. Feeling unable to purge his sense of guilt in the confines of a Holy place, he walked around Santa Maria a dozen times with only his remorse for company. Leonardo arrived at the basilica just as a distressed Carlo was passing.

'Carlo, are you alright? You look like you've seen a ghost.'

'Oh, maestro, save me from the hand of God,' Carlo pleaded, gripping Leonardo's hand.

'My dear man, whatever is the matter?' Unable to control himself, the guilt-ridden man poured forth the events of the night before.

'I didn't think the bravados would kill him,' he vainly said. 'I just thought they would have some sport and be on their way.'

'You are a fool, Carlo. Now go!' Leonardo ushered the distressed man towards the Basilica's entrance. 'Confess, and make your peace with God,' Leonardo said as he shoved him through the doorway.

After a minute or two contemplating Carlo's admission for his part in Alessandro's death, Leonardo entered the eerie confines of the Basilica and made his way to its ornately decorated apse where he lit a candle in Alessandro's memory and offered prayers for his salvation and the safe-keeping of the departed man's wife and child. Prayers Prior Vicenzo observed, and like all who desire some choice gossip, made his way to stand beside Leonardo, where he waited until the artist had completed his supplications. Leonardo rose from his knees and bumped into the Prior.

'I hear rumours concerning Alessandro, are they true?' he asked sharply.

'Good Prior, it is with great sadness of heart that I confess the rumours are true. Alessandro was murdered last night. I heard it from one who witnessed the tragic event.'

'God be praised!' cried the Prior.

'I do not consider the death of any man worthy of giving praise to God.'

'Only the death of heretics,' said Prior Vicenzo, who walked away with a swagger in
  his step.

The armed messenger dispatched to deliver news to Letizia of her husband's death carried with him two letters of condolence, one from Leonardo and the other from the Archbishop. The messenger was also entrusted with the generous amount of money Alessandro had been given by the Duke and the Archbishop, which he had left with Francesco when Leonardo was being treated by the Duke's physician.

There had been an occasion when in the early hours, a drunk Alessandro had arrived with Isabella demanding the monies be returned to him. It was an occasion that caused Leonardo to lie, an act that his pursuit of integrity rarely allowed him to commit. But in this instance, he felt compelled to and told Alessandro the monies had been returned to the Church. It therefore pleased Leonardo to dispatch the monies to Letizia, whom he considered the rightful beneficiary of such a princely sum.

Upon arriving in Bergamo, the messenger was informed by Father Gregory, Letizia had departed for Milan. Upon ascertaining the content of the message, Father Gregory's response was she should be spared the heartache of receiving such tragic news from a stranger. He ordered his housemaid to prepare some food for the messenger and some hay for his horse. He then saddled his old grey mare and set off in pursuit of Letizia.

After riding for two hours, Father Gregory found Letizia in the company of the Dominican monks who had taken her under their care.

'My child, tragedy has struck your household, yet do not fall into despair. Pray the God of hope will revive your spirit,' said Father Gregory taking Letizia by the hand. He read out the letters of condolence from both the Archbishop and the maestro, and informed her too, that a considerable sum of money, by way of compensation for her tragic loss had been delivered along with the letters and was in safekeeping at his home.

'I would still like to journey to Milan, and pray by his graveside,' Letizia said. Her voice was solemn and her face pasty white from the shock of her news.

'My dear child,' said Father Gregory, 'There is no grave to visit. He was removed… to the paupers' pit outside Milan.' Such sensitive information Father Gregory did not learn from the letters in his possession, rather it had been gleaned from the dispatch rider.

'Upon my soul, he will burn in hell if he is not buried in hallowed ground,' cried Letizia.

'Do not concern yourself with the salvation of your husband. It is God who decides our eternal fate.' A bereft Letizia thanked the Dominican monks for their hospitality and journeyed back to Bergamo with Father Gregory. A journey she undertook in silence, save for her sobs.

Finally, Letizia understood the premonitory nature of the feelings that had accompanied her short life with Alessandro. It was the portent of death. She was to be a widow. Her whole being felt besieged by loss and her heart weighed heavy with grief over the man she loved and whose arms would never cradle their son. She had no desire to delve into the gossip that surrounded her husband's life once he had entered Milan, nor ponder a future that promised only the oppressive loneliness of widowhood. It was her preference to remember Alessandro as she had known him, strong, handsome, always teasing her, a man diligent in his work, one who was grateful of her cooking, and a husband, who unlike many, never raised a hand to his wife or treated her with any disrespect.

Their marriage had lasted a year and a half, yet her heartache grieved for the ten, twenty, thirty or more she hoped she would have had, but which fate had denied. A numbness crept over her being, one so strong it stifled out any words she could speak. She attempted to mutter what prayers she could to the Almighty, but her spirit was so broken words failed her. It was as if she had forgotten how to pray. Tears rolled down her cheeks. She felt the hand of Father Gregory console her.

'Peace my child. May our Lord, who knew sorrow in the garden of Gethsemane, comfort you in your grief.'

It was a busy day for Leonardo, who did all he could to order Alessandro's affairs and fend off rumours that he had played some part in his death. For the next few months he adhered to the proverb 'out of sight, out of mind', and rarely ventured into the streets. Instead, he remained in his workshop where he immersed himself in preparations for a cast for the Sforza horse. Once he and his apprentices had made their final arrangements,

Il Moro, keen to exploit an opportunity for self-promotion, ordered a grand unveiling of the giant cast of the Sforza horse to take place in the grounds of the castello. Milan's nobility were invited and, in order to popularize the cult of the Sforza name, commoners too were rounded up and assigned places at the far end of the castello courtyard. It was a position none wished to be in, most held opinion that Il Moro was a jumped-up shoemaker whose family had usurped control of Milan.

Leonardo's clay horse, covered by an enormous drape, sat atop a low-slung cart pulled by two stout black farm horses. Half a dozen men either side of the model steadied it with long poles. Il Moro wrung his hands in anticipation and grinned to his wife.

'Beatrice my love,' Il Moro said affectionately, 'let us hope the maestro is as good as his word.' Unconvinced, Beatrice fiddled with the ruffled collar on her blue taffeta dress. She mistrusted the maestro, believing he often used his superior intellect to gainsay her husband.

Confined to watching the proceedings from her bedroom balcony, well out of sight of the jealous Beatrice, who remained ever watchful for evidence of her husband's infidelity, Cecilia watched Leonardo stand on the cart and inspect the pulleys connected to the drapes. Jumping off the cart he paced round it twice, checking the pulleys once more and joking with several of the workmen.

Francesco approached, and the pair exchanged a few words. Satisfied all was well, Leonardo walked to Il Moro and his invited guests and bowed while Francesco, who was assigned the task of unveiling the Sforza horse, waited for his master's signal. 'Illustrious Lord, upon whose favour Milan rests, it is my honour to unveil a cast of the Sforza horse in recognition of your esteemed family.'

The drape covering *Leonardo's Horse* swung slowly backwards revealing the proud head of a stallion. There was an audible intake of breath as the beast was fully displayed. Even Prior Vicenzo, who had sneaked in to observe the proceedings, gasped in surprise along with everyone else. Cecilia too, from her vantage point was filled with admiration when she caught sight of Leonardo's creation.

Il Moro, proudly ambled forwards with his hands raised gleefully above his head.

'Leonardo, you're a genius!' he exclaimed, but his words were drowned out by clapping and shouts of 'bravo!' from the crowd, all of who were amazed at the grand statue before them.

Leonardo's Horse painted black and varnished to gleam like a mirror was poised elegantly on two legs. Every muscle flexed and accentuated. It was a horse fit for a king. Its aristocratic neck was complemented by a tightly woven mane of curls that fell gracefully on either side of its muscular body. Its back was perfectly arched like all good thoroughbreds, while its tail was slightly raised and proud. Even the crisscrossing of fine hair on its tail glistened in the sunlight. The head was tilted downwards as if snorting to give the impression it was about to rise up, while its eyes glared with an arrogance reserved for the prince of beasts. It was truly a descendant of the Hippoi Athanatoi: offspring of the four wind gods who were said to pull the chariot of Zeus.

'You have surpassed yourself, Leonardo,' raved a delighted Il Moro, who vigorously shook his artist's hand.

'If you provide the bronze my Lord, I would erect the largest statue in Christendom. Something all Italy would marvel at, all in honour of the Sforza name.'

'It is magnificent maestro, the most remarkable sculpture I have ever seen,' praised Beatrice, who was not usually this complimentary towards Leonardo.

'Thank you, my Lady,' replied Leonardo bowing.

'Do you need this model for the bronze statue?' asked Il Moro.

'No my Lord everything I need is set aside in preparation.'

'Then I would like this statue to remain here in the castello grounds until the bronze one can be erected in its place.'

'A charming idea my Lord,' chirped Il Moro's secretary, who threw a rare smile in Leonardo's direction.

'As a reward for your many services to my kingdom a vineyard has been donated to you. I will have the deeds to the land drawn up in your name.' Leonardo kissed the royal ring on the left hand of Il Moro and thanked him for his kindness

Buoyed by his success, the following morning Leonardo headed straight for Santa Maria delle Grazie and renewed working on *The Last Supper*. Days, which turned into weeks and then months while he waited for Il Moro to procure the considerable amount of bronze needed for the Sforza horse were wisely used auditioning men for the roles of the disciples. Considering the spectacle Alessandro had made of his term under the maestro's care, Leonardo thought it would prove difficult to find men willing to be the disciples. In fact, the opposite was true as men gladly came forward to offer themselves to be painted. Some saw it as their civic duty, while others sought a cathartic spiritual experience and deeper understanding of Our Lord's suffering at the hour of his greatest need.

The chosen 'disciples' were an assortment of characters. Some were merchants from the educated classes, while others were traders or artisans. In this respect they mirrored Christ's disciples who too had been a mixture of artisans and professional men. All were cheerful, and none appeared to hold any prejudice towards Leonardo, each acting the role he had assigned to them with due diligence, be they Matthew protesting his innocence, Peter clutching a knife, or Thomas, stabbing the air with his doubting finger, all behaved with courtesy and respect.

In an attempt to capture the moment when Jesus revealed to his disciples that one of them would betray him, Leonardo twisted their bodies into a myriad of angles. No two disciples were seated the same, each had his own unique shape as he burst forth with energy, rising to his feet, leaning towards his friend, pleading with his hands, all begging for answers. Their faces carried an abundance of emotion, shock, fear, disbelief, denial, as each man manifested the questions burning in his mind: *Surely not I? Who can it be? Why Lord, would one of the twelve betray you?*

CHAPTER THIRTY-FOUR

Spring arrived but as if to spite the fair city of Milan, the heavens opened. Father Marco rued his misfortune. He and another brother priest had set off before daybreak on the arduous journey of escorting Alessandro to his new home high in the Swiss Alps.

They were not the only ones venturing out on such a wet day. The Duchess of Milan was also departing for Venice, where along with her father Ercole d'Este, Duke of Ferrara they were to carry out a diplomatic mission on behalf of her husband. One that would hopefully see the Venetians recognize Ludovico Sforza as the rightful Duke of Milan. Something they had been loath to do since Il Moro had usurped the Duchy of Milan from his seven-year-old nephew, Gian Galeazzo Sforza, after the assassination of the boy's father, the cruel and tyrannical Galeazzo Maria Sforza, in 1476. After the assassination, a protracted and bitter dispute arose, one which eventually saw Ludivco Sforza declare himself ruler of Milan.

Like all comings and goings in a large city, today was also a day when another traveller strode into Milan intent on fomenting strife, Father Rodrigo of Salamanca, who still seethed over his failure to bring Leonardo da Vinci to trial. However, any thoughts of vengeance against the maestro would have to wait until the Papal mission for which he had been dispatched had been fulfilled. It was a subtle hand Father Rodrigo was forced to play. To balance on the one hand his desire for a more faithful and godly Pope in Cardinal della Rovere, and on the other, the expediency of his present need, to show himself loyal to Pope Alexander VI.

'Be they Dukes or Borgias, every man has his day of reckoning,' was the dictum Father Rodrigo had relayed to the one man in Milan he could trust, Prior Vicenzo. 'No mortal can thwart the purposes of God,' affirmed Father Rodrigo in a stern voice.

'Artists like our Florentine enemy, they too will suffer. God wills it,' replied Prior Vicenzo.

'God wills it,' repeated his newly arrived guest.

From Prior Vicenzo, the belligerent Spaniard learned of Alessandro's blessing on the steps of the Duomo, how he had disgraced himself with wild living in the company of Caterina Rossetti, and of his subsequent descent into madness and murder at the hands of cutthroats. Prior Vicenzo offered his distraught guest a little brandy to ease his agitation. Father Rodrigo said nothing to Prior Vicenzo that it was he who had paid the Rossetti harlot to ruin Alessandro. It was, he reasoned, his Papal duty to test and lure into temptation those he considered heretics.

'A man with a sacrilegious mind will always choose sin over righteousness, whereas a true Christian would resist temptation and remain blameless,' was the argument he made to his faithful host. 'Evil begets evil. None more so than those like the maestro who are born out of wedlock and therefore more inclined to stir up wickedness. Keep a close watch on him Prior, be my eyes and ears in Milan and, in time, we will strike.'

The following morning, the Sala delle Asse shimmered

with spring brightness. A calm but determined Father Rodrigo was ushered into Il Moro's presence and bowed while he was engaged in a whispered conversation with his secretary.

'I come on business from Rome,' Father Rodrigo hissed while it was still clear Il Moro had not finished his conversation.

'When you come into my court, I expect you to show me the respect my position accords. Now wait.'

'The Holy Father has a message for you,' replied Father Rodrigo, clearly aggrieved.

'Perhaps the good priest would like some wine to quell his mood,' enquired the secretary, who disliked the prevailing tension.

'Wine makes you dull,' the priest rasped.

'Then you're in good company,' Il Moro replied with gusto, igniting a ripple of

laughter from his courtiers. Father Rodrigo flashed a look of disdain at the courtiers then turned slowly to face Il Moro.

'The message I bring is one for your ears alone. But, first, a gift from His Holiness.'

Father Rodrigo clapped his hands and a priest entered with a small chest that he placed on the floor close to Il Moro's feet and opened it. Il Moro's eyes glazed over at the sight of hundreds of gold coins. The mute priest looked up grinning as Il Moro, relishing the clink of coins bent down and plunged his fingers into the chest. Hypnotized by the sight of gold the courtiers inched forward, the sweat of greed causing their slippery fingers to tingle with anticipation. Il Moro looked at them with disdain.

'Greedy pig shitters!' he yelled. The courtiers bowed their heads and reluctantly backed away. 'Follow me,' Il Moro said, to his papal emissary, who was amused by the sight of retreating courtiers. 'Here's a piece of free advice,' said Il Moro, walking towards the doorway of the Sala delle Asse. 'Show those beneath you only two things, contempt and praise. Contempt so they are reminded of their position and praise, for in thinking they have gained your favour, they will fall over themselves in their effort to please you more.'

'Wise words indeed,' replied Father Rodrigo.

Il Moro stopped outside a thick door guarded by two soldiers with stubbly chins and murderous eyes. The soldiers stood aside as Il Moro took a long iron key from his belt and opened the door by its solid bronze handle. He motioned to the secretary to place the chest on an oak table. Il Moro lifted a handful of gold coins to his lips and kissed them.

'What are you still doing here?' he barked at his secretary, who skulked away. Il Moro slammed the door shut. 'What does His Holiness want?'

'Italy is surrounded by enemies. France, it is rumoured has her eyes on Naples and Milan…'

'The French kings are all bastards!' interrupted Il Moro. 'One of these days one of them will lay claim to the kingdom of Heaven and oust the Creator from his throne.'

'It is not only the French who lay claim to Milan. Naples and Spain also have a grievance against you while to the east, the Ottoman Empire threatens the power of Venice. And if Venice falls, the Turkish hordes will come marching to your door. Divided Italy is vulnerable. His Holiness has devised a plan to secure the safety of Italy.'

'Has he indeed,' replied Il Moro.

'It is only possible if Italy is to unite under one banner, Rome. Only unified under the stewardship of His Holiness can we protect Italy. The Pope asks that you recognize his authority by relinquishing your claim to be Duke of Milan and accept Papal governance over the city and her territories. In return, His Holiness will allow you to remain as governor, but the city itself will fall under the jurisdiction of Rome.'

Il Moro pinned his Papal visitor to the door. 'My family have single-handedly resurrected this city and you expect me, Ludovico Sforza, to hand over everything we've worked for!'

'If Italy is to survive, she must unite,' replied the priest as he wrestled free of Il Moro's grip.

'And Lorenzo the Magnificent? He would never relinquish Florence to Rome's control. He is the one man, besides His Holiness, who has the power to unite Italy.'

'Lord Lorenzo is dying and not long for this world. Besides, Florence is beset with unrest as the monk Savonarola fights for control of the city. If you look to Florence to forge an alliance you will be disappointed,' Father Rodrigo said with a faint smile.

Il Moro took a moment to digest this news. 'The Medici will not relinquish Florence to His Holiness without a fight and, if Rome goes to war against Florence, Italy will be more vulnerable to attack, not less.'

'His Holiness speaks for God. Do you doubt his plan is the will of God?'

'Rodrigo Borgia wouldn't know the will of God if it kicked him up the backside.'

'Pope Alexander VI is the Vicar of Christ and you would do well to remember that.'

'You see this?' Il Moro said. 'Porcelain from China, the table and treasure box from India, silver from Germany, this bust from ancient Athens, these scrolls from the library of Alexander, and this stone tablet from King Solomon's Temple. Italy as a nation of city states has enjoyed peace these past fifty years and because of this we are all prospering. Rodrigo Borgia would sell off Italy piece by piece to the highest bidder.'

'His Holiness regrets to inform you that your brother, Cardinal Ascanio, is currently imprisoned in the dungeons of the Castello Gandolfo, accused of the murder of Giovanni Borgia. Unless you agree to the Pope's demands, your brother will be left to rot.'

Il Moro threw the Greek bust he was holding at the Papal

Emissary, who jumped aside as it smashed against the wall and fell to the floor.

'You think you can threaten a Sforza?' Il Moro yelled. 'You come to my city and demand that I hand over the keys of my kingdom to a Spanish usurper!'

'Your brother...' began Father Rodrigo.

'How dare you threaten my family you scabby Spanish cunt!' Il Moro took hold of Father Rodrigo and placed him in a headlock, rubbing his knuckles painfully into the priest's bald head.

Watched by shocked and amused courtiers and guards, Il Moro dragged the priest out of the treasury room – into the outer hall – and out onto the front steps of the palace. Holding Father Rodrigo by the hair, with an arm twisted behind his back, in a loud voice Il Moro addressed the motley crew of traders, shoppers and soldiers that milled about.

'People of Milan. Gather round!' Their response being too slow for his impatient temperament, he blasted out, 'Quick about it!' The soldiers, traders and common folk hurried to assemble beneath the palace steps. 'This Spanish lackey has been sent from Rome to dictate terms to your Duke. What do we say to that?'

The people, knowing reprisals would follow if they did not demonstrate allegiance to their ruler, booed and jeered and hurled the necessary insults to indicate their displeasure at the papal 'lackey' held fast in Il Moro's vice-like grip. 'Go back to Rome, priest, and tell Rodrigo Borgia to keep his nose out of Milan!' With those words, Il Moro hurled Father Rodrigo down the steps, who, with arms and legs flailing wildly about tumbled in a comical way downwards receiving several cuts and bruises and a deep gash on his forehead as he landed in the mud with a thud.

His noviciate servant helped to pick the bedraggled priest off the ground and used the hem of his tunic to dab the cut on Father Rodrigo's forehead.

'Father Rodrigo,' piped up the concerned noviciate.

'Shut up!' Father Rodrigo replied. Furious and utterly humiliated he scurried like a muddied rat out of the castello courtyard, while having to bear the ignominy of those nearby who spat and hurled insults at him.

Not content with chasing him out of the courtyard, the crowd pursued him into the streets. An action that was done more to appease Il Moro than demonstrate any genuine malice against the bloodied priest.

CHAPTER THIRTY-FIVE

Horses' hooves beat heavily off the ground, churning up the earth that splattered against the gold crested carriage they were pulling. Escorting the carriage were a dozen mounted soldiers, determination etched across their faces. There was a full moon and a sky festooned with stars, which shed their silver light on the road ahead. Driving hard through the town of Monza, the carriage, flying the Duke of Milan's crest of arms, passed unhindered. The coach veered off sharply as it passed the seat of local government, the Arengario, with its five porches and stone loggia. Onwards they rode past fields, plentiful vineyards and sleeping villages, waking up neighbourhood dogs as they hastened on their way.

Dawn broke. In the distance, the topmost minarets of the Duomo could be seen welcoming the new day as the light reflected off them like a halo. The soldiers picked up the pace. Entering Milan, they made straight for the castello, causing the occasional early riser to hurry out of their way and almost knocking over a baker with a cartload of bread. The horses' hooves clattered against the stone floor of the castello forecourt then, amidst much shouting and yelling, the carriage came to a halt. Soldiers rushed over and demanded to know what news they brought. Horses snorted and neighed, grateful that their arduous trek was over.

The captain of the escort, a nobleman of thirty with fine black hair and a sizable moustache, slid wearily from his saddle. He paused to catch his breath and straighten his uniform before he opened the door to the carriage. Inside a flustered Duchess of Milan, looked pale and fatigued from her journey.

'My Lady,' said the captain, who held out his hand and helped the Duchess out of her carriage.

'You know what needs to be done,' the Duchess said to the captain, who saluted proudly.

Gathering up her cumbersome blue dress, Beatrice did what no soldier had ever seen a lady of breeding do, she ran across the courtyard and in a blur of fabric, bounded up the steps and disappeared inside the palace.

The door to the Duke's bedroom flew open, but their bed had not been slept in and the balcony door was closed. Alerted by the sound of Beatrice's arrival, the secretary stumbled into the Duke's bedroom, still in his nightgown.

'Where is he?' demanded the Duchess.

'My Lady, please, I am sure there is...' began the secretary before he was roundly slapped across the face. 'Do not take me for a fool!' The secretary stroked his stinging face.

'Where is the room of his mistress?' The embarrassed secretary shrugged his shoulders. 'Ludovico! Ludovico!' shouted the Duchess. Pushing past the secretary an irascible Beatrice proceeded to bang upon every door in the corridor. 'Ludovico! Ludovico!' the Duchess yelled.

Undeterred, she took the stairs at the far end of the corridor and continued to shout and bang upon doors, waking the Duke's cook, chief valet and housemaid. Doing his best to placate everyone was the secretary, whose forehead glistened with beads of sweat in his attempt to keep up with the Duchess as she charged around the castello. She climbed to the very top of a staircase reserved for servants. Midway down the corridor, two guards stood outside a room. Upon hearing the Duchess approach, one of them nudged the other, Beatrice headed straight towards them.

'Out of my way,' she said as they attempted to prevent her entering the room. She beat upon the door with her fists. 'Ludovico!' she shouted, pushing aside a guard as she wrestled with the door handle.

A naked Il Moro jumped out of bed and fumbled with his evening gown just as the Duchess came barging in. She looked scornfully at her naked husband and Cecilia who gave a startled cry.

'My father said I should not expect a Sforza to honour his marriage vows,' Beatrice said bitterly as her husband finally managed to wrap his evening gown around himself.

'My darling, she means nothing to me, just someone to warm the bed.'

'The French are coming,' said the Duchess as if announcing dinner. 'I heard it from the Doge personally. A drunken French General on a diplomatic mission to Venice boasted to one of his mistresses that King Charles aims to claim Milan and Naples. They are already marching through the Alps. You have a week before they lay siege to your city.'

The Duke's legs buckled. 'Bastards! Whoresons! Warty pricks!' he said as he beat his hand against Cecilia's bed post.

'There is no time to lose,' Beatrice said, walking out of the room, just as a panting secretary reached the doorway. 'Fool,' she muttered as she barged past him.

The Castello Sforzesco echoed with orders being barked, a dozen officers all urgently attending to what duties had been assigned to them. Il Moro ran around in a desperate attempt to see his gold and silver ushered safely out of Milan. Beatrice quickly organized an inventory of items and carts for them to be loaded onto. Il Moro's general, General Conti, a proud soldier with square shoulders and distinguished grey hair, approached the Duke.

'My Lord, we have insufficient bronze for the cannons.'

'Then use the bronze set aside for the Sforza horse.'

By this time, the Duke's own spies had entered Milan confirming the news Beatrice had relayed the night before. Outnumbered by twenty to one and facing bigger cannons, defeat was inevitable. Yet the stout General was in no mood to capitulate without a fight. Whilst Il Moro planned his escape, General Conti set about fortifying the city's defences and boosting the morale of his troops. Mounting his black stallion, he rode amongst the ranks of soldiers and instilled in them as much bravery and fortitude for battle as any noble General from the ranks of history.

'The French will think that with their vastly superior numbers they can swat us aside like a man lashing out at a wasp. But let us show them we Milanese have a sting in our tail. Let them taste Milanese steel. Let us spill the blood of our enemy. Let us make them regret the day they marched to our doors and thought they could take our city or violate the dignity of our wives, daughters and mothers. The French have never shown mercy when they have laid siege to a city. Therefore, I demand you show no mercy! Cut them down! Strike a blow for the liberty and freedom of this great city.' He raised himself on his horse and brandished his sword. 'Milan for a thousand years!' yelled General Conti, words his stout-hearted men repeated with gusto.

In the streets of Milan, the populace were seized with terror. The nobility and merchant class packed what belongings they could and along with their womenfolk, set off to stay with relatives in the country until it was safe to return. Knowing even the sanctity of the church was no deterrent to thieving French hands, priests hid gold ornaments, jewelled crosses and other precious artefacts in the secret alcoves of Milan's basilicas. The streets were crammed with carts pulled by donkeys, horses and cows, as the fleeing Milanese took what they could salvage in their urgency to escape the city. Vagabonds helped themselves to the pickings the rich left behind in their desperation to escape. Many souls sought refuge in the castello, only to be turned out by Il Moro's personal guard, causing many to declare that such an ungracious ruler deserved to be taught a lesson by the ghastly French.

In the castello courtyard a dozen wagons laden with the Duke's gold, ornaments, paintings (including *The Virgin of the Rocks*) and the items from his treasury room were being loaded into place under the supervision of Beatrice. Twenty soldiers were assigned to escort the Duke and Duchess to safety. A horse, alarmed by the commotion, bolted, tipping over the cart it was pulling and spilling its contents. A chest burst open scattering gold ducats across the courtyard. Il Moro rushed forward to scoop his gold back into chest.

'Get your thieving hands off my gold,' he snarled at several soldiers who came to assist him.

Tentatively Cecilia entered the courtyard. At first, she went undetected by Il Moro, who was too busy ensuring that all his gold was accounted for to notice his mistress approach.

'My Lord, save me. If the French capture me, they will…'

'…You ridiculous woman, you can't come with me.'

'I know, My Lord. Send me away under your protection, I beg of you.' Il Moro

looked about him. Nearby, a young captain was supervising a group of soldiers.

'Captain!' yelled Il Moro. The young captain turned his horse around.

'What of Leonardo?' Cecilia asked. Il Moro looked at her, puzzled. 'If the French were to capture him?' Cecilia continued. Il Moro took hold of the reins to the young captain's horse. 'Ride to Santa Maria delle Grazie and escort maestro Leonardo to Florence.' The young captain saluted Il Moro.

'My Lord,' cried Cecilia, thinking for a moment she was to be abandoned.

'Take her too,' the Duke ordered, half-heartedly wagging a finger in the direction of his distraught mistress. 'And charge Leonardo with her protection.'

'Thank you, my Lord,' Cecilia said. Grateful for his intervention, she kissed Il Moro's hand.

While the streets of Milan were a hive of activity, Leonardo stood deep in concentration at the top of a scaffold. He stroked his brush on the wall of Santa Maria delle Grazie in a manner that suggested he was oblivious to the tumult outside. Francesco, assisted by Salai, urgently organized an inventory of personal possessions and works of art.

'Maestro, I beg you, the French…' began Francesco.

'Are always coming,' retorted an angry Leonardo.

'But maestro…!'

'I will not abandon my work,' said an emphatic Leonardo.

'Il Moro has fled the city,' replied a frustrated Francesco, who turned to Salai.

'Can't you talk some sense into him?'

'Since when does he take any notice of me?' replied Salai, who marched over to the scaffold. 'Do you plan to get us all killed?' he screamed, shaking the scaffold to ensure he got his papa's attention. 'Do you think the French will spare you if they get their hands on you?'

'What do you think you're doing?' asked Leonardo. Salai shook the scaffold again, only harder. 'Do you plan to kill me?' Leonardo said.

'The French will do a good enough job of that!' shouted Salai, shaking the scaffold

further and causing Leonardo to hang on to the frame for support.

The door to the refectory swung open and in marched the young captain accompanied by two of his men. 'Where will I find the maestro Leonardo da Vinci?' he asked Francesco.

Everyone in the room pointed to the figure stood atop the scaffold. The young captain approached.

'I am Captain Chianti and I am under orders from the Duke to escort you safely to Florence.

'Captain Chianti, that's a Tuscan name,' replied Leonardo.

'You are correct maestro, my family were originally from Radda.' Leonardo looked the earnest young captain up and down.

'As I have already explained, I'm not leaving. You may go.' Leonardo turned back around and picked up his paintbrush.

'Maestro, you will agree to the Duke's request. I insist.' There was the sound of a scuffle in the doorway and a woman's screech echoed around the refectory. Everyone turned to face Cecilia, who entered followed by a soldier.

'I'm sorry, captain,' begged the soldier. 'She refused to stay outside.' Cecilia walked to the scaffold and placed her hand upon the ladder.

'Now is not a time for obstinacy, Leonardo. Do you think the French will show you mercy if they were to get their hands on you?' Then, stepping back and preening her hair, she announced. 'The Duke has placed me under your protection.'

'Is this true?' Leonardo asked.

'It is maestro,' replied Captain Chianti. Leonardo placed his hands upon the wall and, lost in his thoughts, slowly caressed the painting: *I have been undone, again.*

'Papa! We must go!' Salai pleaded. Sighing heavily, Leonardo slowly descended the ladder still holding a brush in his hand.

'Maestro,' implored the captain. Leonardo turned to face his apprentices.

'Salai and Francesco, you will accompany me. But as for you, Nicoli and Romano, you have family in Milan. I urge you to go to them. When it is safe to return I will notify you.' While the apprentices were saying their goodbyes, Leonardo gave instructions to Father Paulo to cover 'The Last Supper' with drapes and hide it from French eyes.

Father Paulo assured the maestro they would do all in their power to preserve the integrity of the painting and hide his additional works of art. This necessity seen to, Leonardo mounted his horse while Francesco and Salai rode pillion with two of the captain's guards.

In the streets of Milan they passed citizens fleeing for their lives or barricading their homes. Outside the basilicas, priests ushered a frightened populace inside for sanctuary from the French. At the city's south gate no soldiers were on guard, all having been assigned to defensive duties elsewhere in the province. The road out of Milan was a pitiful sight of refugee's intent on finding safety in the homes of relations in the country.

Unfortunately, the vast majority of Milanese had neither relatives in Lombardy nor elsewhere in Italy who could harbour them, nor did they have the means to escape. Therefore, they stayed in the city to face the invasion. In the ensuing chaos, vagabonds took advantage of the fleeing rich to rob and violate premises including Leonardo's workshop, which was ransacked.

On the outskirts of the city, there was no time to mourn the brave death of General Conti who, true to his word, was slain with his sword in his hand. Even though he and his men fought valiantly, the sting they promised the French was short-lived. Entering Milan, the French conscripts, plucked from peasant stock and dressed in their tatty dog-eared uniforms, showed no mercy. They raped and slew wantonly, dragged women from churches and houses and ravaged them in the open streets, killing husbands and priests who sought to defend their honour. They stormed and ransacked the Castello Sforzesco but found little of value. Gascon archers used Leonardo's clay Sforza horse for target practice, turning the once-proud statue into an oddly-shaped conglomeration of lumps that bore only a passing resemblance to its former glory.

On the open road, Captain Chianti was pleased with their progress, considering the obstructions presented by numerous carts and slow-moving pedestrians. By nightfall, they had arrived at Piacenza only to find the inns full. However, thanks to Leonardo and Cecilia's status, accommodation was quickly provided in the pink-marbled Palazzo Comunale. Senior Scoto, who acting as provincial ruler on behalf of the Duke of Milan, ordered food for his esteemed guests.

Once Francesco and Salai had retired, and the soldiers had located the nearest tavern, Captain Chianti departed to secure what news he could of the road ahead, leaving Leonardo and Cecilia on their own for the first time since their furtive meeting in Il Moro's prayer room.

'You have hardly spoken two words since we left Milan,' said Cecilia. Leonardo took his goblet of wine and drank it dry.

'I am grateful you are safe,' he replied. 'And spared the abuses the French would no doubt have heaped upon you.'

'I am comforted to know you have regards to my safety,' Cecilia replied.

'Excuse me,' Leonardo said rising from his seat and stepping away.

'Leonardo. What ails you?'

'My dear, you once exhorted me not to abandon 'The Last Supper' as I am accused of having abandoned projects in Florence. I was determined to stay and prove my worth, now everything of value… is… gone.'

'My friend, I know you are aggrieved in this matter. At such times it falls upon us to trust to God.' Ignoring her plea, Leonardo made for the door, stopping on the threshold he turned to look at Cecilia.

'God? What if God is silent and heeds not my prayers?' In no mood for debate, he departed the room.

Seeking to take in the night air, he made his way around the Piazza Cavalli, which throbbed with people who had no other choice but to bed down under the stars. He entered the Basilica of St Francis and prayed to the Almighty to protect his apprentices, their families and the few friends he had. His prayer was uttered more from a spirit of obligation than one of faith, but Leonardo reasoned God, being God, heeds all prayers, regardless of the spirit in which they are spoken.

After conversing with a handful of fellow refugees, he retired to his room where, once again, a dark mood seized him and he descended into melancholy. A feeling of hopelessness gripped him as he considered the fate of Milan and the people left behind. Above all, he felt like a man divorced from their destiny. *The Last Supper* had become to him a symbol of his art, one he feared leaving behind.

His restless mind turned to thoughts of Cecilia: *Is it a game to test my fidelity? Or, has Il Moro consigned Cecilia to my protection hoping I would make her my wife? If I was to bed her, would he pronounce his blessing, or hunt me down and have me killed?*

CHAPTER THIRTY-SIX

A PURPLE HAZE HOVERED OVER THE ROLLING HILLS OF
Tuscany like a wave of magic dust blown into the air by some
mythical genie. The light dangled between mountain peaks as
if cast by an ancient spell. Cecilia was particularly taken by
the vast array of wild flowers, which covered each meadow in
a vivid blanket of colour. The air was thick with the fragrance
of wild roses mixed with thyme, basil, rosemary and fennel,
the smells suffused the many vineyards they rode past. For in
the rich soil of Tuscany, a variety of grapes were grown, and
no two vineyards smelt quite the same. Salai, however, was
unimpressed. Never having ridden a horse until the day they
fled Milan, he spent much of the time travelling through
Tuscany complaining. 'Damn animals.' 'My arse hurts.' 'Even
when I shit I get no relief.'

Accompanied by wispy clouds, infused with the light of
the setting sun, the red cupola of the Basilica di Santa Maria
del Fiore and Giotto's ornate bell tower could be seen rising
above the Florentine skyline. It was a sight that warmed
Leonardo's heart. Cecilia took hold of Leonardo's hand. She
alone knew what returning to Florence meant to him.

A breeze wafted through a small copse of cypress trees

that lay just beyond the boundary of Florence, infusing the air with their familiar oily scent, one that was accompanied by the rhythmic drumming of cicadas filling the early evening landscape with their noisy chatter. Above the trees, the sun was setting over the most beautiful skyline in all Italy when Captain Chianti delivered those under his charges safely into the bosom of Florence. Then, guided by Leonardo, they wove their way through narrow cobbled streets, while he pointed out to Cecilia and Francesco various landmarks. Nothing appeared to have changed in the years he had been away, except a little more work had been done to the Duomo.

They passed through the Piazza opposite Santa Croce just as the watchmen were lighting the lamps and carried on towards the Via de Agnolo. Coming to a halt outside a large double door, Leonardo dismounted and hammered on the door of his former maestro.

The door creaked open to reveal the elderly figure of Verrocchio. Leonardo, Francesco and Salai were ushered inside by a frail yet smiling Verrocchio, who held tightly to the arm of his former pupil. Leonardo, wanting to maintain the honour of Cecilia, had Captain Chianti escort her to the Pitti Palace. An apprentice brought food for Leonardo and his two young travelling companions. When Francesco and Salai retired for the night, Verrocchio poured another glass of wine for Leonardo.

'My eyes are not what they used to be,' Verrocchio said, pulling his chair closer to his old friend, 'but I see your hair is now peppered with streaks of grey. Perhaps the climate in Milan does not suit you.'

'I live modestly,' replied Leonardo.

'It is the only way for an artist,' Verrocchio replied, tapping Leonardo on the knee.

'I'm surprised you still run a studio,' Leonardo said. 'Surely you could have retired by now?'

'It's better to be busy than to sit staring into the street like some old retard from sunrise to sunset.' Leonardo smiled at his old mentor's reply.

'You have a son, I see, but no wife, Leonardo. What of the Lady Cecilia?' Leonardo laughed, perhaps a little too loudly.

'You old rascal! Lady Cecilia is my patron's mistress.' Verrocchio tactfully changed subject. 'But what of the French?'

'In a year or two they will be gone. And if Il Moro returns, then I too will return to complete *The Last Supper.*'

'Leonardo. I have known you thirty years, and in all that time, how many works have you left unfinished? Here...' Verrocchio reached out a hand. 'Help me to my room.' Without responding to Verrocchio's accusation, Leonardo took hold of the old man's arm and led him from the dining room to his chambers.

'Do you need me to help you dress for bed?' asked Leonardo.

'One of the boys will help me. Goodnight my friend. It is good to see you again.'

Later in bed a discontent Leonardo lay awake mulling over Verrocchio's words: *Where he sees abandonment, I see the machinations of fate and the eternal nuisance of being forced to fulfil commissions contrary to my vision.* An agitated Leonardo tossed from side to side, while the nagging voice of doubt assailed his ears throughout the course of the night until the hint of dawn began to permeate his room. It was only then, when the first kiss of daylight arrived that his troubled mind ceased its noisy activity and he drifted off for a few hours' sleep.

CHAPTER THIRTY-SEVEN

WITHIN THE WALLS OF THE PALAZZO MEDICI, THE RULER OF Florence, Piero de' Medici, otherwise known as Piero the Unfortunate (the son of Lorenzo the Magnificent), had capitulated to King Charles VIII's demands as the invading French had entered Tuscany, leaving Florence in disarray. A weak and incapable Piero, who lacked the leadership his father had shown, abandoned the city. In protest, the populous of Florence revolted against the Medici family who fled into exile. Florence was once again a Republic.

Savonarola, the Dominican monk whose fiery preaching and penchant for stirring up the populous had plagued the final years of the reign of Lorenzo the Magnificent, now believed he was free to usher in an era of religious repression. However, not all in Florence had fallen under the sway of the charismatic monk and older powers, families like the Pazzis, whose long-running feud with the Medicis had torn the city apart, now sought to reassert their influence.

Since her arrival in Florence, Cecilia longed for Leonardo to lavish her with the kind of attention too oft denied in Milan. Instead, she found she was largely ignored. The gossip in the Pitti Palace was that Cecilia had been welcomed to keep Leonardo happy, in the belief while he remained in Florence, his talents would be put to service. It was a rumour Cecilia hoped there was an element of truth to. Yet night after night she pined for Leonardo to come to her bed. Yet rather than Leonardo's undivided attention, she regrettably found herself having to fend off the advances of unwanted suitors.

Shuffling on his feet before the unfinished *Adoration of the Magi*, thoughts of Cecilia were far from Leonardo's mind. Instead, there was the regrettable sound of Senior Prodi, the Florentine lawyer who had visited him in Milan.

'It is a fair offer,' the lawyer said, his stern voice only adding to the injury Leonardo felt. 'The monks of San Donato a Scopeto have been most accommodating, as I'm sure you will agree.' Leonardo silently nodded. 'I'll leave the contract for you to sign,' said Senior Prodi, who allowed a satisfied smirk to weave across his thin lips as he placed a document down upon a table. He then wished Leonardo a pleasant day and left just as Verrocchio entered, accompanied by the artist, Filippino Lippi.

'Greetings!' cried an exuberant Filippino.

'Filippino!' yelled Leonardo in return.

'You haven't changed, Leonardo. You're still devilishly handsome.'

'And you're still devilishly ugly,' retorted Leonardo, as the two friends embraced.

In his youth Filippino had wooed many a virgin with his looks, charm and ability to poke fun. Thankfully the years had been kind to him and he still cut a dashing figure with his curly russet hair, neat chin and mischievous pale green eyes. Verrocchio stood before the *Adoration of the Magi* and marvelled at the detail of Leonardo's drawing. He ran a finger over the contours of the Virgin Mary.

'I remember when you first unveiled the cartoon for the Adoration,' said Verrocchio, a hint of sadness in his voice. 'It was the talk of Florence, remember? For weeks people from all walks of life came by to view it.'

'Do you now intend to paint it, Leonardo?' asked Filippino. 'I'm sure the monks of San Donato would be delighted if you did.' Leonardo put an arm around Filippino.

'My brush could not add one iota to the scene I have drawn here. This is the perfect drawing.' Leonardo placed a sheet over the cartoon he had drawn and walked to the door.

'Please forgive me,' he said, turning around to face a baffled Filippino and Verrocchio. 'Dine with me tonight and I will explain, or try to explain, why I cannot finish the Adoration.' For a moment, Verrocchio and Filippino stood there staring at the empty space Leonardo had occupied just seconds ago.

'Still the same old Leonardo,' said Filippino sighing.

'He will never change,' remarked Verrocchio, who stretched out a hand and removed the cloth Leonardo had placed over the Adoration. 'I'll speak to the monks myself, perhaps an arrangement can still be made?' Grateful, Filippino shook Verrocchio's hand.

In a state of agitation following Senior Prodi's visit, Leonardo heeded no one's company but his own. It was not that he had sought to deliberately ignore his old friend Filippino. Rather he felt compelled to find rest in the stillness and solitude of nature. Here he hoped his mind may yet conjure some means out of his legal predicament. The country paths around Florence were well known to Leonardo, and he veered off the beaten track until he found a pleasant meadow secluded from passers-by. Amidst the fauna and flora of the Tuscan countryside, he meditated upon the beauty of nature until a more tranquil mood descended over him. In a state of contemplation, he sat for hours hoping his mind would find a satisfactory solution to the demands of the monks of San Donato a Scopeto.

When Leonardo finally returned to Verrocchio's, he was

handed a note left by Cecilia. 'The rumours of her appearance are true,' remarked Verrocchio. Leonardo chose not to reply and taking the note took himself off to his room. Sitting down upon a chair he held the letter betwixt his forefinger and thumb for some time before he finally overcame his apprehension and read Cecilia's note, which read:

My dearest Leonardo, why have you not come to see me? The court of Florence is in upheaval as men fight over their position in the new Republic. I have no friends here. I am alone, and no thanks to you left in a vulnerable position. Please come soon. Your ever-faithful Cecilia.

CHAPTER THIRTY-EIGHT

THE FOLLOWING MORNING, LEONARDO ENTERED THE PALAZZO
Medici gardens where he found Cecilia seated on a white
bench beneath an intricate floral canopy of red geraniums.
Without an introductory greeting, he launched straight into
his annoyance at the visit of Senior Prodi until he was interrupted by Cecilia, hitting him repeatedly on the arm with her
white fan.

'I am subjected to ridicule by the ladies of the city, and the
unwarranted attention of unscrupulous men, who think with
my protector nowhere to be seen they can part my legs and
treat me like a concubine! And now you come to me without
so much as a kiss on the cheek and all you can talk about is an
unfinished commission that some miserable monks would
have you complete. By my word, I would have been better off
in Milan!'

'Forgive me. I did not mean to offend,' he said
reassuringly.

'What have I done that you act so cruelly towards me?'
Cecilia said, stabbing a finger in Leonardo's chest.

'You are guiltless, my songbird. I find myself so absorbed
by re-acquaintances with old friends catching up on the

Republic's news. Time passes without my being aware of the discourtesy I have demonstrated.'

'Walk with me,' Cecilia said, linking her right arm inside Leonardo's. 'I think you are only telling half the truth. I know men, and you are not a man like other men, who by now would have taken advantage of the fact Il Moro is in Austria to enter my bedroom.' Leonardo wanted to stop and turn around, but Cecilia's arm was firmly locked in his and she was not letting go. 'It is why you show me your ornithopter and complain to me about commissions and conniving lawyers, because to talk to me of anything else risks exposing your true emotions?'

'You have the advantage, Lady Cecilia,' Leonardo said. 'At nights I lie awake and long to come to your bedroom, for I know you would welcome me. But you were entrusted to me for protection, and to violate the trust bestowed upon me would mark me out as a man who lacked integrity.' Cecilia stopped by a Roman figure carved in marble.

'Damn your integrity Leonardo, for once can't you act like a man?' But the honesty of his words touched her, no man, save her father, had ever shown her such respect.

'Is there nothing I can do to dissuade you?' Her hand reached out to caress Leonardo's face.

'Cecilia, in the annals of history you will be remembered as one of Italy's most beautiful of daughters, but I too long to be remembered, not only as an artist and a scientist, but as a man who chose the path of celibacy over his natural inclinations.'

'If we are not to be lovers, do not at the same time forsake your duty towards me,' Cecilia said. Leonardo bowed and kissed her on both hands.

Taking his arm in hers, they continued their conversation. Leonardo explained to her the consequences of the demise of the Medici after the death of Lorenzo the Magnificent, and the grip Savonarola had over the masses. During their discourse they stopped frequently to admire plants the Medici gardeners had cultivated from lands both near and far. When the time came for them to part company Leonardo reiterated his intention.

'I will neglect you no longer and will visit you more often. You have my word.' Satisfied with Leonardo's promise, Cecilia departed more content and at peace than at any time since her arrival in Florence. He, too, felt relief that the feelings he had battled with had now been laid to rest.

Arriving back at Verrocchio's studio, the old man welcomed him to the dining table where he and his apprentices sat.

'There is to be a summer banquet in honour of the Republic,' began Verrocchio to Leonardo. 'You may bring the lady Cecilia.'

'I am sure she will be delighted,' replied Leonardo.

'Do you have any words of wisdom for my apprentices?' Leonardo looked around at the eager young faces sitting at the table.

'Art,' he said, 'is pretty simple. You come up with an idea and do your best to execute it. Most fail. Some work. You do more of what works. If it works well, others quickly copy. Then you do something else. The trick is the doing something else.'

'Excellent advice,' said Verrocchio. 'I have something to tell you, my friend. You have been invited to sit on the committee to choose the artist for the statue of David.'

'Who is the favourite?' Leonardo asked.

'Michelangelo,' Verrocchio replied.

'Michelangelo! That ugly deformed creature,' said Leonardo.

'You cannot allow personal animosity to cloud your judgment. I beg you Leonardo, as the older man to lead by example,' Verrocchio implored.

'That halfwit would sooner throw rocks at me than shake

my hand.' Leonardo stood to his feet. 'Good evening,' he said, and departed for his room.

Verrocchio turned to his apprentices, who along with Francesco and Salai were witnesses to Leonardo's outburst. 'Like the warring Medici and Pazzi families, it would appear Florence cannot accommodate both Leonardo and Michelangelo, at least not at the same time.'

The day arrived for the committee to award their decision. Leonardo, along with Verrocchio, the Archbishop of Florence and other civic dignitaries gathered around a large marble-topped oval table. In front of them was a blueprint for a statue that each man examined in turn. 'It is magnificent, don't you agree?' the Archbishop enquired of Leonardo.

'Absolutely,' said Leonardo with a hint of envy in his voice. All were in agreement. Michelangelo's blueprint was by the far the most ambitious of those presented for consideration. It depicted a young David, with his body turned at an angle accentuating his muscular torso.

To polite applause, Michelangelo entered. He was an odd-looking youth, small and stocky with a permanent scowl on his face and powerful hands like those of a pugilist. The Archbishop of Florence, a wizened old relic, extended a hand to Michelangelo.

'Come,' he said. 'We are pleased that you have returned from Rome. After much debate, it has been agreed that you be given the commission for the statue of David.' A delighted Michelangelo shook hands with all the committee, excluding Leonardo.

'Even Leonardo favoured you,' said Verrocchio.

'Well, of course you voted for me,' Michelangelo said, prodding Leonardo hard in the chest. 'You may be a bastard but you're not blind.'

Leonardo bowed and having no desire to hear Michelangelo gloat further, left him to bask in his moment of glory.

Behind an archway, watching Leonardo make his way out

of the civic building was Father Rodrigo of Salamanca. Alongside the Father were three French mercenaries, hidden in shadow. The priest pointed Leonardo out to his accomplices, who then followed him at a safe distance into the busy streets of Florence. The mercenaries wore long black capes slung over one shoulder and each carried a French long sword rather than the shorter *espada ropera* favoured by Italians.

Leonardo made his way to the Ponte Vecchio where he stopped and purchased a roll of fine white linen and some gold silk thread and needles. Once Leonardo had moved further down the path, the short mercenary (who spoke the best Italian) approached the merchant.

'Wasn't that the artist Leonardo da Vinci?' he said.

'Yes,' replied the merchant. Then seeking an opportunity to boast he continued, 'He has been invited to the summer banquet of the Republic and purchased from me fabric for the costume he has a mind to wear.'

CHAPTER THIRTY-NINE

SEATED AT A TABLE IN THE NEAT AND SPACIOUS ROOM Verrocchio had assigned to him, Leonardo, dressed in only his undergarment, held a needle in his left hand. In front of him was a purple and cream coloured piece of fabric that he was busy stitching to the main body of the garment which was white. Satisfied with his workmanship, he held up the finished toga, slipped off his undergarment and with the aid of one of Verrocchio's apprentices, put on the garment he had just made. Holding a small mirror in his hand, he admired himself from various angles. The hem of the toga was rimmed in gold while sliding elegantly across the left-hand side of his chest was a decorated motif of the symbolic Florentine Giglio.

Several hours later, Leonardo and Verrocchio were in a carriage en route to the summer banquet of the Republic. Under the influence of the zealous monk Savonarola, strict laws had been imposed, which many had opposed, believing them more suited to monks living in a monastery than the free-spirited Florentines who enjoyed their nights of revelry. The austere who sided with Savonarola, believed all such banquets to be signs of immorality. Regardless of their objections, they were many in the tumultuous days of Savonarola's reign who saw such occasions as an opportunity to do business the old ways. The Florentine bankers, merchants and men of commerce who still wielded considerable influence relished any excuse to make a profit, even when dressed in the garb of those intent on an evening of merriment and frolic.

Verrocchio was dressed in a smart blue silk jacket, white ruff and military style breeches.

'With my failing eyesight, I would only make more of a spectacle of myself if I came trussed up to the eyeballs,' had been his answer when Leonardo had offered to make

him something for the occasion. Leonardo poked his head out of the carriage window. There was a gentle breeze scented with the aroma of cypress trees. Leonardo breathed in the sweet smell thankful for nature's simple pleasures.

Arriving at the Palazzo Medici, Leonardo and Verrocchio were joined by Cecilia, dressed for the occasion in a loose flowing brocade dress of gold with a silk sash of red wrapped around the middle. When Leonardo saw her, his thoughts were taken back to the first time they met in his studio: *She is a goddess of sublime proportions.*

Together they were greeted by their civic hosts, who were all splendidly arrayed in costume. Their host for the evening was Senior Pazzi, who sought once again to ingratiate his family into the political elite of Florence now the Medici's were in exile.

'Welcome, Leonardo. May the night be long and may your wishes come true,' he said, with a jovial smile as he shook Leonardo's hand.

'Leonardo, you are more beautiful than any Greek or Roman god,' remarked his daughter Viola.

'Besides you, my fair lady, I am but a pale imitation of beauty,' Leonardo replied to giggles from his host's daughter and a forced smile from Cecilia.

Ignoring Leonardo's escort, the Lady Viola (whose opinion of Cecilia was that she should have stayed in Milan and used her talents to entertain the French,) took Leonardo by the arm and escorted him inside the Palazzo. Wearing the black and white outfit of a harlequin, she was a slim, buxom, hazel-eyed young woman who still retained the squeaky high-pitched tone of a five-year-old. Viola had received an enlightened education and was considered a most elegant lady. Nevertheless, she was used to getting her own way and tonight she was determined to have Leonardo's full attention.

'Age has not added years to you, Leonardo. To what do you attribute your good fortune?' asked Viola coyly. Although married, she was not going to pass up the opportunity to flirt with the man she had been infatuated with since childhood.

'Abstinence from excess,' replied Leonardo, 'and taking regular walks to admire the beauty of nature.'

'Well, tonight it is your sole duty to admire me,' his young escort said.

The Lady Viola led them into a spacious ballroom draped in gold and silver banners. In the middle was a silver fountain filled with red wine from which servants filled goblets, while at the far end a small orchestra played. The dignitaries of Florence, dressed in outlandish costumes, lined up to greet Leonardo and Viola.

Verrocchio shook his head and walked off passing two men wearing the purple robes of the Roman Praetorian Guard. Preoccupied with eyeing Leonardo, the taller of the two bumped into Verrocchio. 'Pardonnez-moi,' he said, giving his nationality away to Verrocchio. The smaller guard hissed. 'In Italian, you imbecile.' The pair loitered on the periphery of those mingling around Leonardo and Viola, never close enough to engage either of them in conversation, but close enough to cringe at the bootlicking they overheard.

'It must feel divine to be the possessor of such extraordinary talent,' said one.

'To be a genius, no less,' offered another.

'Your presence in Florence is like the return of the sun after a long winter,' remarked Viola.

'Any time you need your bed warming at night, I am at your service,' said a young maiden who unveiled the top of her costume to reveal a breast.

'And I, too, maestro,' said a handsome man wearing a shoulder-length wig, 'would offer my attention if you so desired.'

'You flatter me too much,' Leonardo said with false modesty. 'But as many of you will no doubt of have heard, since my unfortunate incarceration in the dungeons of Florence, I have chosen the life of a celibate.' Viola cringed, even though her nether regions pulsated at the thought of Leonardo as a lover, she was at least wise enough to know such infatuations always ended in tears.

Confined to watching events from the side-lines for fear of arousing the jealousy of Viola was Cecilia, who bored took to admiring the ballroom. The room had gilded gold panels along all four walls that were intricately carved by the finest craftsmen. They were higher than any she has seen in Milan and were so polished their reflection could be seen on the marble floor merging with the feet of the dancers, and the light thrown down from half a dozen ornate chandeliers, each holding ten candle holders, which were likewise painted in gold leaf.

'It is the same with Michelangelo,' a despairing Verrocchio said, coming to stand beside her as he pointed to an adoring group busy plying Leonardo with praise. 'Both of them are in competition for the hearts of Florence. It is madness. We're meant to be artists, not demi-gods.'

'I sense you do not approve of such behaviour,' replied Cecilia.

'Leonardo ought to know better.'

'Do you think he will be the victor in this war for Florence's affection?'

'He is too easily distracted by matters other than art. Michelangelo not only burns with ambition but has the force of will to carry projects through to the end. He is the more prolific and Florentines like trophies they can put on display.'

At last the throng of people cavorting around Leonardo moved on. Sensing an opportunity, Cecilia made her way towards him, only to be accosted by a nobleman dressed as Zeus.

'A dance, lady Cecilia?' She curtseyed to her companion and waited for the dance to begin, a lively carola. 'It is easy to understand why Il Moro is besotted with you,' Zeus said. 'The only surprise is that he didn't cart you off to Austria under the nose of his wife.' Cecilia smiled. 'Still, it would be a shame to leave you wanting for affection,' he said pulling Cecilia close. He dropped his right hand over her shoulder and fondled her breast, while his other hand gave her bottom a squeeze.

'I believe you asked for a dance,' an annoyed Cecilia said. Curtseying she walked briskly away to where Leonardo was standing by the food.

'Try these,' he said, popping into Cecilia's mouth a pastry topped with sugared almonds. While the guests helped themselves to food, entertainment was provided by a troupe of Commedia dell'Arte actors who performed in front of a colourful backdrop. Leonardo nudged Cecilia and they slipped quietly away. Together they walked along an ornate corridor and after descending half a dozen carpeted steps, Cecilia pulled Leonardo into an alcove with a stain glass window of the Medici coat of arms.

'Il Moro is raising an army of German and Swiss mercenaries,' he said hurriedly, eager to convey information she had only heard earlier in the day.

'I should have painted you in moonlight,' Leonardo replied, observing the gleam of the silver ornament in her hair. Further down the corridor, the two French mercenaries clung to the walls as they made their way towards the moonlit couple.

'Do you think he will succeed?' Cecilia earnestly implored.

'Just look at your face,' Leonardo replied, gently lifting a hand towards it.

'Leonardo!'

'Huh?'

'Have you listened to a word I've…' Before Cecilia could finish her sentence, Leonardo wrapped her up in his arms. She closed her eyes and raised her lips. Just as their lips touched, from behind came a deliberate cough. Leonardo quickly let go of Cecilia, who stumbled off balance.

'I am dismayed,' replied his former maestro. The two mercenaries halted their advance and once again blended into the background.

'Dismayed?' questioned a surprised Leonardo.

'Why do you allow them to treat you with such pawing adulation?' Verrocchio asked,

pointing in the direction of the ballroom and its assembled guests.

'I cannot be held accountable for the actions of others,' Leonardo replied.

'Do you think yourself worthy of such praise?' Verrocchio planted his feet firmly in front of Leonardo while he waited for an answer.

Leonardo stared guiltily at a small gathering of curious partygoers, who inched their way towards them.

'Verrocchio, please. This discussion is for another day, surely,' Cecilia said, placing a consoling arm on the old man's shoulder. 'Come, enjoy the party.' She took Verrocchio's arm in hers to lead him away, but he turned again to Leonardo, jabbing his finger in his chest.

'I asked you a question. Do you think yourself worthy of such vanity?'

'All artists crave adulation and applause, don't we?' replied Leonardo.

'Have you no manners, Verrocchio?' From behind him, Viola, accompanied by two guards, arrived.

'My lady please, I meant no offence,' Verrocchio said, alarmed.

'You have had too much wine,' replied Viola. 'Make sure he arrives home safely,' she said, addressing the two guards who led Verrocchio away.

'Thank you, my lady,' said Leonardo, bowing to Viola. Cecilia, too, curtseyed, grateful for her intervention. 'The lady Cecilia and I were just discussing the news from Milan.'

'You are in Florence now. There will be plenty of opportunity to gossip about Milan's affairs later. If I may?' Cecilia stepped aside to allow Viola to place her arm in Leonardo's and, without casting Cecilia a sideways glance, escort him away.

The two French mercenaries followed Leonardo and Viola at a discreet distance and watched them enter a room where people were busy playing blind man's bluff.

'It is futile,' said the taller of the two mercenaries to his companion.

'We'll wait a little longer,' replied the shorter mercenary.

'I say we go now.'

'We go when I say so and not before,' the smaller Frenchmen repeated.

In the ballroom, Lady Viola oversaw the evening's entertainment. She handed Leonardo a blindfold just as Cecilia snuck into the room. The partygoers poked and prodded Leonardo, who spun around wildly thrashing his arms about. In an attempt to capture someone, he grabbed hold of Cecilia. Thinking quickly, she swapped her mask with a lady standing nearby. A hush descended upon the room. Tentatively, Leonardo reached out a hand to touch the face and mask of the lady who had accompanied him from Milan.

'It's a woman,' he exclaimed. He ran a hand through her hair, down her neck and above her shoulders. 'Hurry! Hurry!' the crowd urged.

'I don't know,' replied Leonardo, removing his blindfold. Then realising he'd been outsmarted by Cecilia, a smile appeared on his face.

'Forfeit! Forfeit!' yelled the crowd. 'Kiss her!' shouted a voice.

Before Leonardo could react, hands thrust him into Cecilia's waiting arms. After what seemed like an eternity, they kissed. Cecilia's heart exploded as Leonardo pressed his lips firmly against hers. She wanted to scream the joy she felt to the whole world but fearful this may be the only time their lips embrace, she clung to him. Some of those looking on whooped and yelled their encouragement. When at last their lips parted, Cecilia rushed immediately out of the room.

Cecilia ran down a gilded gold corridor where once had hung the proud portraits of the Medici ancestry, but these had all been taken down by the Republic, all that remained where their discoloured outlines on the walls. When she reached the end of the corridor she opened a glass-panelled double-door and found herself in the garden of the Palazzo Medici. Leonardo entered the garden just in time to see Cecilia duck inside the maze. She wove her way through the hedged corridors until she arrived at a small wooden pavilion surrounded by a modest garden of exotic flowers.

Inside the pavilion, Cecilia collapsed on to a chaise longue and holding her head in her hands sobbed uncontrollably. 'My dearest goddess Cecilia,' Leonardo said, bending down to wrap his arms around her. 'Cecilia I...' Before he could continue, she put a finger to his lips.

'Answer me Leonardo, just this once, do you love me?' She buried her head in his shoulder. He placed his arms around her, laid her down and kissed her. Eagerly, Cecilia responded wrapping a leg around his to push him tight against her gently gyrating body. He eagerly tugged on the material of her dress until it parted to reveal her soft breasts. He had forgotten how delicate and warm the breasts of a maiden were, and his fingers delighted in their touch before his tongue reached down to caress her strawberry-coloured nipples. From a place deep within, all of Cecilia's longing for Leonardo burst to the surface. She moaned ecstatically as his gentle, yet firm touch lit a fuse through her orgasmic body.

'Make love to me,' she whispered in his ear, responding to his fingers slowly reaching up between her thighs. Leonardo quivered as he anticipated the joy he would feel the moment their two bodies became one.

Glinting in the moonlight, Cecilia saw out of the corner of her eye, the flash of a silver blade. She screamed but it was too late to alert Leonardo. A hand grabbed him by the scruff of his collar and yanked him to his feet.

'Who are you? What do you want?' demanded Leonardo, hastily attempting to assert his dignity and dress. The tip of a sword wielded by the smaller of the French mercenaries waved dangerously close to his ashen face. Taking hold of a half-naked Cecilia, busy fumbling with her dress, the taller mercenary shook her.

'You're the Duke's slut, aren't you?' he said in French.

'We'll have fun with you later.' With a knife poised in one hand across her throat, he reached down with his spare hand to grope her breasts.

'Filthy pig!' cursed a defiant Cecilia in French.

'Leave her!' his companion ordered. 'It's him we've come for.'

'Another time, *mon cher*,' said the taller of the mercenaries to Cecilia, tossing her to the ground.

'You'll hang for this!' Cecilia shouted in French, just before she was punched in the face.

'Who are you? What do you want with me?' asked Leonardo. The smaller mercenary bound Leonardo's hands tight behind his back and then, at the point of his sword, escorted him back through the maze. At the edge of the maze, he whistled a command. A pock-faced mercenary appeared from the far end of the garden with four horses.

'I demand you let me go,' insisted Leonardo.

'The King of France has need of you,' replied the smaller mercenary in Italian. 'Now get on your horse.'

The smaller mercenary used his surprising strength to lift Leonardo on to his horse, a black mare with a Bordeaux crest embossed on its saddle. As they fastened Leonardo to his horse, Cecilia emerged stumbling from the maze. One hand frantically waving an embroidered handkerchief, while the other wiped blood from a split lip.

'Run, Cecilia!' implored Leonardo. Cecilia made a dash for the double doors.

'Help!' she shouted. Brandishing his sword, the taller mercenary spun his horse around and set out after her.

'We haven't time. Leave her!' ordered his smaller companion.

'Help! Help!' screamed Cecilia, stumbling in her panic.

'Take the reins!' the smaller mercenary shouted to Leonardo. He then gave Leonardo's horse a smack on the flank. The horse bolted at a lightning pace, quickly followed by the three mercenaries.

From the far end of the garden, soldiers with drawn swords and spears appeared. Their captain, a burly middle-aged man with a resplendent beard, ordered his men into two lines, one behind the other, those with the spears in front, those with swords behind.

'Steady,' he ordered. 'Pick your target.' The pock-faced mercenary let go of the reins to Leonardo's horse and drew his sword. The tallest of the trio also drew his sword and in unison, they shouted, 'Vive la France!' before charging at the waiting soldiers. Leonardo swung his body to one side to divert his horse from the waiting spears. The short mercenary drew his sword and aimed for the very end of the line of soldiers, where a youth nervously held a shaking spear. 'For France, the King and glory!' he shouted, and threw his sword at the nervous youth, killing him. Then, urging his horse on, he jumped through the gap left by the fallen soldier. His two companions were not so successful. The taller mercenary was killed outright, a spear piercing his right side and another through the throat. The pock-faced mercenary was disabled by a spear in his left thigh. Unable to make his escape, his head was lopped off his shoulders by the captain's sword.

Leonardo fell backwards off his horse, and with his feet caught in the stirrups, was dragged along the ground as his horse bolted. The terrified horse reared dangerously until the captain took hold of the reins and brought it under control.

'You're a lucky man, maestro,' the captain said, freeing his feet from the stirrups and cutting him loose from his bonds.

'Thank you, captain,' Leonardo said. 'I owe you my life.'

CHAPTER FORTY

THE FOLLOWING MORNING LEONARDO, WHO WAS LATE FOR breakfast, entered rubbing a bruise on his left arm. An incensed Verrocchio approached him.

'You could have got yourself killed last night, and what for? To please your vanity and indulge your… appetites!'

'My appetites were not indulged,' Leonardo replied. 'Now excuse me.' Picking up a roll of bread Leonardo left.

'And what have you to say to the monks of San Donato a Scopeto?' Verrocchio yelled to his departing friend.

Showing no willingness to fulfil his obligations, the monks of San Donato a Scopeto finally wearied of his endless procrastination and once again Senior Prodi was again dispatched to Verrocchio's workshop.

Walking down the Via de Agnolo, Leonardo ducked into a doorway and watched as Senior Prodi exited Verrocchio's workshop. In an attempt to appease the disgruntled monks, Leonardo had previously visited the monastery of San Donato a Scopeto.

'Good brethren, the cartoon I have drawn is 'the' perfect piece of craftsmanship. To paint over it would lessen its beauty.' Like godly men they listened to the maestro explain his artistic inclinations, but they were adamant the commission was unfulfilled and, while they admired the energy and passion of his cartoon, they wanted a finished work.

Leonardo paused in the doorway until Senior Prodi was out of sight before he resumed his walk to Verrocchio's studio.

'Ah, Leonardo. There has been a visitor for you,' Verrocchio said. 'Senior Prodi. He left this for you.' Verrocchio handed Leonardo a document which he opened.

'Is it the final demand from the monks of San Donato?' Verrocchio asked.

'They've obtained a civic hearing. I have either to write confirming I will complete the *Adoration of the Magi* within a year or return the payment I received.'

'Those are fair terms,' Verrocchio said. 'It is not just the monks though. The civic c council is also keen to see you finish the commission.'

'It would appear I am very much in demand,' replied Leonardo teasingly.

'What has got into you? You are dismissive of the monks of San Donato. You show scant regard for the wishes of the civic authorities. Your behaviour at the summer banquet was not worthy of your good name. If Il Moro were to discover news of your dalliance with his mist…'

'… Cecilia is not my lover, we… were… we were…'

'… What are you trying to tell me?' asked Verrocchio.

'I have committed no wrong.'

'Try explaining that to Il Moro,' a curt Verrocchio replied.

Fearful of any of further attempts upon his life from French mercenaries, Leonardo barricaded both his bedroom door and window. As he laid on his bed his mood once more slumped into despondency. His agitated mind raced with recent events and unable to sleep he routinely got out of his bed to pace his room: *I ought to apologise to Verrocchio for the discourtesy I have shown against my old friend. Cecilia too, what must be going through her mind? The noble life of celibacy has been my chosen path. Therefore, I must put to death all carnal urges I hold towards the girl.* He concluded addressing each would have to wait. His mind was further troubled by what demands the court authorities would place upon him if they found in favour of the monks of San Donato, which he suspected they would. The attack of the French mercenaries, this too weighed heavily upon him: *What if they should seek to snatch me a second time?* His mind set, when morning finally arrived, he rose purposefully from his bed.

'Francesco,' Leonardo said, 'pack up the bags we're leaving for Rome.' The diligent Francesco had profited a great deal working alongside Verrocchio's apprentices. It was an altogether more efficient arrangement than the haphazard approach Leonardo took to the acquiring and fulfilling of commissions. Verrocchio's studio had been an environment in which Francesco, who thrived on orderliness, had enjoyed immensely. Being Leonardo's senior apprentice had given him a degree of standing amongst the other boys, who were keen to hear what other great works the maestro was engaged in. All were fascinated to learn of the various inventions they had had to leave behind in Milan.

'What are you telling me?' snapped Salai. 'We are leaving boring boring Florence. But going to bastard sodomise me up the arse Rome! Jupiter's cock, will I ever get home to Milan and stroll along the streets with my friends again?'

'The French are in Milan and they have already made one attempt upon my life,' Leonardo explained to his frustrated son.

'What of Cecilia?' a concerned Francesco asked.

'I will make arrangements with Captain Chianti for her to be safely taken to Mantua.'

'You're not going to see her?' Salai asked.

'No,' replied Leonardo. An astonished look passed between Francesco and Salai.

'Il Moro will have him chopped into little pieces if any harm befalls her,' whispered Salai to Francesco.

In late September, only a few days after his announcement, Leonardo, Francesco and Salai bade farewell to Verrocchio, (with whom Leonardo had made his peace) and took the old Roman road to Rome. The skies were clear, but a mild breeze heralded the arrival of autumn. The ever-present purple mist that covered the undulating hills of Tuscany, hung in the distance as they travelled further away from the land of Leonardo's birth. The path that carried them echoed of history, they could barely travel a mile without stumbling upon some Roman ruin built of travertine stone, whether a temple to some long-forgotten god or the remains of some nobleman's mansion, the remnants of a once glorious past festooned the countryside. Whereas the north of Italy bordering the wild Alps was a haven for bravados, Tuscany was pleasant like its people, and Leonardo journeyed without the need of an armed escort.

It only took a long day of travelling and a cold night beneath a starry sky for Salai to vent his frustrations.

'You drag me from one place to another to freeze my balls off, and what for?'

'Just a few more days and you will be sleeping in a warm bed,' assured Leonardo. But Salai was unrelenting.

'I want to go back to Milan,' he said.

'Roll up your mat and eat breakfast,' Leonardo replied.

After a week's travel, Rome came into view. The three dismounted and stood upon a grassy hillock and gazed into the distance at the sublime skyline, one that has memorised a millennia of people

'Truly she is home to the gods,' said Francesco.

'In Rome, all men can be gods,' replied Leonardo.

'Well, maybe there's hope for me,' said Salai, laughing.

'Here's the money, Francesco, ride ahead and see if the rooms I have rented have been prepared.' Leonardo handed a small pouch to Francesco, who took it, remounted his horse and galloped on his way.

'Why does he get to go with the money and not me?' an indignant Salai asked.

'Do you seriously think I would entrust you with money?' Leonardo replied.

Dusk was settling over the eternal city when Leonardo and his adopted son found their horses treading upon cobbled streets. The lengthening shadows threw their arms around the many sublime Roman ruins. Leonardo took comfort in the geometry of the buildings and found great pleasure in the order and simplicity of the ancient architecture: *Surely, I will prosper here. If ever a city was made for a man of my talents, this must be it.*

As they made their way down a narrow street, they passed a dreary looking hospice with dirty boarded up windows and a badly written sign that read: *Hospice for poor souls needing the blessed guidance of the merciful Saint Jerome.* A dead man was being wheeled out on a cart by an elderly caretaker.

'My good man,' Leonardo said, addressing the caretaker. 'How long has this chap been dead?' Leonardo picked up the dead man's arm, which was dangling over the side of the cart and examined the fingers. Rigor mortis had not yet set in.

'No more than an hour, sir,' replied the caretaker. 'I'm just on my way to take him to the paupers graveyard.' He doffed his grubby hat and Leonardo stepped aside to let the old man pass.

'You make my flesh crawl' said Salai, to Leonardo.

'Death, my young friend is the only certainty in life. And a man should have no fear of it if he has led a virtuous life.'

'Well then I'm buggered, aren't I?' replied Salai with a snigger.

When they reached their lodgings, Francesco had brushed the place clean, laid out food for everyone and prepared the sleeping quarters. There were three rooms downstairs, a bedroom for Leonardo, and another to be shared by Francesco and Salai and a large living room with a hearth for cooking. Upstairs there was one long room to suffice as a studio. All the rooms were basic and the furniture worn with age.

'It's a pigsty,' complained Salai. 'You must be crazy if you think I'm living in this dump.'

'Don't be so ungrateful,' said Francesco. 'What gives you the right to be so high and mighty? There was a time a few years ago when a night's sleep in a room like this would have seemed like a palace to you.'

'Boys,' said Leonardo. 'I know it's not particularly salubrious but…'

'What the hell does that mean?' interrupted Salai.

'Pleasant, of a high standard,' explained Francesco.

'You can say that again,' Salai said.

'I have to be careful with our finances until our situation improves, so for the time being it will have to suffice.'

Leonardo pulled up a chair and helped himself to the food Francesco had prepared and a glass of wine whilst Salai stood by, scowling.

'I'm going out,' he said and headed for the door. Leonardo jumped to his feet.

'You'll do no such thing! Sit down and eat.' But it was too late. Salai had already opened the door and was running down the street.

When he returned several hours later, sporting a black eye, Francesco had already retired to bed. Leonardo, however, was seated at a table. By the light of a candle he was drawing in intricate detail the hand and fingers of the dead man he had seen earlier that evening.

'Another fight?' asked Leonardo.

'Some boys poked fun at my accent.' Leonardo opened his arms, which for once Salai was glad to embrace. 'Can we go home?' the youth said, a tear trapped in his eye.

'We will,' said Leonardo, 'just as soon as the French have left.'

CHAPTER FORTY-ONE

IN A SPARSE CELL WITH HIS FEET CHAINED TO THE WALL, Alessandro was woken by the bell summoning the monks of the Holy Order of Saint Bernard of Montjoux to Lauds. His window gave him a spectacular view of the jagged ridges of the Alpine peaks, where even in summer the mountain tops remained snow-capped. However, his feet had never set foot upon them, for ever since the day of his arrival he had been confined within the monastery. Although it was a balmy morning in summer, he shuddered to think what would await him during hostile winter months when the pass into the mountains was inaccessible, and a fierce Alpine wind blew down the Grand Saint Bernard.

With a monk either side of him, Alessandro was escorted into the chapel where he was coerced by his 'guardians' to participate in all daily offices as though he were a novice preparing for Holy orders. At first, Alessandro had made such an unholy racket he had been muzzled, but this punishment was abandoned at the behest of Abbot Jerome. The Abbot's virtuous nature believed the longer Alessandro was treated like an irredeemable animal, such acts would only prolong any state of repentance.

As penitence for the crimes he had committed, Alessandro was flogged once a month and, under interrogation of the Abbot, asked to renounce his proclamation that he was Jesus. On days when the monastery had nuns visiting or female pilgrims passing through, Alessandro was confined to his cell. Upon his arrival, the Archbishop had given written instructions that exposure to women be strictly prohibited.

Life for Alessandro followed a strict regime of five services a day, followed by instruction from various monks in the Holy Scriptures. All sought to bring about a state of contrition in the errant man. When instruction and prayer failed, which it always did, Alessandro was made to perform hard labour, often at the inducement of a whip.

One morning after Lauds, he was taken by two burly monks to the office of the Abbot. Behind a plain desk piled high with books and manuscripts sat the Abbot, a small grey-haired man with a knowledgeable air. To the right of his desk, an elaborate stain-glass window depicted a lion beside a lamb with the Good Shepherd holding a gold staff in his hand. The Abbot pulled out a chair for Alessandro. The two monks used a length of rope to tie him to the chair. Once they were satisfied he was secure, the two monks left.

'My son, the Archbishop requests news of your progress. Has God healed you of your affliction?'

'But why would I need to be healed? I am who I am. Selah.'

'I see,' said the Abbot, who sat back and made a few notes on a manuscript. 'Our Lord proclaimed a message of peace, hope and salvation for all. What message do you preach?'

'That God will strike down mercilessly all who oppose his chosen vessel!' The Abbot opened the door and waved the two burly monks inside.

The monks untied Alessandro and sought to escort him away. However, he resisted and bit a monk, who screamed in pain and released his grip. Alessandro rushed at the Abbot and wrapped his fingers around his throat. In the struggle that followed, the desk and its contents were tipped over, pinning the distressed Abbot to the floor and destroying a two-hundred-year-old gold leaf copy of the *'Niunconsciouschean Ethics.'*

'I'll tear you apart,' cursed Alessandro.

'Help! Help! Come quickly!' the Abbot yelled.

It took three monks to finally drag a cursing Alessandro away, while a fourth monk lifted the desk from off the Abbot and helped the shaking man to his feet. After taking a moment to compose himself, he reached for his pen and began to write a letter. Distracted by the lashes of a whip, the Abbot put down his pen and rising to his feet, peered through his stain-glass window to the courtyard below where Alessandro, stripped to the waist and tied to a pole, was being flogged. Once twelve lashes had been administered, the Abbot returned to his desk.

A month later, the letter was delivered to the Archbishop of Milan. It read:

Your Grace, there has been no remission of his delusional condition and no repentance of sin. Indeed, I doubt if such a creature as he has become is even capable of true repentance. I regret if this news distresses you and, if your Grace considers I have failed in the execution of my duties, I humbly beg your forgiveness.

Your humble servant of our Lord,

Abbot Jerome

The Archbishop put down the letter and with a heavy heart said *'alea iacta est,'* the die is cast.

CHAPTER FORTY-TWO

Beside himself with rage, Michelangelo Buonarroti's arms gesticulated wildly while curses flew from his mouth as he steamed through the streets of Rome.

'Bastard by birth, bastard by nature!' 'Filthy pig-shitter!' 'Fat-kidneyed prick!'

Ever since he was a youth growing up in Florence, the name of Leonardo da Vinci was spoken in ways which indicated awe at the man's talent. But not by Michelangelo, he had a mind to prove that he alone was the greatest of Florence's artists.

'Why in the name of God has that son of a whore come to Rome? Jupiter's cock! I am the glory of Florence' were the words he had spoken to several artists when they informed him Leonardo da Vinci had arrived in Rome.

Deep inside the Vatican, Pope Alexander VI was being helped into an ornate gold chasuble by two priests. His Holiness was a ruddy-faced man with blemished skin and a considerable girth, which once encased in his chasuble, made him look even more imposing. In spite of the trappings of holy office, one would think twice before deciding who had been the most debauched ruler of the citizens of Rome. If the Emperor Nero was accused of playing the fiddle while Rome burned, then the reign of Rodrigo Borgia as Pope Alexander VI was synonymous with sexual indulgence, mistresses and orgies, often attended by his daughter, Lucrezia, and his son Cesare. To this was added the accusation of incest between Lucrezia and Cesare, to which the father openly colluded, along with his mistress, Vannozza dei Cattanei, whom he kept within the Vatican and who was the mother of four of his children.

Guarding the entrance to the Pope's palatial room with its gold panelled walls and portraits of former Popes were a pair of Swiss guards. Both wore full body armour and red feathers atop their silver helmets, while in their hands each held a gleaming metal pikestaff with a small Vatican insignia tied at the end.

'Out of my way!' demanded a red-faced Michelangelo. The Swiss guards resolutely held their ground. 'I said out of my way, goat shaggers!' Undeterred by the tantrums of petulant artists, the two guards forced Michelangelo back. 'I've heard that bastard Leonardo da Vinci is in town!' Michelangelo shouted.

'Indeed, I have heard the same thing,' replied the Pope, toying with him.

'Did you summon him?'

'What need have I for another son of Florence, when I have you?'

His Holiness signalled to the guards who allowed Michelangelo to enter. He walked briskly into the room, knelt and fleetingly kissed the Papal ring.

'What do you intend to do about him?' Michelangelo demanded.

'Do? Nothing,' said the Pope, winking at the priests in attendance.

'God's bones! Do you just expect me to sit back and watch

him gallivant around Rome like he owns the sodding place? Well, if you won't do anything…'

'You aren't listening,' interrupted the Pope. 'I will have Leonardo do nothing. What do you suppose he will do? Or to whom will he turn if I expressly forbid any commission be offered to him while in Rome?'

A smile crossed the face of Michelangelo. His Holiness continued.

'But a man of Leonardo's talents ought to be put to some use. I have heard he has designed instruments of warfare, which I have no doubt Cesare will be most interested in. And perhaps we can put him in the thick of some battle. Does this meet with your approval, my child?'

'How could I have doubted you, your Holiness? God be with you,' said Michelangelo, bending down to kiss the Papal ring. The Pope patted the head of his temperamental artist.

'Now go and give thanks to God for he has chosen to favour you.'

Considerably calmer, Michelangelo walked backwards out of the presence of His Holiness.

Several days later, Leonardo was summoned to the Vatican for an audience with the most devious offspring of Rodrigo Borgia's loins, his son Cesare. If his father's weakness was women, his son's was murder. He had dispatched enemies, friends and even members of his own family by sword, poison, torture, starvation and whatever foul means satisfied his homicidal nature.

Cesare Borgia was curious about Leonardo's weapons of warfare and had sent word to him to arrive with the evidence. Cesare was a muscular man, with shoulder length black hair and soulless eyes. His nose was crooked, and his sullen mouth had never been known to smile. He wore black gloves from morning until night and like the guardian of the underworld, preferred to dress in black. Even his father, the Pope, was fearful of his temper.

Leonardo chose to dress sombrely for their meeting and wore a dark blue tunic with black tights and boots. It was a wise choice for Cesare detested the more outlandish clothes commonly worn by artists.

'It has come to my attention that you have devised instruments of warfare,' Cesare Borgia said in a cold voice.

'It is true, Sire. I have indeed designed such various instruments.'

'Show me your plans.' Leonardo rolled out several sheets with his designs for a mortar blaster, an armoured vehicle and a giant crossbow, all of which impressed.

'Purchase what you need for these mortars of yours and I will cover the expense,' Cesare said, handing Leonardo a pouch stuffed with coins. Then, picking up Leonardo's designs, he scrutinized them one more time. 'Tell no-one your business, or the mortars you devise. If your machines prove successful, you will be handsomely rewarded. If you cross me, I will cut out your heart and feed it to my dogs.' He removed a black glove from his left hand then using his right-hand slapped Leonardo hard across the cheek with the back of his glove. 'That is to remind you I am not a man to be disloyal to.'

His mind a state of heightened anxiety, Leonardo walked aimlessly pondering the nature of his meeting with Cesare Borgia. Passing the coliseum, he made his way towards the Appian Way and walked out of Rome. Although he had boasted about his weapons of warfare, he had never envisaged he would be forced to oversee their construction for use in battle, especially for a man such as Cesare Borgia. Even the promise of wealth did little to ease his conscience.

'It would have been better for me to stay and face my creditors in Florence,' complained Leonardo to Francesco when he eventually returned home later the same day. At least they would never have threatened to feed my beating heart to their dogs.'

'What will you do, maestro?' asked a worried Francesco.

'I have no choice,' said Leonardo. I must comply.'

With the help of Francesco and Salai, who found the idea of making instruments of warfare more exciting than painting, Leonardo set about constructing three mortar blasters for his new paymaster.

Leonardo's mortar blasters were designed to be lighter, smaller and more versatile than a conventional cannon. They were shaped like a large barrel which was cast in solid iron and housed on two wheels. The barrel could be moved up and down and depended on the trajectory of the missile in relation to its target. Into the barrel could be placed a cannon ball, which Leonardo predicated would travel at a greater velocity than a conventional cannon and thus inflict greater damage on the enemy's defences. Into the barrel could also be placed iron fillings which, when fired at an approaching army, would pierce a soldier's body armour as easily as a hot knife through butter.

It did not take Cesare Borgia long to pick a fight and to enlist Leonardo in a military campaign. The object of Cesare's wrath was Count Orsini, who had spurned the advances of His Holiness to have the principality of Orsini brought under Papal jurisdiction. Cesare obtained 'confessions' from men allied to the Orsinis, who admitted to being party to a plot orchestrated by Count Orsini to poison the Pope. His Holiness duly declared Count Orsini a traitor and dispatched his warmongering son to bring the obdurate Count and the Orsini clan to heel.

A persistent Salai begged Leonardo to take him on the campaign.

'Many a man my age has gone to war,' argued Salai.

'Many a boy your age has died in war too,' replied Leonardo.

'Better to die in glory than grow into a toothless old man,' Salai retorted.

'There is no glory in having your body blown to pieces.

You will remain in Rome under the guardianship of Francesco, who will continue to tutor you in my absence.'

'Bugger the pair of you,' said Salai, who ran out into the street.

'Don't worry about him' said Francesco. 'He'll come back when he's tired and hungry, or after he's suffered another beating.'

'Francesco?'

'Yes?'

'If something was to befall me, can I count on you to see my affairs would be conducted according to my will?'

'The good Lord will protect you,' Francesco said, embracing the maestro.

Less than a week later, Leonardo found himself camped a few miles south of the Orsini castle, which was perched atop a hill. Surrounding the hill was a wood where the army of Cesare Borgia camped. The captains of Cesare Borgi were a joyless bunch of mercenaries. Once they learnt the mechanics of Leonardo's mortars, Leonardo was ostracized. The common soldiers, who eyed Leonardo with suspicion, followed their paymaster's example and likewise ignored him.

Along with everyone else, Leonardo queued for his evening rations of bread, cured sausage, which he gave to the man behind, and a mug of wine. To his right, a group of men were playing cards, the prize being a pair of expensive boots that looked to have been worn by some nobleman. Further to his right a swordsmith was busy sharpening the swords of a steady stream of men, while beyond them lay a makeshift enclosure where servant boys were grooming the cavalry's horses. To his left a fire burned, around which men were huddled in small groups eating their rations and chatting or making repairs to their boots.

Beyond the fire lay the tent of Cesare Borgia and his captains, who were dining on roasted wild boar and drinking superior wine from silver goblets. They studied maps, discussed tactics and assigned duties to each captain. Well away from prying eyes, he sat under the shade of a small crop of Italian Cyprus trees and eat his meagre rations. Happy to keep to himself, Leonardo took out a small knife and whittled on a piece of sycamore, where content to worry the night away in silence, he contemplated whether he would live to see the following day and beseeched the Almighty: *Good Lord, I petition you. Have I been the man I ought to have been? Had I chosen another man as Jesus, would the outcome have been any different? I should have shown more exertion and finished The Last Supper. Then at least there would be one remembrance of me on this joyless earth.* Then getting to his knees he genuflected and whispered a prayer: *God preserve my life so I may do good. Amen.*

Morning came with a flurry of activity. Every man checked his weapons, put on his armour, or helped another comrade into his, whilst swords were thrust first in one direction and then another in mock execution of an enemy soldier. Some cursed while others prayed to whichever saint belonged to their village. Others partook of whatever superstitious ritual had thus far seen them survive previous battles. Men took an extraordinary amount of time over their boots, they stamped up and down, prodded their toes and only moved to join their regiment once they were satisfied their footwear would not betray them at some crucial moment.

Some boasted noisily of what feats they would accomplish on the battlefield, others looked solemn and spoke little. When each man had taken up his position, Cesare Borgia rode up and down on a black stallion, inspecting his soldiers in silence. He gave no speech to rally his men, it was left to each captain to relay the task that had been assigned to them. Once Cesare Borgia's officers had taken up their positions, silence descended.

On Cesare's orders, the mortars were fired at the advancing Orsini infantry. Mercilessly the iron filings ripped through the soldiers' armour. Dozens of men fell instantaneously, their bodies riddled with burning shrapnel. Blood turned the ground crimson.

The noise of battle was so horrific Leonardo felt as if a hole had been blown in his head. He clasped his hands tight to his ears in a vain attempt to drown out the hellish racket. All around him, trees were uprooted and torn into pieces. Lumps of earth caked him from head to toe. Standing nearby, a servant boy no older than Salai was blown up, bits of flesh from the poor boy's body clung to Leonardo's clothes. He could barely think above the din. Men ran screaming in every direction.

A second volley was fired from the mortars. More men fell in a shrieking mass of bones and flesh. The Orsini soldiers, sensing death and defeat were imminent, threw down their weapons and retreated, only to be chased by Cesare Borgia's cavalry who cut them down mercilessly.

A guilt-ridden Leonardo took himself off to stand by the makeshift stable and watched helpless as the shredded bodies of men on the field of battle slipped in blood-curdling throes of suffering from this life and into the next. Leonardo wept. He had witnessed men die before but they had been the peaceful surrender of men on their beds. Now, however, he watched dumbstruck as men littered the field in front of him, screaming and cursing their last breath, knowing it was he who had precipitated their demise.

A passing captain ordered him to help carry the wounded to the hospital tent where two surgeons were performing amputations. One was cutting through a soldier's leg with a sharp narrow-toothed hacksaw. 'Hold him down,' demanded one of the surgeons, a man in his sixties. Leonardo took hold of the man's leg and held it in place while the surgeon sawed through the man's left tibia and fibula. The sound was excruciating yet Leonardo was too fascinated to be squeamish. Once the soldier's leg had been cut off, a hot iron was applied to the open wound to cauterize the arteries. The smell of burning flesh shot up Leonardo's nostrils, it was the only time he baulked. Another man was brought in needing the same treatment. For the next two days, Leonardo held men down while a limb was amputated, or a wound tended to. He noted how the surgeon used a different saw, scalpel or knife for the different injuries being treated, and observed how and where the incisions were made. After the wounded had been attended to, his preoccupation with human anatomy propelled him to draw several sketches of men who lay dead upon or injured on the blood-soaked hospital floor.

Once the smoke had cleared and the terms of the Orsini surrender had been agreed, an ebullient Cesare Borgia, flushed with the glory of victory, sent for Leonardo.

'Maestro, I am a fair man.' Cesare gestured to a table upon which lay a small chest of coins. 'Take these in recognition of your service to His Holiness. If I have need of you again, you will be contacted. You may go.' Leonardo couldn't bring himself to say thank you, instead he nodded meekly to his paymaster, picked up the chest and left. He was richer than he had ever been before, but his heart took no joy in his newly acquired wealth.

Before he left camp, Leonardo made his way to the hospital tent and sought out the surgeon whom he had assisted.

'Excuse me, sir. The various instruments and knives that you employ, where can I purchase the same?

'They are each individually made by the finest of craftsman. Why do you ask, Leonardo? Surely you are not thinking of taking up another profession?' asked the surgeon.

'In my search for understanding of the human body, I have learned much from you. At some point in the future, I may wish to perform some simple surgery on cadavers.' Leonardo paused before continuing. 'That is, if I am ever permitted.'

'I would not have thought a mild inconvenience such as

permission from the Church would obstruct you,' said the surgeon. 'Here, take these, I have others. It will raise fewer questions if I have need of new instruments than if a man of your reputation was to get a set made for him.'

The surgeon picked up a rolled leather case and handed it over. For his kindness, Leonardo gave the surgeon a sum of money that was more than adequate to purchase their replacements.

In a state of deep depression, Leonardo dragged his gloom-filled guilt-ridden body back to Rome. Being a perceptive soul, Francesco could sense the maestro was troubled by melancholy and in no mood to talk. Salai, however, wanted to know every gory detail and pestered his adopted father relentlessly. Leonardo told the youth some of what he had seen but kept the most gruesome realities to himself.

'How many men were killed by your mortars and did you see them die?'

'Leave him be, Salai,' pleaded Francesco, who knew from tales of his father, men returning from battle are often accompanied by a brooding spirit.

'Was it fifty, a hundred or more than a hundred? Two hundred?'

'Salai, enough,' Francesco said.

'To die in battle is not glorious,' Leonardo said.

'I cannot think of anything more exciting than to be plunged into battle.'

'I'm going to bed.' Leonardo took his tired limbs off to his room and left Salai and Francesco to continue their squabbling.

Alone in his room, he turned over a new page in his journal and wrote: *Our life is made by the death of others, while I thought that I was learning how to live, I have been learning how to die.*

CHAPTER FORTY-THREE

ROME WAS RIFE WITH RUMOURS AND SCANDAL, CENTRAL TO them all were the Borgias. The husband of Lucrezia Borgia, Alfonso of Aragon, who was the illegitimate son of the King of Naples was murdered. One day, while walking up the steps of St Peter's Basilica, Alfonso was attacked by unidentified assailants. He survived the attack and was cared for by the Pope's physicians. However, while recovering from his ordeal he was strangled in his bed. Many, including his grieving widow Lucrezia, believed Cesare guilty of his murder.

As reward for his military assistance to Cesare Borgia, Leonardo had hoped His Holiness may have shown him favour and commissioned a work from him. But, alas, there had been not a single approach for a commission since arriving in Rome.

As purchaser for Leonardo's household, Francesco began talking to a group of apprentice artists at the market beside the coliseum.

'Your maestro is wasting his time in Rome,' said a slender youth of fifteen who had been assigned the task of mixing paints for Michelangelo.

'Why is that?' asked Francesco.

'The Pope has given Michelangelo his word that he will not commission a work by Leonardo. If the Pope forbids Leonardo a commission, then everyone else in Rome will do likewise. You should leave.' Upon arriving home, Francesco relayed his gossip.

'Ugly deformed cretin,' snarled Leonardo. 'So, I have been ostracized by the Pope in order to appease that temperamental halfwit.' Leonardo paced the room and was glad for once that Salai had gone for a wander.

'What am I supposed to do with myself, Francesco? Build more infernal weapons for that despot, Cesare Borgia?'

'He did pay handsomely,' said the pragmatic Francesco.

'Better to have one's integrity and be miserable than to prosper at the price of your dignity,' replied Leonardo.

'Perhaps we ought to pray more fervently that God will grant a change in fortune.'

'I'm going for a walk to hopefully clear my head.' Leonardo picked up a notepad and some pens and hurried out into the street.

Walking along the Appian Way, cedars, poplars, fig trees, orange groves and vineyards lined the old Roman road. After he had walked several miles, Leonardo picked a couple of oranges from a tree on the edge of a grove. He peeled a segment and bit into it, savouring the sweet juice. Passing by a cream lily with velvet leaves, he sat down and drew the flower in intricate detail from a variety of angles. After he had examined his specimen, he pressed the petals in between his notepad and ate the second of his oranges.

By the time he decided to head back into the city, the light was fading fast. In the distance, a reminder of its once mighty dominion, the Coliseum dwarfed the twilight skyline. Lost in thought Leonardo took a wrong turn and found himself in the narrow-cobbled street outside the Hospice of Saint Jerome. He opened the door and bumped into the old caretaker.

'Hello, do you remember me? We spoke last September,' Leonardo said.

Looking him up and down the elderly caretaker had his misgivings.

'If you have business here, it's Father Alfonso you'd best speak to. But he, like the rest of the good brothers won't be here 'til sunrise.'

'If you are a man of discretion, then my business is with you and I will pay you handsomely for… your silence.'

'I'm all ears,' said the caretaker. 'Step this way.' He led Leonardo into a small room lit by a single candle on a rickety old table. The room had one window that offered a view of a long room. Inside the room were two rows of ten beds. On each bed was a sick man that the monks of Saint Jerome tended to.

Leonardo took out a pouch of gold ducats that made a thud when they hit the table. He opened it and tossed the caretaker a handful of coins.

'For you,' Leonardo said. 'And there's more if you can be trusted.' Grinning, the caretaker picked up the coins with his knurled fingers.

'You don't want me to murder anyone, do you?' the caretaker said, running a suspicious eye over Leonardo. 'Only I'm a little old for such shenanigans.'

'No, certainly not,' replied Leonardo with a smirk.

'Then what do you want for such a sum of money?'

'I want to be informed whenever one of your patients dies. I have need of their bodies.'

'Why, whatever for?' he said alarmed. Leonardo tipped out a couple more coins on to the table.

'That is my business. Do we have an agreement?' The elderly caretaker licked his lips.

'We do,' he said, holding out his hand.

'Don't breathe a word of this to anyone. Whenever I have need of a body, I will pay you two ducats.'

'But you placed eight on the table.'

'That was to buy your silence. Now, how close to the next life are any of the men in the room yonder?'

'Come and see for yourself.'

The caretaker led Leonardo into the room where the sick and the dying coughed and groaned on their grubby mattresses. On the third bed from the caretaker's room laid a man who shivered and sweated. Leonardo bent down to speak to him.

'What is your name?'

'Water,' the man gasped, 'water!'

'Fetch this man some water,' Leonardo demanded of the caretaker, who returned carrying a large jug. Leonardo poured a mug of water and handed it to the thirsty man. He drank it desperately, his shaking hands spilling as much down his ragged shirt as entered his mouth. 'More,' he begged, taking hold of Leonardo by the arm arm.

'Pour him another drink,' Leonardo said to the caretaker who did as he was instructed.

Next to the thirsty man's bed was a man who shook as he gripped his stomach. He was in violent pain. Leonardo knelt down and cradled him in his arms. He noted the whites of the man's eyes were tinged yellow.

'What is your name?' Leonardo asked. The man opened his mouth as if to speak, but a fit of agonies caused him to lurch backwards and forwards in Leonardo's arms and finally surrender his spirit.

'You have your man,' said the caretaker.

'Be at peace,' Leonardo whispered to the dead man in his arms. He then turned to the caretaker, 'Do you have a cart?' Leonardo asked.

'I do. Follow me.' After a short while, the dead man was loaded into a cart and covered with a blanket.

'I will have the cart returned in the morning.'

Under cover of darkness, Leonardo made his way through

Rome's streets as furtively as possible for a man in possession of a corpse. It was not an easy task for the wooden wheels had a tendency to get caught between ruts in the uneven road. On more than one occasion he was close to tipping the corpse into the street and several times he had to stop for breath.

Upon arriving at his accommodation, he was greeted with gasps of horror from Francesco.

'You will have me excommunicated for sure!' he exclaimed.

'Don't panic, Francesco. I have enough money to buy the old caretaker's silence and, as long as you and Salai keep quiet, there's nothing to worry about.'

'My silence you can count on, but Salai?'

'I'll see to him.' With great reluctance, Francesco helped carry the dead man upstairs.

They laid the corpse on the workbench that ran the length of the far wall. Then, feeling unclean for having touched a corpse, the apprentice washed thoroughly and took himself to his room to pray.

On a hook above the corpse, Leonardo placed a lantern. He then placed a candle on top of some journals by the head of the body. On a table behind he placed several roles of paper, various pens and some chalk. Lastly, he went downstairs and took the small brass candle from the kitchen table and placed it on the table besides his papers and pens.

Calmly and carefully, Leonardo washed down the pitted body of his corpse and rubbed a little almond oil into the body to ward of the stench. He rolled out the leather pouch containing his surgical instruments and removed a long scalpel. He was just about to make an incision to the left of the man's sternum when the door was opened with a clatter.

'The dirty old dog, the dirty old dog, His Holiness is a dirty old dog. For breakfast he shags his mistress, at noon a visiting countess. And at night when the stars do shine, he sings every whore in Rome is mine!' Salai had returned. With no candle to light his way, the drunken boy fell over the dining table bench. Frustrated by his un-timely interruption, Leonardo headed downstairs, carrying the candle stand.

'Salai, Salai, where have you been these past two days? Look at you? Do you need something to eat? Shall I fetch some bread?' Leonardo said, lifting Salai's head off the table.

'Oh my word. Where did you get those bruises?'

'Those were earned defending you, papa. Don't you know you're not welcome in Rome? You've been ost… ostra… ostrac… oh shit!'

'Ostracized. Yes, I know.'

'What are we doing here then? Why aren't we back in Milan, tell me that?'

Leonardo took hold of Salai and carried him the short distance to his bedroom where Francesco, woken by the noise, helped Salai to bed.

By the time Salai had quietened down, the first shafts of daybreak were bursting through the upstairs window. It was too late to retire to bed, so Leonardo again took the scalpel in his left hand. His hand shook a little as he made an incision just to the left of the man's sternum in a straight line. He felt the resistance of the flesh as he cut. Blood trickled from the wound and, using a cloth, Leonardo wiped the blood and proceeded to cut all the way down to below the man's navel, the flesh of which was tinged a yellowish colour.

Once he had cut past the sternum, he found the flesh of the abdomen much easier to cut through. However, far more blood seeped from the incision and stained his hands. Cutting into the abdomen, he prized the flesh apart until he could see the stomach. He made a horizontal incision from right to left through the stomach wall, being careful not to cut through the large intestine. He washed away the copious amounts of blood and wrung the cloth out in a bowl placed between the corpse's legs. Once there was no more blood obstructing his view of the innards, Leonardo put his hands inside the cavity and methodically felt around, exploring the larger and lower intestines. He located the kidneys, liver and the gallbladder, which even to his untrained eye appeared swollen and infected.

Drawing the inner viscera of the human anatomy, Leonardo meticulously noted the veins and arteries that traversed the body's organs. He was so engrossed in his studies he failed to hear footsteps on the stairs.

'Jesus, Mary and Joseph!' exclaimed Salai. 'Francesco, quick! He's killed someone and chopped up the body!'

'Will you desist from your histrionics?' retorted Leonardo. 'The man was already dead. I purchased his body from the Hospice of Saint Jerome.'

'You'll get us all hung.'

'Salai!'

But the youth ignored his father's voice and paraded around the room, shaking his head. 'I always knew you were mad. By the Virgin, to think I slept last night while you were up here chopping up some dead bloke. Why, papa? Why?'

'It is my duty as an artist to have a better understanding of human anatomy if I am ever to represent it truthfully and in perfect proportion.'

'But, papa, what if they find out? What will happen to you?'

'I'm not the first artist who has procured cadavers to study.'

'Yes, but do you have to do it under my nose? You could have at least warned me?' Francesco emerged from the bedroom.

'Salai,' he said. 'There is no need to assume the worst.'

'Assume the worst? In case you've forgotten we're in Rome. And in Rome they tend to burn people accused of witchcraft.'

'But if we are silent on the matter and remain on our guard, no one need ever know,' Leonardo said.

DA VINCI'S LAST SUPPER

'It will cost you,' replied Salai, folding his arms defiantly across his chest.

'I'm ashamed to know you,' said Francesco, who walked away shaking his head.

'Twenty ducats,' demanded Salai.

'Ten,' replied Leonardo. 'All you will use it for is to get drunk.'

'And a whore,' replied Salai with a snigger.

'Expensive whore.'

'I plan to have more than one,' said Salai. 'Fifteen and that's my final offer.'

'Agreed,' said Leonardo.

'And to leave this wretched city and return to Milan.'

'You have my word, Salai. As soon as it is possible to return, we will.'

CHAPTER FORTY-FOUR

A VATICAN OFFICIAL, DISTINGUISHABLE BY A PURPLE BELT TIED around his midriff made his way towards Leonardo's house. He was an irksome creature with pallid skin who appeared to have a constant sliver of grease covering his clammy hands. He looked through a window, seeing no one in the room he tried the door handle and, with the habits of a thief, sneaked into the house. Looking around the large downstairs room nothing suspicious arrested his attention, but upon hearing sounds from upstairs he froze to the spot. The official waited momentarily before carefully making his way one step at a time up the staircase that led to Leonardo's studio.

The door at the top of the studio was partially open. The official tentatively poked his head around the door. The sight that greeted the official's eyes made him clasp his hand against his mouth. On a table not more than seven paces away was a severed human arm. The flesh had been cut to the bone and peeled back. All around the arm were scattered drawings showing the muscle, bone and blood vessels. Leonardo was leant over the corpse with a scalpel in his hand. The official watched as Leonardo made an incision into the shoulder and bicep of the corpse's remaining arm.

Shaking with fear, lest the maestro perform some act of wizardry, the official backed down the stairs. In his haste to depart he slipped on the last step and landed with thud.

'Salai, is that you?' enquired Leonardo. The Vatican official snatched at the door and hurriedly made his way out into the street. Leonardo leaned out of his studio window just in time to see the official flee pass Salai and Francesco in the street. 'Hey, you! Come back! What do you want?' shouted Leonardo. But the official had rounded the corner and was gone. Leonardo bounded down the stairs.

'Who was that man?' asked Salai, who almost collided with his papa hastily opening the door. 'A Vatican official I think,' replied Leonardo.

'God help us,' said Francesco, who nervously made the sign of the cross.

'We're as good as dead,' pronounced a solemn Salai.

The Vatican official ran as though he expected bolts of lightning to come hurtling down from above. Flailing his arms and muttering 'Hail Marys' he hurried on his way. With sweat dripping off his forehead and his face flushed from exertion he bounded up the white steps of the Vatican and hastened down an ornate corridor displaying the portraits of former Pontiffs. The official entered a large square room in which were seated various priests and dignitaries waiting for an audience with the Pope. Beyond this room a door led to an inner sanctum guarded by two Swiss guards.

Seated on a splendid gold cathedra, was the Pope. The throne was intricately carved in gold. At the foot of each armrest was the head of a lion, while above the Pontiff's head, was carved the figure of Jesus appearing to the women in the garden of Gethsemane. His Holiness beckoned the official forward.

'He's practising magic, your Holiness,' the official said, bowing before the Pope. 'Using human sacrifices. I saw him chop up a man's arm.'

'Are you absolutely sure they're human?' asked Father Rodrigo, wetting his lips in anticipation.

'I've seen enough dead bodies,' replied the official.

'Do you have an address?' asked Father Rodrigo.

'He's renting a large house on the edge of the Jewish Quarter in a side street off the Via Arenula. He has hung the sign of an artist above the doorway,' replied the official.

'Thank you for fulfilling your duties with such dedication,' said the Pope, extending his hand for the official to kiss the Fisherman's ring.

'Would you like me to continue to observe Leonardo, your Holiness?' The Pope dismissed this suggestion with a wave of his hand.

'Your humble servant,' said the official who walked backwards out of the room, bowing on his way.

Once the official had left the room, Father Rodrigo holding tightly to the silver cross that hung around his neck prayed silently: *Lord God, may the Holy Father extinguish this Florentine heretic.*

'Is there no limit to the depravity of that man?' hissed Father Rodrigo.

'I doubt Leonardo is practising the dark arts,' replied the Pope. 'Nonetheless, the usen of cadavers is strictly prohibited.'

'Did you know he's left-handed?' Father Rodrigo said.

'Is he really?'

'In my experience Holy Father, those who are left-handed are more prone to malevolent tendencies.'

I have heard such nonsense before.'

'Da Vinci and his ilk are a boil that needs to be lanced.'

'Leonardo has many uses,' replied His Holiness, swatting away a fly. 'None of which would be served if he were dead, at least not yet. Leave him for now. I order it.' Then, taking hold of Father Rodrigo's hand he said, 'There must be no repeat of the French attempt upon his life, not while he is of service to Cesare's military campaigns.' Choking on the Pope's words, Father Rodrigo bade him 'good day' and obediently kissed the Papal ring.

Regardless of the instruction from His Holiness, Father Rodrigo decided that he would make it his duty to discover where Leonardo had obtained his cadavers and pour down such wrath upon those responsible they would fear for their salvation. He made his way towards the Jewish Quarter and soon located a house such as the Vatican official had described.

Reciting a prayer for protection, Father Rodrigo knocked on the door of a house opposite and was greeted by a Jewish man, somewhat alarmed to find a Papal official on his doorstep. The priest learned the man's name was Simon. His hair was styled in traditional payots and he wore a black kippa upon his head. Father Rodrigo offered him a couple of ducats to observe the house across the street from his window. At first, Simon was reluctant but, after consultation with his wife, agreed. Simon pulled up a chair and Father Rodrigo positioned himself until he had a good view of Leonardo's doorway and upstairs window.

Just after midday, Leonardo departed from his house. In keeping with his personal preference, he wore a crimson tunic made of velvet and tights to match that were etched in silver brocade. The moment Father Rodrigo caught sight of him, blood rushed to his head. The one thing he shared in common with Cesare Borgia was a loathing of the fashionable attire artists were prone to wear. Bidding his hosts farewell, Father Rodrigo quickly made his way out into the street. Sticking close to the side of buildings and using the hood from his robe to cover his face, he followed Leonardo through a maze of cobbled streets.

Dotted along the ancient walkway by the Coliseum was a string of busy market traders. Father Rodrigo eyed Leonardo as he approached the store of an apothecary and browsed through his collection of jars and potions. The apothecary was a stout bald fellow. Leonardo picked up a large vial and held it up to the light.

'The best in Rome. Unlike some of my competitors, I don't water it down,' boasted the apothecary. While Leonardo was examining the bottle, it was suddenly snatched from his hand by a young man dressed in a colourful tunic popular with artists. The youth quickly passed the bottle to a smirking Michelangelo.

'Embalming fluid, huh?' Michelangelo sneered. 'So, the rumours are true. You are no artist, you're a butcher. They should name you the Butcher of Florence.' The two young men accompanying Michelangelo laughed raucously. Leonardo attempted to snatch the bottle back from Michelangelo, but his two companions stepped between them and barred his way.

'Michelangelo,' said Leonardo 'Can we strive to be friends, or at least be amicable to one another?'

'You do know if you don't finish 'The Last Supper,' an artist from Rome will finish it for you?' Michelangelo said, indicating to his companions who were jeering and making obscene gestures.

'Are you going to pay for that?' the apothecary asked Michelangelo, who was still holding the embalming fluid. Seizing his moment, Leonardo barged passed the two youths and walked briskly away.

'Leonardo!' yelled Michelangelo, throwing the bottle. It hit Leonardo on the side of the head, fell to the ground and smashed, its pungent odour filling the air. 'I'll be remembered as the greater artist long after you're dead and buried!'

'The greatest deception men suffer, Michelangelo, is from their own opinions.'

By now even the two hot-heads with Michelangelo were

ushering their fiery tempered friend away. 'Butcher!' taunted Michelangelo. Before Leonardo could reply the apothecary raised his hand to Leonardo's chest. 'Leave him be,' he said. Leonardo apologized to the apothecary and purchased two jars of embalming oils as well as paying for the one Michelangelo had smashed. Feeling aggrieved by his encounter, Leonardo hurried home, checking every now and again to ensure he wasn't being followed.

From his vantage position by the Arch of Constantine, Father Rodrigo scratched his head. He'd rather hoped Michelangelo had pulled a knife and cut Leonardo down. It wouldn't have been the first time that artists had killed one another in these streets. He approached the apothecary and asked what Leonardo had purchased.

'What business is it of yours?' replied the apothecary, who was rewarded with a slap across the face. 'I am the Papal Inquisitor, Father Rodrigo of Salamanca. Now answer my question.' The repentant apothecary told the priest what had been purchased. Smarting over the indignity of having his authority questioned by a tradesman, Father Rodrigo ordered the apothecary to attend confession and seek repentance for questioning a man of the cloth.

'If there was a man on Saint Peter's chair worthy of God, such scum would not speak to priests as if they were schoolboys,' he bitterly remarked to himself as he hastily departed in the same direction as Leonardo.

Knocking again on Simon's door, Father Rodrigo was invited in after paying the man a further gold ducat. The Jewish man's wife brought their Papal visitor a small jug of water to drink, some unleavened bread and a bowl of soup. The hours passed slowly. There was no movement from the house and the only event was when Salai returned home, drunk. When it was time for Simon and his wife to retire to bed, Father Rodrigo ventured out into the night. He persisted with his vigil from a doorway further up the street for perhaps an hour before he unwillingly returned to his room in the Vatican. Once inside, he took out a small whip and flagellated himself for his weakness in failing to track down the source of Leonardo's cadavers.

CHAPTER FORTY-FIVE

When the French marched through the Grand Saint Bernard on their way into Italy their generals were disciplined, and the army passed the monastery unhindered. The return home however, was an altogether different affair. The generals having ridden on ahead into France, left only a few junior officers in tow to maintain order of the motley crew of conscripts who had survived the French incursion into Italy.

Wearied from their hike through the Italian Alps, the French army entered the monastery hungry and in a foul temper. They ransacked the kitchen and took everything edible. Not satisfied with food, they also helped themselves to the mead and communion wine from the monks' store room.

Numerous pilgrims, taking advantage of the summer months to pass through the Grand Saint Bernard and enter Italy, also sought shelter within the monastery. The soldiers robbed the pilgrims and when a couple of these pious souls pleaded to be spared, the French, not satisfied with robbing them, murdered them too. Amongst the pilgrims were a handful of nuns of the order of Saint Clair, their destination, Milan. The retreating French soldiers dragged these devout ladies from their prayers and brutally raped each one. When some brothers of the order of Saint Bernard sought to protect the dear sisters, they too were put to the sword by blood-thirsty French soldiers.

An officer, no more than twenty years of age, attempted to subdue the men who were meant to be under his command, but two of them rounded on him and cut him down. The few remaining officers, like their slain comrade, were all young and decided not to interfere lest they too met the same fate.

The venerable Abbot Jerome sought to appease the drunken French horde that had descended upon his monastery and, speaking in his native French, pleaded for the soldiers to cease their vile ways and repent before God. But God and repentance were the last things on the mind of the mob. In vain, he protested when a soldier sought to remove the jewelled cross of Christ from above the Altar. The French soldier snatched the cross of Christ and beat the Abbot with it over the head until he fell to the floor unconscious. The thieving soldier hadn't walked more than four paces from the unconscious Abbot when he, in turn, was set upon by a larger soldier whose eyes burned with gold lust. 'Give it to me,' he demanded, seeking to snatch the cross.

'Over my dead body,' replied the soldier who had stolen the cross.

'So, my friend, you seek death,' said the larger soldier, angrily thrusting his sword in the direction of the soldier in possession of the cross. However, his thrust was executed with the awkwardness and loss of balance of a drunken man and rather than pose a threat, he merely exposed his own weakness. The soldier holding the cross easily parried his assailant's sword and ran the drunken soldier through.

When it became clear French soldiers intended to enter the monastery, Alessandro, being an Italian, had no desire to be seen by the enemies of his country, or risk being impaled on the end of a French bayonet. He headed straight for the kitchen, where he took some bread and a flagon of watered-down wine. In one of the outlying buildings of the monastery, the monks bred a few pigs, enough to supply them with some meat during the long winter months when they were cut off from the world and the supply of food was scarce. Alessandro headed for the pigsty and hid amidst the mud and dirt, hoping the French would not have the foresight to search there.

From behind a loose board in the side of the pigsty, he witnessed the carnage being inflicted on the monastery and its inhabitants. At one point he thought he was about to be undone when several soldiers came towards the pigsty. But, satisfied with bayoneting a couple of pigs that they carried off to the kitchen, they left the rest squealing in panic.

For two days, Alessandro hid amongst the dirt and squalor until the retreating French decided to press on and abandon the monastery to its fate. By the time they left, the stench of death hung heavy in the air as bodies lay unburied. The few surviving monks were far too preoccupied burying their dead and cleaning up to notice the madman who had been under their care and protection these past three years slip quietly away.

CHAPTER FORTY-SIX

After being in Rome for close on two years, Leonardo finally received a summons from the Pope. It was delivered by a priest from the Vatican and bore a red Papal seal. Leonardo scrutinized the words: His Holiness Pope Alexander VI summons you to attend in person on the thirteenth of September. A day away, Leonardo felt a cold dread come over him, his hand trembled and the summons slipped from his fingers to the floor. Francesco picked it up and read it.

'Perhaps he has learned of your work dissecting cadavers?' said a worried Francesco.

'If my studies of human anatomy have offended him, we would have heard long before now.'

The thirteenth of September was a day when Rome was clothed in an azure sky that graced its majestic buildings with the kiss of splendour. Yet as Leonardo walked the streets of the eternal city his mind was too occupied striving to grapple why His Holiness had taken so long to summon him, and whether the news he bore would be good or ill, to pay attention to the delights of the weather.

Ushered into a large ostentatious room, adorned with gilded gold-panelled walls and an elaborately painted ceiling,

Leonardo stopped to admire a portrait of Christ preaching his Sermon on the Mount. He was so engrossed in the painting he failed to hear the Pope's footsteps.

'It is a question that puzzles you deeply, is it not?' His Holiness said, placing a hand upon Leonardo's shoulder. 'How it is possible to truly capture the nature of the divine?' Leonardo faltered a moment before turning around.

'Your Holiness,' he said, bowing before Pope Alexander VI.

'How fares The Last Supper? Is it finished?' His Holiness asked.

'It is almost complete,' replied Leonardo, with some hesitancy in his voice. Feigning a smile the Pope walked on and indicated for Leonardo to follow. Behind them, a small entourage of officials feigned apathy as they admired the way His Holiness dangled Leonardo on a string. The Pope led them out on to an open corridor with a balcony overlooking a well-tended garden. Almost indifferent to Leonardo's presence, His Holiness paused to look at the plants.

'Many a thing left unfinished was almost complete,' he said.

'Your Holiness if I may...,' Leonardo began, only to be cut short by a raised finger.

'It is an unfortunate business, this fascination of yours with cadavers.'

'I humbly beg your forgiveness,' replied a flustered Leonardo.

'Come.' The Pope led Leonardo further along the corridor.

When they approached a large door, His Holiness stopped. A priest dashed forward and opened the door. The Pope led Leonardo out onto the veranda, before stopping to admire the view across the river Tiber and the unique skyline of Rome.

'This is my favourite view of Rome,' said the Pope. Before

them laid the skyline of the eternal city, resplendent with its ancient architecture, an indomitable reminder if ever one were needed of its glorious past. Tucked neatly alongside the many Roman ruins were the new glories to the city of Rome, buildings that popes, wealthy bishops and nobles had built that blended perfectly with the old. These too were ostentatious in design, magnificent monuments that declared the wealth of noble houses that had made Rome the envy of the known world. Below them lay the Vatican garden, a place of beauty where priests came daily to mediate amidst the flora and fauna from around the world, cultivated as a testimony to the extensive hand of the Catholic Church. Also stretching out, the river Tiber meandered through the city, peppered with bridges that spanned this symbol of Roman dominance.

'It is magnificent,' said Leonardo.

'How would you like to be remembered after your death, Leonardo?' asked the Pope. 'As a good artist or as one whose work is immortalized throughout history?'

'You ask me something I dare not answer here,' Leonardo eventually replied.

'I ask you only what you have asked many times of yourself,' replied the Pope, who nodded imperceptibly before leading Leonardo out into an open quadrant with a criss-cross façade.

In the courtyard below, several young artists were erecting their easels and arranging their brushes and paints. Leonardo paused to observe them. With what felt like the weight of a hammer, His Holiness rested an arm on Leonardo's shoulder and left it there.

'Rome is home to many, who like you, possess great skill,' His Holiness said, pointing to the boys below. 'Michelangelo, Raphael and others are all determined to stamp their mark. My son, you have left almost complete one too many commissions.'

'You fear I will not finish The Last Supper?' responded a

shaken Leonardo. Soothingly, like a parent disciplining an errant child, His Holiness replied,

'My fear is for you my son, and what will become of you if you should fail.'

'I will finish it,' blurted Leonardo.

'Good. Then you will be pleased to learn that Il Moro has retaken Milan, so you have no reason to delay your stay in Rome any longer.' Leonardo bowed his head.

'Your Holiness,' said Leonardo with as much composure as he could muster before he turned to walk away.

'Leonardo!' snapped the Pope. Holding out his hand he extended the Fisherman's ring to Leonardo, who took hold of the Pope's hand and kissed the sacred symbol.

On his way out of the Vatican he walked past works of art by artists he had heard since a youth: Giotto, Cimabue and Duccio. Once more Leonardo felt as if fate had conspired against him: *What have I done, Lord, to be dismissed from Rome without leaving behind so much as a footprint that I was ever here?*

When Leonardo told Francesco and Salai they would be returning to Milan, Salai danced around punching the air. Departing Rome had only one consolation for Leonardo, he would be beyond the malicious grasp of Cesare Borgia.

'Had you hoped you would be offered a Papal commission?' asked Francesco.

'A man hopes for many things in his lifetime,' replied a crestfallen Leonardo.

CHAPTER FORTY-SEVEN

THE LAST THING ISABELLA THE FRUIT SELLER SAW AS SHE walked home one autumnal evening was the flash of a knife, and the violent hand of a man yank her head back before the glinting knife slit her throat. Her assailant then held up her hands and pierced each one through the palms. Not satisfied, he plunged the knife deep into the right side of her ribcage and pushed the knife all the way in to the hilt. He dragged the knife towards the stomach and gutted Isabella, watching as her intestine spilt out. He wiped the knife clean on her grubby red dress, stripped her naked and left the bloodied clothes beside her ruined body. He spread her arms out in the shape of the cross, ground the heel of his boot in Isabella's face and departed.

Carlo had been the first to suffer the same fate that befell Isabella: throat slit, hands pierced, gutted like an animal and stripped naked. Some weeks after Carlo, it was the turn of the landlord, Eduardo the Spaniard. He, however, put up a struggle, his arms were covered in deep cuts inflicted by a knife, but the ferocity of his attacker had been too severe for him to defend against. Yet it was the brutal murder of Isabella that most revolted common Milanese folk, who now dreaded to enter the street once darkness fell.

The fact that two men and now a woman had all been butchered in the same gruesome way sent waves of fear throughout the city. Even Il Moro, wishing to curry favour with a population who had suffered two years of French rule ordered the castello guards to patrol the streets at night and offered a reward of a hundred gold ducats to anyone who captured the culprit. Needless to say, for such a princely sum of money every mercenary in Lombardy flocked to Milan.

One of these mercenaries, an ill-tempered man known as Carlos the Giant, on account of the fact he was almost seven feet tall, believed the culprit to be some Frenchman who had decided not to return to France, but instead inflict his barbaric savagery on innocent Italians. Carlos the Giant formed a vigilante group that marched through the streets with burning torches until they arrived at the home of a poor French soldier named Marius, who had married a Milanese girl and was now employed as a tanner by his father-in-law. To screams from his pregnant wife, the young man was carried off into the street and strung up by a jubilant crowd. Several other French men, all of whom would later prove to be innocent, suffered the same fate.

On a dark night in October, when a pale moon slid across the sky in a manner that suggested it would be the only witness to the next murder, Philippe the Hunchback, the owner of the tavern by the castello, played unsuspecting host to the man terrorizing Milan. It had been a quite night. Since the murder of Isabella, business had been slack and most of his customers arrived and left in twos and threes. The only newcomer tonight was a man who sat in the corner to the right of the fireplace. He was tall, well-built and kept a hood over his head. No one paid him any attention, believing him to be one of the mercenaries who had come to the city in the hope of capturing the 'Butcher of Milan', as he was now called.

When time came for Philippe to bid goodnight to the last of his customers and lock up his premises, he noted his unknown guest was no longer in the corner. He had no recollection of seeing the man leave but presumed he most have done so when he was otherwise engaged. Then, while counting the evening's takings, he saw the shadow of a man behind him reflected by the moonlight and the last embers of a dying fire. He jumped to one side just as a knife whistled passed his shoulder and cut his arm. The tavern owner reached for a cudgel that he kept hidden under the bar and, when his attacker came at him with the knife a second time, he hit the man in the arm causing the knife to go spinning across the room.

'Help! Help!' the tavern owner shouted as he ran into the street. Silhouetted in the doorway stood his attacker, the knife in his hand glinted beneath the cold light of the moon. 'Murderer! The Butcher of Milan!' Philippe screamed at the top of his voice. While his attacker hesitated in the doorway, the sound of armour clinking was heard rushing along the cobbled street. 'Help! Come quickly!'

Doors opened, and bleary-eyed people scanned the street to ascertain the cause of such commotion. The tavern owner stood his ground and held up the cudgel ready to defend his life when from the end of the street three soldiers appeared.

'The Butcher of Milan!' yelled Philippe, pointing at his attacker, who ran off down a side street pursued by Il Moro's guards. Within seconds the street was alive with activity. A neighbour came to Philippe's assistance, while several men barefoot and in their nightshirts ran inside to collect a weapon from their home, before they too joined the pursuit. Soon the clank of armour and the shouts and yells of those joining the chase could be heard reverberating around the streets. The man at the centre of this furore ran blindly into the night down deserted alleyways while the sound of the hunt behind him grew ever closer. One of the soldiers was fleet of foot and, no matter where the attacker ran, he could not shake off his tracker who blew a whistle to alert his colleagues behind him to his whereabouts.

Still holding the knife and his lungs bursting from exhaustion, the attacker rounded a corner and collided with a soldier. The two men were sent sprawling to the ground. The fleeing man scrambled to his feet, leaving his knife behind. However, he only managed to take a few steps before the soldier who had been chasing him caught up.

'Stop!' the soldier ordered, brandishing his sword. But the assailant ignored him and picked up the sword of the soldier who was still sprawled out on the floor. The two men stood slightly apart, each holding up their swords and weighing up their options. The alert soldier quickly decided to block off his opponent's means of retreat rather than engage a desperate man in combat, leaving only one route open an alley that led towards the fast-approaching throng of soldiers and citizens. There were about twenty men, some held torches while others wielded cudgels and spades. The cornered man looked the soldier in the face and grimaced.

'You think I frighten easily?' he said, in a guttural voice that sounded as if talking was painful. 'I'll split you in two the same way I split the others.'

'I'd like to see you try,' said the soldier, who lunged at his attacker nicking him on the side and drawing blood. Sensing the soldier before him was more than his match, the cornered man turned and ran headlong towards the approaching mob.

Stunned by this act of madness, some stopped their shouting as the bravery they had shown chanting through the streets evaporated at the sight of a madman hurtling towards them brandishing a sword. Most of the citizens backed into the sides of buildings or hid behind soldiers, who were being hastily marshalled into position by an unflinching captain of the guard.

The captain ordered the half a dozen soldiers under his command to stand their ground. Not all held their nerve. One of them buckled when the man who had struck such fear into Milan pointed his sword directly at him. A terrified young soldier let down his guard and stumbling over his feet retreated. The attacking man seized his opportunity and stabbed the young soldier in the stomach. He would have escaped had it not been for the bravery of a citizen who jumped into the gap and felled the fleeing murderer with a spade. Sent sprawling to the ground by the force of the blow he was quickly disarmed and tied up by the soldiers. Blood from his broken nose poured out on to the cobbled street. The captain ordered two of his men to carry the body of their comrade, while a further two dragged their captive through the streets towards the castello as a jubilant mob applauded.

CHAPTER FORTY-EIGHT

THE COURTHOUSE WAS SMALL AND CRAMPED. INSIDE, commoners were made to stand, while at the front there was a row of chairs reserved for the privileged. On one sat Father Rodrigo of Salamanca, newly arrived in Milan. Opposite him, behind a long table, sat three judges, dressed in black robes all looking appropriately solemn. A prisoner was brought into the crowded courtroom by two guards. Instantly a hullabaloo arose as a jeering crowd threw rotten fruit and vegetables at the shackled man. Several missiles missed their targets and hit the dignitaries seated on the front row, including an indignant Father Rodrigo, who wiped the remains of a cabbage from his shoulder.

The prisoner's hair was so pitted with filth it was impossible to tell its colour, likewise his flesh was thick with grime, while his soulless eyes chilled the Judges as each in turn dared look into them. They examined the papers before them, briefly conferring with one another. The courtroom seethed with anger. Shouts of 'Hang the bastard!' echoed around the room. With tempers at boiling point, people surged forward. Had it not been for a line of guards that came rushing in to separate the prisoner from the mob, a swift and bloody vengeance would have befallen the defendant. Two of the judges rose to their feet and waved their hands to calm an outraged courthouse, while the most senior judge, seated centrally, banged a gavel on the table.

Eventually, calm was restored. The senior judge, an elderly gentleman who wore his position of authority well, spoke first.

'We find the defendant guilty before God and the Holy Church of the most vile and despicable acts of murder. We therefore condemn you to be hung by the neck as an example to others of your godforsaken ilk. May God have mercy on your wretched soul.'

He hit his gavel once more on the table, the sound of which was accompanied by shouts of jubilation. 'Next!' said the senior judge, but as the guards took hold of their prisoner to lead him away, the prisoner rounded upon them.

'I have watched you hump nuns before the statue of Christ,' the prisoner hissed.

'Silence!' demanded the senior judge.

'Fornicating in the house of God!'

The three judges pounded their fists upon the table, while the once noisy public were momentarily silenced by the audacity of the prisoner's accusations. 'Adulterers! Devil worshippers!' screamed the defiant defendant before he was silenced by a blow to the head from the butt of a sword.

'Take him out,' ordered a red-faced senior judge.

The subdued crowd watched the limp body of the prisoner being dragged away. As they absorbed his accusations, old rumours pertaining to the hypocrisy of the ruling elite surfaced. The suspicious common folk now eyed the judges with a new-found malice.

'Court is closed. Now away with you,' ordered the senior judge, dismissing the public with an arrogant wave of his hand. Slowly the common folk filed out of the courthouse. But their mood was changed, and they left disgruntled, weighing up the accusations they had heard.

In a small room that contained a single shelf upon which rested a few books of legal paraphernalia, the three judges poured themselves a much-needed drink.

'Gentlemen,' said the voice of Father Rodrigo, who entered unannounced.

'Who are you? What are you doing here?' asked the senior judge. Their intruder had an air about him that made them ill at ease.

'I am Father Rodrigo of Salamanca.' The judges' reactions were sufficient to indicate it was a name they were familiar with. 'I have reasons for wanting to keep your last prisoner alive,' the priest said slowly, making each word count.

'Alive! Him? Are you deaf?' asked the judge who had been seated right, a man in his forties with a high forehead.

'Did you not hear his vile blasphemy?' quizzed the judge who had been seated left, the shortest and fattest of the three.

'Throw him into some dungeon to rot. But he is not to die, at least not yet. I may have need of him,' Father Rodrigo said in a cold voice. The senior judge stepped forward.

'You have no authority in Milan, Father,' he said. Father Rodrigo removed from his pocket a document bearing the red seal of the Pope.

'My authority comes from the Pope,' he said, handing the senior judge the document.

'Good day gentlemen,' Father Rodrigo said as he exited the room, leaving astonished looks on the judges' faces.

CHAPTER FORTY-NINE

It was an hour past sundown when Leonardo, Francesco and Salai entered Milan by the southern gate. They had barely passed the threshold of the guardhouse when the errant youth dismounted his horse and ran off.

'Salai!' Leonardo shouted half-heartedly.

'I want to see my pals,' came the reply as he hurried on his way.

'Can't that wait till tomorrow?' Leonardo shouted after him. Too intent on seeking out his friends Salai ignored him.

'He'll be back as always when he's hungry, cold or suffered a beating,' reassured Francesco.

'He may call me papa, but I fear the street will always be his real home,' said a weary Leonardo.

Passing familiar haunts, Salai skirted the edge of the Castello Sforzesco, upon passing, the night was greeted by the screams of a woman in labour that resounded around the castello's corridors and drifted into the concourse outside. Salai paid it no attention as he hurried towards the nearby tavern.

'Ludovico!' Beatrice cried. Il Moro, who was nervously biting his nails in the corridor, barged into the room where his wife lay on the bed writhing in agony. Between Beatrice's legs was a pool of blood a maid was wiping with a towel. Il Moro's physician earnestly examined the Duchess, who was breathing frantically in short sharp bursts. Witnessing the final throes of childbirth, Il Moro's face turned pale.

'I'm here' he said, gingerly taking hold of his wife's hand to offer what comfort he could. Gritting her teeth, Beatrice pushed one more time, letting out an ear-piercing screech that chilled Il Moro's blood. Spent of all her strength, she fell backwards on to the bed. Poking out between her legs could be seen the head of a baby. 'One more push,' implored the physician. Beatrice's breathing was shallow and her body too weak to continue.

'Beatrice,' Il Moro said, in a voice that broke with emotion. His wife turned her head towards her husband, her face was deathly pale, and the sparkle had left her eyes. She tried to smile but even this was too great an effort. Holding her husband's hand, she gasped a throaty rattle of death. The physician did what he could to save the child, but alas it was stillborn. Sobbing uncontrollably, Il Moro cradled Beatrice's lifeless body in his arms.

For months, Il Moro was struck down by grief. He barely left his bed chamber; some days he was so bereft he didn't even take the time to wash or dress. For those who thought there had been no great love between them, the manner in which her loss affected his mood made many reconsider. One morning, just like many others that had seen him pace the floor in his bare feet and refuse all advances from his courtiers, his physician arrived.

'My Lord, you are wasting away,' he said firmly. Indeed, since the death of Beatrice the Duke had lost his appetite for food. 'Your Kingdom is in need of a ruler. Much more of this melancholy and people will assume you are weak, and in Italy weak rulers are soon toppled.' The physician sat down upon the edge of the bed and waited for Il Moro to cease his striding up and down. After a period of an hour, during which the physician said no more the Duke finally halted his incessant footsteps. When he spoke, his voice trembled.

'I have… no desire… to be ousted from my throne.'

'Then regain your strength of mind and body and be done with your period of mourning while you still can. I have witnessed such grief before my Lord, and if unchecked the mind is never quite the same.'

Father Paulo, no longer a novice but an ordained priest, escorted Leonardo into the refectory at Santa Maria delle Grazie.

'After you left, we boarded up the far end of the room,' he said, stepping over some of the discarded wood. 'All your other items are safe, too.' Father Paulo said. 'The French ransacked the place but what they took was of little value.'

Leonardo nodded and placed a hand on Father Paulo's shoulder. He then walked silently forward and stood before the painting of *The Last Supper*. The background and fore-ground had been completed, including the table and its contents. The disciples to Jesus' left were finished, while the central figure of Jesus and the disciples to his right remain unpainted. Leonardo rested his hands against the wall and sighed. 'Where the spirit does not work with the hand, there is no art,' muttered Leonardo.

Over the following months, Leonardo would periodically return to Santa Maria delle Grazie. On occasions, his visits were brief. On others, like today he stood, stoic like, not moving from sunrise to sunset without eating or drinking. Fears and doubts assailed his mind: *Do I possess the talent to execute the painting according to the image seared upon my mind? If I do possess the talent, do I have the temperament to continue? Or will fate once more conspire against me as it has done so many times before?* Round and round the debate in his mind continued as he struggled with the belief *The Last Supper* was his destiny – to being riddled with self-doubt and the fear his hands would always fall short of the perfection his mind imagined.

Irritated beyond his limited patience, Prior Vicenzo wrote to Father Rodrigo of Salamanca to ask for his assistance in removing Leonardo. He also petitioned Il Moro until the Duke eventually gave in and summoned Leonardo to give an account of his progress.

Inside the Sala delle Asse, Prior Vicenzo was not the only one bending the Duke's ear for Father Rodrigo had once again arrived in Milan. Since the death of his wife, Il Moro had lost his appetite for the machinations of political intrigue and had no stomach for a further fight with his Papal visitor.

'The Pope has given his authority,' Father Rodrigo said, holding out a document.

'All I need is your signature and, upon my return to Rome, an artist will be dispatched to complete the commission where Leonardo has failed.'

'For many years Leonardo has served me faithfully,' Il Moro said.

'Not faithfully enough,' replied an adamant Father Rodrigo.

'My Lord,' said Cecilia. 'We ought to allow Leonardo to present his case.' She, more than most, knew Il Moro no longer carried the fight of old.

'Like all women, you think too highly of artists and this one in particular,' snapped Father Rodrigo.

'I have no doubt you could pluck some talented young man from the many artists who flock to Rome, but look around you,' Cecilia said, pointing to the wonder of the forest and the myriad creatures Leonardo had painted upon the ceiling of the Sala delle Asse. 'How many artists in Rome could equal this?'

Leonardo entered the Sala delle Asse under the guidance of the Duke's secretary, who could not resist the temptation to gloat.

'The vultures have come to pick over your bones,' he hissed under his breath. Leonardo ignored him, he was too busy looking at Cecilia. Her beauty hadn't diminished. Her eyes still glinted with the intellect and confidence that had captivated him. Although he had been back in Milan for almost a year, neither had thought it prudent to see the other. Looking at her now he felt some shame that he had neglected her companionship.

'My Lord,' Leonardo said, bowing. But before Il Moro had time to speak, Leonardo turned on Prior Vicenzo, who was standing resolutely beside Father Rodrigo. 'Have you got nothing better to do than petition the Duke with needless complaints?' Prior Vicenzo flushed with anger stuttered as he prepared to speak. Il Moro lazily waved his hand in the direction of the flustered priest to silence him.

'Forgive me, my Lord, but I fail to see why I should be called to explain myself to an ignoramus,' Leonardo said, pointing at Prior Vicenzo. By now the cheeks of the agitated prior were a shade of purple and his eyes bulged with consternation.

'Using the wisdom passed down by my ancestor, the great King Solomon…'

'I was not aware King Solomon was one of your ancestors, my Lord,' interrupted Leonardo.

'The Duke's genealogist has been able to trace a line on his mother's side,' the secretary peevishly replied. Il Moro gestured for Prior Vicenzo to speak.

'My Lord, four years have elapsed since…'

'Five!' said Father Rodrigo.

'Five?' asked Il Moro.

'Yes, my Lord, five,' replied the secretary.

'Yet does the artist work diligently towards the completion of The Last Supper?' asked Prior Vicenzo. 'No, he does not.'

'He does not?' Il Moro asked.

'For over a year now all he has done is stand and stare at it,' replied Prior Vicenzo.

'It?' asked a bemused Il Moro.

'The painting, my Lord. The Prior accuses me of doing nothing other than stare at it,' said Leonardo.

'Leonardo, how do you answer your accuser?' asked Il Moro.

'An artist,' Leonardo said, rolling up his sleeves, 'must first conceive in his imagination that which he is to later create with his hands. Only after an artist is satisfied in his mind can he proceed.'

'Happy, Prior?' asked Il Moro, hoping the matter would now be concluded. The Prior stood gawping at Leonardo as if he were a man possessed, whereas Father Rodrigo was of no doubt that the maestro was indeed possessed by a malevolent spirit.

'My Lord, may I offer an example that may help the good Prior?' interjected Cecilia calmly, much to the surprise of the men gathered around Il Moro's throne, who hitherto had only paid scant attention to the presence of the woman by his side. Smiling benignly the Duke nodded his consent.

'Good Prior,' she said looking him in the face, 'how many days did it take God to create the Earth?'

'Six,' he replied

'I do not need lessons in theology from a kept woman!' blurted an indignant Father Rodrigo who lifted up his silver cross and brandished it in Cecilia's direction.

'Enough! I would like to know where this is going, Cecilia?' said Il Moro.

'Thank you, my Lord. Your answer is, of course, correct. Six,' continued Cecilia.

'But how many days, or indeed years, did God take while he was thinking about creating the earth?' Leonardo smiled at the intelligence of her answer.

'My Lady,' said Leonardo bowing. 'Your beauty is surpassed only by your wisdom.'

'Ignorant strumpet,' snapped a vexed Father Rodrigo.

'Father, I have warned you once before,' replied Il Moro.

'Lady Cecilia,' said a chaste Father Rodrigo bowing. 'Since God is omnipotent, such questions pertaining to how much time the Almighty took to design creation are insignificant. The question at hand is rather how much longer should your Duke tolerate the foibles of a wayward artist incapable of completing the commission entrusted to him?'

The hairs on Leonardo's neck bristled at the effrontery of his Spanish menace, whom he believed more familiar with the wiles of the Devil than the good graces of God. While all eyes fastened upon him, awaiting a response, he slowly stroked the tip of his beard.

'You do me an injustice, Father Rodrigo,' responded Leonardo. 'Where you and Prior Vicenzo see inactivity and a lack of ambition, I see faithfulness to my patron. For entrusting this commission into my hands, a burden of expectation has been placed upon me to paint something that truly captures the divine. Therefore, the time I have thus far taken to exercise my obligation is not due to lack of ambition. Rather the opposite. *The Last Supper* must be executed with the utmost attention to detail.'

'See how difficult situations can be resolved when you possess the wisdom of King Solomon?' said Il Moro, hoping to placate Father Rodrigo. Sensing the tide was turning in his favour, Leonardo bowed before Il Moro.

'My Lord, I would like to add I have trudged through the city at all hours of the day and night, visiting places where virtuous men fear to tread in search of a suitable model to paint as Judas. Perhaps if I remain unsuccessful, the good Prior might offer to sit as Judas for me?'

The suggestion brought laughter from Il Moro. Resenting

the inference, Prior Vicenzo's face turned crimson and he huffed loudly.

'I have the means to a solution,' began Father Rodrigo. 'Recently, I had occasion to be at court when presented before the judges was the most foul and evil reprobate I have encountered. Notorious for murder he has shown no remorse for his heinous crimes. I am sure this man could be the Judas you seek.' Having spoken his Peace Father Rodrigo bowed, a glint of menace in his dark Spanish eyes.

CHAPTER FIFTY

MARCHING THROUGH COBBLED STREETS ON A BITTERLY COLD day in February, Maria passed few people. Those she did were all hurrying to get out of the snow-covered ground and the biting wind that blew into Milan from the Alps to the north. Only a group of children throwing snowballs seemed to be enjoying themselves. Maria wrapped her fur coat around her and headed in the direction of Leonardo's workshop.

Inside the workshop Francesco, engaged in painting the baby John the Baptist for the second *Madonna of the Rocks*, let the weight of his brush fall gently on the babe's chubby face. Apart from the baby John, the background had been painted but the figures of the infant Jesus, the Madonna and angel had still to be executed and remained in cartoon form.

'Let more light breathe on your subject,' Leonardo said. The main door opened, and a blast of cold air blew in as a shivering Maria entered. 'Yes, Maria' said Leonardo. Maria curtseyed.

'My mistress waits at Santa Maria delle Grazie. She bids you to come at once.'

'Just a moment while I fetch my coat.' While she waited, Maria looked with rapt curiosity at a bizarre contraption a few feet away from her. Putting on his warmest coat, Leonardo departed the workshop in the company of Maria, who took one last look at the machine that so fascinated her. Once outside in the street, she plucked up the courage to ask.

'Maestro, what was that strange looking machine?' asked Maria.

'An ornithopter,' replied Leonardo. 'I want to see if it is possible for man to fly aided by such a machine.'

'Fly? You mean like a bird?' the astonished maid asked. All the long-held superstitions that were ingrained in Maria's mind came bursting to the surface.

'Is it true you're a wizard?' she blurted, before clasping a hand over her mouth. Leonardo laughed.

'I beg your forgiveness, maestro. I am a poor working girl.' She paused for a moment then added rather excitedly. 'Maestro, do you truly believe it is possible to one day fly?' Leonardo gave a warm smile which caused the maid to look away bashfully.

'The knowledge of all things is possible Maria, even the knowledge of flight.'

The awe-struck maid felt sure one day she would regale her children and grandchildren with tales of the maestro and his flying machine. The two of them walked through the walled garden by the refectory and entered Santa Maria delle Grazie. Leonardo opened the door to Il Moro's private prayer room, while Maria stood guard outside.

'Cecilia, my dear. A joy to see you,' Leonardo said, holding out his arms to embrace her. Cecilia stepped away and placed her back against the wall.

'It has been so long. Too long,' she said in an uncompromising tone. Looking at her, still striking in her vulnerable femininity, Leonardo felt shame for his abandonment of her.

'I had no choice, I had to leave...'

'Without even having the decency to say goodbye,' Cecilia snapped. 'Do you know how many unwanted propositions were foisted upon me by the men of Florence. All eager to boast they had bedded the Duke of Milan's mistress?'

'I am sorry.'

'You should be more than sorry. There were days when I hated you.' Confronted by the consequence of his actions, Leonardo's face flushed with embarrassment.

'After the events of... when I was almost kidnapped by the French, I realised pursuing you was futile and resolved the only woman I want to be tethered to is my art.'

'Is that how you see marriage, Leonardo? To be tethered?' Her words spoken curtly, momentarily took him by surprise. To his shame he slowly nodded his head.

'I have since come to the conclusion that intellectual passion drives out sensuality and I wish to be free from such emotions.'

'Was there ever a man like you?'

'Surely you haven't invited me here just to castigate me.'

'I asked you to come because I wish to know of your progress on 'The Last Supper.' Leonardo looked away. 'Leonardo, talk to me.' He chose to remain silent. 'You haven't been to the dungeon to see this man, have you?' Leonardo walked to the window and looked out into the street. 'Why haven't you been to see this man?' Cecilia said, her tone of voice indicative of her annoyance.

'I think it will snow again,' he said. Cecilia looked at him, horrified.

'You're not going to finish it, are you?' Cecilia said.

'Art is never finished, only abandoned,' replied Leonardo. Cecilia took hold of Leonardo and gripped him firmly by the arms.

'Don't be a fool. Il Moro is a man subdued since the death of Beatrice, but he will not forgive you if you fail to complete *The Last Supper.*'

'My dear Cecilia, I am enslaved by the fear my hands can

never create that which my mind can conceive.' A knock on the door alerted them that their time was up.

'Leonardo,' said Cecilia, gently taking hold of his hand and raising it to her lips. 'You once said to me "he who is fixed to a star does not change his mind". The Last Supper is your star. You once believed it to be so. Do not let despair master you. Prove to yourself, that you truly are the master of your destiny.'

Cecilia slipped out into the church, leaving Leonardo alone. He spun around several times in the darkness while Cecilia's words rung in his ears. His eyes fell upon the small wood-panelled painting of the crucifixion that hung to the right of the window, and he did something he had not done in a long time. He knelt on the stool and, looking at the painting of Christ, genuflected. 'Lord,' he said. 'Grant me the determination to complete that which you have entrusted to my hands.'

On his way out of the basilica, he entered the bitterly cold refectory. What immediately struck Leonardo about the painting he had given his strength to was its grace and simplicity, the depth of movement and feeling he had managed to convey. The individuality of Christ's disciples, their very personalities captured by the conviction that surely, they were not the betrayer spoken of. Energized by the calm manner in which Jesus had delivered his stark revelation, eyes, faces, hands, fingers all questioned their neighbour on the truth of Jesus's words. Even though there was still much to be done, he nonetheless felt a sense of pride as the fire of inspiration took hold of him.

Propped up against the wall to the left of the painting was his discarded scaffold. Leonardo set about erecting it. Father Paulo entered the refectory and offered to assist.

'Father Paulo,' said Leonardo once the scaffold was in place. 'Will you do me one more kindness? Run to the dungeon at the Castello Sforzesco and speak to the jailer and say that I wish to see the prisoner whose life Father Rodrigo spared.'

The dust of Leonardo's neglect covered the painting and no work could be done until it had been cleaned and was in pristine condition. With daylight fading fast, Leonardo took up a bucket and cloth and methodically set about cleaning every inch of the fresco. He was still engrossed in this task when Father Paulo returned.

'You can go,' he said. Unmoved, Leonardo continued to clean the refectory wall.

'I will be ready within the hour,' he replied without turning around.

'No, maestro Leonardo, he said to come right away,' answered Father Paulo, taking a deep breath. 'He wants two ducats.' Leonardo slowly turned around and nodded briefly to Father Paulo before descending the ladder.

Entering the grounds of the castello, they clung to the walls as Father Paulo led them towards a secluded doorway. Through a window on the opposite side of the courtyard, the shadowy figure of Father Rodrigo was watching. Plucking a torch from the wall, Father Paulo led Leonardo down a dimly lit staircase. At the bottom of the staircase they were met by a giant of a jailer. He held out a plate-sized hand into which Leonardo placed two coins. The jailer bit into each. Satisfied the coins were genuine, he put them into a purse tied around his waist. The jailer picked up a torch and using a large brass key, opened a gate leading to a small cell. Leonardo squinted in the darkness.

'Come here, scoundrel!' yelled the jailer. With one hand, he thrust a torch into the face of the prisoner and, with the other lifted him up by his matted hair. The man screamed. Leonardo recoiled in shock, but not quickly enough to prevent the prisoner from gripping him around his neck. Leonardo's head rocked from side to side under the ferocity of the man's grasp, while from his vile smelling mouth came unintelligible curses mingled with grunts of rage. With the butt of a bull-whip the jailer hit the prisoner twice on the back, but he reso-lutely refused to release Leonardo. The jailer hit the prisoner again, this time on the back of the head causing him to release his grip around Leonardo's throat.

'Are you hurt?' a white-faced Father Paulo asked.

'Vile dog!' cursed the jailer, who lashed the prisoner with his whip.

'I'll kill you!' screamed the prisoner. Father Paulo grabbed hold of a shaken Leonardo and ushered him out of the dungeon. Behind them they could hear the crack of the whip. At the top of the stairs, Father Paulo replaced the torch on the hook by the door and taking a key, frantically fought to open it.

'Hurry up,' a breathless Leonardo implored. But the door refused to open. Leonardo pushed Father Paulo to one side and attempted to open the door himself, but in his panic the key slipped from his hand. 'God get me out of this infernal place!' he yelled, beating his fists against the door. Father Paulo picked up the key and once again tried the lock, this time the door gave way.

Gasping for breath Leonardo lurched into the courtyard, his head spun, and the dark shapes of the castello buildings appeared like black ghosts cascading around him. Observing Leonardo's distressed condition from the safety of his secluded window, a malevolent Father Rodrigo kissed the silver cross that hung around his neck.

CHAPTER FIFTY-ONE

A WEEK LATER, THE NECESSARY ARRANGEMENTS WERE IN PLACE for the prisoner to be delivered to Leonardo's workshop. Lest his identity be made known, he would be muzzled, manacled and escorted in the back of a covered wagon. At the discretion of the guards, Leonardo would be permitted to paint him for as long as they deemed the situation acceptable. If the prisoner became violent, or if the chief guard felt they were in danger of his identity being revealed, he would be returned to the dungeon immediately.

The cart holding Leonardo's Judas rattled through the streets of Milan on a fresh spring day in March. By the sides of the castello, daffodils and crocuses had sprouted on the lawn lining the moat, but none of these spring delights were seen by the prisoner, who journeyed with a hood over his head. Against his flesh the prisoner felt the joy of a mild breeze, one that brought him pleasure after the stale dampness of his dungeon. Even though he was blind to the sights around him, he could hear ordinary folk going about their business, the shouts of traders, the lewd comments of his guards whenever they passed an attractive maiden and the clatter of horse's hoofs on the cobbled streets he had terrorized.

The prospect of meeting his debased visitor filled Leonardo with dread. His hands fidgeted with his beard as he nervously marched up and down his workshop.

'Is he a murderer?' asked Salai.

'Yes, of children who ask too many questions,' was Leonardo's apt reply.

'I don't want to see him,' insisted Francesco, taking himself off to his room.

'I think you had best go and attend to your studies,' Leonardo said to Salai.

'Not on your life,' he replied.

The cart carrying the prisoner arrived midway through the morning and was backed up as far as it could go to the double doors at the far end of the workshop.

'This way, please,' said Leonardo, directing the guards inside. The prisoner's manacles rattled off the stone floor as he hobbled through the workshop. Salai, his mouth open wide searched for clues as to the identity of the hooded man. Leonardo led the guards and their prisoner into his personal studio.

'You may seat him here.' Leonardo pointed to a simple chair that rested beside a small sturdy table. The chief guard stroked his mottled grey beard.

'Do you have any rope?' he asked. Leonardo rummaged around his studio until he produced a small length of rope.

'Will this do?' The chief guard took the rope and sat his prisoner down. Along with his companion, a tall, bald-headed man, he fastened the robe around the prisoner and tied it to the back of the chair. The disgruntled prisoner shook his head and grunted through his muzzle.

Still lurking in the doorway was Salai, who much to his annoyance, was pushed out of the way by the bald-headed guard who closed the door in his face. The chief guard removed the prisoner's hood. Leonardo looked fretfully into the hate-filled eyes of the muzzled man, who strained on his manacles. Spittle gathered at the sides of his mouth and his nose flared. His hair was a wiry matted mess and his skin was pitted with a thick coat of filth. He strained and pushed and rocked in an attempt to free himself from his restraints. But it was his wide bulging eyes, brimming with hatred, which caused Leonardo to quake in his shoes.

'When you're ready maestro,' the chief guard said. Leonardo was breathing rapidly and drumming his fingers on the table top. 'Maestro?' the chief guard repeated.

'Take him away,' replied a flustered Leonardo.

'What?' answered the chief guard.

'Give me one more week.'

'Maestro, he cannot harm you. He is under our protection,' the taller guard said.

'Please, take him away.'

'Il Moro will not like your postponement when I report to him,' said the chief guard, who reluctantly untied the prisoner. They grudgingly led their hooded captive through Leonardo's workshop and passed Salai, eavesdropping outside Leonardo's door.

'Satan's breath! What a pimply-arsed coward,' said the chief guard as they bundled the prisoner into the cart. 'Dozy cunt wouldn't last half a day in your outfit, boss,' said the taller guard. Once their prisoner had been bundled into the back of the cart, the chief guard yanked him down by his manacled feet, causing his captive to groan in protest as his head bounced off the board at the end of the cart.

Oblivious to the mockery of Il Moro's guards, a shaking Leonardo sat down on the chair that had been occupied by the prisoner. Moments later his studio door swung open and Salai stood there grinning. 'You couldn't do it, could you?' snapped Salai. 'The captain's right about you. You're a pimply-arsed coward.' Having uttered his insult, the young miscreant strutted arrogantly away.

'What's going on?' Francesco asked. 'Where's that awful man?'

'I couldn't do it,' Leonardo replied, sinking his head into his hands.

'What are you going to do now?' his chief apprentice asked.

Francesco's question was answered by a wet and bedraggled Father Rodrigo of Salamanca, who paid the artist a visit late in the day amidst a thunderstorm. A surprised Francesco opened the door to the Spanish Inquisitor.

'Is your maestro home?' Father Rodrigo asked in a voice that chilled Francesco's blood.

'He is, Father. Please, step this way.' Francesco led the soaking wet priest into the workshop and then went to fetch the maestro. A somewhat perplexed Leonardo entered, to be greeted by a firm handshake from the man who had once sought to have him burnt as a heretic.

'Good evening, maestro. I trust I have not interrupted you from your work?'

'Not at all. Here, take a towel,' said Leonardo.

'Thank you' said Father Rodrigo wiping his face. 'You are probably wondering why I have chosen to pay you a visit?'

'Well, yes, it had crossed my mind,' replied Leonardo, hoping there was not too much of quake in his voice. 'Please, be seated,' he said, offering the priest a chair.

'Are these designs for a flying machine?' Father Rodrigo asked, eyeing several discarded sheets of paper with sketches of an ornithopter.

'They are,' said Leonardo.

'Remarkable,' replied the priest, sitting down.

'Wine?' said Leonardo.

'Delightful,' replied a smiling Father Rodrigo.

Leonardo poured his guest a goblet of wine. 'Maestro,' the priest began in a measured tone. 'You and I have not seen eye to eye. In fact, it would be fair to say my attitude towards you has at times been... unsympathetic. But tonight, I come to your aid and I hope you will receive my good intentions.' Leonardo sipped his wine and scrutinized the face of his uninvited guest.

'I am intrigued,' he said.

'The man we agreed to be painted as Judas is a despicable murderer whose life I spared because I felt prompted by God that there was some service, some act of redemption, which he would yet be central to. My instincts proved true. Today I have spoken to him in my capacity as the guardian of his soul. He will not harm you. I have made him swear this before Almighty God.' The Father kissed the silver cross that hung around his neck while Leonardo stepped back for a moment and absorbed the priest's words.

'Father Rodrigo, experience has taught me when my enemies seek to climb into bed with me, they do so because they hold a dagger underneath.'

'There is no knife maestro, just an opportunity to be part of God's noble purpose.' Leonardo looked into the eyes that had sentenced a hundred souls to death and examined them for a sign his nemesis had come with trickery to outwit him, but he saw none.

'If you guarantee he will keep good his promise, I will paint him as Judas.'

CHAPTER FIFTY-TWO

TWO DAYS LATER, LEONARDO STUDIED THE EYES OF HIS manacled prisoner for evidence of treachery. To his relief, he was calm and obliged Leonardo with a lopsided smile. The guards secured a rope to the back of the chair. The prisoner's left arm was positioned to rest atop a sturdy table, while in his right hand, the prisoner held a pouch of coins. Leonardo positioned him with the right side of his face and body turned in profile, so as to hide the scar that ran down the left-hand side of his neck. 'What is your name?' Leonardo asked.

'You're wasting your time,' said the chief guard. 'He refuses to talk. We call him the Butcher of Milan, but you can call him Judas if you like.' The chief guard slapped the shoulder of his colleague as both chortled at his little joke. His eyebrows furrowed by concentration, Leonardo studied the contours on the face of his 'Judas'. His nose had once been broken and, judging by his protruding jaw and the lump on the left side of it, that too had been broken. Thankfully, the misshapen features of his appearance were largely concealed by the man's dark beard. Each nook and cranny of his malicious face gave rise to him being the personification of every villain from childhood that had been told to him by his uncle. Nevertheless, it was the man's eyes that agitated him most, they seemed to be the eyes of a man who had died many years ago, for whom living had merely become a means to perpetuate the hatred he felt towards mankind.

An anxious Leonardo drew sketches of the prisoner from a variety of angles, but none satisfied him. He decided to swap his silver-point pen for a piece of charcoal and began drawing Judas in profile. In his haste, he applied too much pressure and the charcoal snapped. Rolling across the stone floor it came to a stop beside a manacled foot. Leonardo looked apprehensively into the prisoner's eyes before he bent down to pick it up. The moment he touched the piece of charcoal, the prisoner shook his manacles.

'I'll kill you,' he whispered in a guttural voice. Leonardo bolted upright, the colour draining from his face. Reacting to the artist's histrionics, the prisoner threw his head back and roared hysterically.

'Is he bothering you?' asked the chief guard, taking hold of the whip on his belt.

'That's enough for today,' replied Leonardo. 'Tomorrow, can you bring him to the studio I have prepared at Santa Maria delle Grazie?'

'Makes no difference to me where you want him,' replied the chief guard, as he and his accomplice put down their cards, checked their prisoner's shackles and escorted him away.

Habitually, Leonardo reached for a jug of wine and poured himself a drink into an old brass goblet. He downed it in one and poured another: *Can this evil man be trusted to keep his word? Can I trust Father Rodrigo too? What if there is violence?* His mind racked with the premonition that his Judas might indeed succeed in killing him despite Father Rodrigo's assurances, he rolled out his medical kit and took out a small, sharp knife, which he stabbed with force on top of the table. The knife cut into the wood and oscillated from side to side. He drew the knife from the table and tucked it inside his tunic.

Partially satisfied by his false sense of security, he picked up the drawings he had made of Judas and examined them. He could not look at them for long, there was something about the deranged man's demeanour that disturbed him. Around his head, a chorus of complaints sang: *Nothing good will come of this. You are a dangerous heretic. If you fail now, not even your genius will save you.*

Even after he had drunk another goblet of wine and fallen into a slumber, his sleep was beset with premonitions of his impending death. A knock at the door snapped him out of his despondency. He opened it to find Maria. 'Maestro,' she said and handed Leonardo a note.

'What is it, Maria?' Leonardo asked, but Maria ran down the corridor and out through the door. Leonardo hastily opened the note, it read:

Please come at once. I am in the castello garden and forbidden to leave the grounds. Your dearest songbird, Cecilia.

Twilight had arrived and the sight of a pale moon hovering lazily on the horizon greeted Leonardo as he dashed through the city's cobbled streets. Overhead a brace of nimbus grey clouds threatened rain. Panting for breath, he entered the garden by the southern entrance and saw Cecilia, wrapped in a fur coat standing under a canopy by the summer house. Her shelter offered her a degree of anonymity from prying eyes inside the Castello.

'My dear, what is the meaning of this?' Leonardo asked, holding out the note.

'Il Moro has arranged for me to be married to the young Count Bergamo,' Cecilia said, choking on her words. Leonardo's heart jumped and felt his mouth go dry.

'What? Why now? I've almost finished.'

'Why does everything have to be about you?'

'I'm sorry. When do you leave?'

'In the morning, at first light.' Fighting back her tears, Cecilia turned away. Leonardo reached out a hand to touch her on the shoulder but even though she wanted to feel his arms around her, she instead stepped backward to avoid his touch.

'How is your Judas? Is he as evil as that malevolent priest prophesized?'

'I do not think evil men of bad habits and little intelligence deserve such a fine instrument as the human body.'

'A little longer and this task will be complete. God wills it.'

'I am glad you have such faith in God.'

'Not only in God but you too, Leonardo.'

'When will I see you again?'

'After this hour I do not expect to see you again… ever.'

'Do you get to keep your portrait?'

'Yes,' she said, the faint flicker of a smile lighting up her tearful face.

'Leonardo?' she asked, taking hold of his hand. 'Had we met under different circumstances, could you have loved me enough to… make me your wife?'

It was the one question Cecilia had for years wanted to ask but had never dared until now. Stalling for an answer, Leonardo looked up at the night sky and watched his breath disappear in long thin wisps. He had known for some time the day would come when she would ask such a question, but he had never been able to succeed in coming to a reply that would not grieve the one woman he held affection for.

'My dearest goddess, I could not inflict myself upon any woman, least of all you. If you are alone, you belong entirely to yourself. If you are accompanied by a wife, you belong only half to yourself. And I am afraid, even if I were married to someone as remarkable as you, in the end I would neglect you for the sake of my many fascinations.' Cecilia reached out a hand that almost touched Leonardo's face.

'It is as I feared,' she said, letting her hand fall to her side.

For a while they stood in silence, both content not to speak rather just savour their bittersweet moment. Oblivious to the lengthening shadows of fading light, which like the relentless march of time, crept into the night. Each desired to say more but as creatures of instinct, both knew the day for words had come to an end.

'I must go now,' she said. With a heavy heart Cecilia turned and half-walked half-ran towards a side entrance of the castello. After a short distance she stopped and turned around. 'Leonardo, each time I look at my portrait, I will think of you.'

He stared at her as she hurried inside a doorway. Only once she was out of sight did he allow a trickle of tears to slip down his face. Knowing his eyes would never grace Cecilia's countenance again equalled the most agonizing moment of his life, when as a boy aged five he had been taken from his mother's home and made to live with his uncle. Afterwards, he only saw his mother on rare occasions, but like Cecilia's departure that too had been foisted upon him. His heart felt as it were made of wood, a hallow thud beat loudly inside his aching chest, whilst his stomach churned, sickened by the grief of Cecilia's parting. The thought of never seeing sunlight filter its way through the silken strands of her hair, nor hear the nightingale tone of her soft voice was an anguish greater than he had imagined possible.

The world now seemed void of the one thing, all people, whether great or small needed to sustain them – love.

CHAPTER FIFTY-THREE

WITH A TORCH IN HIS HAND, FATHER RODRIGO OF SALAMANCA climbed down the stairs that led to the castello dungeon at a time of night when only the guards, diligent in their nightly watch were still awake. The jailer, hearing someone approach, stood at the bottom ready to confront his intruder. 'Who goes there?' he barked. Father Rodrigo reached the last step and held up the burning torch.

'Oh, it's you, Father,' the jailer said. 'I wasn't expecting anyone at this hour. Step this way.' He opened the door to his guard room and offered a chair to Father Rodrigo, who declined.

'Show me the Butcher of Milan,' the Inquisitor demanded. The jailer held out his palm to receive his customary payment for such services, but all he received was a rap over the knuckles. 'I am here on the will of God. Now open the door and less of your impertinence!' In an act of defiance, the jailer deliberately placed several wrong keys in the dungeon door. 'You incompetent fool!' scolded the priest, just as the jailer wisely decided to use the correct key to open the dungeon door, which clanked and scraped upon the stone floor.

'Leave us,' ordered the priest.

'He's a madman,' replied the jailer.

'Leave us,' reiterated Father Rodrigo, pushing him out through the door. Satisfied they were alone, Father Rodrigo drew out a small, thick-bladed knife from inside his tunic.

'You mean to kill me?' asked the prisoner, with no fear on his hardened face.

'I am here on a mission from God. Kill the maestro Leonardo and I will personally guarantee you safe passage to anywhere in the land.' He then tucked the knife inside the prisoner's right boot. 'If you do, not only will I grant you your freedom, I will pay you a hundred gold ducats. Can you be trusted?' Father Rodrigo demanded. He grabbed hold of the prisoner by his beard and looked into his eyes. The prisoner let out a hollow laugh and rocking his head back and forth shook his chains.

The following morning the prisoner was led out of the dungeon, up the narrow stair and out into the castello's courtyard. A hood was placed over his head before he was bundled into the back of the cart. Lying down he swivelled his arms down to beside his feet and felt around until he could lift the blade above his boot. Carefully, he hooked the rope over the blade and began to gently inch back and forth until he could feel the sinews of the rope begin to fray. When he was satisfied a good tug from his hand would snap the remaining threads, he pushed the knife back down into his boot.

The chief guard knocked on the studio door at Santa Maria delle Grazie, but there was no answer. 'Maestro!' he shouted several times. 'Are you in?' Just as the chief guard was about to concede no one was in, the door was opened by a haggard Leonardo, his bloodshot eyes blinked uncontrollably in the daylight.

'Do you wish to paint your 'Judas'?' the chief guard asked. Leonardo lifted the hood off the prisoner, who grinned maliciously at the maestro's dishevelled appearance. Before Leonardo could respond, Salai came running up the street.

'Papa, where have you been all this time?' he demanded.

'Salai, please, will you fetch me something to eat?' Salai ignored Leonardo and stood to gawp at the prisoner. 'Bring him in,' Leonardo said.

The taller guard, who stood on the threshold of the studio door, stepped aside to let Salai pass. As he did so, the prisoner broke free of the rope and in one swift movement bent down, snatched hold of the knife tucked inside his boot and stabbed the taller guard in the stomach. The man screamed in agony and slumped down on to the stone floor, blood spilling from his guts. Salai spun around in horror to see the prisoner holding in one hand the blood-stained knife, while with the other he slammed shut the studio door, trapping the chief guard and Leonardo inside.

The chief guard drew his sword, but he wasn't quick enough. Leonardo looked on aghast as the prisoner lunged at the chief guard, piercing his chest. The guard reacted and shoved his attacker away. Arms and legs were tangled together as the two men fought for possession of the knife. The guard hit the prisoner's head against a table top, stunning his attacker momentarily, who dropped the knife to the floor. Moving at speed the prisoner took a hold of knife and as the guard sought to prevent him picking it off the floor, in a deft movement the prisoner unbalanced the guard and twisted the knife into the chest of the wounded guard. Blood gurgled from the chief guard's mouth and he crashed heavily to his knees. The prisoner smashed the kneeling man in the face with the back of his hands and, coughing up more blood, the chief guard fell to the floor. The prisoner leapt forward, his eyes wide with maniacal intent, and plunged the knife repeatedly into the chest cavity of the chief guard, not stopping even after it was clear the man was dead.

Leonardo backed into the wall as far away as was possible

from the killer in his midst. He thought of retrieving the knife from his tunic but was too frozen by fear. The prisoner, whose tattered rags were splattered in blood, took hold of the keys tied to the dead guard's leather belt and unfastened his fetters. He then removed the muzzle from his mouth.

'My God! Don't kill me!' pleaded Leonardo, as the prisoner brandished the knife in his face.

'Who am I?' the prisoner demanded in his throaty voice as he took hold of Leonardo's head and yanked it back. His breath reeked of death as his blood-stained hands forcibly gripped Leonardo. 'Look at me!' he demanded. 'Who am I?'

'I don't know. I swear to God.' The prisoner took the knife and held it against Leonardo's throat. He squeezed the sharp blade against the maestro's flesh and a slither of blood trickled down his neck.

'Five years ago, you painted me as the face of Jesus.'

'Alessandro?' said a shaken Leonardo. 'It can't be, he's…

'… Jesus of Milan!' screamed Alessandro, with his arms outstretched. The madness of his declaration sent shivers down Leonardo's spine. Alessandro grabbed Leonardo by neck and threw him over the table where he landed with a thud against the body of the chief guard.

Like a lion stalking its kill he prowled around the studio. 'Jesus! Jesus! Jesus!' he yelled, puncturing the air with the knife.

'Mercy, Alessandro. Mercy!' begged Leonardo, rocked to the very core of his being by the resurrection of a man he had long presumed dead. In no mood to demonstrate mercy, Alessandro smote Leonardo hard across the face and placed the knife over the maestro's pounding heart.

'Alessandro, please mercy.'

'Everyone called me 'Jesus of Milan,' I woke as Jesus. Ate, drank as Jesus, blessed people as Jesus, healed people as Jesus, until the day you betrayed me,' he said, throwing Leonardo's head back. 'My knife knows no mercy,' he hissed, slashing it across Leonardo's chest ripping the pink and purple tunic he was wearing.

'I thought you were dead. What happened to you after I… I… ?'

'You mean after you kicked me out in the street like a dog?' There was pity in his voice. Looking at the man before him, a shadow of the Alessandro he once knew, Leonardo felt remorse.

'I am sorry,' he said. 'I never meant any harm to befall you.'

'You lie! I am a servant of God, and God has delivered you into my hands to avenge the wrong done to me.'

'We are each in our own way servants of God,' replied Leonardo. Alessandro lifted Leonardo up by his hair and let the knife rest on his throat.

'Make your peace with God,' he said. From a place of insight born of genius, Leonardo's face came alive.

'Have you ever asked yourself, Jesus of Milan, whether the death of Christ would have been more or less significant had he been crucified as a man in his fifties or sixties?' While Alessandro contemplated the question, Leonardo continued, 'What do Jesus Christ, Alexander the Great and Joan of Arc have in common?' Alessandro looked apprehensively around, all three were names he had heard since childhood. 'They all died tragically,' Leonardo said. 'And society creates idols out of those whose fame and glory touched the world yet were tragically snatched from it before their time. And the more tragic…'

'Is their death…' interrupted Alessandro.

'… the greater the myth will become. So in death they receive even greater glory than they received…'

'…in life,' said a hesitant Alessandro.

'Who is being painted here?' Leonardo asked. 'Judas, who betrayed Jesus to his death. And now the artist who painted

Jesus is destroyed once again in an act of revenge by you, Judas!'

Rising to his feet, Leonardo looked Alessandro in the eye. 'If you kill me, no one will remember you as Jesus of Milan. You will be remembered as the scheming, vengeful Judas who threw eternity away for thirty pieces of silver.' Recoiling, Alessandro withdrew the knife from the artist's throat. Dazed and confused by the accusation of Leonardo's words, he spun aimlessly around.

'But I am Jesus of Milan,' replied Alessandro pitifully.

'Not if you kill me. I will be remembered throughout history as the artist who emulated our Lord and who too was killed by Judas. Does anyone revere or worship Judas? No. And neither will they worship you. Save yourself, show mercy.'

The ebb and flow of Alessandro's hatred subsided, and confused by the veracity of Leonardo's argument, he fell face down, his body heaving with bewilderment in deep, anguished breaths. Had Leonardo the inclination, he could have brought his captivity to a swift end but he had never held a knife in violence and could not bring himself to take out the one from his tunic and turn it upon Alessandro.

'Your name,' Leonardo said measured and calm, 'is Alessandro da Canegrate.'

'No, no, you lie! I am Jesus of Mil...'

'No Alessandro. Repeat after me, Alessandro da Canegrate.'

'Jesus of Milan.'

'Alessandro da Canegrate.'

'Jesus of...'

'...Alessandro da Canegrate, say it,' ordered Leonardo. His voice firm and uncompromising. 'Alessandro da Canegrate.' The mind of Alessandro swooned under the authority of Leonardo's words. Leonardo took hold of Alessandro and lifting up his head continued.

'Repeat after me, Alessandro da Canegrate.'

'Al… ess… an… dro.'

'Yes, you are Alessandro da Canegrate.'

'Al… ess… no you lie I am…'

'Alessandro da Canegrate. Repeat after me, Alessandro da Canegrate.'

'Alessandro da Canegrate,' whispered Alessandro.

'Yes. You are Alessandro da Canegrate, a weaver from Bergamo, who has a wife, Letizia.'

'Letizia,' spoke Alessandro, breaking into sobs.

'She bore you a son. You are a father Alessandro, a father.'

'Father,' repeated Alessandro in a weak voice.

'Good. You must believe me. Your name is Ale…'

'Alessandro da Canegrate, a weaver from Bergamo,' replied Alessandro.

'This is the truth,' affirmed Leonardo. 'And the light of truth is stronger than the lies of any darkness.'

There was a smile on Alessandro's face, one illuminated by the truth that had finally penetrated his mind, which for too long had been imprisoned in darkness.

'Where is Letizia?' Alessandro asked. 'Do you know what became of my wife and child?' Before Leonardo could answer, the door was flung off its hinges as three soldiers rushed in. One shoved the maestro aside, while his companions put Alessandro to the sword, stabbing him in the chest and abdomen. Blood gushed from his wounds and he slumped forwards. Leonardo held a bloodied Alessandro in his arms.

'Find her for me,' whispered Alessandro. 'Tell her…' his voice failed, and he passed from this life into the next. Moments later Salai and Prior Vicenzo gasped in horror as they surveyed the sight of Leonardo cradling a dead man in his arms.

'You were right, Prior Vicenzo,' said Leonardo, his voice quivering. 'You once said nothing good will come of this. Here lies Alessandro, the man I painted as Jesus but more tragically as... Judas.' Prior Vicenzo, knelt down and read the Last Rites.

Once he had administered his ministerial function the Prior ordered two monks to take Alessandro's body away.

'My God, what have I done?' Leonardo said, as Alessandro's body was carried out of the studio.

'For one truly repentant, there is always redemption.' Leonardo listened to Prior Vicenzo's words, each one spoken without malice. With his arm around the Prior, Leonardo stumbled on his shaking legs out of the studio down the cold stone corridor and into the church. Following behind was Salai, who said nothing, the youth being more interested in the soldiers taking the bodies of their comrades away than the distress of his adopted father.

Under the nave of Santa Maria delle Grazie, Leonardo gazed upwards as if hoping some angel would descend from heaven to pour myrrh into his broken spirit. Finding strength from somewhere he stumbled off in the direction of the refectory. Francesco, who arrived panting for breath was of a mind to follow him, but Prior Vicenzo halted him.

'Leave him alone for now,' he said in a pastoral voice. 'A man in such distress needs no other company than his own misery and God. The best thing you can do is go home and maintain his affairs. The maestro will speak when he is ready.'

The door to the refectory was swung open by a despairing Leonardo. Upon the wall, the unfinished *The Last Supper* looked accusingly out at him. Leonardo beat his fists against the wall with such relentless anger he skinned his knuckles. Like Samson holding the pillars in the Philistine temple until they gave way and crushed his enemies, so now it seemed Leonardo hoped the wall would cave in and engulf him in an avalanche of rubble.

A heaviness of spirit settled over Leonardo and sank deep into his soul. Over the years he had become familiar with bouts of melancholy that plunged him into despair, where the only thoughts that penetrated his mind were those dominated by his fears: *Oh God, why for all my undoubted talent, I am forever doomed to fail at my attempts of a master work? Why do you allow fate and doubt to have mastery over me? My life is cursed, as has been proven with the resurrection from the dead of Alessandro and his now unfortunate death.*

With his head resting against the refectory wall, Leonardo pondered the dualism of forever balancing the joys of one's art and ambition with the reality of a cruel world, which foisted upon men of greatness, greater and greater stumbling blocks. Alone in the darkness of his own mind, the enormity of his predicament sank in: *I am undone. Fate has once more delivered a cruel blow.*

Early the next morning, with the sun just beginning to cast the first glow of a new day, a fatigued Leonardo slumped to the ground. Holding his knees tight against his chest he rested his head upon the refectory wall. Languishing in the juices of his many miseries, he felt bereft of hope and prayed like one at the end of their tether.

'Forgive me Father, for I have sinned,' he said clearly and respectfully, just as a long tentacle of light burst through the windows of the refectory and reached the tips of his feet. 'Alessandro's tragic death was the desolate end to a soul destroyed by my hubris. For all these things, Lord, I am deeply sorry.' He looked out in the direction of a window, gazed at the inviting sky and genuflected. 'In honour of Alessandro's memory, it would be shameful now for me to complete *The Last Supper*. Grant me forgiveness Father, and I promise I will paint no more. Amen.'

A tangible sense of relief washed over Leonardo's body as the healing balm of God's forgiveness washed over his grief-stricken soul. His head slowly cleared, and a semblance of clarity returned to his thinking. His countenance too, lifted. There was now a sense of peace, even though he knew he would have to answer to Il Moro for his failure to complete the commission.

For once, Salai acted with gravitas and waited until late morning before interrupting his papa. He entered the refectory with a plate of cooked vegetables, took a seat beside Leonardo and placed his hand in that of his father's.

'Papa, what will you do now?'

'I have no idea. The only thing I know is that I cannot continue with The Last Supper.'

'Il Moro will have you flogged or worse.'

'Il Moro can feed me to the dogs if he so desires. All is finished. I am finished.'

'Please, papa, do not give up now. You have come too far and laboured too long to abandon her at the last hour. I will help you. Whatever you ask in order to help finish the painting, I will do. Please, I have no desire to see you punished, banished or left to some tragic fate.'

'That is very gracious of you, Salai, but I have made a vow before God that I will not put brush to the painting again. Since the death of Alessandro…'

'That was not your fault!' interrupted the youth.

'Salai, my dear son. If it were not for me, he would still be a humble weaver.' Francesco too came and stood beside them.

'Salai is right,' he said. 'You cannot give up now. If you do, you will lose everything.'

'All is lost. I cannot go on,' Leonardo replied without looking at either of them.

'Now please, leave me to continue with my devotions.'

Resigned to the maestro's wishes, they left him to contemplate his future and pray. There was one final act of redemption Leonardo needed to discharge, notably to fulfil Alessandro's dying wish. Once he had eaten the food Salai had prepared and drank a little water, he sent Father Paulo on an errand of mercy.

Tucked behind the altar of Santa Maria delle Grazie was

a small statue of the Virgin Mary. Her body was turned at an angle as if someone had called out her name. The Virgin's face was tranquil, and her tender eyes spoke of forgiveness. It was to them Leonardo now looked as he knelt and prayed that she would intercede on behalf of Alessandro, and for God to show him mercy for the crimes he had committed in the madness of his fallen state. Leonardo vowed to remain in prayer and abstain from food and water until Father Paulo returned from his errand. Prior Vicenzo gave instructions the maestro be granted any assistance he requested, yet he asked for none and instead remained humbled in prayer.

The morning was still young when, on the third day, Father Paulo approached a prostrate Leonardo and placed a hand upon his shoulder.

'Maestro,' he said softly. 'She is here.' On a pew halfway down the main aisle of the church sat Alessandro's widow, Letizia. She wore a black veil over her head and held a candle. Seated next to her was a boy aged five years of age with curly blond hair like his father and rosy cheeks. Leonardo straightened out his dishevelled purple and pink smock and, after he had composed himself, followed Father Paulo down the aisle.

Letizia passed the boy the candle in her hand and lifted the veil over her head. Her body shook as a ripple of grief worked its way through her slender frame. Leonardo wondered what misery she must have suffered. When Father Paulo introduced her to Leonardo, she took hold of his cloak.

'Forgive me, maestro Leonardo,' she sobbed, 'Forgive me, forgive...' Unable to continue, she fell against Leonardo's body. He awkwardly embraced her, while he gently raised her up until she stood upright with his arms protectively around her.

'Letizia, it is I who should ask you for forgiveness. Had it not been for me, perhaps you would still have a husband.'

'I do not blame you, maestro. Such things are in the hands

of the Almighty,' she said, composing herself and holding the child close.

The boy reached out to touch Leonardo's beard. Without thinking, Leonardo tickled him. The sound of his laughter echoed around the stillness of the church.

'Maestro, may I see the painting?' Letizia asked.

'I am not sure that's a good idea,' replied Leonardo, casting Father Paulo an anxious glance. 'Please,' she begged. 'I will not leave until I have seen it.'

'I think maestro, she ought to be granted this request,' Father Paulo said.

'Very well,' replied Leonardo after hesitating a moment. 'Follow me.'

Hand in hand with her son, Letizia walked forwards until they were both stood before the painting of *The Last Supper*. The background and foreground had been painted including the disciples to Jesus' left. The disciples to Jesus' right, including Judas, were drawn in detail but remained unpainted. Of Jesus, only his face and hair had been painted. Letizia took hold of the boy's hand and pointed his index finger at the image of Jesus.

'That's your papa. Isn't he handsome?' The boy nodded. Letizia walked forward and stretched out her hand towards the face of Jesus, which was too high for her to touch. Tears swept down her cheeks and she rested a hand where the feet of Jesus stuck out from under the table. 'Mama,' said the boy. Letizia wiped her eyes and turned around. She held her arms out to the boy and cuddled him close.

'I see it is not finished, maestro,' she said without accusation.

'No, and it will not be for me to finish,' Leonardo replied.

'Why is that, when it is almost complete?'

'Since the death of...' Leonardo hesitated.

'Alessandro,' she said.

'Yes. There are more important things to attend to now.'

'You are mistaken, maestro. Nothing is more important,' she replied.

'After all that has happened you would have me finish it?' asked Leonardo.

'God has not allowed such suffering for you to lose heart now. Have faith. It is your duty to finish it, can you not see that?' Leonardo's mind swirled with a dozen sensations: hope, fear, opportunity; this was not the reaction he had expected.

'You mean to say, you sincerely believe it is God's will I complete it?' he asked bewildered.

'What glory does God receive in your failure? No, Maestro. You have begun this journey and if you do not finish it, what memory will there be of Alessandro? But more importantly, what memory will there be of you?'

CHAPTER FIFTY-FOUR

HIS HOLINESS WAS SEATED BEHIND A LARGE OAK TABLE UPON A tall gold chair covered in red velvet. He too had caught wind of the rumour that his errant Inquisitor had attempted to have Leonardo da Vinci assassinated by the lunatic who was being painted as Judas. Beside His Holiness, and engaged in some matter of a private nature, stood his mistress and mother of four of his children, Vannozza die Cattanei.

'Father Rodrigo, come,' His Holiness said, indicating for him to step forward. The Spaniard kissed the Fisherman's ring and bowed grudgingly to Vannozza, who smiled politely before she departed. 'How was your journey from Milan? Not too taxing, I hope?' His Holiness said, insincerely.

'No, your Holiness,' replied Father Rodrigo.

'I am glad,' responded the Pope with even more insincerity. He proceeded to make a show of straightening out his purple and cream chasuble.

'Are we in some discomfort, your Holiness?' enquired Father Rodrigo.

'Fanaticism is something well understood by the Church,' said His Holiness, finally sitting himself down. 'But you, Rodrigo, have lost sight of this for an altogether different kind of fanaticism. Hate.' His Holiness reached into a drawer, pulled out a document and pushed it across the desk.

'What is this, your Holiness?' Father Rodrigo asked.

'I am making you a Cardinal.'

'Your Holiness, I am forever at your service.'

'There is a mission ship leaving from Spain in four months' time, bound for the New World. It is where I believe a man of your talents can be best employed.' Four months later, Cardinal Rodrigo of Salamanca set sail for the New World from Cadiz, never to be heard of again.

CHAPTER FIFTY-FIVE

NESTLED IN A NEAT PLOT OF LAND TO THE WEST OF MILAN WAS Leonardo's vineyard, the one Il Moro had allocated to him as payment for his services. Laid in a secluded corner, underneath some over-hanging fig trees, rested Alessandro's grave, around which, Leonardo, Letizia and her son stood with their heads bowed in prayer. Father Paulo held a Bible and committed Alessandro's soul to the Almighty.

'May you grant Alessandro eternal peace,' prayed Father Paulo, making the sign of the cross above Alessandro's grave. 'And may the light of your glory perpetually shine upon him. May all the souls of the faithfully departed, through the mercy of God, rest in peace, both now and for evermore. Amen.'

'Thank you, Father Paulo, for your kindness,' said Letizia, lifting a black veil from above her face to wipe her misty eyes.

'It is only fitting Alessandro should be buried here in your vineyard,' Leonardo said.

'I do not understand,' responded Letizia. Leonardo removed a document from his coat.

'I have had my lawyers transfer the deeds of ownership into your name. The vineyard, cottage and outlying buildings are now yours, Letizia.'

'No, Maestro, no!' Letizia thrust the document back at Leonardo.

'Please,' pleaded Leonardo. 'After all that has happened, I insist.' Leonardo placed the document firmly in the hand of Letizia.

'What is it, mama?' the boy asked.

'A miracle, my son. A miracle.' She hugged him one more time then rose to her feet.

'I do not know the words to thank you enough for your generosity,' she said, bowing to Leonardo, who kissed her upon the hand.

'You deserve relief from the harshness of this life. It is my prayer that from now on your days are filled with happiness and, if God wills it, you will find joy again.'

'Thank you, maestro. The gift of this vineyard is a gesture I will cherish and in return, I will ensure a large barrel of wine is delivered to your home each year.'

'I wish you well Letizia. Goodbye.'

'Goodbye, maestro.'

At the far end of the vineyard, Letizia stopped to admire her cottage. The building was made of stone, had a terracotta roof and large windows with pretty shutters painted in bright yellow. To the side of the cottage was a sizable stable, big enough to accommodate a horse or two. Next to this was a large building for pressing and storing the grapes, while to the side of the cottage lay a neatly tilled stretch of earth for growing vegetables.

'Look,' she said to her son, pointing to the cottage. 'This will soon be our new home.'

'Just for us?' the boy said amazed.

Having spent her working life in the vineyards of Lombardy Letizia had picked up enough knowledge on viticulture to know how to produce good wine. With a sense of pride, she surveyed the land that was now hers. The vineyard gifted to her was of a size sufficient to afford a modest income.

Relishing the future, she walked with confidence to the edge of the road where she turned to Father Paulo walking silently by her side.

'There is no need to accompany me any further, Father. I can find my own way home.'

Watched by Father Paulo, Leonardo stood in silent contemplation by the graveside. When the afternoon sun was at its peak he turned around.

'Come Father,' he said, 'there is work to be done.' Leonardo walked out of the vineyard and headed into Milan. Both walked silently side by side, each lost in their own thoughts. Father Paulo prayed that Letizia and her son would be protected upon the open road, while Leonardo contemplated the effort needed to complete *The Last Supper*.

When at last they headed up the concourse that led towards Santa Maria delle Grazie, they bumped into a drunken Salai, accompanied by some friends propping up a wall with several jugs of grappa between them. Leonardo nodded to Father Paulo, who continued on while he stopped to talk with Salai.

'Salai, how sincere are you?' Leonardo asked.

'What do you mean?' replied Salai.

'You said you would do anything to help me finish The Last Supper, is that so?

'Yes, why? Have you had a change of heart?'

'Follow me.' Without a backwards glance at his friends, Salai followed his papa into Santa Maria delle Grazie.

The following days merged together as Leonardo painted the disciples to Jesus' right. James, Andrew, Bartholomew, and John. He painted with a passion and an energy that was relentless. It was if his will had been marshalled for one final effort and he pushed all else aside in the pursuit of his goal, neither eating nor sleeping. Every sinew in his body pulsed to the rhythm of the brush in his hand. Sometimes the brush beat against the wall as fevered as the fist he had beaten on the night of Alessandro's death, other times his strokes were as gentle as the breath upon a lover's neck in the midst of sleep.

The face of Judas grimaced as if he was grinding his teeth and his right hand clasped covetously onto a pouch of coins. His body was taut, as if he knew some dark secret and was in terror of it being revealed. There was hardness about his face. He stared menacingly across at the face of Jesus, all reverence for his Saviour abolished by the act of betrayal he had committed.

The refectory was a mess. Jars of paint lay everywhere as paint hastily mixed by Francesco, and at other times by Salai littered the floor. Portraits of the disciples lay discarded. Ash from the braziers was scattered over the floor alongside plates of uneaten food, which Salai brought regularly but which Leonardo repeatedly ignored.

'Francesco, have you prepared the blue I asked for?'

'Yes, maestro,' replied a flustered Francesco, struggling to keep pace with the demand for paints to be mixed. Prior Vicenzo entered the refectory and walked slowly forward as if admiring the beauty of the painting for the first time. Leonardo took the blue jar Francesco had handed to him and mixed a small amount with another blue. He then applied the two blues to different parts of the garment worn by Jesus.

'Good day, Prior,' said Leonardo. 'Which blue do you prefer? This one... or this one?' Prior Vicenzo walked forward and, standing below Jesus, scrutinized the two blues.

'This one,' he responded after a short contemplation.

'Why?' asked Leonardo. The Prior shrugged his heavy shoulders.

'I shall enlighten you,' said Leonardo. 'More light reflects off the blue you chose than the other, thus creating the impression that underneath the robe of Christ, his glory is shining through.' Prior Vicenzo and Francesco both looked on amazed.

'Maestro da Vinci, I have witnessed your recent troubles and have observed how graciously you have dealt with them.'

'Thank you, Father. In my weakness I fear I have offended God and mankind because my art didn't reach the quality it should have.'

Walking forward, Prior Vicenzo waited for Leonardo to put down his brush and climb down the scaffold. 'No man can paint our Lord with the majesty I witness before me who does not have faith,' said the Prior.

'Thank you kindly,' replied Leonardo.

'As the Prior of this church, I want you to know you are my son and, if there are any matters of a private nature you wish to discuss with me, you will find my door is always open.'

'Dear Prior Vicenzo,' Leonardo said, bowing his head slightly. 'The lesson I have learned these past years is that the purpose of painting is to transform the painter's mind into a resemblance of the Divine mind. Only then can what he creates truly be for the glory of God.' He stretched out his right hand towards the contemplative Prior, who clasped his hand firmly in Leonardo's.

Prior Vicenzo shook Leonardo's hand once more before he turned to make his way out of the refectory. In the doorway he stopped and made the sign of the cross, leant against a wall and looking heavenward mumbled in Latin. Salai noisily approached, disturbing the Prior from his meditation.

'You have slipped back into the habit of not attending Mass,' said the Prior, taking hold of Salai, who squirmed uncomfortably. 'I expect to see you tomorrow.' Still smarting from his encounter with the Prior, a surly Salai entered the refectory and made his way over to stand beside Francesco.

'Go talk to him, Salai,' said Francesco, 'he might listen to you.' Salai tried to talk his papa into taking a few hours rest, but to no avail.

Together, the two youths looked on as Leonardo painted

Jesus, whose head was tilted slightly to his left giving him the look of a man who had a great weight pressing down upon his shoulders. His hands extended outwards to demonstrate his surrender to the cross, while his eyes were cast to his left hand, as if in anticipation of the nail that would soon pierce his flesh. His eyes, too, revealed the depth of loneliness and the agony that would soon hold him slave to a wooden Roman beam.

While Leonardo busied himself perfecting the golden glow in Jesus' hair, Salai entered with a basket of bread, cheese, apples and a cup of weak wine.

'I've brought you some food,' the young man said, placing the basket at the foot of the scaffold. Leonardo ignored him and continued to paint. 'Eat, damn it. Eat,' demanded Salai.

'I'm not hungry,' replied an irritated Leonardo.

'You've not slept or eaten in two days. You're tired, Papa. Eat and get some rest tonight.' Salai reached upwards and passed some bread to Leonardo, who took it and bit into it.

Half-heartedly, Leonardo descended the scaffold and sat beside a relieved Salai. Moments later, his eyes rolled in their sockets and his head slumped forward on his chin.

'You're exhausted,' said Francesco, coming to sit beside them. But Leonardo was already gently snoring.

'What shall we do with him?' asked Salai.

'Try and make him comfortable,' replied Francesco, who took off his coat and, laying Leonardo down on the floor, propped it under his head.

'Are we just going to leave him here like this?' asked Salai.

'Well we can't carry him home, can we? Here, pass me those sheets,' Francesco said, pointing to some discarded sheets near a brazier. Salai picked them up and placed them over his papa. They then pushed a brazier nearer to let its heat warm the sleeping artist.

'I guess I've slept in worse places,' joked Salai, who picked up an apple each for him and Francesco and arm around one others shoulders, they left Leonardo to sleep.

Leonardo slept soundly on the refectory floor until he was woken by daylight and the sound of monks chanting their early morning devotions. The hum of voices echoed in the stillness like a paean of harmony, uniting the worship of their voices with the worship of Leonardo's craftsmanship on the refectory wall. It was a tranquil start to the day, contemplative, spiritual.

He scrambled up the ladder and set about putting the last remaining touches. He mixed some pale red for the garment of Jesus. The instant he dipped the tip of his brush into the paint he had prepared, euphoria swept through his tired limbs. The brush in his hand seemed to come alive with the excitement of the moment. He focused on the technicality of his art, to weight perfectly the folds in the red shirt of Jesus' right arm. His touch was deliberate as he stroked the brush to create the sense that the fabric hung from the arm of Jesus. Hours later, each crease, fold and indent in the fabric was shaped according to the natural order of clothes worn by a seated man.

Lastly, he mixed a natural tone, for the flesh on Jesus' left hand, the only part of his body still to be painted. From the basilica of Santa Maria delle Grazie, the comforting sound of a congregation at worship and the priests chanting their missals reverberated around the refectory. Leonardo paused to admire the soft voices at prayer before he applied his brush one last time to the left hand of Jesus. In the very centre of the palm, he darkened the flesh, almost imperceptibly, the fore-taste of an imprint from a nail that would pierce the Saviour's flesh.

When no more paint needed to be applied, Leonardo climbed down from his scaffold to judge his work. A sense of jubilation, which he thought he would feel, did not occur.

Instead, he felt humbled for having honoured the Almighty with the labour of his hands.

Like all artists, there was a mixture of both amazement and criticism at his finished work. In taking in the scope and energy of the painting, both praise and dissatisfaction were held like scales in equal balance: *There is a simplicity and vigour hitherto unseen in my efforts at art. Perhaps now I have painted a master-work my name will be forever remembered?* Alongside this was his critical self: *Can you hand on heart declare you have executed The Last Supper to the image of perfection imprinted upon your mind these past five years?* While the pendulum in his mind swung from one opinion to the other – the gentle hymn of voices coming from the adjacent room soothed his troubled soul.

Exhausted he fell to his knees and prayed: **Oh Lord, you hand us everything at the price of our effort. Take therefore what I have laboured for in your name and reveal your glory. Amen.**

Dear reader,

We hope you enjoyed reading *Da Vinci's Last Supper*. Please take a moment to leave a review, even if it's a short one. Your opinion is important to us.

Discover more books by Paul Arrowsmith at

https://www.nextchapter.pub/authors/paul-arrowsmith

Want to know when one of our books is free or discounted? Join the newsletter at

http://eepurl.com/bqqB3H

Best regards,

Paul Arrowsmith and the Next Chapter Team

ABOUT THE AUTHOR

Ever since I was a child I have been fascinated with words as a means to express myself through the medium of storytelling. In my late teens I formed an amateur drama group along with other young people from various churches in my home town of Darlington. We performed in churches, community halls, fetes and even some street theatre. The majority of the material was either written by me or adapted by me from other sources.

Not long after turning thirty I was approached by local Christian organisations to form a Theatre in Education company to tour local schools and take Christian themed assemblies, Religious Education classes and various workshops. Over a seven-year period we regularly visited 20-30 schools in an academic year and had contact with 10,000 plus children and young people. We used a variety of mediums; puppets, drama sketches, magic tricks, visual aids, story boards. Once again, the majority of the material we used was either written by myself or adapted from original sources.

From there I was accepted onto the MA in 'Screenwriting for Television & Film' at the 'Northern Film School,' Leeds, UK. To assist with the cost of my MA I was given a bursary by Channel Four for a student with a disability who demonstrated industry potential.

Since graduating I have been supported by the former UK Film Council, Northern Film & Media and The Lottery Fund.

Of the eight screenplays and two TV drama series I have written, I have been optioned five times and have had the privilege to have my work in development with several production companies including Factor Films, Hurricane Films, Tiger Aspect, Jeep productions and Rotunda Films.

Printed in Great Britain
by Amazon

81949899R00212